Time and Time Again

Time and Time Again

SIXTEEN TRIPS IN TIME

BY

Robert Silverberg

THREE ROOMS PRESS
New York, NY

TIME AND TIME AGAIN
Sixteen Trips in Time by Robert Silverberg

ISBN 978-1-941110-72-0 (trade paperback)
ISBN 978-1-941110-73-7 (ebook)
Library of Congress Control Number: 2018940809

BISAC Coding:
FIC028080 Science Fiction Time Travel
FIC029000 Science Fiction Short Stories (single author)
FIC028000 Science Fiction General

BOOK DESIGN:
KG Design International | www.katgeorges.com

DISTRIBUTED BY:
Publishers Group West / Ingram Content Group | www.pgw.com

Visit our website at www.threeroomspress.com or
write us at info@threeroomspress.com

For H. G. Wells, H. P. Lovecraft, Eric Temple Bell, and Robert A. Heinlein,
who showed the way.

Time present and time past
Are both perhaps present in time future

—T. S. ELIOT, *Burnt Norton*

TABLE OF CONTENTS

INTRODUCTION
BY ROBERT SILVERBERG

TIME AND TIME AGAIN, YES: throughout a career of nearly sixty years I would return almost obsessively to the theme of traveling freely in time. It has always seemed to me the essence of what science fiction is about, offering liberation from the bonds of the quotidian, the freedom to move in unhindered leaps through the unknown realms of the future and the nearly-as-mysterious realms of the past. Even though one could argue with some justification that the space-travel story also provides such freedom, I still think that a fictional space voyage, even if it takes us to the ends of the universe, still ties us to our three-dimensional world, whereas an imagined trip in time, sending us backward even to the moment of creation or forward to the final day of all, or, indeed, down some parallel track in a reality that is not our reality, adds a fourth dimension, a sense of boundless adventure, of infinite possibility.

And so for me, time travel has always been the basic theme. I have assembled here an assortment of my time travel stories, spanning the full length of a long writing career. One story from my earliest days as a writer is in this book, and one of the last that I wrote before I decided, around the year 2009, that I had written enough fiction for one lifetime—and in the decades between "Absolutely Inflexible" of 1955 and "Against the Current" of 2009 I rang every imaginable change I could on the idea that it might somehow be possible to move forward or backward along the stream of time. Which is an idea, by the way, that I happen to think is scientifically impossible, a violation of the laws of thermodynamics, and one which I think is philosophically implausible as well, running us aground on the shoals of paradox whichever way we try to go. But science fiction is not necessarily limited by the boundaries of the possible: quite the contrary. As Robert A. Heinlein once suggested, it really ought to be called *speculative* fiction. There often isn't much science in it, but there's a powerful element of speculation, a *what-if* element, that allows a sufficiently skillful writer to transcend mere scientific or philosophical implausibility for the sake of telling a good story and to arouse the reader's sense of wonder. The trick is to make one's speculations *seem* plausible: to achieve what Samuel Taylor Coleridge called, long ago, the willing suspension of disbelief. It is by achieving that suspension of disbelief that we can make the gateway swing open and undertake the otherwise impossible journey to some otherwise inaccessible distant reach of time.

Four works of science fiction in particular imprinted this lifelong fascination with time travel on me before I was thirteen years old.

The first, which I encountered in the Brooklyn Public Library when I was ten or eleven, was H.G. Wells' short novel *The Time Machine.* I had already read Jules Verne's *Twenty Thousand Leagues Under the Sea,* which only marginally qualifies as science fiction but which does convey the kind of extraordinary venture into the unknown that science fiction would later provide for me, and when a librarian suggested that I might want to try some H.G. Wells next, I pounced eagerly on the slender volume that was *The Time Machine.*

The opening page or two must have been tough going for me, precocious reader though I was. The book opens with a fairly dry mathematical discussion: "You know of course that a mathematical line, a line of the thickness *nil,* has no real existence. They taught you that? Neither has a mathematical plane. These things are mere abstractions." I wonder how much of that I, who had had my first experience of multiplication and division only three or four years earlier, was able to follow. But I must have pushed gamely on, into a discussion of space as having three dimensions, "length, breadth, and thickness," and then the suggestion that time could be understood as a fourth dimension at right angles to the other three. Such things as dimensions and even right angles surely still were mysteries to me, terms from the unknown world of mathematics that lay some years in my future, but I had at least heard of the famous Fourth Dimension, which popped up often enough in comic books, where villains, for example, tended to escape by jumping off into something blithely labeled the Fourth Dimension, without further explanation. So I kept going, and was told that the protagonist of the story, whom we know only by the name of the Time Traveler, had developed a machine that traveled in four dimensions, capable of journeys not just in the three dimensions that make up our tangible existence, but in the fourth dimension, time, as well. And then he revealed the machine itself, "a glittering metallic framework, scarcely larger than a small clock, and very delicately made. There was ivory in it, and some transparent crystalline substance." It had two levers. One, said the Time Traveler, sent the machine forward in time. The other reversed the direction.

He demonstrated; and the little machine disappeared. "You mean to say that the machine has traveled into the future?" one onlooker asked. And the Time Traveler said, "Into the future or the past—I don't, for certain, know which." He went on to declare that he had nearly finished constructing a full-sized version of his device. "Upon that machine," he said, "I intend to explore time."

I was hooked. I read on and on, and within a few pages, the preliminary disquisitions were over and the Time Traveler was telling his friends about his successful voyage to the far reaches of time.

Wells had begun writing his story around 1887, when he was 21, and it went through six drafts before it finally appeared in book form, the first of his many published novels, in 1895. Though I had no way of knowing it then, it had not been his intention simply to tell an adventure tale in the manner of such popular writers of the day as Jules Verne and H. Rider Haggard. He wanted it to be a novel of ideas as well. He had read Karl Marx and was interested in the history of class struggle, and had some strong notions of how class warfare would transform the civilization of the millennia ahead. He knew his Darwin, too, so the novel would explore the future of human evolution. But none of that meant much to me then. What interested me was the look and feel of the future Wells was depicting, a future that I knew I myself could never live to see, but which had, for me, the absolute reality of the most powerful and vivid of visions. So onward I went, following the Time Traveler into the years to come. "I saw trees growing and changing like puffs of vapor, now brown, now green; they grew, shivered, and passed away. I saw tall buildings rise up faint and fair, and pass like dreams. The whole surface of the earth seemed changed—melting and flowing under my eyes. The little hands that registered my speed raced round faster and faster. . . ."

Eventually the Time Traveler's vehicle came to rest in what the dials indicated was the year 802,701: the world of our successor humans, the gentle, effete Eloi and the bestial Morlocks. I wandered that world, agog. The class strife between the Eloi and the Morlocks was of very little interest to me, but the beauty of the future world certainly held my attention, its soaring towers and its porcelain palaces with gates of bronze.

Then—after a bit of romance with a delicate Eloi girl named Weena, which interested my prepubescent self not at all—it was onward again, deeper and deeper into time, into an epoch when the sun was red and feeble and the world was plainly dying, and finally the Time Traveler gave me a view of Earth's last denizens, monstrous crabs crawling slowly about at the edge of a chilly sea under a somber, swollen sun that had come to its final days. That image, the huge crabs, the bloated red sun, the desolate landscape, has remained with me all my life. I will never live to see any such thing, of course— but Wells had shown it to me in his astounding little tale, and once I had made that journey to the end of time with his voyager, I would never be the same again.

My encounter with the second of those four powerful time travel stories came a year or so later. I discovered that the book department of Macy's vast department store in Manhattan had a little group of books of what I was only just learning to call science fiction, a term that had not yet come into wide popular usage. There my parents, always generous in allowing me to acquire books, bought me a small, thick volume called *The Portable Novels of Science,* edited by Donald A. Wollheim, which contained four long stories, three of which would burn their way into my soul forever. The opening novel, *The First Men in the Moon* by Wells, again, had surprisingly little impact on me. But the book also contained Olaf Stapledon's *Odd John,* a haunting, tragic story of a strange young boy of high intelligence with whom I found it only too easy to identify, and H. P. Lovecraft's *The Shadow Out of Time,* a novella poised on the brink between science fiction and fantasy. I had already encountered a couple of Lovecraft's stories in an anthology called *Great Tales of Terror and the Supernatural,* and they had made a strong impression on me, but they had been horror stories, and *The Shadow Out of Time* was science fiction, a genre that was rapidly becoming of major importance in my developing reading tastes.

And what science fiction it was! A professor at Miskatonic University in the New England town of Arkham—both of them, I would later discover, Lovecraftian inventions—had suddenly become subject to terrifying hallucinations that had sent him, for six years, into a psychotic state. Awakening finally from his madness as his old rational self, he realized that some sort of alien entity had taken possession of his mind during those six lost years, and then he began to have dreams of a vast library, "holding what seemed to be volumes of immense size with strange hieroglyphs on their backs," situated in a steamy tropical jungle that he perceived after a while to be the Earth of a remote prehistoric era, 150 million years or more in the past. As the complicated story unfolds, it becomes clear that his mind had been invaded by a denizen of that ancient world that had thrown its consciousness forward into the twentieth century; and he himself comes to visit the alien civilization of the Permian or Triassic Age in dreams, moving among its grotesque inhabitants and exploring the books in that strange library. As the story develops, Lovecraft unfolded visions of remote time that provided exactly what I was looking for in science fiction: a gateway out of the here-and-now world into the unknown and unknowable.

The biggest moment for me came when the dreaming protagonist encounters other time-wanderers who, like him, had drifted back into that lost world:

> There was a mind from the planet we know as Venus, which would live incalculable epochs to come, and one from an outer moon of Jupiter six million years in the past. Of earthly minds there were some from the winged, star-headed, half-vegetable race of paleogean Antarctica; one from the reptile people of fabled Valusia; three from the furry prehuman Hyperborean worshippers of Tsathoggua; one from the wholly abominable Tcho-Tchos. . . .

And so on for three staggering paragraphs:

> I talked with the mind of Nug-Soth, a magician of the dark conquerors of 16,000 A.D.; with that of a Roman named Titus Cempronius Blaesus, who had been a quaestor in Sulla's time; with that of Khepnes, an Egyptian of the 14th Dynasty, who told me the hideous secret of Nyarlathotep. . . . with that of Crom-Ya, a Cimmerian chieftain of 15,000 B.C.; and with so many others that my brain cannot hold the shocking secrets and dizzying marvels I learned from them.

Those dizzying marvels dizzied me, too, and have continued to do so, every time in the past seventy years that I have re-read that amazing page. It seemed to me that all of time lay open before me: there were no barriers, no mysteries of worlds gone by or worlds yet to come. By way of Lovecraft's stupendous imagination, I was treated to the sort of revelations that only time travel fiction can provide.

And then another story in that astonishing little collection of science fiction novellas clinched the deal for me: John Taine's *Before the Dawn*, which took me back to one of the obsessions of my earlier childhood, the vanished world of the dinosaurs. As a small boy growing up in New York City, I had ready access to the American Museum of Natural History and the spectacular collection of dinosaur fossils displayed on its fourth floor; and, like many other small boys then and now, I had been utterly captivated by those great beasts and learned all I could about them, diligently mastering such mouth-filling names as Tyrannosaurus and Stegosaurus and Triceratops before I was eight years old. It was my early fascination with dinosaurs and the remote epoch in which they had lived, I think, that made it so easy for me to tumble into a love for time travel fiction, which I swiftly discovered would take me into distant reaches of time in the only way available to me.

John Taine was, in reality, Eric Temple Bell, a professor of mathematics at the California Institute of Technology, who under his own name published books on mathematical and technical subjects, and under the pseudonym wrote a dozen or so superb science fiction novels, mainly in the 1920s and 1930s. *Before the Dawn*, which dated from 1934, had an unusual publishing history, having been brought out not by a company noted for works of fiction, or in a science fiction magazine, but rather by Williams and Wilkins, a Baltimore-based publisher of scientific texts. Many years later after encountering it in the Wollheim collection, I would acquire a copy of the Williams and Wilkins edition, the jacket of which proclaimed it to be a novel of "TELEVISION IN TIME," television then being something more in the province of science fiction than commercial reality. And in a somewhat apologetic preface, the publishers declared:

> When a house that has devoted its attention wholly to factual books and journals in the realm of research science or its applications publishes a romance, it is no more than reasonable to explain the phenomenon. Dr. Bell's *Before the Dawn* is fiction, written for the love and fun of the thing, and to be read in the same spirit. It is a romance. But it is not mere unguided romancing. There is scientific background for everything he writes. . . . If there is no television in time as a matter of sober fact, it is also a matter of sober fact that the thing is possible; science has sown the seeds. The conjecture lies in guessing which way the seeds will grow.

The commodity that *Before the Dawn* delivered was precisely that which I had been hungering for ever since my first glimpse, at the age of six or seven, of the mighty dinosaur skeletons in the American Museum of Natural History. I would never see a living Brontosaurus or Tyrannosaurus; but here was a book in which a plausibly described device could focus a beam of light on some ancient object and bring forth television images showing scenes that had been imprinted on that object at some distant point in time. We are marched step by step through a series of tests that reveal a gigantic bloody claw, and then, from a shapeless lump of stone, a crudely-executed statuette of a woman, carved far back in prehistory by a Mayan sculptor; and then, finally, a nest of reptile eggs out of which a small creature that is unmistakably a baby dinosaur emerges.

As they gain more control of their instrument, the experimenters are able to bring forth a coherent narrative of dinosaur life, following the growth of their baby dinosaur, his development as a warrior, his battles, his migrations. Belshazzar, they call him. Other dinosaurs enter the narrative, and are given names: Jezebel, Satan, Bartholomew. And I, that not-quite-teenage reader, was held entranced, as though I myself were looking on these living dinosaurs as they moved across the television screen. At last, in a chapter that bore what to me was the wondrous heading of "Sunset and Evening Star," death comes to the titanic creature that the baby dinosaur Belshazzar has become: "The last light died in his eyes as the head dropped back, the unconquerable jaws still wide in their last snarl of defiance." And I, deeply shaken by what I had read, put the book down with the feeling that this work of fiction had actually conveyed me, however briefly, into the actual Age of Reptiles. Just as Wells had given me a vision of the unreachable eons to come, and Lovecraft had shown me the full range of astonishing pasts and futures, so had Taine taken me into a remote era that had been vivid in my mind for most of my life but which I had never seen with such clarity before.

It remained for one more story to show me the complete possibilities of the time travel story. This I came upon about a year after the first three. By now—the year was 1949, and I was a sophomore in high school—I was a regular reader of the science fiction magazines of the day, *Astounding Science Fiction* and *Amazing Stories* and five or six more—and I had learned that certain writers, Isaac Asimov and A. E. van Vogt and Lewis Padgett and, particularly, Robert A. Heinlein, were reliable producers of superior work. So when I discovered, in Macy's ever-delightful science fiction department, a bulky anthology called *Adventures in Time and Space* that had stories by all those people plus many more of my new favorites, I knew that revelations were in store for me.

And so they were. I read and re-read *Adventures in Time and Space,* and it became one of the great books of my lifetime, and even now, when I take my copy down from the shelf seventy years later, I feel the original thrill all over again. I would not want to choose any one favorite from its three dozen stories, but it was Heinlein's time travel dazzler, "By His Bootstraps," that had the greatest impact on my career to come. For this was my first encounter with the time paradox story.

As I said many pages ago, I don't believe that time travel is scientifically possible, and one reason for that belief is that it asks us to accept the notion that someone can be in more than one place at once along the stream of time. Heinlein began his story with a mysterious stranger materializing out of nowhere in the room where a graduate student named Bob Wilson is working on a thesis that proves that time travel is a mathematically-impossible concept. The stranger is about the same age as Wilson, with a black eye, a three-day growth of beard, and a cut and swollen upper lip. Wilson demands to know who he is, and the stranger replies, "Don't you recognize me?" Wilson does not. He is told that the stranger has just arrived through a Time Gate—a circle hovering in the air behind him, "a great disk of nothing, of the color one sees when the eyes are shut tight." The visitor tosses Wilson's beloved hat through the gate and it disappears. Wilson protests. They argue; while that is happening, a third man, who looks very much like the other one but has no black eye, steps through the gate.

And then the fun begins, for one thing leads to another, there is a fistfight, and one of the strangers knocks Wilson through the gate. He lands in a strange place that turns out to be more than twenty thousand years in the future, and the story unfolds a complex series of adventures involving four characters who, we eventually learn, are—well, I hesitate to spoil the surprise that landed on me at my first reading of the story in 1949. Suffice it to say that Heinlein methodically and brilliantly presents us with a spectacular demonstration of the paradoxical nature of time travel. I would, in many stories to be written decades into my own future, devote much mental energy to the time paradox issue myself.

The earliest of them is before me right now, in the form of the battered 19-page manuscript of a story called "Vanguard of Tomorrow," which bears a penciled notation indicating that I wrote it when I was fourteen. It has never been published, and, no, it isn't ever going to be published, either, because although it's a reasonably decent job for a fourteen-year-old writer, that kid was still some years away from producing publishable copy. It starts off with a scene that is as close to a plagiarism of Heinlein's opening in "By His Bootstraps" as makes very little difference: "Bill Ferris was putting the finishing touches on the story when four men popped out of nowhere and stared coldly at him." Ferris is a would-be writer, not a graduate student of philosophy, and the four men are nothing like the various visitors that Heinlein's Bob Wilson has to deal with, but they have come to him from the future through a time gate, and—well, never mind. It's not a very good story. But I was only fourteen.

I went on writing stories, many of them time travel stories, and by the time I was seventeen or so, they *were* good enough to be published, and were. The earliest one that I sold dates from June 1954, when I was finishing my junior year at Columbia. It was called "Hopper." It was about unemployed workers traveling to the past to find jobs, and it was almost good enough—not quite—to be worth using as the lead-off story for this collection. (I did expand it, a dozen years later, into a novel called *The Time Hoppers* that is a good deal better.) There were plenty of other time travel stories from me after that, as you will see, and not just short ones. Over the years there were novellas as well, some of them reprinted here. As though caught in some compulsion to wrestle with this stuff, I grappled at greater length in such novels as *Shadow on the Stars* (1958), *Up the Line* (1969), and *The Stochastic Man* (1975) with the philosophical questions Heinlein had raised in "By His Bootstraps." And, as I noted above, one of the last stories I wrote before I retired from the literary arena, "Against the Current" of 2009, was, once more, a story of travel through time.

Wells had given me my first taste of the visionary splendor a fictional voyage into the far future could provide. Lovecraft had shown me how a time travel story could unfold an infinity of possibilities in all directions. Taine had allowed me to think I was actually visiting the Mesozoic of my childhood dreams. And Heinlein had revealed the dizzying paradoxes inherent in the assumption that time travel could be achieved at all. As I continued my youthful reading of the science fiction magazines and anthologies, I came upon many other remarkable stories that provided further variations on the time travel concept: Murray Leinster's "Sidewise in Time," pioneering the alternative world idea; P. Schuyler Miller's "As Never Was," posing a nasty little circular reality paradox; Ross Rocklynne's "Time Wants a Skeleton," a time travel murder mystery; and Henry Kuttner's "Line to Tomorrow," in which a telephone is mysteriously connected to the future, among many others. Then, by 1954, I began to sell stories to the science fiction magazines myself, and, year in, year out, I chose frequently to deal with the narrative challenges of time travel, beginning with such works as 1954's "Hopper" and 1955's "Absolutely Inflexible" and continuing on, decade after decade as I was making my own long journey through time. Here, now, is the full spectrum of them, my adventures in time travel brought together in one book from first to last.

—Robert Silverberg

Time and Time Again

ABSOLUTELY INFLEXIBLE

Here is a story from the dawn of my career as a professional writer that shows I was concerned with the time travel concept right from the outset.

I was just beginning to sell my stories to the science fiction magazines from 1954 on, but progress was slow and often discouraging. Despite that, and the rigors of college work—I was still an undergraduate, in my junior year at Columbia—I wrote short stories steadily all year—one in April, two in May, three in June, two in October after the summer break. And I eventually sold them all, too. But it wasn't until the summer of 1955 that there was any pattern of consistent sales.

By then I was beginning to believe that I might actually be able to earn a modest living of some sort as a professional science fiction writer after I graduated in June of 1956. But the evidence in favor of that, so far, was pretty slim: a handful of sales to a couple of minor SF magazines. My total income from all of that was $352.60 spread over a year and a half—not a great deal even in those days. But I was finding it easier and easier to construct short stories that—to me—seemed at least as good as most of those that the innumerable SF magazines of the day were publishing. With hope in my heart, I stepped up my pace of production as the college year came to its close, and by June of 1955 I was writing a story a week.

"Absolutely Inflexible" was among them—one of my first successful tries at the time paradox theme. I suppose it's more than a little indebted to Robert A. Heinlein's classic "By His Bootstraps," but what time paradox story isn't? And it has some strength of its own, enough to have seen it through an assortment of anthology appearances over the years, and even, for a while, to be something

of a best-seller for one of the pioneering online publishers of the 1990s. It was bought, after making the rounds of the various higher-paying magazines for about six months, by the veteran editor-publisher Leo Margulies, who ran it in the July 1956 issue of the underrated magazine he had founded and edited, Fantastic Universe.

THE DETECTOR OVER IN ONE corner of Mahler's little office gleamed a soft red. He indicated it with a weary gesture of his hand to the sad-eyed time jumper who sat slouched glumly across the desk from him, looking cramped and uncomfortable in the bulky spacesuit he was compelled to wear.

"You see," Mahler said, tapping his desk. "They've just found another one. We're constantly bombarded with you people. When you get to the Moon, you'll find a whole Dome full of them. I've sent over four thousand there myself since I took over the bureau. And that was eight years ago—in 2776. An average of five hundred a year. Hardly a day goes by without someone dropping in on us."

"And not one has been set free," the time jumper said. "Every time traveler who's come here has been packed off to the Moon immediately. Every one."

"Every one," Mahler said. He peered through the thick shielding, trying to see what sort of man was hidden inside the spacesuit. Mahler often wondered about the men he condemned so easily to the Moon. This one was small of stature, with wispy locks of white hair pasted to his high forehead by perspiration. Evidently he had been a scientist, a respected man of his time, perhaps a happy father (although very few of the time jumpers were family men). Perhaps he possessed some bit of scientific knowledge that would be invaluable to the twenty-eighth century; perhaps not. It did not matter. Like all the rest, he would have to be sent to the Moon, to live out his remaining days under the grueling, primitive conditions of the Dome.

"Don't you think that's a little cruel?" the other asked. "I came here with no malice, no intent to harm whatsoever. I'm simply a scientific observer from the past. Driven by curiosity, I took the Jump. I never expected that I'd be walking into life imprisonment."

"I'm sorry," Mahler said, getting up. He decided to end the interview; he had to get rid of this jumper because there was another coming right up. Some days they came thick and fast, and this looked like one of them. But the efficient mechanical tracers never missed one.

"But can't I live on Earth and stay in this spacesuit?" the time-jumper asked, panicky now that he saw his interview with Mahler was coming to an end. "That way I'd be sealed off from contact at all times."

"Please don't make this any harder for me," Mahler said. "I've explained to you why we must be absolutely inflexible about this. There cannot—must not—be any exceptions. It's two centuries since last there was any occurrence of disease on Earth. In all this time we've lost most of the resistance acquired over the previous countless generations of disease. I'm risking my life coming so close to you, even with the spacesuit sealing you off."

Mahler signaled to the tall, powerful guards waiting in the corridor, grim in the casings that protected them from infection. This was always the worst moment.

"Look," Mahler said, frowning with impatience. "You're a walking death-trap. You probably carry enough disease germs to kill half the world. Even a cold, a common cold, would wipe out millions now. Resistance to disease has simply vanished over the past two centuries; it isn't needed, with all diseases conquered. But you time travelers show up loaded with potentialities for all the diseases the world used to have. And we can't risk having you stay here with them."

"But I'd—"

"I know. You'd swear by all that's holy to you or to me that you'd never leave the confines of the spacesuit. Sorry. The word of the most honorable man doesn't carry any weight against the safety of the lives of Earth's billions. We can't take the slightest risk by letting you stay on Earth. It's unfair, it's cruel, it's everything else. You had no idea you would walk into something like this. Well, it's too bad for you. But you knew you were going on a one-way trip to the future, and you're subject to whatever that future wants to do with you, since there's no way of getting back."

Mahler began to tidy up the papers on his desk in a way that signaled finality. "I'm terribly sorry, but you'll just have to see our way of thinking about it. We're frightened to death at your very presence here. We can't allow you to roam Earth, even in a spacesuit. No; there's nothing for you but the Moon. I have to be absolutely inflexible. Take him away," he said, gesturing to the guards. They advanced on the little man and began gently to ease him out of Mahler's office.

Mahler sank gratefully into the pneumochair and sprayed his throat with laryngogel. These long speeches always left him feeling exhausted, his throat feeling raw and scraped. Someday I'll get throat cancer from all this talking, Mahler thought. And that'll mean the nuisance of an operation. But if I don't do this job, someone else will have to.

Mahler heard the protesting screams of the time jumper impassively. In the beginning he had been ready to resign when he first witnessed the inevitable frenzied reaction of jumper after jumper as the guards dragged them away, but eight years had hardened him.

They had given him the job because he was hard, in the first place. It was a job that called for a hard man. Condrin, his predecessor, had not been the same sort of man Mahler was, and for that reason Condrin was now himself on the Moon. He had weakened after heading the Bureau for a year and had let a jumper go; the jumper had promised to secrete himself at the tip of Antarctica, and Condrin, thinking that Antarctica was as safe as the Moon, had foolishly released him. That was when they called Mahler in. In eight years Mahler had sent four thousand men to the Moon. (The first was the runaway jumper, intercepted in Buenos Aires after he had left a trail of disease down the hemisphere from Appalachia to Argentine Protectorate. The second was Condrin.)

It was getting to be a tiresome job, Mahler thought. But he was proud to hold it. It took a strong man to do what he was doing. He leaned back and awaited the arrival of the next jumper.

The door slid smoothly open as the burly body of Dr. Fournet, the Bureau's chief medical man, broke the photo-electronic beam. Mahler glanced up. Fournet carried a time-rig dangling from one hand.

"Took this away from our latest customer," Fournet said. "He told the medic who examined him that it was a two-way rig, and I thought I'd bring it to show you."

Mahler came to full attention quickly. A two-way rig? Unlikely, he thought. But it would mean the end of the dreary jumper prison on the Moon if it were true. Only how could a two-way rig exist?

He reached out and took it from Fournet. "It seems to be a conventional twenty-fourth century type," he said.

"But notice the extra dial here," Fournet said, pointing. Mahler peered and nodded.

"Yes. It *seems* to be a two-way rig. But how can we test it? And it's not really very probable," Mahler said. "Why should a two-way rig suddenly show up from the twenty-fourth century when no other traveler's had one? We don't even have two-way time travel ourselves, and our scientists don't think it's possible. Still," he mused, "it's a nice thing to dream about. We'll have to study this a little more closely. But I don't seriously think it'll work. Bring him in, will you?"

As Fournet turned to signal the guards, Mahler asked him, "What's his medical report, by the way?"

"From here to here," Fournet said somberly. "You name it, he's carrying it. Better get him shipped off to the Moon as soon as possible. I won't feel safe until he's off this planet." The big medic waved to the guards.

Mahler smiled. Fournet's overcautiousness was proverbial in the Bureau. Even if a jumper were to show up completely free from disease, Fournet would probably insist that he was carrying everything from asthma to leprosy.

The guards brought the jumper into Mahler's office. He was fairly tall, Mahler saw, and young. It was difficult to see his face clearly through the dim plate of the protective spacesuit all jumpers were compelled to wear, but Mahler could tell that the young time-jumper's face had much of the lean, hard look of Mahler's own. It seemed that the jumper's eyes had widened in surprise as he entered the office, but Mahler was not sure.

"I never dreamed I'd find you here," the jumper said. The transmitter of the spacesuit brought his voice over deeply and resonantly. "Your name is Mahler, isn't it?"

"That's right," Mahler agreed.

"To go all these years—and find you. Talk about improbabilities!"

Mahler ignored him, declining to take up the gambit. He had found it was good practice never to let a captured jumper get the upper hand in conversation. His standard procedure was firmly to explain to the jumper the reasons why it was imperative that he be sent to the Moon, and then send him, as quickly as possible.

"You say this is a two-way time-rig?" Mahler asked, holding up the flimsy-looking piece of equipment.

"That's right," the other agreed. "Works both ways. If you pressed the button, you'd go straight back to 2360 or thereabouts."

"Did you build it?"

"Me? No, hardly," said the jumper. "I found it. It's a long story, and I don't have time to tell it. In fact, if I tried to tell it, I'd only make things ten times worse than they are, if that's possible. No. Let's get this over with, shall we? I know I don't stand much of a chance with you, and I'd just as soon make it quick."

"You know, of course, that this is a world without disease—" Mahler began sonorously.

"And that you think I'm carrying enough germs of different sorts to wipe out the whole world. And therefore you have to be absolutely inflexible with me. I won't try to argue with you. Which way is the Moon?"

Absolutely inflexible. The phrase Mahler had used so many times, the phrase that summed him up so neatly. He chuckled to himself; some of the younger technicians must have tipped the jumper off about the usual procedure, and the jumper was resigned to going peacefully, without bothering to plead. It was just as well.

Absolutely inflexible.

Yes, Mahler thought, the words fit him well. He was becoming a stereotype in the Bureau. Perhaps he was the only Bureau chief who had never relented and let a jumper go. Probably all the others, bowed under the weight of the hordes of curious men flooding in from the past, had finally cracked and taken the risk. But not Mahler; not Absolutely Inflexible Mahler. He knew the deep responsibility that rode on his shoulders, and he had no intention of failing what amounted to a sacred trust. His job was to find the jumpers and get them off Earth as quickly and as efficiently as possible. Every one. It was a task that required unsoftening inflexibility.

"This makes my job much easier," Mahler said. "I'm glad I won't have to convince you of the necessity of my duty."

"Not at all," the other agreed. "I understand. I won't even waste my breath. You have good reasons for what you're doing, and nothing I say can alter them." He turned to the guards. "I'm ready. Take me away."

Mahler gestured to them, and they led the jumper away. Amazed, Mahler watched the retreating figure, studying him until he could no longer be seen.

If they were all like that, Mahler thought.

I could have got to like that one. That was a sensible man—one of the few. He knew he was beaten, and he didn't try to argue in the face of absolute necessity. It's too bad he had to go; he's the kind of man I'd like to find more often these days.

But I mustn't feel sympathy, Mahler told himself.

He had performed his job so well so long because he had managed to suppress any sympathy for the unfortunates he had to condemn. Had there been someplace else to send them—back to their own time, preferably—he would have been the first to urge abolition of the Moon prison. But, with no place else to send them, he performed this job efficiently and automatically.

He picked up the jumper's time-rig and examined it. A two-way rig would be the solution, of course. As soon as the jumper arrives, turn him around and send him back. They'd get the idea soon enough. Mahler found himself wishing it were so; he often wondered what the jumpers stranded on the Moon must think of him.

A two-way rig could change the world completely; its implications were staggering. With men able to move with ease backward and forward in time, past, present, and future would blend into one mind-numbing new entity. It was impossible to conceive of the world as it would be, with free passage in either direction.

But even as Mahler fondled the confiscated time-rig he realized something was wrong. In the six centuries since the development of time travel, no one had yet developed a known two-way rig. And, more important, there were no documented reports of visitors from the future. Presumably, if a two-way rig existed, such visitors would be commonplace.

So the jumper had been lying, Mahler thought with regret. The two-way rig was an impossibility. He had merely been playing a game with his captors. This couldn't be a two-way rig, because the past held no record of anyone's going back.

Mahler examined the rig. There were two dials on it, one the conventional forward dial and the other indicating backward travel. Whoever had prepared this hoax had gone to considerable extent to document it. Why?

Could it be that the jumper had told the truth? Mahler wished he could somehow test the rig in his hands; there was always that one chance that it might actually work, that he would no longer have to be the rigid dispenser of justice, Absolutely Inflexible Mahler.

He looked at it. As a time machine, it was fairly crude. It made use of the standard distorter pattern, but the dial was the clumsy wide-range twenty-fourth-century one; the vernier system, Mahler reflected, had not been introduced until the twenty-fifth.

Mahler peered closer to read the instruction label. PLACE LEFT HAND HERE, it said. He studied it carefully. The ghost of a thought wandered into his mind; he pushed it aside in horror, but it recurred. It would be so simple. What if—?

No.

But—

PLACE LEFT HAND HERE.

He reached out tentatively with his left hand.

Just a bit—

No.

PLACE LEFT HAND HERE.

He touched his hand gingerly to the indicated place. There was a little crackle of electricity. He let go, quickly, and started to replace the time-rig on his desk when the desk abruptly faded out from under him.

THE AIR WAS FOUL AND grimy. Mahler wondered what had happened to the conditioner. Then he looked around.

Huge, grotesque buildings raised to the sky. Black, despairing clouds of smoke overhead. The harsh screech of an industrial society.

He was in the middle of an immense city, with streams of people rushing past him on the street at a furious pace. They were all small, stunted creatures, angry-looking, their faces harried, neurotic. It was the same black, frightened expression Mahler had seen so many times on the faces of jumpers escaping to what they hoped might be a more congenial future.

He looked at the time-rig clutched in one hand, and knew what had happened.

The two-way rig.

It meant the end of the Moon prisons. It meant a complete revolution in civilization. But he had no further business back in this age of nightmare. He reached down to activate the time-rig.

Abruptly someone jolted him from behind. The current of the crowd swept him along, as he struggled to regain his control over himself. Suddenly a hand reached out and grabbed the back of his neck.

"Got a card, Hump?"

He whirled to face an ugly, squinting-eyed man in a dull-brown uniform with a row of metallic buttons.

"Hear me? Where's your card, Hump? Talk up or you get Spotted."

Mahler twisted out of the man's grasp and started to jostle his way through the crowd, desiring nothing more than a moment to set the time-rig and get out of this disease-ridden squalid era. As he shoved people out of his way, they shouted angrily at him.

"There's a Hump!" someone called. "Spot him!"

The cry became a roar. "Spot him! Spot him!"

Wherever—whenever—he was, it was no place to stay in long. He turned left and went pounding down a side street, and now it was a full-fledged mob that dashed after him, shouting wildly.

"Send for the Crimers!" a deep voice boomed. "They'll Spot him!"

Someone caught up to him, and without looking Mahler reached behind and hit out, hard. He heard a dull grunt of pain, and continued running. The unaccustomed exercise was tiring him rapidly.

An open door beckoned. He stepped inside, finding himself inside a machine store of sorts, and slammed the door shut. They still had manual doors, a remote part of his mind observed coldly.

A salesman came towards him. "Can I help you, sir? The latest models, right here."

"Just leave me alone," Mahler panted, squinting at the time-rig. The sales- man watched uncomprehendingly as Mahler fumbled with the little dial.

There was no vernier. He'd have to chance it and hope he hit the right year. The salesman suddenly screamed and came to life, for reasons Mahler would never understand. Mahler averted him and punched the stud viciously.

It was wonderful to step back into the serenity of twenty-eighth-century Appalachia. Small wonder so many time jumpers come here, Mahler reflected, as he waited for his overworked heart to calm down. Almost anything would be preferable to *then*.

He looked around the quiet street for a Convenience where he could repair the scratches and bruises he had acquired during his brief stay in the past. They would scarcely be able to recognize him at the Bureau in his present battered condition, with one eye nearly closed, a great livid welt on his cheek, and his clothing hanging in tatters.

He sighted a Convenience and started down the street, pausing at the sound of a familiar soft mechanical whining. He looked around to see one of the low-running mechanical tracers of the Bureau purring up the street towards him, closely followed by the two Bureau guards, clad in their protective casings.

Of course. He had arrived from the past, and the detectors had recorded his arrival, as they would that of any time traveler. They never missed.

He turned and walked towards the guards. He failed to recognize either one, but this did not surprise him; the Bureau was a vast and wide-ranging organization, and he knew only a handful of the many guards who accompanied the tracers. It was a pleasant relief to see the tracer; the use of tracers had been instituted during his administration, so at least he knew he hadn't returned too early along the time-stream.

"Good to see you," he called to the approaching guards. "I had a little accident in the office."

They ignored him and methodically unpacked a spacesuit from the storage trunk of the mechanical tracer. "Never mind talking," one said. "Get into this."

He paled. "But I'm no jumper," he said. "Hold on a moment, fellows. This is all a mistake. I'm Mahler—head of the Bureau. Your boss."

"Don't play games with us, fellow," the taller guard said, while the other forced the spacesuit down over Mahler. To his horror, Mahler saw that they did not recognize him at all.

"If you'll just come peacefully and let the Chief explain everything to you, without any trouble—" the short guard said.

"But I *am* the Chief," Mahler protested. "I was examining a two-way time-rig in my office and accidentally sent myself back to the past. Take this thing off me and I'll show you my identification card; that should convince you."

"Look, fellow, we don't want to be convinced of anything. Tell it to the Chief if you want. Now, are you coming, or do we bring you?"

There was no point, Mahler decided, in trying to prove his identity to the clean-faced young medic who examined him at the Bureau office. That would only add more complications, he realized. No; he would wait until he reached the office of the Chief.

He saw now what had happened: apparently he had landed somewhere in his own future, shortly after his own death. Someone else had taken over the Bureau, and he, Mahler, was forgotten. (Mahler suddenly realized with a shock that at this very moment his ashes were probably reposing in an urn at the Appalachia Crematorium.)

When he got to the Chief of the Bureau, he would simply and calmly explain his identity and ask for permission to go back the ten or twenty or thirty years to the time in which he belonged, and where he could turn the two-way rig over to the proper authorities and resume his life from his point of departure. And when that happened, the jumpers would no longer be sent to the Moon, and there would be no further need for Absolutely Inflexible Mahler.

But, he realized, if I've already done this then why is there still a Bureau now? An uneasy fear began to grow in him.

"Hurry up and finish that report," Mahler told the medic.

"I don't know what the rush is," the medic said. "Unless you like it on the Moon."

"Don't worry about me," Mahler said confidently. "If I told you who I am, you'd think twice about—"

"Is this thing your time-rig?" the medic asked boredly, interrupting.

"Not really. I mean—yes, yes it is," Mahler said. "And be careful with it. It's the world's only two-way rig."

"Really, now?" said the medic. "Two ways, eh?"

"Yes. And if you'll take me in to your Chief—"

"Just a minute. I'd like to show this to the Head Medic."

In a few moments the medic returned. "All right, let's go to the Chief now. I'd advise you not to bother arguing; you can't win. You should have stayed where you came from."

Two guards appeared and jostled Mahler down the familiar corridor to the brightly lit little office where he had spent eight years. Eight years on the other side of the fence.

As he approached the door of what had once been his office, he carefully planned what he would say to his successor. He would explain the accident, demonstrate his identity as Mahler, and request permission to use the two-way rig to return to his own time. The Chief would probably be belligerent at first, then curious, finally amused at the chain of events that had ensnarled Mahler. And, of course, he would let him go, after they had exchanged anecdotes about their job, the job they both held at the same time and across a gap of years. Mahler swore never again to touch a time machine, once he got back. He would let others undergo the huge job of transmitting the jumpers back to their own eras.

He moved forward and broke the photoelectronic beam. The door to the Bureau Chief's office slid open. Behind the desk sat a tall, powerful-looking man, lean, hard.

Me.

Through the dim plate of the spacesuit into which he had been stuffed, Mahler saw the man behind the desk. Himself. Absolutely Inflexible Mahler. The man who had sent four thousand men to the Moon, without exception, in the unbending pursuit of his duty.

And if he's Mahler—

Who am I?

Suddenly Mahler saw the insane circle complete. He recalled the jumper, the firm, deep-voiced, unafraid time jumper who had arrived claiming to have a two-way rig and who had marched off to the Moon without arguing. Now Mahler knew who that jumper was.

But how did the cycle start? Where did the two-way rig come from in the first place? He had gone to the past to bring it to the present to take it to the past to—

His head swam. There was no way out. He looked at the man behind the desk and began to walk towards him, feeling a wall of circumstance growing around him, while he, in frustration, tried impotently to beat his way out.

It was utterly pointless to argue. Not with Absolutely Inflexible Mahler. It would just be a waste of breath. The wheel had come full circle, and he was as good as on the Moon. He looked at the man behind the desk with a new, strange light in his eyes.

"I never dreamed I'd find you here," the jumper said. The transmitter of the spacesuit brought his voice over deeply and resonantly.

◆

NEEDLE IN A TIMESTACK

In the summer of 1981 I was at a science fiction convention, chatting with my good friend Bill Rotsler, when a young man came up to us and started making himself obnoxious. Bill turned to him and said, "Go away, kid, or I'll change your future." At which I said, "No, tell him that you'll change his past," and suddenly I realized that I had handed myself a nice story idea. An intricate time travel plot unfolded itself for me with marvelous clarity, one that very vividly demonstrates the perils of being able to fool around with things that have already happened if one postulates that the past is not a sealed book, but is, in fact, a fluid thing subject to retroactive manipulation. I wrote it in January 1982 and sent it to Alice Turner, Playboy's *brilliant fiction editor in those days, who bought it immediately and published it in the July 1983 issue.*

Some years later, a major American movie company bought it also. They gave me quite a lot of money, which was very pleasant, but did nothing about actually making the movie and eventually gave me back the rights. Then, a few years later, they bought it again and once again did not get around to filming it. Now a different company is planning to do the film. This is a very jolly loop to be caught in, bringing me one nice paycheck after another, but I hope some-one does finally make the movie, sooner or later. It's one science fiction movie I'd actually like to see.

BETWEEN ONE MOMENT AND THE next, the taste of cotton came into his mouth, and Mikkelsen knew that Tommy Hambleton had been tinkering with his past again. The cotton-in-the-mouth sensation was the standard tip-off for Mikkelsen. For other people it might be a ringing in the ears, a tremor of the little finger, a tightness in the shoulders. Whatever the symptom, it always meant the same thing: your time track has been meddled with, your life has been retroactively transformed. It happened all the time. One of the little annoyances of modern life, everyone always said. Generally, the changes didn't amount to much.

But Tommy Hambleton was out to destroy Mikkelsen's marriage, or, more accurately, he was determined to unhappen it altogether, and that went beyond Mikkelsen's limits of tolerance. In something close to panic, he phoned home to find out if he still had Janine.

Her lovely features blossomed on the screen—glossy dark hair, elegant cheekbones, cool sardonic eyes. She looked tense and strained, and Mikkelsen knew she had felt the backlash of this latest attempt too.

"Nick?" she said. "Is it a phasing?"

"I think so. Tommy's taken another whack at us, and Christ only knows how much chaos he's caused this time."

"Let's run through everything."

"All right," Mikkelsen said. "What's your name?"

"Janine."

"And mine?"

"Nick. Nicholas Perry Mikkelsen. You see? Nothing important has changed."

"Are you married?"

"Yes, of course, darling. To you."

"Keep going. What's our address?"

"11 Lantana Crescent."

"Do we have children?"

"Dana and Elise. Dana's five, Elise is three. Our cat's name is Minibelle, and—"

"Okay," Mikkelsen said, relieved. "That much checks out. But I tasted the cotton, Janine. Where has he done it to us this time? What's been changed?"

"It can't be anything major, love. We'll find it if we keep checking. Just stay calm."

"Calm. Yes." He closed his eyes. He took a deep breath. The little annoyances of modern life, he thought. In the old days, when time was just a linear flow from *then* to *now,* did anyone get bored with all that stability? For better or for worse it was different now. You go to bed a Dartmouth man and wake up Columbia, never the wiser. You board a plane that blows up over Cyprus, but then your insurance agent goes back and gets you to miss the flight. In the new fluid way of life there was always a second chance, a third, a fourth, now that the past was open to anyone with the price of a ticket. But what good is any of that, Mikkelsen wondered, if Tommy Hambleton can use it to disappear me and marry Janine again himself?

They punched for readouts and checked all their vital data against what they remembered. When your past is altered through time-phasing, all records of your life are automatically altered too, of course, but there's a period of two or three hours when memories of your previous existence still linger in your brain, like the phantom twitches of an amputated limb. They checked the date of Mikkelsen's birth, parents' names, his nine genetic coordinates, and his educational record. Everything seemed right. But when they got to their wedding date the readout said 8 Feb 2017, and Mikkelsen heard warning chimes in his mind. "I remember a summer wedding," he said. "Outdoors in Dan Levy's garden, the hills all dry and brown, the 24th of August."

"So do I, Nick. The hills wouldn't have been brown in February. But I can see it—that hot dusty day—"

"Then five months of our marriage are gone, Janine. He couldn't un-marry us altogether, but he managed to hold us up from summer to winter." Rage made his head spin, and he had to ask his desk for a quick buzz of tranks. Etiquette called for one to be cool about a phasing. But he couldn't be cool when the phasing was a deliberate and malevolent blow at the center of his life. He wanted to shout, to break things, to kick Tommy Hambleton's ass. He wanted his marriage left alone. He said, "You know what I'm going to do one of these days?

I'm going to go back about fifty years and eradicate Tommy completely. Just arrange things so his parents never get to meet, and—"

"No, Nick. You mustn't."

"I know. But I'd love to." He knew he couldn't, and not just because it would be murder. It was essential that Tommy Hambleton be born and grow up and meet Janine and marry her, so that when the marriage came apart she would meet and marry Mikkelsen. If he changed Hambleton's past, he would change hers too, and if he changed hers, he would change his own, and anything might happen. Anything. But all the same he was furious. "Five months of our past, Janine—"

"We don't need them, love. Keeping the present and the future safe is the main priority. By tomorrow we'll always think we were married in February of 2017, and it won't matter. Promise me you won't try to phase him."

"I hate the idea that he can simply—"

"So do I. But I want you to promise you'll leave things as they are."

"Well—"

"Promise."

"All right," he said. "I promise."

LITTLE PHASINGS HAPPENED ALL THE time. Someone in Illinois makes a trip to eleventh-century Arizona and sets up tiny ripple currents in time that have a tangential and peripheral effect on a lot of lives, and someone in California finds himself driving a silver BMW instead of a gray Toyota. No one minded trifling changes like that. But this was the third time in the last twelve months, so far as Mikkelsen was able to tell, that Tommy Hambleton had committed a deliberate phasing intended to break the chain of events that had brought about Mikkelsen's marriage to Janine.

The first phasing happened on a splendid spring day—coming home from work, sudden taste of cotton in mouth, sense of mysterious disorientation. Mikkelsen walked down the steps looking for his old ginger tomcat, Gus, who always ran out to greet him as though he thought he was a dog. No Gus. Instead a calico female, very pregnant, sitting placidly in the front hall.

"Where's Gus?" Mikkelsen asked Janine.

"Gus? Gus who?"

"Our cat."

"You mean Max?"

"Gus," he said. "Sort of orange, crooked tail—"

"That's right. But Max is his name. I'm sure it's Max. He must be around somewhere. Look, here's Minibelle." Janine knelt and stroked the fat calico. "Minibelle, where's Max?"

"Gus," Mikkelsen said. "Not Max. And who's this Minibelle?"

"She's our cat, Nick," Janine said, sounding surprised. They stared at each other.

"Something's happened, Nick."

"I think we've been time-phased," he said.

Sensation as of dropping through trapdoor—shock, confusion, terror. Followed by hasty and scary inventory of basic life-data to see what had changed. Everything appeared in order except for the switch of cats. He didn't remember having a female calico. Neither did Janine, although she had accepted the presence of the cat without surprise. As for Gus—Max—he was getting foggier about his name, and Janine couldn't even remember what he looked like. But she did recall that he had been a wedding gift from some close friend, and Mikkelsen remembered that the friend was Gus Stark, for whom they had named him, and Janine was then able to dredge up the dimming fact that Gus was a close friend of Mikkelsen's and also of Hambleton and Janine in the days when they were married, and that Gus had introduced Janine to Mikkelsen ten years ago when they were all on holiday in Hawaii.

Mikkelsen accessed the household callmaster and found no Gus Stark listed. So the phasing had erased him from their roster of friends. The general phone directory turned up a Gus Stark in Costa Mesa. Mikkelsen called him and got a freckle-faced man with fading red hair, who looked more or less familiar. But he didn't know Mikkelsen at all, and only after some puzzling around in his memory did he decide that they had been distantly acquainted way back when, but had had some kind of trifling quarrel and had lost touch with each other years ago.

"That's not how I think I remember it," Mikkelsen said. "I remember us as friends for years, really close. You and Donna and Janine and I were out to dinner only last week, is what I remember, over in Newport Beach."

"Donna?"

"Your wife."

"My wife's name is Karen. Jesus, this has been one hell of a phasing, hasn't it?" He didn't sound upset.

"I'll say. Blew away your marriage, our friendship, and who knows what-all else."

"Well, these things happen. Listen, if I can help you any way, fella, just call. But right now Karen and I were on our way out, and—"

"Yeah. Sure. Sorry to have bothered you," Mikkelsen told him.

He blanked the screen.

Donna. Karen. Gus. Max. He looked at Janine.

"Tommy did it," she said.

She had it all figured out. Tommy, she said, had never forgiven Mikkelsen for marrying her. He wanted her back. He still sent her birthday cards, coy little gifts, postcards from exotic ports.

"You never mentioned them," Mikkelsen said.

She shrugged. "I thought you'd only get annoyed. You've always disliked Tommy."

"No," Mikkelsen said, "I think he's interesting in his oddball way, flamboyant, unusual. What I dislike is his unwillingness to accept the notion that you stopped being his wife a dozen years ago."

"You'd dislike him more if you knew how hard he's been trying to get me back."

"Oh?"

"When we broke up," she said, "he phased me four times. This was before I met you. He kept jaunting back to our final quarrel, trying to patch it up so that the separation wouldn't have happened. I began feeling the phasings and I knew what must be going on, and I told him to quit it or I'd report him and get his jaunt-license revoked. That scared him, I guess, because he's been pretty well-behaved ever since, except for all the little hints and innuendoes and invitations to leave you and marry him again."

"Christ," Mikkelsen said. "How long were you and he married? Six months?"

"Seven. But he's an obsessive personality. He never lets go."

"And now he's started phasing again?"

"That's my guess. He's probably decided that you're the obstacle, that I really do still love you, that I want to spend the rest of my life with you. So he needs to make us unmeet. He's taken his first shot by somehow engineering a breach between you and your friend Gus a dozen years back, a breach so severe that you never really became friends and Gus never fixed you up with me. Only it didn't work out the way Tommy hoped. We went to that party at Dave Cushman's place and I got pushed into the pool on top of you and you introduced yourself and one thing led to another and here we still are."

"Not all of us are," Mikkelsen said. "My friend Gus is married to somebody else now."

"That didn't seem to trouble him much."

"Maybe not. But he isn't my friend any more, either, and that troubles *me*. My whole past is at Tommy Hambleton's mercy, Janine! And Gus the cat is gone too. Gus was a damned good cat. I miss him."

"Five minutes ago you weren't sure whether his name was Gus or Max. Two hours from now you won't know you ever had any such cat, and it won't matter at all."

"But suppose the same thing had happened to you and me as happened to Gus and Donna?"

"It didn't, though."

"It might the next time," Mikkelsen said.

BUT IT DIDN'T. THE NEXT time, which was about six months later, they came out of it still married to each other. What they lost was their collection of twentieth-century artifacts—the black-and-white television set and the funny old dial telephone and the transistor radio and the little computer with the typewriter keyboard. All those treasures vanished between one instant and the next, leaving Mikkelsen with the telltale cottony taste in his mouth, Janine with a short-lived tic below her left eye, and both of them with the nagging awareness that a phasing had occurred.

At once they did what they could to see where the alteration had been made. For the moment they both remembered the artifacts they once had owned, and how eagerly they had collected them in '21 and '22, when the craze for such things was just beginning. But there were no sales receipts in their files and already their memories of what they had bought were becoming blurry and contradictory. There was a grouping of glittery sonic sculptures to the corner, now, where the artifacts had been. What change had been effected in the pattern of their past to put those things in the place of the others?

They never really were sure—there was no certain way of knowing—but Mikkelsen had a theory. The big expense he remembered for 2021 was the time jaunt that he and Janine had taken to Aztec Mexico, just before she got pregnant with Dana. Things had been a little wobbly between the Mikkelsens back then, and the time jaunt was supposed to be a second honeymoon. But their guide on the jaunt had been a hot little item named Elena Schmidt, who had made a very determined play for Mikkelsen and who had had him considering, for at least half an hour of lively fantasy, leaving Janine for her.

"Suppose," he said, "that on our original time track we never went back to the Aztecs at all, but put the money into the artifact collection. But then Tommy went back and maneuvered things to get us interested in time jaunting, and at the same time persuaded that Schmidt cookie to show an interest in me. We couldn't afford both the antiques and the trip; we opted for the trip, Elena did her little number on me, it didn't cause the split that Tommy was hoping for, and now we have some gaudy memories of Moctezuma's empire and no collection of early electronic devices. What do you think?"

"Makes sense," Janine said.

"Will you report him, or should I?"

"But we have no proof, Nick!"

He frowned. Proving a charge of time-crime, he knew, was almost impossible, and risky besides. The very act of investigating the alleged crime could cause an even worse phase-shift and scramble their pasts beyond repair. To enter the past is like poking a baseball bat into a spider web: it can't be done subtly or delicately.

"Do we just sit and wait for Tommy to figure out a way to get rid of me that really works?" Mikkelsen asked.

"We can't just confront him with suspicions, Nick."

"You did it once."

"Long ago. The risks are greater now. We have more past to lose. What if he's not responsible? What if he gets scared of being blamed for something that's just coincidence, and *really* sets out to phase us? He's so damned volatile, so unstable—if he feels threatened, he's likely to do anything. He could wreck our lives entirely."

"If *he* feels threatened? What about—"

"Please, Nick. I've got a hunch Tommy won't try it again. He's had two shots and they've both failed. He'll quit it now. I'm sure he will."

Grudgingly Mikkelsen yielded, and after a time he stopped worrying about a third phasing. Over the next few weeks, other effects of the second phasing kept turning up, the way losses gradually make themselves known after a burglary. The same thing had happened after the first one. A serious attempt at altering the past could never have just one consequence; there was always a host of trivial—or not so trivial—secondary shifts, a ramifying web of transformations reaching out into any number of other lives. New chains of associations were formed in the Mikkelsens' lives as a result of the erasure of their plan to collect electronic artifacts and the substitution of a trip to pre-Columbian Mexico. People they had met on that trip now were good friends, with whom they exchanged gifts, spent other holidays, and shared the burdens and joys of parenthood. A certain hollowness at first marked all those newly ingrafted old friendships, making them seem curiously insubstantial and marked by odd inconsistencies. But after a time everything felt real again, everything appeared to fit.

Then the third phasing happened, the one that pushed the beginning of their marriage from August to the following February, and did six or seven other troublesome little things, as they shortly discovered, to the contours of their existence.

"I'm going to talk to him," Mikkelsen said.

"Nick, don't do anything foolish."

"I don't intend to. But he's got to be made to see that this can't go on."

"Remember that he can be dangerous if he's forced into a corner," Janine said. "Don't threaten him. Don't push him."

"I'll tickle him," Mikkelsen said.

HE MET HAMBLETON FOR DRINKS at the Top of the Marina, Hambleton's favorite pub, swiveling at the end of a jointed stalk a thousand feet long rising from the harbor at Balboa Lagoon. Hambleton was there when Mikkelsen came in—a small sleek man, six inches shorter than Mikkelsen, with a slick confident manner. He was the richest man Mikkelsen knew, gliding through life on one of the big microprocessor fortunes of two generations back, and that in itself made him faintly menacing, as though he might try simply to buy back, one of these days, the wife he had loved and lost a dozen years ago when all of them had been so very young.

Hambleton's overriding passion, Mikkelsen knew, was time travel. He was an inveterate jaunter—a compulsive jaunter, in fact, with that faintly hyperthyroid goggle-eyed look that frequent travelers get. He was always either just back from a jaunt or getting his affairs in order for his next one. It was as though the only use he had for the humdrum real-time event horizon was to serve as his springboard into the past. That was odd. What was odder still was where he jaunted. Mikkelsen could understand people who went zooming off to watch the battle of Waterloo, or shot a bundle on a first-hand view of the sack of Rome. If he had anything like Hambleton's money, that was what he would do. But according to Janine, Hambleton was forever going back seven weeks in time, or maybe to last Christmas, or occasionally to his eleventh birthday party. Time travel as tourism held no interest for him. Let others roam the ferny glades of the Mesozoic: he spent fortunes doubling back along his own time track, and never went anywhen other. The purpose of Tommy Hambleton's time travel, it seemed, was to edit his past to make his life more perfect. He went back to eliminate every little contretemps and faux pas, to recover fumbles, to take advantage of the new opportunities that hindsight provides—to retouch, to correct, to emend. To Mikkelsen that was crazy, but also somehow charming. Hambleton was nothing if not charming. And Mikkelsen admired anyone who could invent his own new species of obsessive behavior, instead of going in for the standard hand-washing routines, or stamp-collecting, or sitting with your back to the wall in restaurants.

The moment Mikkelsen arrived, Hambleton punched the autobar for cocktails and said, "Splendid to see you, Mikkelsen. How's the elegant Janine?"

"Elegant."

"What a lucky man you are. The one great mistake of my life was letting that woman slip through my grasp."

"For which I remain forever grateful, Tommy. I've been working hard lately to hang on to her, too."

Hambleton's eyes widened. "Yes? Are you two having problems?"

"Not with each other. Time track troubles. You know, we were caught in a couple of phasings last year. Pretty serious ones. Now there's been another one. We lost five months of our marriage."

"Ah, the little annoyances of—"

"—modern life," Mikkelsen said. "Yes. A very familiar phrase. But these are what I'd call frightening annoyances. I don't need to tell you, of all people, what a splendid woman Janine is, how terrifying it is to me to think of losing her in some random twitch of the time track."

"Of course. I quite understand."

"I wish I understood these phasings. They're driving us crazy. And that's what I wanted to talk to you about."

He studied Hambleton closely, searching for some trace of guilt or at least uneasiness. But Hambleton remained serene.

"How can I be of help?"

Mikkelsen said, "I thought that perhaps you, with all your vast experience in the theory and practice of time-jaunting, could give me some clue as to what's causing them, so that I can head the next one off."

Hambleton shrugged elaborately. "My dear Nick, it could be anything! There's no reliable way of tracing phasing effects back to their cause. All our lives are interconnected in ways we never suspect. You say this last phasing delayed your marriage by a few months? Well, then, suppose that as a result of the phasing you decided to take a last bachelor fling and went off for a weekend in Banff, say, and met some lovely person with whom you spent three absolutely casual and nonsignificant but delightful days, thereby preventing her from meeting someone else that weekend with whom in the original time track she had fallen in love and married. You then went home and married Janine, a little later than originally scheduled, and lived happily ever after; but the Banff woman's life was totally switched around, all as a consequence of the phasing that delayed your wedding. Do you see? There's never any telling how a shift in one chain of events can cause interlocking upheavals in the lives of utter strangers."

"So I realize. But why should we be hit with three phasings in a year, each one jeopardizing the whole structure of our marriage?"

"I'm sure I don't know," said Hambleton. "I suppose it's just bad luck, and bad luck always changes, don't you think? Probably you've been at the edge of some nexus of negative phases that has just about run its course." He smiled dazzlingly. "Let's hope so, anyway. Would you care for another filtered rum?"

He was smooth, Mikkelsen thought. And impervious. There was no way to slip past his defenses, and even a direct attack—an outright accusation that he was the one causing the phasings—would most likely bring into play a whole new line of defense. Mikkelsen did not intend to risk that. A man who used time jaunting so ruthlessly to tidy up his past was too slippery to confront. Pressed, Hambleton would simply deny everything and hasten backward to clear away any traces of his crime that might remain. In any case, making an accusation of time-crime stick was exceedingly difficult, because the crime by definition had to have taken place on a track that no longer existed. Mikkelsen chose to retreat. He accepted another drink from Hambleton; they talked in a desultory way for a while about phasing theory, the weather, the stock market, the excellences of the woman they both had married, and the good old days of 2014 or so when they all used to hang out down in dear old La Jolla, living golden lives of wondrous irresponsibility. Then he extricated himself from the conversation and headed for home in a dark and brooding mood. He had no doubt that Hambleton would strike again, perhaps quite soon. How could he be held at bay? Some sort of preemptive strike, Mikkelsen wondered? Some bold leap into the past that would neutralize the menace of Tommy Hambleton forever? Chancy, Mikkelsen thought. You could lose as much as you gained, sometimes, in that sort of maneuver. But perhaps it was the only hope.

He spent the next few days trying to work out a strategy. Something that would get rid of Hambleton without disrupting the frail chain of circumstance that bound his own life to that of Janine—was it possible? Mikkelsen sketched out ideas, rejected them, and tried again. He began to think he saw a way.

Then came a new phasing on a warm and brilliantly sunny morning that struck him like a thunderbolt and left him dazed and numbed. When he finally shook away the grogginess, he found himself in a bachelor flat ninety stories above Mission Bay, a thick taste of cotton in his mouth, and bewildering memories already growing thin of a lovely wife and two kids and a cat and a sweet home in mellow old Corona del Mar.

Janine? Dana? Elise? Minibelle?

Gone. All gone. He knew that he had been living in this condo since '22, after the breakup with Yvonne, and that Melanie was supposed to be dropping in about six. That much was reality. And yet another reality still lingered in his mind, fading vanishing.

So it had happened. Hambleton had really done it this time.

THERE WAS NO TIME FOR panic or even for pain. He spent the first half hour desperately scribbling down notes, every detail of his lost life that he still remembered, phone numbers, addresses, names, descriptions. He set down whatever he could recall of his life with Janine and of the series of phasings that had led up to this one. Just as he was running dry the telephone rang. Janine, he prayed.

But it was Gus Stark. "Listen," he began, "Donna and I got to cancel for tonight, on account of she's got a bad headache, but I hope you and Melanie aren't too disappointed, and—" He paused. "Hey, guy, are you okay?"

"There's been a bad phasing," Mikkelsen said.

"Uh-oh."

"I've got to find Janine."

"Janine?"

"Janine—Carter," Mikkelsen said. "Slender, high cheekbones, dark hair—you know."

"Janine," said Stark. "Do I know a Janine? Hey, you and Melanie on the outs? I thought—"

"This has nothing to do with Melanie," said Mikkelsen.

"Janine Carter." Gus grinned. "You mean Tommy Hambleton's girl? The little rich guy who was part of the La Jolla crowd ten-twelve years back when—"

"That's the one. Where do you think I'd find her now?"

"Married Hambleton, I think. Moved to the Riviera, unless I'm mistaken. Look, about tonight, Nick—"

"Screw tonight," Mikkelsen said. "Get off the phone. I'll talk to you later."

He broke the circuit and put the phone into search mode, all directories worldwide, Thomas and Janine Hambleton. While he waited, the shock and anguish of loss began at last to get to him, and he started to sweat, his hands shook, his heart raced in double time. I won't find her, he thought. He's got her hidden behind seven layers of privacy networks and it's crazy to think the phone number is listed, for Christ's sake, and—

The telephone. He hit the button. Janine calling, this time.

She looked stunned and disoriented, as though she were working hard to keep her eyes in focus. "Nick?" she said faintly. "Oh, God, Nick, it's you, isn't it?"

"Where are you?"

"A villa outside Nice. In Cap d'Antibes, actually. Oh, Nick—the kids—they're gone, aren't they? Dana. Elise. They never were born, isn't that so?"

"I'm afraid it is. He really nailed us, this time."

"I can still remember just as though they were real—as though we spent ten years together—oh, Nick—"

"Tell me how to find you. I'll be on the next plane out of San Diego."

She was silent a moment.

"No. No, Nick. What's the use? We aren't the same people we were when we were married. An hour or two more and we'll forget we ever were together."

"Janine—"

"We've got no past left, Nick. And no future."

"Let me come to you!"

"I'm Tommy's wife. My past's with him. Oh, Nick, I'm so sorry, so awfully sorry—I can still remember, a little, how it was with us, the fun, the running along the beach, the kids, the little fat calico cat—but it's all gone, isn't it? I've got my life here, you've got yours. I just wanted to tell you—"

"We can try to put it back together. You don't love Tommy. You and I belong with each other. We—"

"He's a lot different, Nick. He's not the man you remember from the La Jolla days. Kinder, more considerate, more of a human being, you know? It's been ten years, after all."

Mikkelsen closed his eyes and gripped the edge of the couch to keep from falling. "It's been two hours," he said. "Tommy phased us. He just tore up our life, and we can't ever have that part of it back, but still we can salvage something, Janine, we can rebuild, if you'll just get the hell out of that villa and—"

"I'm sorry, Nick." Her voice was tender, throaty, distant, and almost unfamiliar. "Oh, God, Nick, it's such a mess. I loved you so. I'm sorry, Nick. I'm so sorry."

The screen went blank.

MIKKELSEN HAD NOT TIME-JAUNTED IN years, not since the Aztec trip, and he was amazed at what it cost now. But he was carrying the usual credit cards and evidently his credit lines were okay, because they approved his application in five minutes. He told them where he wanted to go and how he wanted to look, and for another few hundred the makeup man worked him over, taking that dusting of early gray out of his hair and smoothing the lines from his face and spraying him with the good old Southern California tan that you tend to lose when you're in your late thirties and spending more time in your office than on the beach. He looked at least eight years younger, close enough to pass. As long as he took care to keep from running into his own younger self while he was back there, there should be no problems.

He stepped into the cubicle and sweet-scented fog enshrouded him and when he stepped out again it was a mild December day in the year 2012, with a faint hint of rain in the northern sky. Only fourteen years back, and yet the world looked prehistoric to him, the clothing and the haircuts and the cars all wrong, the buildings heavy and clumsy, the advertisements floating overhead offering archaic and absurd products in blaring gaudy colors. Odd that the world of 2012 had not looked so crude to him the first time he had lived through it; but then the present never looks crude, he thought, except through the eyes of the future. He enjoyed the strangeness of it: it told him that he had really gone backward in time. It was like walking into an old movie. He felt very calm. All the pain was behind him now; he remembered nothing of the life that he had lost, only that it was important for him to take certain countermeasures against the man who had stolen something precious from him. He rented a car and drove quickly up to La Jolla. As he expected, everybody was at the beach club except for young Nick Mikkelsen, who was back in Palm Beach with his parents. Mikkelsen had put this jaunt together quickly but not without careful planning.

They were all amazed to see him—Gus, Dan, Leo, Christie, Sal, the whole crowd. How young they looked! Kids, just kids, barely into their twenties, all that hair, all that baby fat. He had never before realized how young you were when you were *young*. "Hey," Gus said, "I thought you were in Florida!" Someone handed him a popper. Someone slipped a capsule to his ear and raucous overload music began to pound against his cheekbone. He made the rounds, grinning, hugging, explaining that Palm Beach had been a bore, that he had come back early to be with the gang. "Where's Yvonne?" he asked.

"She'll be here in a little while," Christie said.

Tommy Hambleton walked in five minutes after Mikkelsen. For one jarring instant Mikkelsen thought that the man he saw was the Hambleton of his own time, thirty-five years old, but no: there were little signs, and certain lack of tension in this man's face, a certain callowness about the lips, that marked him as younger. The truth, Mikkelsen realized, is that Hambleton had *never* looked really young, that he was ageless, timeless, sleek and plump and unchanging. It would have been very satisfying to Mikkelsen to plunge a knife into that impeccably shaven throat, but murder was not his style, nor was it an ideal solution to his problem. Instead, he called Hambleton aside, bought him a drink and said quietly, "I just thought you'd like to know that Yvonne and I are breaking up."

"Really, Nick? Oh, that's so sad! I thought you two were the most solid couple here!"

"We were. We were. But it's all over, man. I'll be with someone else New Year's Eve. Don't know who, but it won't be Yvonne."

Hambleton looked solemn. "That's so sad, Nick."

"No. Not for me and not for you." Mikkelsen smiled and nudged Hambleton amiably. "Look, Tommy, it's no secret to me that you've had your eye on Yvonne for months. She knows it too. I just wanted to let you know that I'm stepping out of the picture, I'm very gracefully withdrawing, no hard feelings at all. And if she asks my advice, I'll tell her that you're absolutely the best man she could find. I mean it, Tommy."

"That's very decent of you, old fellow. That's extraordinary!"

"I want her to be happy," Mikkelsen said.

Yvonne showed up just as night was falling. Mikkelsen had not seen her for years, and he was startled at how uninteresting she seemed, how bland, how unformed, almost adolescent. Of course, she was very pretty, close-cropped blonde hair, merry greenish-blue eyes, pert little nose, but she seemed girlish and alien to him, and he wondered how he could ever have become so involved with her. But of course all that was before Janine. Mikkelsen's unscheduled return from Palm Beach surprised her, but not very much, and when he took her down to the beach to tell her that he had come to realize that she was really in love with Hambleton and he was not going to make a fuss about it, she blinked and said sweetly, "In love with Tommy? Well, I suppose I *could* be—though I never actually saw it like that. But I could give it a try, couldn't I? That is, if you truly are tired of me, Nick." She didn't seem offended. She didn't seem heartbroken. She didn't seem to care much at all.

He left the club soon afterward and got an expresSFax message off to his younger self in Palm Beach: *Yvonne has fallen for Tommy Hambleton. However upset you are, for God's sake get over it fast, and if you happen to meet a young woman named Janine Carter, give her a close look. You won't regret it, believe me. I'm in a position to know.*

He signed it *A Friend,* but added a little squiggle in the corner that had always been his own special signature-glyph. He didn't dare go further than that. He hoped young Nick would be smart enough to figure out the score.

Not a bad hour's work, he decided. He drove back to the jaunt-shop in downtown San Diego and hopped back to his proper point in time.

THERE WAS THE TASTE OF cotton in his mouth when he emerged. So it feels that way even when you phase *yourself,* he thought. He wondered what changes he had brought about by his jaunt. As he remembered it, he had made the hop in order to phase himself back into a marriage with a woman named Janine, who apparently he had loved quite considerably until she had been snatched away from him in a phasing. Evidently the unphasing had not happened, because he knew he was still unmarried, with three or four regular companions—Cindy, Melanie, Elena and someone else—and none of them was named Janine. Paula, yes, that was the other one. Yet he was carrying a note, already starting to fade, that said: *You won't remember any of this, but you were married in 2016 or 17 to the former Janine Carter, Tommy Hambleton's ex-wife, and however much you may like your present life, you were a lot better off when you were with her.* Maybe so, Mikkelsen thought. God knows he was getting weary of the bachelor life, and now that Gus and Donna were making it legal, he was the only singleton left in the whole crowd. That was a little awkward. But he hadn't ever met anyone he genuinely wanted to spend the rest of his life with, or even as much as a year with. So he had been married, had he, before the phasing? Janine? How strange, how unlike him.

He was home before dark. Showered, shaved, dressed, headed over to the Top of the Marina. Tommy Hambleton and Yvonne were in town, and he had agreed to meet them for drinks. Hadn't seen them for years, not since Tommy had taken over his brother's villa on the Riviera. Good old Tommy, Mikkelsen thought. Great to see him again. And Yvonne. He recalled her clearly, little snub-nosed blonde, good game of tennis, trim compact body. He'd been pretty hot for her himself, eleven or twelve years ago, back before Adrienne, before Charlene, before Georgiana, before Nedra, before Cindy, Melanie, Elena, Paula. Good to see them both again. He stepped into the skylift and went shooting blithely up the long swivel-stalk to the gilded little cupola high above the lagoon. Hambleton and Yvonne were already there.

Tommy hadn't changed much—same old smooth, slickly-dressed little guy—but Mikkelsen was astonished at how time and money had altered Yvonne. She was poised, chic, sinuous, all that baby-fat burned away, and when she spoke there was the smallest hint of a French accent in her voice. Mikkelsen embraced them both and let himself be swept off to the bar.

"So glad I was able to find you," Hambleton said. "It's been years! Years, Nick!"

"Practically forever."

"Still going great with the women, are you?"

"More or less," Mikkelsen said. "And you? Still running back in time to wipe your nose three days ago, Tommy?"

Hambleton chuckled. "Oh, I don't do much of that any more. Yvonne and I went to the Fall of Troy last winter, but the short-hop stuff doesn't interest me these days. I—oh. How amazing!"

"What is it?" Mikkelsen asked, seeing Hambleton's gaze go past him into the darker corners of the room.

"An old friend," Hambleton said. "I'm sure it's she! Someone I once knew—briefly, glancingly—" He looked toward Yvonne and said, "I met her a few months after you and I began seeing each other, love. Of course, there was nothing to it, but there could have been—there could have been—" A distant wistful look swiftly crossed Hambleton's features and was gone. His smile returned. He said, "You should meet her, Nick. If it's really she, I know she'll be just your type. How amazing! After all these years! Come with me, man!"

He seized Mikkelsen by the wrist and drew him, astounded, across the room.

"Janine?" Hambleton cried. "Janine Carter?"

She was a dark-haired woman, elegant, perhaps a year or two younger than Mikkelsen, with cool perceptive eyes. She looked up, surprised. "Tommy? Is that you?"

"Of course, of course. That's my wife, Yvonne, over there. And this—this is one of my oldest and dearest friends, Nick Mikkelsen. Nick—Janine—"

She stared up at him. "This sounds absurd," she said, "but don't I know you from somewhere?"

Mikkelsen felt a warm flood of mysterious energy surging through him as their eyes met. "It's a long story," he said. "Let's have a drink and I'll tell you all about it."

◆

TRIPS

During the most active phase of my career in the 1960s and 1970s, I wrote novels with almost obsessive regularity, but after 1972 or so I often needed to be prodded into writing short stories. Every one of the sixteen stories in this volume was written at some editor's direct request. It was all too easy, in that troubled era, for me not to write at all; but I had *to write such novels as* The Stochastic Man *and* Shadrach in the Furnace, *even so, because I was contractually bound to do them, and I have always honored my contracts. But waking up in the morning and saying, "Hi ho, I think I'll write a short story for somebody today!"—no, I stopped feeling such impulses decades ago. Only when some friend or colleague who was editing an anthology of new fiction asked me to contribute something could I push myself into tackling the job.*

I have always responded to a good challenge, though, and the one that came from Barry Malzberg and Ed Ferman in the winter of 1972–73 was a beauty. They were editing a book called Final Stage: The Ultimate Science Fiction Anthology, *and each story in it was supposed to be the definitive statement of its theme—time travel, immortality, space exploration, robots and androids, the future of sex, etc. Malzberg and Ferman offered a list of themes to a select group of writers and asked them to pick the one that held the greatest personal appeal.*

Isaac Asimov, of course, took robots, and who would begrudge that choice to him? Harlan Ellison and Joanna Russ tackled the future of sex from very different viewpoints. I wanted time travel, but I think Philip K. Dick beat me to it, or else I simply opted right away for alternative universes and left the time travel theme free for him; I don't quite remember. In any case, the alternative universe concept is a kind of time travel, taking the voyager sidewise in time to other possible contemporary worlds. The task I set for myself was to send my protagonist to a dozen alternative Californias in the space of some 12,000 words. And so I did, in March 1973, with a profligacy of invention that would serve to fill a pair of trilogies today. I threw in one twist that might have been too subtle, because no one appears to have noticed it in all the years since the book appeared in the Ferman-Malzberg anthology Final Stage*: the place where the protagonist arrives at the end, which I assert is the world from which he departed at the outset, is not exactly the world we ourselves live in. I can demonstrate that by pointing to the evidence, but I will leave that to perceptive readers.*

Does this path have a heart? All paths are the same: they lead nowhere. They are paths going through the bush, or into the bush. In my own life I could say I have traversed long, long paths, but I am not anywhere . . . Does this path have a heart? If it does, the path is good; if it doesn't, it is of no use. Both paths lead nowhere; but one has a heart, the other doesn't. One makes for a joyful journey; as long as you follow it, you are one with it. The other will make you curse your life.

—The Teachings of Don Juan

1.

THE SECOND PLACE YOU COME to—the first having proved unsatisfactory, for one reason and another—is a city which could almost be San Francisco. Perhaps it is, sitting out there on the peninsula between the ocean and the bay, white buildings clambering over improbably steep hills. It occupies the place in your psychic space that San Francisco has always occupied, although you don't really know yet what this city calls itself. Perhaps you'll find out before long.

You go forward. What you feel first is the strangeness of the familiar, and then the utter heartless familiarity of the strange. For example the automobiles, and there are plenty of them, are all halftracks: low, sleek, sexy sedans that have the flashy Detroit styling, the usual chrome, the usual streamlining, the low-raked windows all agleam, but there are only two wheels, both of them in front, with a pair of treadbelts circling endlessly in back. Is this good design for city use? Who knows? Somebody evidently thinks so, here. And then the newspapers: the format is the same, narrow columns, gaudy screaming headlines, miles of black type on coarse grayish-white paper, but the names and the places have been changed. You scan the front page of a newspaper in the window of a curbside vending machine. Big photo of Chairman DeGrasse, serving as host at a reception for the Patagonian Ambassador. An account of the tribal massacres in the highlands of Dzungaria. Details of the solitude epidemic that is devastating Persepolis. When the halftracks stall on the hillsides, which is often, the other drivers ring silvery chimes, politely venting their impatience. Men who look like Navahos chant what sound like sutras in the intersections. The traffic lights are blue and orange. Clothing tends toward the prosaic, grays and dark blues, but the cut and slope of men's jackets has an angular, formal, eighteenth-century look, verging on pomposity.

You pick up a bright coin that lies in the street; it is vaguely metallic but rubbery, as if you could compress it between your fingers, and its thick edges bear incuse lettering: TO GOD WE OWE OUR SWORDS. On the next block, a squat two-story building is ablaze, and agitated clerks do a desperate dance. The fire engine is glossy green and its pump looks like a diabolical cannon embellished with sweeping flanges; it spouts a glistening yellow foam that eats the flames and, oxidizing, runs off down the gutter, a trickle of sluggish blue fluid. Everyone wears eyeglasses here, everyone. At a sidewalk cafe, pale waitresses offer mugs of boiling-hot milk into which the silent tight-faced patrons put cinnamon, mustard, and what seems to be Tabasco sauce. You offer your coin and try a sample, imitating what they do, and everyone bursts into laughter. The girl behind the counter pushes a thick stack of paper currency at you by way of change: UNITED FEDERAL COLUMBIAN REPUBLIC, each bill declares, GOOD FOR ONE EXCHANGE. Illegible signatures. Portrait of early leader of the republic, so famous that they give him no label of identification, bewigged, wall-eyed, ecstatic. You sip your milk, blowing gently. A light scum begins to form on its speckled surface. Sirens start to wail. About you, the other milk-drinkers stir uneasily. A parade is coming. Trumpets, drums, far-off chanting. Look! Four naked boys carry an open brocaded litter on which there sits an immense block of ice, a great frosted cube, mysterious, impenetrable. "Patagonia!" the onlookers cry sadly. The word is wrenched from them: "Patagonia!" Next, marching by himself, a mitered bishop advances, all in green, curtseying to the crowd, tossing hearty blessings as though they were flowers. "Forget your sins! Cancel your debts! All is made new! All is good!" You shiver and peer intently into his eyes as he passes you, hoping that he will single you out for an embrace. He is terribly tall but white-haired and fragile, somehow, despite his agility and energy. He reminds you of Norman, your wife's older brother, and perhaps he *is* Norman, the Norman of this place, and you wonder if he can give you news of Elizabeth, the Elizabeth of this place, but you say nothing and he goes by.

And then comes a tremendous wooden scaffold on wheels, a true juggernaut, at the summit of which rests a polished statue carved out of gleaming black stone: a human figure, male, plump, arms intricately folded, face complacent. The statue emanates a sense of vast Sumerian calm. The face is that of Chairman DeGrasse. "He'll die in the first blizzard," murmurs a man to your left. Another, turning suddenly, says with great force, "No, it's going to be done the proper way. He'll last until the time of the accidents, just as he's supposed to. I'll bet on that." Instantly they are nose to nose, glaring, and then they are wagering—a tense complicated ritual involving slapping of palms, interchanges of slips of paper, formal voiding of spittle, hysterical appeals to witnesses. The emotional climate here seems a trifle too intense. You decide to move along. Warily you leave the café, looking in all directions.

2.

Before you began your travels you were told how essential it was to define your intended role. Were you going to be a tourist, or an explorer, or an infiltrator? Those are the choices that confront anyone arriving at a new place. Each bears its special risks.

To opt for being a tourist is to choose the easiest but most contemptible path; ultimately it's the most dangerous one, too, in a certain sense. You have to accept the built-in epithets that go with the part: they will think of you as a *foolish* tourist, an *ignorant* tourist, a *vulgar* tourist, a *mere* tourist. Do you want to be considered mere? Are you able to accept that? Is that really your preferred self-image—baffled, bewildered, led about by the nose? You'll sign up for packaged tours, you'll carry guidebooks and cameras, you'll go to the cathedral and the museums and the marketplace, and you'll remain always on the outside of things, seeing a great deal, experiencing nothing. What a waste! You will be diminished by the very traveling that you thought would expand you. Tourism hollows and parches you. All places become one: a hotel, a smiling, swarthy, sunglassed guide, a bus, a plaza, a fountain, a marketplace, a museum, a cathedral. You are transformed into a feeble shriveled thing made out of glued-together travel folders; you are naked but for your visas; the sum of your life's adventures is a box of leftover small change from many indistinguishable lands.

To be an explorer is to make the macho choice. You swagger in, bent on conquest; for isn't any discovery a kind of conquest? Your existential position, like that of any mere tourist, lies outside the heart of things, but you are unashamed of that. And while tourists are essentially passive, the explorer's role is active: an explorer intends to grasp that heart, take possession, squeeze. In the explorer's role you consciously cloak yourself in the trappings of power: self-assurance, thick bankroll, stack of credit cards. You capitalize on the glamour of being a stranger. Your curiosity is invincible; you ask unabashed questions about the most intimate things, never for an instant relinquishing eye contact. You open locked doors and flash bright lights into curtained rooms. You are Magellan; you are Malinowski; you are Captain Cook. You will gain much, but—ah, here is the price!—you will always be feared and hated, you will never be permitted to attain the true core. Nor is superficiality the worst peril. Remember that Magellan and Captain Cook left their bones on tropic beaches. Sometimes the natives lose patience with explorers.

The infiltrator, though? His is at once the most difficult role and the most rewarding one. Will it be yours? Consider. You'll have to get right with it when you reach your destination, instantly learn the regulations, find your way around like an old hand, discover the location of shops and freeways and hotels, figure out the units of currency, the rules of social intercourse—all of this knowledge mastered surreptitiously, through observation alone, while moving about silently, camouflaged, never asking for help. You must become a part of the world you have entered, and the way to do it is to encourage a general assumption that you already are a part of it, have always been a part of it. Wherever you land, you need to recognize that life has been going on for millions of years, life goes on there steadily, with you or without you; you are the intrusive one, and if you don't want to feel intrusive you'd better learn fast how to fit in.

Of course, it isn't easy. The infiltrator doesn't have the privilege of buying stability by acting dumb. You won't be able to say, "How much does it cost to ride on the cable car?" You won't be able to say, "I'm from somewhere else, and this is the kind of money I carry–dollars, quarters, pennies, halves, nickels—is any of it legal tender here?" You don't dare identify yourself in any way as an outsider. If you don't get the idioms or the accent right, you can tell them you grew up out of town, but that's as much as you can reveal. The truth is your eternal secret, even when you're in trouble, *especially* when you're in trouble. When your back's to the wall you won't have time to say, "Look, I wasn't born in this universe at all, you see, I came zipping in from some other place, so pardon me, forgive me, excuse me, pity me." No, no, no, you can't do that. They won't believe you, and even if they do, they'll make it all the worse for you once they know. If you want to infiltrate, Cameron, you've got to fake it all the way. Jaunty smile; steely, even gaze. And you have to infiltrate. You know that, don't you? You don't really have any choice.

Infiltrating has its dangers, too. The rough part comes when they find you out, and they always will find you out. Then they'll react bitterly against your deception; they'll lash out in blind rage. If you're lucky, you'll be gone before they learn your sweaty little secret. Before they discover the discarded phrasebook hidden in the boarding-house room, before they stumble on the torn-off pages of your private journal. They'll find you out. They always do. But by then you'll be somewhere else, you hope, beyond the reach of their anger and their sorrow, beyond their reach.

3.

SUPPOSE I SHOW YOU, FOR Exhibit A, Cameron reacting to an extraordinary situation. You can test your own resilience by trying to picture yourself in his position. There has been a sensation in Cameron's mind very much like that of the extinction of the cosmos: a thunderclap, everything going black, a blankness, a total absence. Followed by the return of light, flowing inward upon him like high tide on the celestial shore, a surging stream of brightness moving with inexorable certainty. He stands flat-footed, dumbfounded, high on a bare hillside in warm early-hour sunlight. The house—redwood timbers, picture window, driftwood sculptures, paintings, books, records, refrigerator, gallon jugs of red wine, carpets, tiles, avocado plants in wooden tubs, carport, car, driveway—is gone. The neighboring houses are gone. The winding street is gone. The eucalyptus forest that ought to be behind him, rising toward the crest of the hill, is gone. Downslope there is no Oakland, there is no Berkeley, only a scattering of crude squatter's shacks running raggedly along unpaved switchbacks toward the pure blue bay. Across the water there is no Bay Bridge; on the far shore there is no San Francisco. The Golden Gate Bridge does not span the gap between the city and the Marin headland—Cameron is astonished, not that he didn't expect something like this, but that the transformation is so complete, so absolute. "If you don't want your world anymore," the old man had said, "you can drop it, can't you? Let go of it, let it drop. Can't you? Of course you can."

And so Cameron has let go of it. He's in another place entirely, now. Wherever this place is, it isn't home. The sprawling Bay Area cities and towns aren't here, never were. Goodbye, San Leandro, San Mateo, El Cerrito, Walnut Creek. He sees a landscape of gentle bare hills, rolling meadows, the dry brown grass of summer; the scarring hand of man is evident only occasionally. He begins to adapt. This is what he have wanted, after all; and though he has been jarred by the shock of transition, he is recovering quickly; he is settling in; he feels already that he could belong here. He will explore this unfamiliar world, and if he finds it good, he will discover a niche for himself. The air is sweet. The sky is cloudless. Has he really gone to some new place, or is he still in the old place and has everything else that was there simply gone away? Easy. He has gone. Everything else has gone. The cosmos has entered into a transitional phase. Nothing's stable any more. From this moment onward, Cameron's existence is a conditional matter, subject to ready alteration. What did the old man say? *Go wherever you like. Define your world as you would like it to be, and go there, and if you discover that you don't care for this or don't need that, why, go somewhere else. It's all trips, this universe.* What else is there? There isn't anything but trips. Just trips. So here you are, friend. New frameworks! New patterns! New!

4.

There is a sound to his left, the crackling of dry brush underfoot, and Cameron turns, looking straight into the morning sun, and sees a man on horseback approaching him. He is tall, slender, about Cameron's own height and build, it seems, but perhaps a shade broader through the shoulders. His hair, like Cameron's, is golden, but it is much longer, descending in a straight flow to his shoulders and tumbling onto his chest. He has a soft, full, curling beard, untrimmed but tidy. He wears a wide-brimmed hat, buckskin chaps, and a light fringed jacket of tawny leather. Because of the sunlight, Cameron has difficulty at first making out his features, but after a moment his eyes adjust and he sees that the other's face is very much like his own: thin lips, jutting high-bridged nose, cleft chin, cool blue eyes below heavy brows. Of course. Your face is my face. You and I, I and you, drawn to the same place at the same time across the many worlds. Cameron had not expected this, but now that it has happened it seems to have been inevitable.

They look at each other. Neither speaks. During that silent moment Cameron invents a scene for them. He imagines the other dismounting, inspecting him in wonder, walking around him, peering into his face, studying it, frowning, shaking his head, finally grinning and saying:

—I'll be damned. I never knew I had a twin brother. But here you are. It's just like looking in the mirror.

—We aren't twins.

—We've got the same face. Same everything. Trim away a little hair and nobody could tell me from you, you from me. If we aren't twins, what are we?

—We're closer than brothers.

—I don't follow your meaning, friend.

—This is how it is: I'm you. You're me. One soul, one identity. What's your name?

—Cameron.

—Of course. First name?

—Kit.

—That's short for Christopher, isn't it? My name is Cameron too. Chris. Short for Christopher. I tell you, we're one and the same person, out of two different worlds. Closer than brothers. Closer than anything.

None of this is said, however. Instead, the man in the leather clothing rides slowly toward Cameron, pauses, gives him a long incurious stare, and says simply, "Morning. Nice day." And continues onward.

"Wait," Cameron says.

The man halts. Looks back. "What?"

Never ask for help. Fake it all the way. Jaunty smile; steely, even gaze.

Yes. Cameron remembers all that. Somehow, though, infiltration seems easier to bring off in a city. You can blend into the background there. More difficult here, exposed as you are against the stark, unpeopled landscape.

Cameron says, as casually as he can, using what he hopes is a colorless neutral accent, "I've been traveling out from inland. Came a long way."

"Umm. Didn't think you were from around here. Your clothes."

"Inland clothes."

"The way you talk. Different. So?"

"New to these parts. Wondered if you could tell me a place I could hire a room till I got settled."

"You come all this way on foot?"

"Had a mule. Lost him back in the valley. Lost everything I had with me."

"Umm. Indians cutting up again. You give them a little gin, they go crazy." The other smiles faintly; then the smile fades and he retreats into impassivity, sitting motionless with hands on thighs, face a mask of patience that seems merely to be a thin covering for impatience or worse.

—Indians—?

"They gave me a rough time," Cameron says, getting into the fantasy of it.

"Umm."

"Cleaned me out, let me go."

"Umm. Umm."

Cameron feels his sense of a shared identity with this man lessening. There is no way of engaging him. I am you, you are I, and yet you take no notice of the strange fact that I wear your face and body, you seem to show no interest in me at all. Or else you hide your interest amazingly well.

Cameron says, "You know where I can get lodging?"

"Nothing much around here. Not many settlers this side of the bay, I guess."

"I'm strong. I can do most any kind of work. Maybe you could use—"

"Umm. No." Cold dismissal glitters in the frosty eyes. Cameron wonders how often people in the world of his former life saw such a look in his own. A tug on the reins. Your time is up, stranger. The horse swings around and begins picking its way daintily along the path.

Desperately Cameron calls, "One thing more!"

"Umm?"

"Is your name Cameron?"

A flicker of interest. "Might be."

"Christopher Cameron. Kit. Chris. That you?"

"Kit." The other's eyes drill into his own. The mouth compresses until the lips are invisible: not a scowl but a speculative, pensive movement. There is tension in the way the other man grasps his reins. For the first time Cameron feels that he has made contact. "Kit Cameron, yes. Why?"

"Your wife," Cameron says. "Her name Elizabeth?"

The tension increases. The other Cameron is cloaked in explosive silence. Something terrible is building within him. Then, unexpectedly, the tension snaps. The other man spits, scowls, slumps in his saddle. "My woman's dead," he mutters. "Say, who the hell are you? What do you want with me?"

"I'm—I'm—" Cameron falters. He is overwhelmed by fear and pity. A bad start, a lamentable start. He trembles. He had not thought it would be anything like this. With an effort he masters himself. Fiercely he says, "I've got to know. Was her name Elizabeth?" For an answer the horseman whacks his heels savagely against his mount's ribs and gallops away, fleeing as though he has had an encounter with Satan.

5.

Go, THE OLD MAN SAID. You know the score. This is how it is: everything's random, nothing's fixed unless we want it to be, and even then the system isn't as stable as we think it is. So go. Go. Go, he said, and, of course, hearing something like that, Cameron went. What else could he do, once he had his freedom, but abandon his native universe and try a different one? Notice that I didn't say a better one, just a different one. Or two or three or five different ones. It was a gamble, certainly. He might lose everything that mattered to him, and gain nothing worth having. But what of it? Every day is full of gambles like that: you stake your life whenever you open a door. You never know what's heading your way, not ever, and still you choose to play the game. How can a man be expected to become all he's capable of becoming if he spends his whole life pacing up and down the same courtyard? Go. Make your voyages. Time forks, again and again and again. New universes split off at each instant of decision. Left turn, right turn, honk your horn, jump the traffic light, hit your gas, hit your brake, every action spawns whole galaxies of possibility. We move through a soup of infinities. If repressing a sneeze generates an alternative continuum, what, then, are the consequences of the truly major acts, the assassinations and inseminations, the conversions, the renunciations? Go. And as you travel, mull these thoughts constantly. Part of the game is discerning the precipitating factors that shaped the worlds you visit. What's the story here? Dirt roads, donkey-carts, handsewn clothes. No Industrial Revolution, is that it? The steam-engine man—what was his name, Savery, Newcomen Watt?—smothered in his cradle? No mines, no factories, no assembly lines, no dark satanic mills. That must be it. The air is so pure here: you can tell by that, it's a simpler era. Very good, Cameron. You see the patterns swiftly. But now try somewhere else. Your own self has rejected you here; besides, this place has no Elizabeth. Close your eyes. Summon the lightning.

6.

The parade has reached a disturbing level of frenzy. Marchers and floats now occupy the side streets as well as the main boulevard, and there is no way to escape from their demonic enthusiasm. Streamers cascade from office windows, and gigantic photographs of Chairman DeGrasse have sprouted on every wall, suddenly, like dark infestations of lichen. A boy presses close against Cameron, extends a clenched fist, opens his fingers: on his palm rests a glittering jeweled case, egg-shaped, thumbnail-sized. "Spores from Patagonia," he says. "Let me have ten exchanges and they're yours." Politely Cameron declines. A woman in a blue and orange frock tugs at his arm and says urgently, "All the rumors are true, you know. They've just been confirmed. What are you going to do about that? What are you going to do?" Cameron shrugs and smiles and disengages himself. A man with gleaming buttons asks, "Are you enjoying the festival? I've sold everything, and I'm going to move to the highway next Godsday." Cameron nods and murmurs congratulations, hoping congratulations are in order. He turns a corner and confronts, once more, the bishop who looks like Elizabeth's brother, who is, he concludes, indeed Elizabeth's brother. "Forget your sins!" he is crying still. "Cancel your debts!" Cameron thrusts his head between two plump girls at the curb and attempts to call to him, but his voice fails, nothing coming forth but a hoarse wordless rasp, and the bishop moves on. Moving on is a good idea, Cameron tells himself. This place exhausts him. He has come to it too soon, and its manic tonality is more than he wants to handle. He finds a quiet alleyway, presses his cheek against a cool brick wall, and stands there breathing deeply until he is calm enough to depart. All right. Onward.

7.

EMPTY GRASSLANDS SPREAD TO THE horizon. This could be the Gobi steppe. Cameron sees neither cities nor towns nor even villages, just six or seven squat black tents pitched in a loose circle in the saddle between two low gray-green hummocks, a few hundred yards from where he stands. He looks beyond, across the gently folded land, and spies dark animal figures at the limits of his range of vision: about a dozen horses, close together, muzzle to muzzle, flank to flank, horses with riders. Or perhaps they are a congregation of centaurs. Anything is possible. He decides, though, that they are Indians, a war party of young braves, maybe, camping in these desolate plains. They see him. Quite likely they saw him some while before he noticed them. Casually they break out of their grouping, wheel, ride in his direction.

He awaits them. Why should he flee? Where could he hide? Their pace accelerates from trot to canter, from canter to wild gallop; now they plunge toward him with fluid ferocity and a terrifying eagerness. They wear open leather jackets and rough rawhide leggings; they carry lances, bows, battle-axes, long curved swords; they ride small, agile horses, hardly more than ponies, tireless packets of energy. They surround him, pulling up, the fierce little steeds rearing and whinnying; they peer at him, point, laugh, exchange harsh derisive comments in a mysterious language. Then, solemnly, they begin to ride slowly in a wide circle around him. They are flat-faced, small-nosed, bearded, with broad, prominent cheekbones; the crowns of their heads are shaven but long black hair streams down over their ears and the napes of their necks. Heavy folds in the upper lids give their eyes a slanted look. Their skins are copper-colored but with an underlying golden tinge, as though these are not Indians at all, but—what? Japanese? A samurai corps? No, probably not Japanese. But not Indians either.

They continue to circle him, gradually moving more swiftly. They chatter to one another and occasionally hurl what sound like questions at him. They seem fascinated by him, but also contemptuous. In a sudden demonstration of horsemanship one of them cuts from the circular formation and, goading his horse to an instant gallop, streaks past Cameron, leaning down to jab a finger into his forearm. Then another does it, and another, streaking back and forth across the circle, poking him, plucking at his hair, tweaking him, nearly running him down. They draw their swords and swish them through the air just above his head. They menace him, or pretend to, with their lances. Throughout it all they laugh. He stands perfectly still. This ordeal, he suspects, is a test of his courage. Which he passes, eventually. The lunatic galloping ceases; they rein in, and several of them dismount.

They are little men, chest-high to him but thicker through the chest and shoulders than he is. One unships a leather pouch and offers it to him with an unmistakable gesture: take, drink. Cameron sips cautiously. It is a thick grayish fluid, both sweet and sour. Fermented milk? He gags, winces, forces himself to sip again; they watch him closely. The second taste isn't so bad. He takes a third more willingly and gravely returns the pouch. The warriors laugh, not derisively now but more in applause, and the man who had given him the pouch slaps Cameron's shoulder admiringly. He tosses the pouch back to Cameron. Then he leaps to his saddle, and abruptly they all take off. Mongols, Cameron realizes. The sons of Genghis Khan, riding to the horizon. A worldwide empire? Yes, and this must be the Wild West for them, the frontier, where the young men enact their rites of passage. Back in Europe, after seven centuries of Mongol dominance, they have become citified, domesticated, sippers of wine, theatregoers, cultivators of gardens, but here they follow the ways of their all-conquering forefathers. Cameron shrugs. Nothing for him here. He takes a last sip of the milk and drops the pouch into the tall grass. Onward.

8.

No grass here. He sees the stumps of buildings, the blackened trunks of dead trees, mounds of broken tile and brick. The smell of death is in the air. All the bridges are down. Fog rolls in off the bay, dense and greasy, and becomes a screen on which images come alive. These ruins are inhabited. Figures move about. They are the living dead. Looking into the thick mist he sees a vision of the shock wave, he recoils as alpha particles shower his skin. He beholds the survivors emerging from their shattered houses, straggling into the smoldering streets, naked, stunned, their bodies charred, their eyes glazed, some of them with their hair on fire. The walking dead. No one speaks. No one asks why this has happened. He is watching a silent movie. The apocalyptic fire has touched the ground here; the land itself is burning. Blue phosphorescent flames rise from the earth. The final judgment, the day of wrath.

Now he hears a dread music beginning, a death march, all cellos and basses, the dark notes coming at wide intervals: *ooom ooom ooom ooom ooom.* And then the tempo picks up, the music becomes a danse macabre, syncopated, lively, the timbre still dark, the rhythms funereal: *ooom ooom ooom-de-ooom de-ooom de-ooom de-ooom-de-ooom,* jerky, chaotic, wildly gay. The distorted melody of the Ode to Joy lurks somewhere in the ragged strands of sound. The dying victims stretch their fleshless hands toward him. He shakes his head. What service can I do for you? Guilt assails him. He is a tourist in the land of their grief. Their eyes reproach him. He would embrace them, but he fears they will crumble at his touch, and he lets the procession go past him without doing anything to cross the gulf between himself and them. "Elizabeth?" he murmurs. "Norman?" They have no faces, only eyes. "What can I do? I can't do anything for you." Not even tears will come. He looks away. Though I speak with the tongues of men and of angels, and have not charity, I am become as sounding brass or a tinkling cymbal. And though I have the gift of prophecy, and understand all mysteries and all knowledge; and though I have all faith, so that I could remove mountains, and have not charity, I am nothing. But this world is beyond the reach of love. He looks away. The sun appears. The fog burns off. The visions fade. He sees only the dead land, the ashes, the ruins. All right. Here we have no continuing city, but we seek one to come. Onward. Onward.

9.

AND NOW, AFTER THIS SERIES of brief, disconcerting intermediate stops, Cameron has come to a city that is San Francisco beyond doubt, not some other city on San Francisco's site but a true San Francisco, a recognizable San Francisco. He pops into it atop Russian Hill, at the very crest, on a dazzling, brilliant, cloudless day. To his left, below, lies Fisherman's Wharf; ahead of him rises the Coit Tower; yes, and he can see the Ferry Building and the Bay Bridge. Familiar landmarks—but how strange all the rest seems! Where is the eye-stabbing Transamerica pyramid? Where is the colossal somber stalk of the Bank of America? The strangeness, he realizes, derives not so much from substitutions as from absences. The big Embarcadero developments are not there, nor the Chinatown Holiday Inn, nor the miserable tentacles of the elevated freeways, nor, apparently, anything else that was constructed in the last twenty years. This is the old short-shanked San Francisco of his boyhood, a sparkling miniature city, un-Manhattanized, skyline-less. Surely he has returned to the place he knew in the sleepy 1950s, the tranquil Eisenhower years.

He heads downhill, searching for a newspaper box. He finds one at the corner of Hyde and North Point, a bright-yellow metal rectangle. *San Francisco Chronicle,* ten cents? Is that the right price for 1954? One Roosevelt dime goes into the slot. The paper, he finds, is dated Tuesday, August 19, 1975. In what Cameron still thinks of, with some irony now, as the real world, the world that has been receding rapidly from him all day in a series of discontinuous jumps, it is also Tuesday, the 19th of August, 1975. So he has not gone backward in time at all; he has come to a San Francisco where time had seemingly been standing still. Why? In vertigo he eyes the front page. A three-column headline declares: FUEHRER ARRIVES IN WASHINGTON

Under it, to the left, a photograph of three men, smiling broadly, positively beaming at one another. The caption identifies them as President Kennedy, Fuehrer Goering, and Ambassador Togarashi of Japan, meeting in the White House Rose Garden. Cameron closes his eyes. Using no data other than the headline and the caption, he attempts to concoct a plausible speculation. This is a world, he decides, in which the Axis must have won the war. The United States is a German fiefdom. There are no high rise buildings in San Francisco because the American economy, shattered by defeat, has not yet in thirty years of peace returned to a level where it can afford to erect them, or perhaps because American venture capital, prodded by the financial ministers of the Third Reich (Hjalmar Schacht? The name drifts out of the swampy recesses of memory) now tends to flow toward Europe. But how could it have happened? Cameron remembers the war years clearly, the tremendous surge of patriotism, the vast mobilization, the great national effort. *Rosie the Riveter. Lucky Strike Green Goes to War. Let's Remember Pearl Harbor, As We Did the Alamo.* He doesn't see any way the Germans might have brought America to her knees. Except one. The bomb, he thinks. The bomb. The Nazis get the bomb in 1940 and Wernher von Braun invents a transatlantic rocket, and New York and Washington are nuked one night and that's it, we've been pushed beyond the resources of patriotism; we cave in and surrender within a week. And so—

He studies the photograph. President Kennedy, grinning, standing between Reichsfuehrer Goering and a suave youthful-looking Japanese. Kennedy? Ted? No, this is Jack, looking jowly, heavy bags under his eyes, deep creases in his face—he must be almost sixty years old, nearing the end of what is probably his second term of office. Jacqueline waiting none too patiently for him upstairs. Get done with your Japs and Nazis, love, and let's have a few drinkies together before the concert. Yes. John-John and Caroline are somewhere on the premises too, the nation's darlings, models for young people everywhere. Yes. And Goering? Indeed, the very same

Goering. Well into his eighties, monstrously fat, chin upon chin, multitudes of chins, vast bemedaled bosom, little mischievous eyes glittering with a long lifetime's cheery recollections of gratified lusts. How happy he looks! And how amiable! It was always impossible to hate Goering the way one loathed Goebbels, say, or Himmler or Streicher; Goering had charm, the outrageous charm of a *monstre sacré,* of a Nero, of a Caligula, and here he is alive in the 1970s, a mountain of immoral flesh, having survived Adolf to become—Cameron assumes—second Fuehrer and to be received in pomp at the White House, no less. Perhaps a state banquet tomorrow night, rollmops, sauerbraten, kassler rippchen, koenigsberger klopse, washed down with flagons of Bernkasteler Doktor '69, Schloss Johannisberg '71, or does the Fuehrer prefer beer? We have the finest lagers on tap, Löwenbrau, Würzburger Hofbrau—

But wait. Something rings false in Cameron's historical construct. He is unable to find in John F. Kennedy those depths of opportunism that would allow him to serve as puppet President of a Nazi-ruled America, taking orders from some slick-haired hard-eyed gauleiter and hopping obediently when the Fuehrer comes to town. Bomb or no bomb, there would have been a diehard underground resistance movement, decades of guerrilla warfare, bitter hatred of the German oppressor and of all collaborators. No surrender, then. The Axis has won the war, but the United States has retained its autonomy. Cameron revises his speculations. Suppose, he tells himself, Hitler in this universe did not break his pact with Stalin and invade Russia in the summer of 1941, but led his forces across the Channel instead to wipe out Britain. And the Japanese left Pearl Harbor alone, so the United States never was drawn into the war, which was over in fairly short order—say, by September of 1942. The Germans now rule Europe from Cornwall to the Urals and the Japanese have the whole Pacific, west of Hawaii; the United States, lost in dreamy neutrality, is an isolated nation, a giant Portugal, economically stagnant, largely cut off from world trade. There are no skyscrapers in San Francisco because no one sees reason to build anything in this country. Yes? Is this how it is?

He seats himself on the stoop of a house and explores his newspaper. This world has a stock market, albeit a sluggish one: the Dow-Jones Industrials stand at 354.61. Some of the listings are familiar—IBM, AT&T, General Motors—but many are not. Litton, Syntex, and Polaroid all are missing; so is Xerox, but he finds its primordial predecessor, Haloid, in the quotations. There are two baseball leagues, each with eight clubs; the Boston Braves have moved to Milwaukee but otherwise the table of teams could have come straight out of the 1940s. Brooklyn is leading in the National League, Philadelphia in the American. In the news section he finds recognizable names: New York has a Senator Rockefeller, Massachusetts has a Senator Kennedy. (Robert, apparently. He is currently in Italy. Yesterday he toured the majestic Tomb of Mussolini near the Colosseum, today he has an audience with Pope Benedict.) An airline advertisement invites San Franciscans to go to New York via TWA's glorious new Starliners, now only twelve hours with only a brief stop in Chicago. The accompanying sketch indicates that they have about reached the DC-4 level here, or is that a DC-6, with all those propellers?

The foreign news is tame and sketchy: not a word about Israel vs. the Arabs, the squabbling republics of Africa, the People's Republic of China, or the war in South America. Cameron assumes that the only surviving Jews are those of New York and Los Angeles, that Africa is one immense German colonial tract with a few patches under Italian rule, that China is governed by the Japanese, not by the heirs of Chairman Mao, and that the South American nations are torpid and unaggressive. Yes? Reading this newspaper is the strangest experience this voyage has given him so far, for the pages *look* right, the tone of the writing *feels* right, there is the insistent texture of unarguable reality about the whole paper, and yet everything is subtly off, everything has undergone a slight shift along the spectrum of events. The newspaper has the quality of a dream, but he has never known a dream to have such overwhelming substantive density.

He folds the paper under his arm and strolls toward the bay. A block from the waterfront he finds a branch of the Bank of America—some things withstand all permutations—and goes inside to change some money. There are risks, but he is curious. The teller unhesitatingly takes his five-dollar bill and hands him four singles and a little stack of coins. The singles are unremarkable, and Lincoln, Jefferson, and Washington occupy their familiar places on the cent, nickel, and quarter; but the dime shows Ben Franklin and the fifty-cent piece bears the features of a hearty-looking man, youngish, full-faced, bushy-haired, whom Cameron is unable to identify at all.

On the next corner eastward he comes to a public library. Now he can confirm his guesses. An almanac! Yes, and how odd the list of Presidents looks. Roosevelt, he learns, retired in poor health in 1940, and that, so far as he can discover, is the point of divergence between this world and his. The rest follows predictably enough. Wendell Willkie, defeating John Nance Garner in the 1940 election, maintains a policy of strict neutrality while—yes, it was as he imagined—the Germans and Japanese quickly conquer most of the world. Willkie dies in office during the 1944 Presidential campaign—Aha! That's Willkie on the half dollar!—and is briefly succeeded by Vice President McNary, who does not want the Presidency; a hastily-recalled Republican convention nominates Robert Taft. Two terms then for Taft, who beats James Byrnes, and two for Thomas Dewey, and then in 1960 the long Republican era is ended at last by Senator Lyndon Johnson of Texas. Johnson's running mate—it is an amusing reversal, Cameron thinks—is Senator John F. Kennedy of Massachusetts. After the traditional two terms, Johnson steps down and Vice President Kennedy wins the 1968 Presidential election. He has been re-elected in 1972, naturally; in this placid world incumbents always win. There is, of course, no UN here, there has been no Korean War, no movement of colonial liberation, no exploration of space. The almanac tells Cameron that Hitler lived until 1960, Mussolini until 1958. The world seems to have adapted remarkably readily to Axis rule, although a German army of occupation is still stationed in England.

He is tempted to go on and on, comparing histories, learning the transmuted destinies of such figures as Hubert Humphrey, Dwight Eisenhower, Harry Truman, Nikita Khrushchev, Lee Harvey Oswald, Juan Peron. But suddenly a more intimate curiosity flowers in him. In a hallway alcove he consults the telephone book. There is one directory covering both Alameda and Contra Costa counties, and it is a much more slender volume than the directory which in his world covers Oakland alone. There are two dozen Cameron listings, but none at his address, and no Christophers or Elizabeths or any plausible permutations of those names. On a hunch he looks in the San Francisco book. Nothing promising there either; but then he checks Elizabeth under her maiden name, Dudley, and yes, there is an Elizabeth Dudley at the familiar old address on Laguna. The discovery causes him to tremble. He rummages in his pocket, finds his Ben Franklin dime, drops it in the slot. He listens. There's the dial tone. He makes the call.

10.

THE APARTMENT, WHAT HE CAN see of it by peering past her shoulder, looks much as he remembers it: well-worn couches and chairs upholstered in burgundy and dark green, stark whitewashed walls, elaborate sculptures—her own—of gray driftwood, huge ferns in hanging containers. To behold these objects in these surroundings wrenches powerfully at his sense of time and place and afflicts him with an almost unbearable nostalgia. The last time he was here, if indeed he has ever been "here" in any sense, was in 1969; but the memories are vivid, and what he sees corresponds so closely to what he recalls that he feels transported to that earlier era. She stands in the doorway, studying him with cool curiosity tinged with unmistakable suspicion. She wears unexpectedly ordinary clothes, a loose-fitting embroidered white blouse and a short, pleated blue skirt, and her golden hair looks dull and carelessly combed, but surely she is the same woman from whom he parted this morning, the same woman with whom he has shared his life these past seven years, a beautiful woman, a tall woman, nearly as tall as he—on some occasions taller, it has seemed—with a serene smile and steady green eyes and smooth, taut skin. "Yes?" she says uncertainly. "Are you the man who phoned?"

"Yes. Chris Cameron." He searches her face for some flicker of recognition. "You don't know me? Not at all?"

"Not at all. Should I know you?"

"Perhaps. Probably not. It's hard to say."

"Have we once met? Is that it?"

"I'm not sure how I'm going to explain my relationship to you."

"So you said when you called. Your *relationship* to me? How can strangers have had a relationship?"

"It's complicated. May I come in?"

She laughs nervously, as though caught in some embarrassing faux pas. "Of course," she says, not without giving him a quick appraisal, making a rapid estimate of risk. The apartment is in fact almost exactly as he knew it, except that there is no stereo phonograph, only a bulky archaic Victrola, and her record collection is surprisingly scanty, and there are rather fewer books than his Elizabeth would have had. They confront one another stiffly. He is as uneasy over this encounter as she is, and finally it is she who seeks some kind of social lubricant, suggesting that they have a little wine. She offers him red or white.

"Red, please," he says.

She goes to a low sideboard and takes out two cheap, clumsy-looking tumblers. Then, effortlessly she lifts a gallon jug of wine from the floor and begins to unscrew its cap. "You were awfully mysterious on the phone," she says, "and you're still being mysterious now. What brings you here? Do we have mutual friends?"

"I think it wouldn't be untruthful to say that we do. At least in a manner of speaking."

"Your own manner of speaking is remarkably roundabout, Mr. Cameron."

"I can't help that right now. And call me Chris, please." As she pours the wine he watches her closely, thinking of that other Elizabeth, *his* Elizabeth, thinking how well he knows her body, the supple play of muscles in her back, the sleek texture of her skin, the firmness of her flesh, and he flashes instantly to their strange, absurdly romantic meeting years ago, that June when he had gone off alone into the Sierra high country for a week of backpacking and, following heaps of stones that he had wrongly taken to be trail markers, had come to a place well off the path, a private place, a cool dark glacial lake rimmed by brilliant patches of late-lying snow, and had begun to make camp, and had become suddenly aware of someone else's pack thirty yards away, and a pile of discarded clothing on the shore, and then had seen her, swimming just beyond a pine-tipped point, heading toward land, rising like Venus from the water, naked, noticing him, startled by his presence, apprehensive for a moment but then immediately making the best of it, relaxing, smiling, standing unashamed shin-deep in the chilly shallows and inviting him to join her for a swim.

These recollections of that first contact and all that ensued excite him terribly, for this person before him is at once the Elizabeth he loves, familiar, joined to him by the bond of shared experience, and also someone new, a complete stranger, from whom he can draw fresh inputs, that jolting gift of novelty which his Elizabeth can never again offer him. He stares at her shoulders and back with fierce, intense hunger; she turns toward him with the glasses of wine in her hands, and, before he can mask that wild gleam of desire, she receives it with full force. The impact is immediate. She recoils. She is not the Elizabeth of the Sierra Lake; she seems unable to handle such a level of unexpected erotic voltage. Jerkily she thrusts the wine at him, her hands shaking so that she spills a little on her sleeve. He takes the glass and backs away, a bit dazed by his own frenzied upwelling of emotion. With an effort, he calms himself. There is a long moment of awkward silence while they drink. The psychic atmosphere grows less torrid; a certain mood of remote, businesslike courtesy develops between them.

After the second glass of wine she says, "Now. How do you know me and what do you want from me?"

Briefly he closes his eyes. What can he tell her? How can he explain? He has rehearsed no strategies. Already he has managed to alarm her with a single unguarded glance; what effect would a confession of apparent madness have? But he has never used strategies with Elizabeth, has never resorted to any tactics except the tactic of utter candidness. And this is Elizabeth. Slowly he says, "In another existence you and I are married, Elizabeth. We live in the Oakland hills and we're extraordinarily happy together."

"Another existence?"

"In a world apart from this, a world where history took a different course a generation ago, where the Axis lost the war, where John Kennedy was President in 1963 and was killed by an assassin, where you and I met beside a lake in the Sierras and fell in love. There's an infinity of worlds, Elizabeth, side by side, worlds in which all possible variations of every possible event take place. Worlds in which you and I are married happily, in which you and I have been married and divorced, in which you and I don't exist, in which you exist and I don't, in which we meet and loathe one another, in which—in which—do you see, Elizabeth, there's a world for everything, and I've been traveling from world to world. I've seen nothing but wilderness where San Francisco ought to be, and I've met Mongol horsemen in the East Bay hills, and I've seen this whole area devastated by atomic warfare, and—does this sound insane to you, Elizabeth?"

"Just a little." She smiles. The old Elizabeth, cool, judicious, performing one of her specialities, the conditional acceptance of the unbelievable for the sake of some amusing conversation. "But go on. You've been jumping from world to world. I won't even bother to ask you how. What are you running away from?"

"I've never seen it that way. I'm running *toward.*"

"Toward what?"

"An infinity of worlds. An endless range of possible experience."

"That's a lot to swallow. Isn't one world enough for you to explore?"

"Evidently not."

"You had all infinity," she says. "Yet you chose to come to me. Presumably I'm the one point of familiarity for you in this otherwise strange world. Why come here? What's the point of your wanderings, if you seek the familiar? If all you wanted to do was find your way back to your Elizabeth, why did you leave her in the first place? Are you as happy with her as you claim to be?"

"I can be happy with her and still desire her in other guises."

"You sound driven."

"No," he says. "No more driven than Faust. I believe in searching as a way of life. Not searching *for,* just searching. And it's impossible to stop. To stop is to die, Elizabeth. Look at Faust, going on and on, going to Helen of Troy herself, experiencing everything the world has to offer, and always seeking more. When Faust finally cries out, *This is it, this is what I've been looking for, this is where I choose to stop,* Mephistopheles wins his bet."

"But that was Faust's moment of supreme happiness."

"True. When he attains it, though, he loses his soul to the devil, remember?"

"So you go on, on, and on, world after world, seeking you know not what, just seeking, unable to stop. And yet you claim you're not driven."

He shakes his head. "Machines are driven. Animals are driven. I'm an autonomous human being operating out of free will. I don't make this journey because I have to, but because I want to."

"Or because you think you ought to want to."

"I'm motivated by feelings, not by intellectual calculations and preconceptions."

"That sounds very carefully thought out," she tells him. He is stung by her words, and looks away, down into his empty glass. She indicates that he should help himself to the wine. "I'm sorry," she says, her tone softening a little.

He says, "At any rate, I was in the library and there was a telephone directory and I found you. This is where you used to live in my world too, before we were married." He hesitates. "Do you mind if I ask—"

"What?"

"You're not married?"

"No. I live alone. And like it."

"You always were independent-minded."

"You talk as though you know me so well."

"I've been married to you for seven years."

"No. Not to me. Never to me. You don't know me at all."

He nods. "You're right. I don't really know you, Elizabeth, however much I think I do. But I want to. I feel drawn to you as strongly as I was to the other Elizabeth, that day in the mountains. It's always best right at the beginning, when two strangers reach toward one another, when the spark leaps the gap—" Tenderly he says, "May I spend the night here?"

"No."

Somehow the refusal comes as no surprise. He says, "You once gave me a different answer when I asked you that."

"Not I. Someone else."

"I'm sorry. It's so hard for me to keep you and her distinct in my mind, Elizabeth. But please don't turn me away. I've come so far to be with you."

"You came uninvited. Besides, I'd feel so strange with you—knowing you were thinking of her, comparing me with her, measuring our differences, our points of similarities—"

"What makes you think I would?"

"You would."

"I don't think that's sufficient reason for sending me away."

"I'll give you another," she says. Her eyes sparkle mischievously. "I never let myself get involved with married men."

She is teasing him now. He says, laughing, confident that she is beginning to yield. "That's the damnedest far-fetched excuse I've ever heard, Elizabeth!"

"Is it? I feel a great kinship with her. She has all my sympathies. Why should I help you deceive her?"

"Deceive? What an old-fashioned word! Do you think she'd object? She never expected me to be chaste on this trip. She'd be flattered and delighted to know that I went looking for you here. She'd be eager to hear about everything that went on between us. How could she possibly be hurt by knowing that I had been with you, when you and she are—"

"Nevertheless, I'd like you to leave. Please."

"You haven't given me one convincing reason."

"I don't need to."

"I love you. I want to spend the night with you."

"You love someone else who resembles me," she replies. "I keep telling you that. In any case, I don't love you. I don't find you attractive, I'm afraid."

"Oh. She does, but you—don't. I see. How do you find me then? Ugly? Overbearing? Repellent?"

"I find you disturbing," she says. "A little frightening. Much too intense, much too controlled, perhaps dangerous. You aren't my type. I'm probably not yours. Remember, I'm not the Elizabeth you met by that mountain lake. Perhaps I'd be happier if I were, but I'm not. I wish you had never come here. Now please go. Please."

11.

Onward. This place is all gleaming towers and airy bridges, a glistening fantasy of a city. High overhead float glassy bubbles, silent airborne passenger vehicles, containing two or three people apiece who sprawl in postures of elegant relaxation. Bronzed young boys and girls lie naked beside soaring fountains spewing turquoise-and-scarlet foam. Giant orchids burst in tropical voluptuousness from the walls of colossal hotels. Small mechanical birds wheel and dart in the soft air like golden bullets, emitting sweet pinging sounds. From the tips of the tallest buildings comes a darker music, a ground bass of swelling hundred-cycle notes oscillating around an insistent central rumble. This is a world two centuries ahead of his, at the least. He could never infiltrate here. He could never even be a tourist. The only role available to him is that of visiting savage. Jemmy Button among the Londoners, and what, after all, was Jemmy Button's fate? Not a happy one. Patagonia! Patagonia! Thees ticket eet ees no longer good here, sor. Colored rays dance in the sky, red, green, blue, exploding, showering the city with transcendental images. Cameron smiles. He will not let himself be overwhelmed, though this place is more confusing than the world of the halftrack automobiles. Jauntily he plants himself at the center of a small park between two lanes of flowing, noiseless traffic. It is a formal garden lush with toothy orange-fronded ferns and thorny skyrockets of looping cactus. Lovers stroll past him arm in arm, offering one another swigs from glossy sweat-beaded green flasks that look like tubes of polished jade. Delicately they dangle blue grapes before each other's lips; playfully they smile, arch their necks, take the bait with eager pounces; then they laugh, embrace, tumble into the dense moist grass, which stirs and sways and emits gentle thrumming melodies. This place pleases him. He wanders through the garden, thinking of Elizabeth, thinking of springtime, and, coming ultimately to a sinuous brook in which the city's tallest towers are reflected as inverted needles, he kneels to drink. The water is cool, sweet, tart, much like young wine. A moment after it touches his lips, a mechanism rises from the spongy earth, five slender brassy columns, three with eye-sensors sprouting on all sides, one marked with a pattern of dark gridwork, one bearing an arrangement of winking colored lights. Out of the gridwork come ominous words in an unfathomable language. This is some kind of police machine, demanding his credentials: that much is clear. "I'm sorry," he says. "I can't understand what you're saying." Other machines are extruding themselves from trees, from the bed of the stream, from the hearts of the sturdiest ferns. "It's all right," he says. "I don't mean any harm. Just give me a chance to learn the language and I promise to become a useful citizen." One of the machines sprays him with a fine azure mist. Another drives a tiny needle into his forearm and extracts a droplet of blood. A crowd is gathering. They point, snicker, wink. The music of the building tops has become higher in pitch, more sinister in texture, it shakes the balmy air and threatens him in a personal way. "Let me stay," Cameron begs, but the music is shoving him, pushing him with a flat irresistible hand, inexorably squeezing him out of this world. He is too primitive for them. He is too coarse; he carries too many obsolete microbes. Very well. If that's what they want, he'll leave, not out of courtesy alone. In a flamboyant way he bids them farewell, bowing with a flourish worthy of Raleigh, blowing a kiss to the five-columned machine, smiling, even doing a little dance. Farewell. Farewell. The music rises to a wild crescendo. He hears celestial trumpets and distant thunder. Farewell. Onward.

12.

Here some kind of oriental marketplace has sprung up, foul-smelling, cluttered, medieval. Swarthy old men, white-bearded, in thick gray robes, sit patiently behind open burlap sacks of spices and grains. Lepers and cripples roam everywhere, begging importunately. Slender long-legged men wearing only tight loincloths and jingling dangling earrings of bright copper stalk through the crowd on solitary orbits, buying nothing, saying nothing; their skins are dark red; their faces are gaunt; their solemn features are finely modeled. They carry themselves like Inca princes. Perhaps they are Inca princes. In the haggle and babble of the market Cameron hears no recognizable tongue spoken. He sees the flash of gold as transactions are completed. The women balance immense burdens on their heads and show brilliant teeth when they smile. They favor patchwork skirts that cover their ankles, but they leave their breasts bare. Several of them glance provocatively at Cameron but he dares not return their quick dazzling probes until he knows what is permissible here. On the far side of the squalid plaza he catches sight of a woman who might well be Elizabeth; her back is to him, but he would know those strong shoulders anywhere: that erect stance, that cascade of unbound golden hair. He starts toward her, sliding with difficulty between the close-packed marketgoers. When he is still halfway across the marketplace from her he notices a man at her side, tall, a man of his own height and build. He wears a loose black robe and a dark scarf covers the lower half of his face. His eyes are grim and sullen and a terrible cicatrice, wide and glaringly cross-hatched with stitch marks, runs along his left cheek up to his hairline. The man whispers something to the woman who might be Elizabeth; she nods and turns, so that Cameron now is able to see her face, and yes, the woman does seem to be Elizabeth, but she bears a matching scar, angry and hideous, up the right side of her face. Cameron gasps. The scar-faced man suddenly points and shouts. Cameron senses motion to one side, and swings around just in time to see a short thick-bodied man come rushing toward him wildly waving a scimitar. For an instant Cameron sees the scene as though in a photograph: he has time to make a leisurely examination of his attacker's oily beard, his hooked hairy-nostriled nose, his yellowed teeth, the cheap, glassy-looking inlaid stones on the haft of the scimitar. Then the frightful blade descends, while the assassin screams abuse at Cameron in what might be Arabic.

It is a sorry welcome. Cameron cannot prolong this investigation. An instant before the scimitar cuts him in two, he takes himself elsewhere, with regret.

13.

ONWARD. TO A PLACE WHERE there is no solidity, where the planet itself has vanished, so that he swims through space, falling peacefully, going from nowhere to nowhere. He is surrounded by a brilliant green light that emanates from every point at once, like a message from the fabric of the universe. In great tranquility he drops through this cheerful glow for days on end, or what seems like days on end, drifting, banking, checking his course with small motions of his elbows or knees. It makes no difference where he goes; everything here is like everything else here. The green glow supports and sustains and nourishes him, but it makes him restless. He plays with it. Out of its lambent substance he succeeds in shaping images, faces, abstract patterns; he conjures up Elizabeth for himself, he evokes his own sharp features, he fills the heavens with a legion of marching Chinese in tapered straw hats, he obliterates them with forceful diagonal lines, he causes a river of silver to stream across the firmament and discharge its glittering burden down a mountainside a thousand miles high. He spins. He floats. He glides. He releases all his fantasies. This is total freedom, here in this unworldly place. But it is not enough. He grows weary of emptiness. He grows weary of serenity. He has drained this place of all it has to offer, too soon, too soon. He is not sure whether the failure is in himself or in the place, but he feels he must leave. Therefore: onward.

14.

TERRIFIED PEASANTS RUN SHRIEKING AS he materializes in their midst. This is some sort of farming village along the eastern shore of the bay: neat green fields, a cluster of low wicker huts radiating from a central plaza, naked children toddling and crying, a busy sub-population of goats and geese and chickens. It is midday; Cameron sees the bright gleam of water in the irrigation ditches. These people work hard. They have scattered at his approach, but now they creep back warily, crouching, ready to take off again if he performs any more miracles. This is another of those bucolic worlds in which San Francisco has not happened, but he is unable to identify these settlers, nor can he isolate the chain of events that brought them here. They are not Indians, nor Chinese, nor Peruvians; they have a European look about them, somehow Slavic, but what would Slavs be doing in California? Russian farmers, maybe, colonizing by way of Siberia? There is some plausibility in that—their dark complexions, their heavy facial structure, their squat powerful bodies—but they seem oddly primitive, half-naked, in furry leggings or less, as though they are no subjects of the Tsar but rather Scythians or Cimmerians transplanted from the prehistoric marshes of the Vistula.

"Don't be frightened," he tells them, holding his upraised outspread arms toward them. They do seem less fearful of him now, timidly approaching, staring with big dark eyes. "I won't harm you. I'd just like to visit with you." They murmur. A woman boldly shoves a child forward, a girl of about five, bare, with black greasy ringlets, and Cameron scoops her up, caresses her, tickles her, lightly sets her down. Instantly the whole tribe is around him, no longer afraid; they touch his arm, they kneel, they stroke his shins. A boy brings him a wooden bowl of porridge. An old woman gives him a mug of sweet wine, a kind of mead. A slender girl drapes a stole of auburn fur over his shoulders. They dance; they chant; their fear has turned into love; he is their honored guest. He is more than that: he is a god. They take him to an unoccupied hut, the largest in the village. Piously they bring him offerings of incense and acorns. When it grows dark they build an immense bonfire in the plaza, so that he wonders in vague concern if they will feast on him when they are done honoring him, but they feast on slaughtered cattle instead, and yield to him the choicest pieces, and afterward they stand by his door, singing discordant, energetic hymns. That night three girls of the tribe, no doubt the fairest virgins available, are sent to him, and in the morning he finds his threshold heaped with newly plucked blossoms. Later two tribal artisans, one lame and the other blind, set to work with stone adzes and chisels, hewing an immense and remarkably accurate likeness of him out of a redwood stump that has been mounted at the plaza's center.

So he has been deified. He has a quick Faustian vision of himself living among these diligent people, teaching them advanced methods of agriculture, leading them eventually into technology, into modern hygiene, into all the contemporary advantages without the contemporary abominations. Guiding them toward the light, molding them, creating them. This world, this village, would be a good place for him to stop his transit of the infinities, if stopping were desirable: god, prophet, king of a placid realm, teacher, inculcator of civilization, a purpose to his existence at last. But there is no place to stop. He knows that. Transforming happy primitive farmers into sophisticated twentieth-century agriculturalists is ultimately as useless a pastime as training fleas to jump through hoops. It is tempting to live as a god, but even divinity will pall, and it is dangerous to become attached to an unreal satisfaction, dangerous to become attached at all. The journey, not the arrival, matters. Always.

So Cameron does godhood for a little while. He finds it pleasant and fulfilling. He savors the rewards until he senses that the rewards are becoming too important to him. He makes his formal renunciation of his godhead. Then: onward.

15.

And this place he recognizes. His street, his house, his garden, his green car in the carport, Elizabeth's yellow one parked out front. Home again, so soon? He hadn't expected that; but every leap he has made, he knows, must in some way have been a product of deliberate choice, and evidently whatever hidden mechanism within him that has directed these voyages has chosen to bring him home again. All right, touch base. Digest your travels, examine them, allow your experiences to work their alchemy on you: you need to stand still a moment for that. Afterward you can always leave again. He slides his key into the door.

Elizabeth has one of the Mozart quartets on the phonograph. She sits curled up in the living-room window seat, leafing through a magazine. It is late afternoon, and the San Francisco skyline, clearly visible across the bay through the big window, is haloed by the brilliant retreating sunlight. There are freshly-cut flowers in the little crystal bowl on the redwood-burl table; the fragrance of gardenias and jasmine dances past him. Unhurriedly she looks up, brings her eyes into line with his, dazzles him with the warmth of her smile, and says, "Well, hello!"

"Hello, Elizabeth."

She comes to him. "I didn't expect you back this quickly, Chris, I don't know if I expected you to come back at all, as a matter of fact."

"This quickly? How long have I been gone, for you?"

"Tuesday morning to Thursday afternoon. Two and a half days." She eyes his coarse new beard, his ragged, sun-bleached shirt. "It's been longer for you, hasn't it?"

"Weeks and weeks. I'm not sure how long. I was in eight or nine different places, and I stayed in the last one quite some time. They were villagers, farmers, some primitive Slavonic tribe living down by the bay. I was their god, but I got bored with it."

"You always did get bored so easily," she says, and laughs, and takes his hands in hers and pulls him toward her. She brushes her lips lightly against him, a peck, a play-kiss, their usual first greeting, and then they kiss more passionately, bodies pressing close, tongue seeking tongue. He feels a pounding in his chest, the old inextinguishable throb. When they release each other he steps back, a little dizzied, and says, "I missed you, Elizabeth. I didn't know how much I'd miss you until I was somewhere else and aware that I might never find you again."

"Did you seriously worry about that?"

"Very much."

"I never doubted we'd be together again, one way or another. Infinity's such a big place, darling. You'd find your way back to me, or to someone very much like me. And someone very much like you would find his way to me, if you didn't. How many Chris Camerons do you think there are, on the move between worlds right now? A thousand? A trillion trillion?" She turns toward the sideboard and says, without breaking the flow of her words, "Would you like some wine?" and begins to pour from a half-empty jug of red. "Tell me where you've been," she says.

He comes up behind her and rests his hands on her shoulders, and draws them down the back of her silk blouse to her waist, holding her there, kissing the nape of her neck. He says, "To a world where there was an atomic war here, and to one where there still were Indian raiders out by Livermore, and one that was all fantastic robots and futuristic helicopters, and one where Johnson was President before Kennedy and Kennedy is alive and President now, and one where—oh, I'll give you all the details later. I need a chance to unwind first." He releases her and kisses the tip of her earlobe and takes one of the glasses from her, and they salute each other and drink, draining the wine quickly. "It's so good to be home," he says softly. "Good to have gone where I went, good to be back." She fills his glass again. The familiar domestic ritual: red wine is their special drink, cheap red wine out of gallon jugs. A sacrament, more dear to him than the burnt offerings of his recent subjects. Halfway through the second glass he says, "Come. Let's go inside."

The bed has fresh linens on it, cool, inviting. There are three thick books on the night table: she's set up for some heavy reading in his absence. Cut flowers in here, too, fragrance everywhere. Their clothes drop away. She touches his beard and chuckles at the roughness, and he kisses the smooth cool place along the inside of her thigh and draws his cheek lightly across it, sandpapering her lovingly, and then she pulls him to her and their bodies slide together and he enters her. Everything thereafter happens quickly, much too quickly; he has been long absent from her, if not she from him, and now her presence excites him, there is a strangeness about her body, her movements, and it hastens him to his ecstasy. He feels a mild pang of regret, but no more: he'll make it up to her soon enough, they both know that. They drift into a sleepy embrace, neither of them speaking, and eventually uncoil into tender new passion, and this time all is as it should be. Afterward they doze. A spectacular sunset blazes over the city when he opens his eyes. They rise, they take a shower together, much giggling, much playfulness. "Let's go across the bay for a fancy dinner tonight," he suggests. "Trianon, Blue Fox, Ernie's, anywhere. You name it. I feel like celebrating."

"So do I, Chris."

"It's good to be home again."

"It's good to have you here," she tells him. She looks for her purse. "How soon do you think you'll be heading out again? Not that I mean to rush you, but—"

"You know I'm not going to be staying?"

"Of course I know."

"Yes. You would." She had never questioned his going. They both tried to be responsive to each other's needs; they had always regarded one another as equal partners, free to do as they wished. "I can't say how long I'll stay. Probably not long. Coming home this soon was really an accident, you know. I just planned to go on and on and on, world after world, and I never programmed my next jump, at least not consciously. I simply leaped. And the last leap deposited me on my own doorstep, somehow, so I let myself into the house. And there you were to welcome me home."

She presses his hand between hers. Almost sadly she says, "You aren't home, Chris."

"What?"

He hears the sound of the front door opening. Footsteps in the hallway.

"You aren't home," she says.

Confusion seizes him. He thinks of all that has passed between them this evening.

"Elizabeth?" calls a deep voice from the living room.

"In here, darling. I have company!"

"Oh? Who?" A man enters the bedroom, halts, grins. He is clean-shaven and dressed in the clothes Cameron had worn on Tuesday; otherwise they could be twins. "Hey, hello!" he says warmly, extending his hand.

Elizabeth says, "He comes from a place that must be very much like this one. He's been here since five o'clock, and we were just going out for dinner. Have you been having an interesting time?"

"Very," the other Cameron says. "I'll tell you all about it later. Go on, don't let me keep you."

"You could join us for dinner," Cameron suggests helplessly.

"That's all right. I've just eaten. Breast of passenger pigeon—they aren't extinct everywhere. I wish I could have brought some home for the freezer. So you two go and enjoy. I'll see you later. Both of you, I hope. Will you be staying with us? We've got notes to compare, you and I."

16.

He rises just before dawn, in a marvelous foggy stillness. The Camerons have been wonderfully hospitable, but he must be moving along. He scrawls a thank-you note and slips it under their bedroom door. Let's get together again someday. Somewhere. Somehow. They wanted him as a house guest for a week or two, but no, he feels like a bit of an intruder here, and anyway the universe is waiting for him. He has to go. The journey, not the arrival, matters, for what else is there but trips? Departing is unexpectedly painful, but he knows the mood will pass. He closes his eyes. He breaks his moorings. He gives himself up to his sublime restlessness. Onward. Onward. *Goodbye, Elizabeth. Goodbye, Chris. I'll see you both again.* Onward.

MANY MANSIONS

Here's an example of mainstream contemporary literature modes carried over into science fiction, something I've done now and again throughout my entire career. (A very early story called "The Songs of Summer" owed a great deal to Faulkner's As I Lay Dying. *I've channeled Joseph Conrad on a number of occasions. One passage in my novel* Son of Man *employs William Burroughs' cut-up technique. And so forth.) This is another, and I think it was a successful transplantation.*

Somewhere in the mid-1960s Robert Coover wrote a funny, frantic story called "The Babysitter," in which a narrative situation is dissected and refracted in an almost Cubist fashion into dozens of short scenes, some of which are deliberately contradictory of others. I read it and admired it and saw what Coover had done as a perfect way to approach the paradoxes of the time travel story, in which a single act of transit through time can generate a host of parallel time tracks. I had written plenty of time travel stories before, of course—but Coover had shown me a completely new way to do it.

So off I went, killing off grandfathers and having characters meeting themselves both coming and going, in what is probably the most complex short story of temporal confusion since Robert A. Heinlein's "By His Bootstraps." (Or Heinlein's much later "—All You Zombies—"). I had a wonderful time doing it, which was important, because in that complicated segment of my life—this was February 1972, when I was midway through the chaotic transition from a lifetime in New York to a wholly new incarnation as a Californian—writing usually was neither easy nor particularly pleasant for me.

Terry Carr published the story in the third of his Universe *anthologies, and it has been reprinted several times since. I can't read it even now without chuckling over its dizzy pace and lunatic inventiveness.*

The debt to Coover's original story, I thought, was obvious. But over the past forty-plus years a grand total of one reader has asked me whether I had had "The Babysitter" in mind when I wrote "Many Mansions." (I never do learn. Many years later, when I wrote a story called "The Secret Sharer" that translated the plot of Conrad's classic novella into science fictional terms, and hung Conrad's original title on my story just so everyone would understand what I was doing, a reader wrote an angry letter to the editor of the magazine where my story appeared, complaining that I had stolen the title of a famous story by Joseph Conrad. Maybe I should attach explanatory footnotes to these things.)

It's been a rough day. Everything gone wrong. A tremendous tie-up on the freeway going to work, two accounts cancelled before lunch, now some inconceivable botch by the weather programmers. It's snowing outside. Actually snowing. He'll have to go out and clear the driveway in the morning. He can't remember when it last snowed. And of course a fight with Alice again. She never lets him alone. She's at her most deadly when she sees him come home exhausted from the office. Ted why don't you this, Ted get me that. Now, waiting for dinner, working on his third drink in forty minutes, he feels one of his headaches coming on. Those miserable killer headaches that can destroy a whole evening. What a life! He toys with murderous fantasies. Take her out by the reservoir for a friendly little stroll, give her a quick hard shove with his shoulder. She can't swim. Down, down, down. Glub. Goodbye, Alice. Free at last.

In the kitchen she furiously taps the keys of the console, programming dinner just the way he likes it. Cold vichyssoise, baked potato with sour cream and chives, sirloin steak blood-rare inside and charcoal-charred outside. Don't think it isn't work to get the meal just right, even with the autochef. All for him. The bastard. Tell me, why do I sweat so hard to please him? Has he made me happy? What's he ever done for me except waste the best years of my life? And he thinks I don't know about his other women. Those lunchtime quickies. Oh, I wouldn't mind at all if he dropped dead tomorrow. I'd be a great widow—so dignified at the funeral, so strong, hardly crying at all. And everybody thinks we're such a close couple. Married eleven years and they're still in love. I heard someone say that only last week. If they only knew the truth about us. If they only knew.

Martin peers out the window of his third-floor apartment in Sunset Village. Snow. I'll be damned. He can't remember the last time he saw snow. Thirty, forty years back, maybe, when Ted was a baby. He absolutely can't remember. White stuff on the ground when? The mind gets wobbly when you're past eighty. He still can't believe he's an old man. It rocks him to realize that his grandson Ted, Martha's boy, is almost forty. I bounced that kid on my knee and he threw up all over my suit. Four years old then. Nixon was President. Nobody talks much about Tricky Dick these days. Ancient history. McKinley, Coolidge, Nixon. Time flies. Martin thinks of Ted's wife, Alice. What a nice tight little ass she has. What a cute pair of jugs. I'd like to get my hands on them. I really would. You know something, Martin? You're not such an old ruin yet. Not if you can get it up for your grandson's wife.

His dreams of drowning her fade as quickly as they came. He is not a violent man by nature. He knows he could never do it. He can't even bring himself to step on a spider; how then could he kill his wife? If she'd die some other way, of course, without the need of his taking direct action, that would solve everything. She's driving to the hairdresser on one of those manual-access roads she likes to use, and her car swerves on an icy spot, and she goes into a tree at eighty kilometers an hour. Good. She's shopping on Union Boulevard, and the bank is blown up by an activist; she's nailed by flying debris. Good. The dentist gives her a new anesthetic and it turns out she's fatally allergic to it. Puffs up like a blowfish and dies in five minutes. Good.

The police come, long faces, snuffly noses. Terribly sorry, Mr. Porter. There's been an awful accident. Don't tell me it's my wife, he cries. They nod lugubriously. He bears up bravely under the loss, though.

"You can come in for dinner now," she says. He's sitting slouched on the sofa with another drink in his hand. He drinks more than any man she knows, not that she knows all that many. Maybe he'll get cirrhosis and die. Do people still die of cirrhosis, she wonders, or do they give them liver transplants now? The funny thing is that he still turns her on, after eleven years. His eyes, his face, his hands. She despises him but he still turns her on.

The snow reminds him of his young manhood, of his days long ago in the East. He was quite the ladies' man then. And it wasn't so easy to get some action back in those days, either. The girls were always worried about what people would say if anyone found out. What people would say! As if doing it with a boy you liked was something shameful. Or they'd worry about getting knocked up. They made you wear a rubber. How awful that was: like wearing a sock. The pill was just starting to come in, the original pill, the old one-a-day kind. Imagine a world without the pill! ("Did they have dinosaurs when you were a boy, grandpa?") Still, Martin had made out all right. Big muscular frame, strong earnest features, warm inquisitive eyes. You'd never know it to look at me now. I wonder if Alice realizes what kind of stud I used to be. If I had the money I'd rent one of those time machines they've got now and send her back to visit myself around 1950 or so. A little gift to my younger self. He'd really rip into her. It gives Martin a quick riffle of excitement to think of his younger self ripping into Alice. But of course he can't afford any such thing.

As he forks down his steak he imagines being single again. Would I get married again? Not on your life. Not until I'm good and ready, anyway, maybe when I'm fifty-five or sixty. Me for bachelorhood for the time being, just screwing around like a kid. To hell with responsibilities. I'll wait two, three weeks after the funeral, a decent interval, and then I'll go off for some fun. Hawaii, Tahiti, Fiji, someplace out there. With Nolie. Or Maria. Or Ellie. Yes, with Ellie. He thinks of Ellie's pink thighs, her soft heavy breasts, her long, radiant auburn hair. Two weeks in Fiji with Ellie. Two weeks in Ellie with Fiji. Yes. Yes. Yes. 'Is the steak rare enough for you, Ted?' Alice asks. 'It's fine,' he says.

She goes upstairs to check the children's bedroom. They're both asleep, finally. Or else faking it so well that it makes no difference. She stands by their beds a moment, thinking, I love you, Bobby, I love you, Tink. Tink and Bobby, Bobby and Tink. I love you even though you drive me crazy sometimes. She tiptoes out. Now for a quiet evening of television. And then to bed. The same old routine. Christ. I don't know why I go on like this. There are times when I'm ready to explode. I stay with him for the children's sake, I guess. Is that enough of a reason?

He envisions himself running hand in hand along the beach with Ellie. Both of them naked, their skins bronzed and gleaming in the tropical sunlight. Palm trees everywhere. Grains of pink sand under foot. Soft transparent wavelets lapping the shore. A quiet cove. "No one can see us here," Ellie murmurs. He sinks down on her firm sleek body and enters her.

A blazing band of pain tightens like a strip of hot metal across Martin's chest. He staggers away from the window, dropping into a low crouch as he stumbles toward a chair. The heart. Oh, the heart! That's what you get for drooling over Alice. Dirty old man. "Help," he calls feebly. "Come on, you filthy machine, help me!" The medic, activated by the key phrase, rolls silently toward him. Its sensors are already at work scanning him, searching for the cause of the discomfort. A telescoping steel-jacketed arm slides out of the medic's chest and, hovering above Martin, extrudes an ultrasonic injection snout. "Yes," Martin murmurs, "that's right, damn you, hurry up and give me the drug!" Calm. I must try to remain calm. The snout makes a gentle whirring noise as it forces the relaxant into Martin's vein. He slumps in relief. The pain slowly ebbs. Oh, that's much better. Saved again. Oh. Oh. Oh. Dirty old man. Ought to be ashamed of yourself.

TED KNOWS HE WON'T GET to Fiji with Ellie or anybody else. Any realistic assessment of the situation brings him inevitably to the same conclusion. Alice isn't going to die in an accident, any more than he's likely to murder her. She'll live forever. Unwanted wives always do. He could ask for a divorce, of course. He'd probably lose everything he owned, but he'd win his freedom. Or he could simply do away with himself. That was always a temptation for him. The easy way out, no lawyers, no hassles. So it's that time of the evening again. It's the same every night. Pretending to watch television, he secretly indulges in suicidal fantasies.

BARE-BODIED DANCERS IN GAUDY LUMINOUS paint gyrate lasciviously on the screen, nearly large as life. Alice scowls. The things they show on TV nowadays! It used to be that you got this stuff only on the X-rated channels, but now it's everywhere. And look at him, just lapping it up! Actually she knows she wouldn't be so stuffy about the sex shows except that Ted's fascination with them is a measure of his lack of interest in her. Let them show screwing and all the rest on TV, if that's what people want. I just wish Ted had as much enthusiasm for me as he does for the television stuff. So far as sexual permissiveness in general goes, she's no prude. She used to wear nothing but trunks at the beach, until Tink was born and she started to feel a little less proud of her figure. But she still dresses as revealingly as anyone in their crowd. And gets stared at by everyone but her own husband. He watches the TV cuties. His other women must use him up. Maybe I ought to step out a bit myself, Alice thinks. She's had her little affairs along the way. Not many, nothing very serious, but she's had some. Three lovers in eleven years, that's not a great many, but it's a sign that she's no puritan. She wonders if she ought to get involved with somebody now. It might move her life off dead center while she still has the chance, before boredom destroys her entirely. "I'm going up to wash my hair," she announces. "Will you be staying down here till bedtime?"

There are so many ways he could do it. Slit his wrists. Drive his car off the bridge. Swallow Alice's whole box of sleeping tabs. Of course those are all old-fashioned ways of killing yourself. Something more modern would be appropriate. Go into one of the black taverns and start making loud racial insults? No, nothing modern about that. It's very 1975. But something genuinely contemporary does occur to him. Those time machines they've got now: suppose he rented one and went back, say, sixty years, to a time when one of his parents hadn't yet been born. And killed his grandfather. Find old Martin as a young man and slip a knife into him. If I do that, Ted figures, I should instantly and painlessly cease to exist. I would never have existed, because my mother wouldn't ever have existed. Poof. Out like a light. Then he realizes he's fantasizing a murder again. Stupid: if he could ever murder anyone, he'd murder Alice and be done with it. So the whole fantasy is foolish. Back to the starting point is where he is.

She is sitting under the hair-dryer when he comes upstairs. He has a peculiarly smug expression on his face, and as soon as she turns the dryer off she asks him what he's thinking about. 'I may have just invented a perfect murder method,' he tells her. "Oh?" she says. He says, "You rent a time machine. Then you go back a couple of generations and murder one of the ancestors of your intended victim. That way you're murdering the victim too, because he won't ever have been born if you kill off one of his immediate progenitors. Then you return to your own time. Nobody can trace you because you don't have any fingerprints on file in an era before your own birth. What do you think of it?" Alice shrugs. "It's an old one," she says. "It's been done on television a dozen times. Anyway, I don't like it. Why should an innocent person have to die just because he's the grandparent of somebody you want to kill?"

They're probably in bed together right now, Martin thinks gloomily. Stark naked side by side. The lights are out. The house is quiet. Maybe they're smoking a little grass. Do they still call it grass, he wonders, or is there some new nickname now? Anyway the two of them turn on. Yes. And then he reaches for her. His hands slide over her cool, smooth skin. He cups her breasts. Plays with the hard little nipples. Sucks on them. The other hand wandering down to her parted thighs. And then she. And then he. And then they. And then they. Oh, Alice, he murmurs. Oh, Ted, Ted, she cries. And then they. Go to it. Up and down, in and out. Oh. Oh. Oh. She claws his back. She pumps her hips. Ted! Ted! Ted! The big moment is arriving now. For her, for him. Jackpot! Afterward they lie close for a few minutes, basking in the afterglow. And then they roll apart. Goodnight, Ted. Goodnight, Alice. Oh, Jesus. They do it every night, I bet. They're so young and full of juice. And I'm all dried up. Christ, I hate being old. When I think of the man I once was. When I think of the women I once had. Jesus. Jesus. God, let me have the strength to do it just once more before I die. And leave me alone for two hours with Alice.

She has trouble falling asleep. A strange scene keeps playing itself out obsessively in her mind. She sees herself stepping out of an upright coffin-size box of dark gray metal, festooned with dials and levers. The time machine. It delivers her into a dark, dirty alleyway, and when she walks forward to the street she sees scores of little antique automobiles buzzing around. Only they aren't antiques, they're the current models. This is the year 1947. New York City. Will she be conspicuous in her futuristic clothes? She has her breasts covered, at any rate. That's essential back here. She hurries to the proper address, resisting the temptation to browse in shop windows along the way. How quaint and ancient everything looks. And how dirty the streets are. She comes to a tall building of red brick. This is the place. No scanners study her as she enters. They don't have annunciators yet or any other automatic home-protection equipment. She goes upstairs in an elevator so creaky and unstable that she fears for her life. Fifth floor. Apartment 5-J. She rings the doorbell. *He* answers. He's terribly young, only twenty-four, but she can pick out signs of the Martin of the future in his face, the strong cheekbones, the searching blue eyes. "Are you Martin Jamieson?" she asks. "That's right," he says. She smiles. "May I come in?" "Of course," he says. He bows her into the apartment. As he momentarily turns his back on her to open the coat closet she takes the heavy steel pipe from her purse and lifts it high and brings it down on the back of his head. *Thwock.* She takes the heavy steel pipe from her purse and lifts it high and brings it down on the back of his head. *Thwock.* She takes the heavy steel pipe from her purse and lifts it high and brings it down on the back of his head. *Thwock.*

Ted and Alice visit him at Sunset Village two or three times a month. He can't complain about that; it's as much as he can expect. He's an old, old man and no doubt a boring one, but they come dutifully, sometimes with the kids, sometimes without. He's never gotten used to the idea that he's a great-grandfather. Alice always gives him a kiss when she arrives and another when she leaves. He plays a private little game with her, copping a feel at each kiss. His hand quickly stroking her butt. Or sometimes when he's really rambunctious it travels lightly over her breast. Does she notice? Probably. She never lets on, though. Pretends it's an accidental touch. Most likely she thinks it's charming that a man of his age would still have at least a vestige of sexual desire left. Unless she thinks it's disgusting, that is.

The time-machine gimmick, Ted tells himself, can be used in ways that don't quite amount to murder. For instance. "What's that box?" Alice asks. He smiles cunningly. "It's called a panchronicon," he says. "It gives you a kind of televised reconstruction of ancient times. The salesman loaned me a demonstration sample." She says, "How does it work?" "Just step inside," he tells her. "It's all ready for you." She starts to enter the machine, but then, suddenly suspicious, she hesitates on the threshold. He pushes her in and slams the door shut behind her. *Wham!* The controls are set. Off goes Alice on a one-way journey to the Pleistocene. The machine is primed to return as soon as it drops her off. That isn't murder, is it? She's still alive, wherever she may be, unless the sabre-tooth tigers have caught up with her. So long, Alice.

In the morning she drives Bobby and Tink to school. Then she stops at the bank and post office. From ten to eleven she has her regular session at the identity-reinforcement parlor. Ordinarily she would go right home after that, but this morning she strolls across the shopping center plaza to the office that the time-machine people have just opened. TEMPONAUTICS, LTD, the sign over the door says. The place is empty except for two machines, no doubt demonstration models, and a bland-faced, smiling salesman. "Hello," Alice says nervously. "I just wanted to pick up some information about the rental costs of one of your machines."

MARTIN LIKES TO IMAGINE ALICE coming to visit him by herself some rainy Saturday afternoon. "Ted isn't able to make it today," she explains. "Something came up at the office. But I knew you were expecting us, and I didn't want you to be disappointed. Poor Martin, you must lead such a lonely life." She comes close to him. She is trembling. So is he. Her face is flushed and her eyes are bright with the unmistakable glossiness of desire. He feels a sense of sexual excitement too, for the first time in ten or twenty years: that tension in the loins, that throbbing of the pulse. Electricity. Chemistry. His eyes lock on hers. Her nostrils flare, her mouth goes taut. "Martin," she whispers huskily. "Do you feel what I feel?" "You know I do," he tells her. She says, "If only I could have known you when you were in your prime!" He chuckles. "I'm not altogether senile yet," he cries exultantly. Then she is in his arms and his lips are seeking her fragrant breasts.

"YES, IT CAME AS A terrible shock to me," Ted tells Ellie. "Having her disappear like that. She simply vanished from the face of the earth, as far as anyone can determine. They've tried every possible way of tracing her and there hasn't been a clue." Ellie's flawless forehead furrows in a fitful frown. "Was she unhappy?" she asks, "Do you think she may have done away with herself?" Ted shakes his head. "I don't know. You live with a person for eleven years and you think you know her pretty well, and then one day something absolutely incomprehensible occurs and you realize how impossible it is ever to know another human being at all. Don't you agree?" Ellie nods gravely. "Yes, oh, yes, certainly!" she says. He smiles down at her and takes her hands in his.

Softly he says, "Let's not talk about Alice any more, shall we? She's gone and that's all I'll ever know." He hears a pulsing symphonic crescendo of shimmering angelic choirs as he embraces her and murmurs, "I love you, Ellie. I love you."

SHE TAKES THE HEAVY STEEL pipe from her purse and lifts it high and brings it down on the back of his head. *Thwock.* Young Martin drops instantly, twitches once, lies still. Dark blood begins to seep through the dense blond curls of his hair. How strange to see Martin with golden hair, she thinks, as she kneels beside his body. She puts her hand to the bloody place, probes timidly, feels the deep indentation. Is he dead? She isn't sure how to tell. He isn't moving. He doesn't seem to be breathing. She wonders if she ought to hit him again, just to make certain. Then she remembers something she's seen on television, and takes her mirror from her purse. Holds it in front of his face. No cloud forms. That's pretty conclusive: you're dead, Martin. R.I.P. Martin Jamieson, 1923–1947. Which means that Martha Jamieson Porter (1948–) will never now be conceived, and that automatically obliterates the existence of her son Theodore Porter (1968–) . Not bad going, Alice, getting rid of unloved husband and miserable shrewish mother-in-law all in one shot. Sorry, Martin. Bye-bye, Ted. (R.I.P. Theodore Porter, 1968–1947. Eh?) She rises, goes into the bathroom with the steel pipe and carefully rinses it off. Then she puts it back into her purse. Now to go back to the machine and return to 2006, she thinks. To start my new life. But as she leaves the apartment, a tall, lean man steps out of the hallway shadows and clamps his hand powerfully around her wrist. "Time Patrol," he says crisply, flashing an identification badge. "You're under arrest for temponautic murder, Mrs. Porter."

TODAY HAS BEEN A BETTER day than yesterday, low on crises and depressions, but he still feels a headache coming on as he lets himself into the house. He is braced for whatever bitchiness Alice may have in store for him this evening. But, oddly, she seems relaxed and amiable. "Can I get you a drink, Ted?" she asks. "How did your day go?" He smiles and says, "Well, I think we may have salvaged the Hammond account after all. Otherwise nothing special happened. And you? What did you do today, love?" She shrugs. "Oh, the usual stuff," she says. "The bank, the post office, my identity-reinforcement session."

If you had the money, Martin asks himself, how far back would you send her? 1947, that would be the year, I guess. My last year as a single man. No sense complicating things. Off you go, Alice baby, to 1947. Let's make it March. By June I was engaged and by September Martha was on the way, though I didn't find that out until later. Yes: March, 1947. So Young Martin answers the doorbell and sees an attractive girl in the hall, a woman, really, older than he is, maybe thirty or thirty-two. Slender, dark-haired, nicely constructed. Odd clothing: a clinging gray tunic, very short, made of some strange fabric that flows over her body like a stream. How it achieves that liquid effect around the pleats is beyond him. "Are you Martin Jamieson?" she asks. And quickly answers herself. "Yes, of course, you must be. I recognize you. How handsome you were!" He is baffled. He knows nothing, naturally, about this gift from his aged future self. "Who are you?" he asks. "May I come in first?" she says. He is embarrassed by his lack of courtesy and waves her inside. Her eyes glitter with mischief. "You aren't going to believe this," she tells him, "but I'm your grandson's wife."

"Would you like to try out one of our demonstration models?" the salesman asks pleasantly. "There's absolutely no cost or obligation." Ted looks at Alice. Alice looks at Ted. Her frown mirrors his inner uncertainty. She also must be wishing that they had never come to the Temponautics showroom. The salesman, pattering smoothly onward, says, "In these demonstrations we usually send our potential customers fifteen or twenty minutes into the past. I'm sure you'll find it fascinating. While remaining in the machine, you'll be able to look through a viewer and observe your own selves actually entering this very showroom a short while ago. Well? Will you give it a try? You go first, Mrs. Porter. I assure you it's going to be the most unique experience you've ever had." Alice, uneasy, tries to back off, but the salesman prods her in a way that is at once gentle and unyielding, and she steps reluctantly into the time machine. He closes the door. A great business of adjusting fine controls ensues. Then the salesman throws a master switch. A green glow envelopes the machine and it disappears, although something transparent and vague—retinal after-image? the ghost of the machine?—remains dimly visible. The salesman says, "She's now gone a short distance into her own past. I've programmed the machine to take her back eighteen minutes and keep her there for a total elapsed interval of six minutes, so she can see the entire opening moments of your visit here. But when I return her to Now Level, there's no need to match the amount of elapsed time in the past, so that from our point of view she'll have been absent only some thirty seconds. Isn't that remarkable, Mr. Porter? It's one of the many extra ordinary paradoxes we encounter in the strange new realm of time travel." He throws another switch. The time machine once more assumes solid form. "Voila!" cries the salesman. "Here is Mrs. Porter, returned safe and sound from her voyage into the past." He flings open the door of the time machine. The passenger compartment is empty. The salesman's face crumbles. "Mrs. Porter?" he shrieks in consternation. "Mrs. Porter? I don't understand! How could there have been a malfunction? This is impossible! Mrs. Porter? *Mrs. Porter?*"

She hurries down the dirty street toward the tall brick building. This is the place. Upstairs. Fifth floor, apartment 5-J. As she starts to ring the doorbell, a tall, lean man steps out of the shadows and clamps his hand powerfully around her wrist. "Time Patrol," he says crisply, flashing an identification badge. "You're under arrest for contemplated temponautic murder, Mrs. Porter."

"But I haven't any grandson," he sputters. "I'm not even mar—" She laughs. "Don't worry about it!" she tells him. "You're going to have a daughter named Martha and she'll have a son named Ted and I'm going to marry Ted and we'll have two children named Bobby, and Tink. And you're going to live to be an old, old man. And that's all you need to know. Now let's have a little fun." She touches a catch at the side of her tunic and the garment falls away in a single fluid cascade. Beneath it she is naked. Her nipples stare up at him like blind pink eyes. She beckons to him. "Come on!" she says hoarsely. "Get undressed, Martin! You're wasting time!"

Alice giggles nervously. "Well, as a matter of fact," she says to the salesman, "I think I'm willing to let my husband be the guinea pig. How about it, Ted?" She turns toward him. So does the salesman. "Certainly, Mr. Porter. I know you're eager to give our machine a test run, yes?" No, Ted thinks, but he feels the pressure of events propelling him willy-nilly. He gets into the machine. As the door closes on him he fears that claustrophobic panic will overwhelm him; he is reassured by the sight of a handle on the door's inner face. He pushes on it and the door opens, and he steps out of the machine just in time to see his earlier self coming into the Temponautics showroom with Alice. The salesman is going forward to greet them. Ted is now eighteen minutes into his own past. Alice and the other Ted stare at him, aghast. The salesman whirls and exclaims, "Wait a second, you aren't supposed to get out of—" How stupid they all look! How bewildered! Ted laughs in their faces. Then he rushes past them, nearly knocking his other self down, and erupts into the shopping-center plaza. He sprints in a wild frenzy of exhilaration toward the parking area. Free, he thinks. I'm free at last. And I didn't have to kill anybody.

Suppose I rent a machine, Alice thinks, and go back to 1947 and kill Martin? Suppose I really do it? What if there's some way of tracing the crime to me? After all, a crime committed by a person from 2006 who goes back to 1947 will have consequences in our present day. It might change all sorts of things. So they'd want to catch the criminal and punish him, or better yet prevent the crime from being committed in the first place. And the time machine company is bound to know what year I asked them to send me to. So maybe it isn't such an easy way of committing a perfect crime. I don't know. God, I can't understand any of this. But perhaps I can get away with it. Anyway, I'm going to give it a try. I'll show Ted he can't go on treating me like dirt.

They lie peacefully side by side, sweaty, drowsy, exhausted in the good exhaustion that comes after a first-rate screw. Martin tenderly strokes her belly and thighs. How smooth her skin is, how pale, how transparent! The little blue veins so clearly visible. "Hey," he says suddenly. "I just thought of something. I wasn't wearing a rubber or anything. What if I made you pregnant? And if you're really who you say you are. Then you'll go back to the year 2006 and you'll have a kid and he'll be his own grandfather, won't he?" She laughs. "Don't worry much about it," she says.

A wave of timidity comes over her as she enters the Temponautics office. This is crazy, she tells herself. I'm getting out of here. But before she can turn around, the salesman she spoke to the day before materializes from a side room and gives her a big hello. Mr. Friesling. He's practically rubbing his hands together in anticipation of landing a contract. "So nice to see you again, Mrs. Porter." She nods and glances worriedly at the demonstration models. "How much would it cost," she asks, "to spend a few hours in the spring of 1947?"

Sunday is the big family day. Four generations sitting down to dinner together: Martin, Martha, Ted and Alice, Bobby and Tink. Ted rather enjoys these reunions, but he knows Alice loathes them, mainly because of Martha. Alice hates her mother-in-law. Martha has never cared much for Alice, either. He watches them glaring at each other across the table. Meanwhile old Martin stares lecherously at the gulf between Alice's breasts. You have to hand it to the old man, Ted thinks. He's never lost the old urge. Even though there's not a hell of a lot he can do about gratifying it, not at his age. Martha says sweetly, "You'd look ever so much better, Alice dear, if you'd let your hair grow out to its natural color." A sugary smile from Martha. A sour scowl from Alice. She glowers at the older woman. "This *is* its natural color," she snaps.

Mr. Friesling hands her the standard contract form. Eight pages of densely-packed type. "Don't be frightened by it, Mrs. Porter. It looks formidable but actually it's just a lot of empty legal rhetoric. You can show it to your lawyer, if you like. I can tell you, though, that most of our customers find no need for that." She leafs through it. So far as she can tell, the contract is mainly a disclaimer of responsibility. Temponautics, Ltd, agrees to bear the brunt of any malfunction caused by its own demonstrable negligence, but wants no truck with acts of God or with accidents brought about by clients who won't obey the safety regulations. On the fourth page Alice finds a clause warning the prospective renter that the company cannot be held liable for any consequences of actions by the renter which wantonly or willfully interfere with the already determined course of history. She translates that for herself: *If you kill your husband's grandfather, don't blame us if you get in trouble.* She skims the remaining pages. "It looks harmless enough," she says. "Where do I sign?"

As Martin comes out of the bathroom he finds Martha blocking his way. "Excuse me," he says mildly, but she remains in his path. She is a big fleshy woman. At fifty-eight she affects the fashions of the very young, with grotesque results; he hates that aspect of her. He can see why Alice dislikes her so much. "Just a moment," Martha says. "I want to talk to you, Father." "About what?" he asks. "About those looks you give Alice. Don't you think that's a little too much? How tasteless can you get?" "Tasteless? Are you anybody to talk about taste, with your face painted green like a fifteen-year old?" She looks angry: he's scored a direct hit. She replies, "I just think that at the age of eighty-two you ought to have a greater regard for decency than to go staring down your own grandson's wife's front." Martin sighs. "Let me have the staring, Martha. It's all I've got left."

He is at the office, deep in complicated negotiations, when his autosecretary bleeps him and announces that a call has come in from a Mr. Friesling, of the Union Boulevard Plaza office of Temponautics, Ltd. Ted is puzzled by that: what do the time machine people want with him? Trying to line him up as a customer? "Tell him I'm not interested in time trips," Ted says. But the autosecretary bleeps again a few moments later. Mr. Friesling, it declares, is calling in reference to Mr. Porter's credit standing. More baffled than before, Ted orders the call switched over to him. Mr. Friesling appears on the desk screen. He is small-featured and bright-eyed, rather like a chipmunk. "I apologize for troubling you, Mr. Porter," he begins. "This is strictly a routine credit check, but it's altogether necessary. As you surely know, your wife has requested rental of our equipment for a fifty-nine-year time jaunt, and inasmuch as the service fee for such a trip exceeds the level at which we extend automatic credit, our policy requires us to ask you if you'll confirm the payment schedule that she has requested us to—" Ted coughs violently. "Hold on," he says. "My wife's going on a time jaunt? What the hell, this is the first time I've heard of that!"

SHE IS SURPRISED BY THE extensiveness of the preparations. No wonder they charge so much. Getting her ready for the jaunt takes hours. They inoculate her to protect her against certain extinct diseases. They provide her with clothing in the style of the mid-twentieth century, ill-fitting and uncomfortable. They give her contemporary currency, but warn her that she would do well not to spend any except in an emergency, since she will be billed for it at its present-day numismatic value, which is high. They make her study a pamphlet describing the customs and historical background of the era and quiz her in detail. She learns that she is not under any circumstances to expose her breasts or genitals in public while she is in 1947. She must not attempt to obtain any mind-stimulating drugs other than alcohol. She should not say anything that might be construed as praise of the Soviet Union or of Marxist philosophy. She must bear in mind that she is entering the past solely as an observer, and should engage in minimal social interaction with the citizens of the era she is visiting. And so forth. At last they decide it's safe to let her go. "Please come this way, Mrs. Porter," Friesling says.

AFTER STARING AT THE TELEPHONE a long while, Martin punches out Alice's number. Before the second ring he loses his nerve and disconnects. Immediately he calls her again. His heart pounds so furiously that the medic, registering alarm on its delicate sensing apparatus, starts toward him. He waves the robot away and clings to the phone. Two rings. Three. Ah. "Hello?" Alice says. Her voice is warm and rich and feminine. He has his screen switched off. "Hello? Who's there?" Martin breathes heavily into the mouthpiece. *Ah. Ah. Ah. Ah.* "Hello? Hello? Hello? Listen, you pervert, if you phone me once more—" *Ah. Ah. Ah.* A smile of bliss appears on Martin's withered features. Alice hangs up. Trembling, Martin sags in his chair. Oh, that was good! He signals fiercely to the medic. "Let's have the injection now, you metal monster!" He laughs. Dirty old man.

TED REALIZES THAT IT ISN'T necessary to kill a person's grandfather in order to get rid of that person. Just interfere with some crucial event in that person's past, is all. Go back and break up the marriage of Alice's grandparents, for example. (How? Seduce the grandmother when she's eighteen? "I'm terribly sorry to inform you that your intended bride is no virgin, and here's the documentary evidence." They were very grim about virginity back then, weren't they?) Nobody would have to die. But Alice wouldn't ever be born.

MARTIN STILL CAN'T BELIEVE ANY of this, even after she's slept with him. It's some crazy practical joke, most likely. Although he wishes all practical jokes were as sexy as this one. "Are you really from the year 2006?" he asks her. She laughs prettily. "How can I prove it to you?" Then she leaps from the bed. He tracks her with his eyes as she crosses the room, breasts jiggling gaily. What a sweet little body. How thoughtful of my older self to ship her back here to me. If that's what really happened. She fumbles in her purse and extracts a handful of coins. "Look here," she says. "Money from the future. Here's a dime from 1993. And this is a two-dollar piece from 2001. And here's an old one, a 1979 Kennedy half-dollar." He studies the unfamiliar coins. They have a greasy look, not silvery at all. Counterfeits? They won't necessarily be striking coins out of silver forever. And the engraving job is very professional. A two-dollar piece, eh? Well, you never can tell. And this. The half-dollar. A handsome young man in profile. "Kennedy?" he says. "Who's Kennedy?"

So this is it at last. Two technicians in gray smocks watch her, soberfaced, as she clambers into the machine. It's very much like a coffin, just as she imagined it would be. She can't sit down in it; it's too narrow. Gives her the creeps, shut up in here. Of course, they've told her the trip won't take any apparent subjective time, only a couple of seconds. *Woosh!* And she'll be there. All right. They close the door. She hears the lock clicking shut. Mr. Friesling's voice comes to her over a loud speaker. "We wish you a happy voyage, Mrs. Porter. Keep calm and you won't get into any difficulties." Suddenly the red light over the door is glowing. That means the jaunt has begun: she's traveling backward in time. No sense of acceleration, no sense of motion. One, two, three. The light goes off. That's it. I'm in 1947, she tells herself. Before she opens the door, she closes her eyes and runs through her history lessons. World War II has just ended. Europe is in ruins. There are forty-eight states. Nobody has been to the moon yet or even thinks much about going there. Harry Truman is President. Stalin runs Russia, and Churchill—is Churchill still Prime Minister of England? She isn't sure. Well, no matter. I didn't come here to talk about prime ministers. She touches the latch and the door of the time machine swings outward.

He steps from the machine into the year 2006. Nothing has changed in the showroom. Friesling, the two poker-faced technicians, the sleek desks, the thick carpeting, all the same as before. He moves bouncily. His mind is still back there with Alice's grandmother. The taste of her lips, the soft urgent cries of her fulfillment. Who ever said all women were frigid in the old days? They ought to go back and find out. Friesling smiles at him. "I hope you had a very enjoyable journey, Mr.—ah—" Ted nods. "Enjoyable and useful," he says. He goes out. Never to see Alice again—how beautiful! The car isn't where he remembers leaving it in the parking area. You have to expect certain small peripheral changes, I guess. He hails a cab, gives the driver his address. His key does not fit the front door. Troubled, he thumbs the annunciator. A woman's voice, not Alice's, asks him what he wants. "Is this the Ted Porter residence?" he asks. "No, it isn't," the woman says, suspicious and irritated. The name on the doorplate, he notices now, is McKenzie. So the changes are not all so small. Where do I go now? If I don't live here, then where? "Wait!" he yells to the taxi, just pulling away. It takes him to a downtown cafe, where he phones Ellie. Her face, peering out of the tiny screen, wears an odd frowning expression. "Listen, something very strange has happened," he begins, "and I need to see you as soon as—" "I don't think I know you," she says. "I'm Ted," he tells her. "Ted who?" she asks.

How peculiar this is, Alice thinks. Like walking into a museum diorama and having it come to life. The noisy little automobiles. The ugly clothing. The squat, dilapidated twentieth-century buildings. The chaos. The oily, smoky smell of the polluted air. Wisps of dirty snow in the streets. Cans of garbage just sitting around as if nobody's ever heard of the plague. Well, I won't stay here long. In her purse she carries her kitchen carver, a tiny nickel-jacketed laser-powered implement. Steel pipes are all right for dream fantasies, but this is the real thing, and she wants the killing to be quick and efficient. Criss, cross, with the laser beam, and Martin goes. At the street corner she pauses to check the address. There's no central info number to ring for all sorts of useful data, not in these primitive times; she must use a printed telephone directory, a thick tattered book with small smeary type. Here he is: Martin Jamieson, 504 West Forty-fifth. That's not far. In ten minutes she's there. A dark brick structure, five or six stories high, with spidery metal fire escapes running down its face. Even for its day it appears unusually run down. She goes inside. A list of tenants is posted just within the front door. Jamieson, 3-A. There's no elevator and of course no lift shaft. Up the stairs. A musty hallway lit by a single dim incandescent bulb. This is Apartment 3-A. Jamieson. She rings the bell.

Ten minutes later Friesling calls back, sounding abashed and looking dismayed: "I'm sorry to have to tell you that there's been some sort of error, Mr. Porter. The technicians were apparently unaware that a credit check was in process, and they sent Mrs. Porter off on her trip while we were still talking." Ted is shaken. He clutches the edge of the desk. Controlling himself with an effort, he says, "How far back was it that she wanted to go?" Friesling says, "It was fifty-nine years. To 1947." Ted nods grimly. A horrible idea has occurred to him. 1947 was the year that his mother's parents met and got married. What is Alice up to?

THE DOORBELL RINGS. MARTIN, FRESHLY showered, is sprawled out naked on his bed, leafing through the new issue of Esquire and thinking vaguely of going out for dinner. He isn't expecting any company. Slipping into his bathrobe, he goes toward the door. "Who's there?" he calls. A youthful, pleasant female voice replies, "I'm looking for Martin Jamieson." Well, okay. He opens the door. She's perhaps twenty-seven, twenty-eight years old, very sexy, on the slender side but well built. Dark hair, worn in a strangely boyish short cut. He's never seen her before. "Hi," he says tentatively. She grins warmly at him. "You don't know me," she tells him, "but I'm a friend of an old friend of yours. Mary Chambers? Mary and I grew up together in—ah—Ohio. I'm visiting New York for the first time, and Mary once told me that if I ever come to New York I should be sure to look up Martin Jamieson, and so—may I come in?" "You bet," he says. He doesn't remember any Mary Chambers from Ohio. But what the hell, sometimes you forget a few. What the hell.

He's much more attractive than she expected him to be. She has always known Martin only as an old man, made unattractive as much by his coarse lechery as by what age has done to him. Hollow-chested, stoop-shouldered, pleated jowly face, sparse strands of white hair, beady eyes of faded blue—a wreck of a man. But this Martin in the doorway is sturdy, handsome, untouched by time, brimming with life and vigor and virility. She thinks of the carver in her purse and feels a genuine pang of regret at having to cut this robust boy off in his prime. But there isn't such a great hurry, is there? First we can enjoy each other, Martin. And then the laser.

"WHEN IS SHE DUE BACK?" Ted demands. Friesling explains that all concepts of time are relative and flexible; so far as elapsed time at Now Level goes, she's already returned. "What?" Ted yells. "Where is she?" Friesling does not know. She stepped out of the machine, bade the

Temponautics staff a pleasant goodbye, and left the showroom. Ted puts his hand to his throat. What if she's already killed Martin? Will I just wink out of existence? Or is there some sort of lag, so that I'll fade gradually into unreality over the next few days? "Listen," he says raggedly, "I'm leaving my office right now and I'll be down at your place in less than an hour. I want you to have your machinery set up so that you can transport me to the exact point in space and time where you just sent my wife." "But that won't be possible," Friesling protests. "It takes hours to prepare a client properly for—" Ted cuts him off. "Get everything set up, and to hell with preparing me properly," he snaps. "Unless you feel like getting slammed with the biggest negligence suit since this time-machine thing got started, you better have everything ready when I get there."

He opens the door. The girl in the hallway is young and good-looking, with close-cropped dark hair and full lips. Thank you, Mary Chambers, whoever you may be. "Pardon the bathrobe," he says, "but I wasn't expecting company." She steps into his apartment. Suddenly he notices how strained and tense her face is. Country girl from Ohio, suddenly having second thoughts about visiting a strange man in a strange city? He tries to put her at her ease. "Can I get you a drink?" he asks. "Not much of a selection, I'm afraid, but I have scotch, gin, some blackberry cordial—" She reaches into her purse and takes something out. He frowns. Not a gun, exactly, but it does seem like a weapon of some sort, a little glittering metal device that fits neatly in her hand. "Hey," he says, "what's—" "I'm so awfully sorry, Martin," she whispers, and a bolt of terrible fire slams into his chest.

She sips the drink. It relaxes her. The glass isn't very clean, but she isn't worried about picking up a disease, not after all the injections Friesling gave her. Martin looks as if he can stand some relaxing too. "Aren't you drinking?" she asks. "I suppose I will," he says. He pours himself some gin. She comes up behind him and slips her hand into the front of his bathrobe. His body is cool, smooth, hard. "Oh, Martin," she murmurs. "Oh! Martin!"

Ted takes a room in one of the commercial hotels downtown. The first thing he does is try to put a call through to Alice's mother in Chillicothe. He still isn't really convinced that his little time-jaunt flirtation has retroactively eliminated Alice from existence. But the call convinces him, all right. The middle-aged woman who answers is definitely not Alice's mother. Right phone number, right address—he badgers her for the information—but wrong woman. "You don't have a daughter named Alice Porter?" he asks three or four times. "You don't know anyone in the neighborhood who does? It's important." All right. Cancel the old lady, ergo cancel Alice. But now he has a different problem. How much of the universe has he altered by removing Alice and her mother? Does he live in some other city, now, and hold some other job? What has happened to Bobby and Tink? Frantically he begins phoning people. Friends, fellow workers, the man at the bank. The same response from all of them: blank stares, shakings of the head. We don't know you, fellow. He looks at himself in the mirror. Okay, he asks himself. Who am I?

Martin moves swiftly and purposefully, the way they taught him to do in the army when it's necessary to disarm a dangerous opponent. He lunges forward and catches the girl's arm, pushing it upward before she can fire the shiny whatzis she's aiming at him. She turns out to be stronger than he anticipated, and they struggle fiercely for the weapon. Suddenly it fires. Something like a lightning bolt explodes between them and knocks him to the floor, stunned. When he picks himself up he sees her lying near the door with a charred hole in her throat.

The telephone's jangling clatter brings Martin up out of a dream in which he is ravishing Alice's luscious young body. Dry-throated, gummy-eyed, he reaches a palsied hand toward the receiver. "Yes?" he says. Ted's face blossoms on the screen. "Grandfather!" he blurts. "Are you all right?" "Of course I'm all right," Martin says testily. "Can't you tell? What's the matter with you, boy?" Ted shakes his head. "I don't know," he mutters. "Maybe it was only a bad dream. I imagined that Alice rented one of those time machines and went back to 1947. And tried to kill you so that I wouldn't ever have existed." Martin snorts. "What idiotic nonsense! How can she have killed me in 1947 when I'm here alive in 2006?"

NAKED, ALICE SINKS INTO MARTIN'S arms. His strong hands sweep eagerly over her breasts and shoulders and his mouth descends to hers. She shivers with desire. "Yes," she murmurs tenderly, pressing herself against him. "Oh, yes, yes, yes!" They'll do it and it'll be fantastic. And afterward she'll kill him with the kitchen carver while he's lying there savoring the event. But a troublesome thought occurs. If Martin dies in 1947, Ted doesn't get to be born in 1968. Okay. But what about Tink and Bobby? They won't get born either, not if I don't marry Ted. I'll be married to someone else when I get back to 2006, and I suppose I'll have different children. Bobby? Tink? What am I doing to you? Sudden fear congeals her, and she pulls back from the vigorous young man nuzzling her throat. "Wait," she says. "Listen, I'm sorry. It's all a big mistake. I'm sorry, but I've got to get out of here right away!"

SO THIS IS THE YEAR 1947. Well, well, well. Everything looks so cluttered and grimy and ancient. He hurries through the chilly streets toward his grandfather's place. If his luck is good, and if Friesling's technicians have calculated things accurately, he'll be able to head Alice off. That might even be her now, that slender woman walking briskly half a block ahead of him. He steps up his pace. Yes, it's Alice, on her way to Martin's. Well done, Friesling! Ted approaches her warily, suspecting that she's armed. If she's capable of coming back to 1947 to kill Martin, she'd kill him just as readily. Especially back here where neither one of them has any legal existence. When he's close to her he says in a low, hard, intense voice, "Don't turn around, Alice. Just keep walking as if everything's perfectly normal." She stiffens. "Ted?" she cries, astonished. "Is that you, Ted?" "Damned right it is." He laughs harshly. "Come on. Walk to the corner and turn to your left around the block. You're going back to your machine and you're going to get the hell out of the twentieth century without harming anybody. I know what you were trying to do, Alice. But I caught you in time, didn't I?"

Martin is just getting down to real business when the door of his apartment bursts open and a man rushes in. He's middle-aged, stocky, with weird clothes—the ultimate in zoot suits, a maze of vividly contrasting colors and conflicting patterns, shoulders padded to resemble shelves—and a wild look in his eyes. Alice leaps up from the bed. "Ted!" she screams. "My God, what are you doing here?" "You murderous bitch," the intruder yells. Martin, naked and feeling vulnerable, his nervous system stunned by the interruption, looks on in amazement as the stranger grabs her and begins throttling her. "Bitch! Bitch! Bitch!" he roars, shaking her in a mad frenzy. The girl's face is turning black. Her eyes are bugging. After a long moment Martin breaks finally from his freeze. He stumbles forward, seizes the man's fingers, peels them away from the girl's throat. Too late. She falls limply and lies motionless. "Alice!" the intruder moans. "Alice, Alice, what have I done?" He drops to his knees beside her body, sobbing. Martin blinks. "You killed her," he says, not believing that any of this can really be happening. "You actually killed her?"

Alice's face appears on the telephone screen. Christ, how beautiful she is, Martin thinks, and his decrepit body quivers with lust. "There you are," he says. "I've been trying to reach you for hours. I had such a strange dream that something awful had happened to Ted—and then your phone didn't answer, and I began to think maybe the dream was a premonition of some kind, an omen, you know—" Alice looks puzzled. "I'm afraid you have the wrong number, sir," she says sweetly, and hangs up.

She draws the laser and the naked man cowers back against the wall in bewilderment. "What the hell is this?" he asks, trembling. "Put that thing down, lady. You've got the wrong guy." "No," she says. "You're the one I'm after. I hate to do this to you, Martin, but I've got no choice. You have to die." "Why?" he demands. "*Why?*" "You wouldn't understand it even if I told you," she says. She moves her finger toward the discharge stud. Abruptly there is a frightening sound of cracking wood and collapsing plaster behind her, as though an earthquake has struck. She whirls and is appalled to see her husband breaking down the door of Martin's apartment. "I'm just in time!" Ted exclaims. "Don't move, Alice!" He reaches for her. In panic she fires without thinking. The dazzling beam catches Ted in the pit of the stomach and he goes down, gurgling in agony, clutching at his belly as he dies.

The door falls with a crash and this character in peculiar clothing materializes in a cloud of debris, looking crazier than Napoleon. It's incredible, Martin thinks. First an unknown broad rings his bell and invites herself in and takes her clothes off, and then, just as he's about to screw her, this happens. It's pure Marx Brothers, only dirty. But Martin's not going to take any crap. He pulls himself away from the panting, gasping girl on the bed, crosses the room in three quick strides, and seizes the newcomer. "Who the hell are you?" Martin demands, slamming him hard against the wall. The girl is dancing around behind him. "Don't hurt him!" she wails. "Oh, please, don't hurt him!"

Ted certainly hadn't expected to find them in bed together. He understood why she might have wanted to go back in time to murder Martin, but simply to have an affair with him, no, it didn't make sense. Of course, it was altogether likely that she had come here to kill and had paused for a little dalliance first. You never could tell about women, even your own wife. Alley cats, all of them. Well, a lucky thing for him that she had given him those few extra minutes to get here. "Okay," he says. "Get your clothes on, Alice. You're coming with me." "Just a second, mister," Martin growls. "You've got your goddamned nerve, busting in like this." Ted tries to explain, but the words won't come. It's all too complicated. He gestures mutely at Alice, at himself, at Martin. The next moment Martin jumps him and they go tumbling together to the floor.

"Who are you?" Martin yells, banging the intruder repeatedly against the wall. "You some kind of detective? You trying to work a badger game on me?" Slam. Slam. Slam. He feels the girl's small fists pounding on his own back. "Stop it!" she screams. "Let him alone, will you? He's my husband!" *"Husband!"* Martin cries. Astounded, he lets go of the stranger and swings around to face the girl. A moment later he realizes his mistake. Out of the corner of his eye he sees that the intruder has raised his fists high above his head like clubs. Martin tries to get out of the way, but no time, no time, and the fists descend with awful force against his skull.

Alice doesn't know what to do. They're rolling around on the floor, fighting like wildcats, now Martin on top, now Ted. Martin is younger and bigger and stronger, but Ted seems possessed by the strength of the insane; he's gone berserk. Both men are bloody-faced, and furniture is crashing over everywhere. Her first impulse is to get between them and stop this crazy fight somehow. But then she remembers that she has come here as a killer, not as a peacemaker. She gets the laser from her purse and aims it at Martin, but then the combatants do a flip-flop and it is Ted who is in the line of fire. She hesitates. It doesn't matter which one she shoots, she realizes after a moment. They both have to die, one way or another. She takes aim. Maybe she can get them both with one bolt. But as her finger starts to tighten on the discharge stud, Martin suddenly gets Ted in a bear-hug and, half lifting him, throws him five feet across the room. The back of Ted's neck hits the wall and there is a loud *crack*. Ted slumps and is still. Martin gets shakily to his feet. "I think I killed him," he says. "Christ, who the hell was he?" "He was your grandson," Alice says and begins to shriek hysterically.

Ted stares in horror at the crumpled body at his feet. His hands still tingle from the impact. The left side of Martin's head looks as though a pile-driver has crushed it. "Good God in heaven," Ted says thickly, "what have I done? I came here to protect him and I've killed him! I've killed my own grandfather!" Alice, wide-eyed, futilely trying to cover her nakedness by folding one arm across her breasts and spreading her other hand over her loins, says, "If he's dead, why are you still here? Shouldn't you have disappeared?" Ted shrugs. "Maybe

I'm safe as long as I remain here in the past. But the moment I try to go back to 2006, I'll vanish as though I've never been. I don't know. I don't understand any of this. What do you think?"

Alice steps uncertainly from the machine into the Temponautics showroom. There's Friesling. There are the technicians. Friesling says, smiling, "I hope you had a very enjoyable journey, Mrs.—ah—uh. . . . " He falters. "I'm sorry," he says, reddening, "but your name seems to have escaped me." Alice says, "It's, ah, Alice—uh—do you know, the second name escapes me too?"

The whole clan has gathered to celebrate Martin's eighty-third birthday. He cuts the cake, and then one by one they go to him to kiss him. When it's Alice's turn, he deftly spins her around so that he screens her from the others and gives her rump a good hearty pinch. "Oh, if I were only fifty years younger!" he sighs.

It's a warm spring-like day. Everything has been lovely at the office—three new accounts all at once—and the trip home on the freeway was a breeze. Alice is waiting for him, dressed in her finest and most sexy outfit, all ready to go out. It's a special day. Their eleventh anniversary. How beautiful she looks! He kisses her, she kisses him, he takes the tickets from his pocket with a grand flourish. "Surprise," he says. "Two weeks in Hawaii, starting next Tuesday! Happy anniversary!" "Oh, Ted!" she cries. "How marvelous! I love you, Ted darling!" He pulls her close to him again. "I love you, Alice dear."

◆

HOMEFARING

I had always had a sneaking desire to write the definitive giant-lobster story. Earlier science fiction writers had preempted most of the other appealing monstrosities—including giant aunts (sic!), dealt with by Isaac Asimov in his classic story "Dreamworld," which I have just ruined forever for you by giving away its punchline. But giant lobsters remained fair game. And when George Scithers, the new editor of the venerable science fiction magazine Amazing Stories, *asked me in the autumn of 1982 to do a lengthy story for him, I decided that it was time at last for me to give lobsters their due.*

The obvious giant-lobster story, in which horrendous pincer-wielding monsters twenty feet long come ashore at Malibu and set about the conquest of Los Angeles by terrorizing the surfers, might work well enough in a cheap Hollywood sci-fi epic, but it wouldn't have stood much chance of delighting a sophisticated science fiction reader like Scithers. Nor did it have a lot of appeal for me as a writer. Therefore, following the advice of the brilliant, cantankerous editor Horace Gold, one of my early mentors, I searched for my story idea by turning the obvious upside down. Lobsters are pretty nasty things, after all. They're tough, surly, dangerous, and ugly—surely the ugliest food objects ever to be prized by mankind. A creature so disagreeable in so many ways must have some redeeming feature. (Other than the flavor of its meat, that is.) And so, instead of depicting them as the savage and hideous-looking critters they really are, what about putting them through a few hundred million years of evolution and turning them into wise and thoughtful civilized beings—the dominant life-form, in fact, of a vastly altered Earth?

A challenging task, yes. And made even more challenging for me, back there in the otherwise sunny and pleasant November of 1982, by the fact that I had just made the great leap from typewriter to computer. "Homefaring" marked my initiation into the world of floppy disks and soft hyphens, of backup copies and automatic pagination. It's all second nature to me now, of course, but in 1982 I found myself timidly stumbling around in a brave and very strange new world. Each day's work was an adventure in terror for me. My words appeared in white letters on a black screen, frighteningly impermanent: one electronic sneeze, I thought, and a whole day's brilliant prose could vanish like a time traveler who has just defenestrated his own grandfather. The mere making of backups didn't lull my fears: how could I be sure that the act of backing up itself wouldn't erase what I had just written? Pushing the button marked "Save"—did that really save anything? Switching the computer off at the end of my working day was like a leap into the abyss. Would the story be there the next morning when I turned the machine on again? Warily, I printed out each day's work when it was done, before backing up, saving, or otherwise jiggling with it electronically. I wanted to see it safely onto paper first.

Sometimes when I put a particularly difficult scene together—for example, the three-page scene at the midpoint of the story, beginning with the line, "The lobsters were singing as they marched"—I would stop right then and there and print it out before proceeding, aware that if the computer somehow were to destroy it I would never be able to reconstruct it at that level of accomplishment. (It's an axiom among writers that material written to replace inadvertently destroyed copy can't possibly equal the lost passage—which gets better and better in one's memory all the time.)

Somehow, in fear and trembling, I tiptoed my way through the entire 88-page manuscript of "Homefaring" without any major disasters. The computer made it marvelously easy to revise the story as I went along; instead of typing out an 88-page first draft, then covering it with handwritten alterations and grimly typing the whole thing out again to make it fit to show an editor, I brought every paragraph up to final-draft status with painless little maneuvers of the cursor. When I realized that I had chosen a confusing name for a minor character, I ordered the computer to correct my error, and sat back in wonder as "Eitel" became "Bleier" throughout the story without my having to do a thing. And then at the end came the wondrous moment when I pushed the button marked "Print"—computers had such buttons, in those pre-Microsoft days—and page after page of immaculate typed copy began to come forth while I occupied myself with other and less dreary tasks.

The story appeared in the November 1983 issue of Amazing Stories, *though its actual first publication was as a slender limited-edition volume published in July of that year by Phantasia Press. The readers liked it and it was a finalist in that year's Nebula Award voting—perhaps might even have won, if it had been published in a magazine less obscure than dear old* Amazing, *which at that stage of its long existence had only a handful of readers. That same year the veteran connoisseur of science fiction, Donald A. Wollheim, chose it for his annual* World's Best SF *anthology, an honor that particularly pleased me. I had deliberately intended "Homefaring" as a sleek and modern version of the sort of imagination-stirring tale of wonder that Wollheim had cherished in the SF magazines of the 1930s, and his choice of the story for his book confirmed my feeling of working within a great tradition.*

McCulloch was beginning to molt. The sensation, inescapable and unarguable, horrified him—it felt exactly as though his body was going to split apart, which it was—and yet it was also completely familiar, expected, welcome. Wave after wave of keen and dizzying pain swept through him. Burrowing down deep in the sandy bed, he waved his great claws about, lashed his flat tail against the pure white sand, scratched frantically with quick worried gestures of his eight walking-legs.

He was frightened. He was calm. He had no idea what was about to happen to him. He had done this a hundred times before.

The molting prodrome had overwhelming power. It blotted from his mind all questions, and, after a moment, all fear. A white line of heat ran down his back—no, down the top of his carapace—from a point just back of his head to the first flaring segments of his tail-fan. He imagined that all the sun's force, concentrated through some giant glass lens, was being inscribed in a single track along his shell. And his soft inner body was straining, squirming, expanding, filling the carapace to overflowing. But still that rigid shell contained him, refusing to yield to the pressure. To McCulloch it was much like being inside a wet suit that was suddenly five times too small.

—What is the sun? What is glass? What is a lens? What is a wet suit?

The questions swarmed suddenly upward in his mind like little busy many-legged creatures springing out of the sand. But he had no time for providing answers. The molting prodrome was developing with astounding swiftness, carrying him along. The strain was becoming intolerable. In another moment he would surely burst. He was writhing in short angular convulsions. Within his claws, his tissues now were shrinking, shriveling, drawing back within the ferocious shell-hulls, but the rest of him was continuing inexorably to grow larger.

He had to escape from this shell, or it would kill him. He had to expel himself somehow from this impossibly constricting container. Digging his front claws and most of his legs into the sand, he heaved, twisted, stretched, pushed. He thought of himself as being pregnant with himself, struggling fiercely to deliver himself of himself.

Ah. The carapace suddenly began to split.

The crack was only a small one, high up near his shoulders—*shoulders?*—but the imprisoned substance of him surged swiftly toward it, widening and lengthening it, and in another moment the hard horny covering was cracked from end to end. *Ah. Ah.* That felt so good, that release from constraint! Yet McCulloch still had to free himself. Delicately he drew himself backward, withdrawing leg after leg from its covering in a precise, almost fussy way, as though he were pulling his arms from the sleeves of some incredibly ancient and frail garment.

Until he had his huge main claws free, though, he knew he could not extricate himself from the sundered shell. And freeing the claws took extreme care. The front limbs still were shrinking, and the limy joints of the shell seemed to be dissolving and softening, but nevertheless he had to pull each claw through a passage much narrower than itself. It was easy to see how a hasty move might break a limb off altogether.

He centered his attention on the task. It was a little like telling his wrists to make themselves small, so he could slide them out of handcuffs.

—Wrists? Handcuffs? What are those?

McCulloch paid no attention to that baffling inner voice. Easy, easy, there—ah—yes, there, like that! One claw was free. Then the other, slowly, carefully. Done. Both of them retracted. The rest was simple: some shrugging and wiggling, exhausting but not really challenging, and he succeeded in extending the breach in the carapace until he could crawl backward out of it. Then he lay on the sand beside it, weary, drained, naked, soft, terribly vulnerable. He wanted only to return to the sleep out of which he had emerged into this nightmare of shell-splitting.

But some force within him would not let him slacken off. A moment to rest, only a moment. He looked to his left, toward the discarded shell. Vision was difficult—there were peculiar, incomprehensible refraction effects that broke every image into thousands of tiny fragments—but despite that, and despite the dimness of the light, he was able to see that the shell, golden-hued with broad arrow-shaped red markings, was something like a lobster's, yet even more intricate, even more bizarre. McCulloch did not understand why he had been inhabiting a lobster's shell. Obviously because he was a lobster; but he was not a lobster. That was so, was it not? Yet he was under water. He lay on fine white sand, at a depth so great he could not make out any hint of sunlight overhead. The water was warm, gentle, rich with tiny tasty creatures and with a swirling welter of sensory data that swept across his receptors in bewildering abundance.

He sought to learn more. But there was no further time for resting and thinking now. He was unprotected. Any passing enemy could destroy him while he was like this. Up, up, seek a hiding place: that was the requirement of the moment.

First, though, he paused to devour his old shell. That, too, seemed to be the requirement of the moment; so he fell upon it with determination, seizing it with his clumsy-looking but curiously versatile front claws, drawing it toward his busy, efficient mandibles. When that was accomplished—no doubt to recycle the lime it contained, which he needed for the growth of his new shell—he forced himself up and began a slow scuttle, somehow knowing that the direction he had taken was the right one.

Soon came the vibrations of something large and solid against his sensors—a wall, a stone mass rising before him—and then, as he continued, he made out with his foggy vision the sloping flank of a dark broad cliff rising vertically from the ocean floor. Festoons of thick, swaying red and yellow water plants clung to it, and a dense stippling of rubbery-looking finger-shaped sponges, and a crawling, gaping, slithering host of crabs and mollusks and worms, which vastly stirred McCulloch's appetite. But this was not a time to pause to eat, lest he be eaten. Two enormous green anemones yawned nearby, ruffling their voluptuous membranes seductively, hopefully. A dark shape passed overhead, huge, tubular, tentacular, menacing. Ignoring the thronging populations of the rock, McCulloch picked his way over and around them until he came to the small cave, the McCulloch-sized cave, that was his goal.

Gingerly he backed through its narrow mouth, knowing there would be no room for turning around once he was inside. He filled the opening nicely, with a little space left over. Taking up a position just within the entrance, he blocked the cave mouth with his claws. No enemy could enter now. Naked though he was, he would be safe during his vulnerable period.

For the first time since his agonizing awakening, McCulloch had a chance to halt: rest, regroup, consider.

It seemed a wise idea to be monitoring the waters just outside the cave even while he was resting, though. He extended his antennae a short distance into the swarming waters, and felt at once the impact, again, of a myriad sensory inputs, all the astounding complexity of the reef world. Most of the creatures that moved slowly about on the face of the reef were simple ones, but McCulloch could feel, also, the sharp pulsations of intelligence coming from several points not far away: the anemones, so it seemed, and that enormous squid-like thing hovering overhead. Not intelligence of a kind that he understood, but that did not trouble him: for the moment, understanding could wait, while he dealt with the task of recovery from the exhausting struggles of his molting. Keeping the antennae moving steadily in slow sweeping circles of surveillance, he began systematically to shut down the rest of his nervous system, until he had attained the rest state that he knew—how?—was optimum for the rebuilding of his shell. Already his soft new carapace was beginning to grow rigid as it absorbed water, swelled, filtered out and utilized the lime. But he would have to sit quietly a long while before he was fully armored once more.

He rested. He waited. He did not think at all.

After a time his repose was broken by that inner voice, the one that had been trying to question him during the wildest moments of his molting. It spoke without sound, from a point somewhere within the core of his torpid consciousness.

—*Are you awake?*

—*I am now,* McCulloch answered irritably.

—*I need definitions. You are a mystery to me. What is a McCulloch?*

—*A man.*

—*That does not help.*

—*A male human being.*

—*That also has no meaning.*

—*Look, I'm tired. Can we discuss these things some other time?*

—*This is a good time. While we rest, while we replenish ourself.*

—*Ourselves,* McCulloch corrected.

—Ourself *is more accurate.*

—*But there are two of us.*

—*Are there? Where is the other?*

McCulloch faltered. He had no perspective on his situation, none that made any sense.

—*One inside the other, I think. Two of us in the same body. But definitely two of us. McCulloch and not-McCulloch.*

—*I concede the point. There are two of us. You are within me. Who are you?*

—*McCulloch.*

—*So you have said. But what does that mean?*

—*I don't know.*

The voice left him alone again. He felt its presence nearby, as a kind of warm node somewhere along his spine, or whatever was the equivalent of his spine, since he did not think invertebrates had spines. And it was fairly clear to him that he was an invertebrate.

He had become, it seemed, a lobster, or, at any rate, something lobster-like. Implied in that was transition: *he had become.* He had once been something else. Blurred, tantalizing memories of the something else that he once had been danced in his consciousness. He remembered hair, fingers, fingernails, flesh. Clothing: a kind of removable exoskeleton. Eyelids, ears, lips: shadowy concepts all, names without substance, but there was a certain elusive reality to them, a volatile, tricky plausibility. Each time he tried to apply one of those concepts to himself—"fingers," "hair," "man," "McCulloch"—it slid away, it would not stick. Yet all the same, those terms had some sort of relevance to him.

The harder he pushed to isolate that relevance, though, the harder it was to maintain his focus on any part of that soup of half-glimpsed notions in which his mind seemed to be swimming. The thing to do, McCulloch decided, was to go slow, try not to force understanding, wait for comprehension to seep back into his mind. Obviously he had had a bad shock, some major trauma, a total disorientation. It might be days before he achieved any sort of useful integration.

A gentle voice from outside his cave said, "I hope that your Growing has gone well."

Not a voice. He remembered voice: vibration of the air against the eardrums. No air here, maybe no eardrums. This was a stream of minute chemical messengers spurting through the mouth of the little cave and rebounding off the thousands of sensory filaments on his legs, tentacles, antennae, carapace, and tail. But the effect was one of words having been spoken. And it was distinctly different from that other voice, the internal one, that had been questioning him so assiduously a little while ago.

"It goes extremely well," McCulloch replied: or was it the other inhabitant of his body that had framed the answer? "I grow. I heal. I stiffen. Soon I will come forth."

"We feared for you." The presence outside the cave emanated concern, warmth, intelligence. Kinship. "In the first moments of your Growing, a strangeness came from you."

"Strangeness is within me. I am invaded."

"Invaded? By what?"

"A McCulloch. It is a man, which is a human being."

"Ah. A great strangeness indeed. Do you need help?"

McCulloch answered, "No. I will accommodate to it."

And he knew that it was the other within himself who was making these answers, though the boundary between their identities was so indistinct that he had a definite sense of being the one who shaped these words. But how could that be? He had no idea how one shaped words by sending squirts of body fluid into the all-surrounding ocean fluid. That was not his language. His language was—

—words—

—English words—

He trembled in sudden understanding. His antennae thrashed wildly, his many legs jerked and quivered. Images churned in his suddenly boiling mind: bright lights, elaborate equipment, faces, walls, ceilings. People moving about him, speaking in low tones, occasionally addressing words to him, English words—

—Is English what all McCullochs speak?

—Yes.

—So English is human-language?

—Yes. But not the only one, said McCulloch. I speak English, and also German and a little—French. But other humans speak other languages.

—Very interesting. Why do you have so many languages?

—Because—because—we are different from one another, we live in different countries, we have different cultures—

—This is without meaning again. There are many creatures, but only one language, which all speak with greater or lesser skill, according to their destinies.

McCulloch pondered that. After a time he replied:

—Lobster is what you are. Long body, claws and antennae in front, many legs, flat tail in back. Different from, say, a clam. Clams have shell on top, shell on bottom, soft flesh in between, hinge connecting. You are not like that. You have lobster body. So you are lobster.

Now there was silence from the other.

Then—after a long pause—

—Very well. I accept the term. I am lobster. You are human. They are clams.

—*What do you call yourselves in your own language?*

Silence.

—*What's your own name for yourself? Your individual self, the way my individual name is McCulloch and my species name is human being?*

Silence.

—*Where am I, anyway?*

Silence, still, so prolonged and utter that McCulloch wondered if the other being had withdrawn itself from his consciousness entirely. Perhaps days went by in this unending silence, perhaps weeks: he had no way of measuring the passing of time. He realized that such units as days or weeks were without meaning now. One moment succeeded the next, but they did not aggregate into anything continuous.

At last came a reply.

—*You are in the world, human McCulloch.*

Silence came again, intense, clinging, a dark warm garment. McCulloch made no attempt to reach the other mind. He lay motionless, feeling his carapace thicken. From outside the cave came a flow of impressions of passing beings, now differentiating themselves very sharply: he felt the thick fleshy pulses of two anemones, the sharp stabbing presence of the squid, the slow ponderous broadcast of something dark and winged, and, again and again, the bright, comforting, unmistakable output of other lobster creatures. It was a busy, complex world out there. The McCulloch part of him longed to leave the cave and explore it. The lobster part of him rested, content within its tight shelter.

He formed hypotheses. He had journeyed from his own place to this place, damaging his mind in the process, though now his mind seemed to be reconstructing itself steadily, if erratically. What sort of voyage? To another world? No: that seemed wrong. He did not believe that conditions so much like the ocean floor of Earth would be found on another—

Earth.

All right: significant datum. He was human, he came from Earth. And he was still on Earth. In the ocean. He was—what?—a land-dweller, an air-breather, a biped, a flesh-creature, a human. And now he was within the body of a lobster. Was that it? The entire human race, he thought, has migrated into the bodies of lobsters, and here we are on the ocean floor, scuttling about, waving our claws and feelers, going through difficult and dangerous moltings—

Or maybe I'm the only one. A scientific experiment, with me as the subject: man into lobster. That brightly-lit room that he remembered, the intricate gleaming equipment all about him—that was the laboratory, that was where they had prepared him for his transmigration, and then they had thrown the switch and hurled him into the body of—

No. No. Makes no sense. Lobsters, McCulloch reflected, are low-phylum creatures with simple nervous systems, limited intelligence. Plainly the mind he had entered was a complex one. It asked thoughtful questions. It carried on civilized conversations with its friends, who came calling like ceremonious Japanese gentlemen, offering expressions of solicitude and goodwill.

New hypothesis: that lobsters and other low-phylum animals are actually quite intelligent, with minds roomy enough to accept the sudden insertion of a human being's entire neural structure, but we in our foolish anthropocentric way have up till now been too blind to perceive—

No. Too facile. You could postulate the secretly lofty intelligence of the world's humble creatures, all right: you could postulate anything you wanted. But that didn't make it so. Lobsters did not ask questions. Lobsters did not come calling like ceremonious Japanese gentlemen. At least, not the lobsters of the world he remembered.

Improved lobsters? Evolved lobsters? Super-lobsters of the future?

—When am I?

Into his dizzied broodings came the quiet disembodied internal voice of not-McCulloch, his companion:

—Is your displacement, then, one of time rather than space?

—I don't know. Probably both. I'm a land creature.

—That has no meaning.

—I don't live in the ocean. I breathe air.

From the other consciousness came an expression of deep astonishment tinged with skepticism.

—Truly? That is very hard to believe. When you are in your own body you breathe no water at all?

—None. Not for long, or I would die.

—But there is so little land! And no creatures live upon it. Some make short visits there. But nothing can dwell there very long. So it has always been. And so will it be, until the time of the Molting of the World.

McCulloch considered that. Once again he found himself doubting that he was still on Earth. A world of water? Well, that could fit into his hypothesis of having journeyed forward in time, though it seemed to add a layer of implausibility upon implausibility. How many millions of years, he wondered, would it take for nearly all the Earth to have become covered with water? And he answered himself: In about as many as it would take to evolve a species of intelligent invertebrates.

Suddenly, terribly, it all fit together. Things crystallized and clarified in his mind, and he found access to another segment of his injured and redistributed memory; and he began to comprehend what had befallen him, or, rather, what he had willingly allowed himself to undergo. With that comprehension came a swift stinging sense of total displacement and utter loss, as though he were drowning and desperately tugging at strands of seaweed in a futile attempt to pull himself back to the surface. All that was real to him, all that he was part of, everything that made sense—gone, gone, perhaps irretrievably gone, buried under the weight of uncountable millennia, vanished, drowned, forgotten, reduced to mere geology. It was unthinkable, it was unacceptable, it was impossible, and as the truth of it bore in on him, he found himself choking on the frightful vastness of time past.

But that bleak sensation lasted only a moment and was gone. In its place came excitement, delight, confusion, and a feverish throbbing curiosity about this place he had entered. He was here. That miraculous thing that they had strived so fiercely to achieve had been achieved—rather too well, perhaps, but it had been achieved, and he was launched on the greatest adventure he would ever have, that anyone would ever have. This was not the moment for submitting to grief and confusion. Out of that world, lost and all but forgotten to him, came a scrap of verse that gleamed and blazed in his soul: *Only through time time is conquered.*

McCulloch reached toward the mind that was so close to his within this strange body.

—*When will it be safe for us to leave this cave?* he asked.

—*It is safe any time, now. Do you wish to go outside?*

—*Yes. Please.*

The creature stirred, flexed its front claws, slapped its flat tail against the floor of the cave, and in a slow ungraceful way began to clamber through the narrow opening, pausing more than once to search the waters outside for lurking enemies. McCulloch felt a quick hot burst of terror, as though he were about to enter some important meeting and had discovered too late that he was naked. Was the shell truly ready? Was he safely armored against the unknown foes outside, or would they fall upon him and tear him apart like furious shrikes? But his host did not seem to share those fears. It went plodding on and out, and in a moment more it emerged on an algae-encrusted tongue of the reef wall, a short distance below the two anemones. From each of those twin masses of rippling flesh came the same sullen pouting hungry murmurs: "Ah, come closer, why don't you come closer?"

"Another time," said the lobster, sounding almost playful, and turned away from them.

McCulloch looked outward over the landscape. Earlier, in the turmoil of his bewildering arrival and the pain and chaos of the molting prodrome, he had not had time to assemble any clear and coherent view of it. But now—despite the handicap of seeing everything with the alien perspective of the lobster's many-faceted eyes—he was able to put together an image of the terrain.

His view was a shortened one, because the sky was like a dark lid, through which came only enough light to create a cone-shaped arena spreading just a little way. Behind him was the face of the huge cliff, occupied by plant and animal life over virtually every square inch, and stretching upward until its higher reaches were lost in the dimness far overhead. Just a short way down from the ledge where he rested was the ocean floor, a broad expanse of gentle, undulating white sand streaked here and there with long widening gores of some darker material. Here and there bottom-growing plants arose in elegant billowy clumps, and McCulloch spotted occasional creatures moving among them over the sand that were much like lobsters and crabs, though with some differences. He saw also some starfish and snails and sea urchins that did not look at all unfamiliar. At higher levels he could make out a few swimming creatures: a couple of the squid-like animals—they were hulking-looking ropy-armed things, and he disliked them instinctively—and what seemed to be large jellyfish. But something was missing, and after a moment McCulloch realized what it was: fishes. There was a rich population of invertebrate life wherever he looked, but no fishes as far as he could see.

Not that he could see very far. The darkness clamped down like a curtain perhaps two or three hundred yards away. But even so, it was odd that not one fish had entered his field of vision in all this time. He wished he knew more about marine biology. Were there zones on Earth where no sea animals more complex than lobsters and crabs existed? Perhaps, but he doubted it.

Two disturbing new hypotheses blossomed in his mind. One was that he had landed in some remote future era where nothing out of his own time survived except low-phylum sea creatures. The other was that he had not traveled to the future at all, but had arrived by mischance in some primordial geological epoch in which vertebrate life had not yet evolved. That seemed unlikely to him, though. This place did not have a prehistoric feel to him. He saw no trilobites; surely there ought to be trilobites everywhere about, and not these oversize lobsters, which he did not remember at all from his childhood visits to the natural history museum's prehistory displays.

But if this was truly the future—and the future belonged to the lobsters and squids—

That was hard to accept. Only invertebrates? What could invertebrates accomplish, what kind of civilization could lobsters build, with their hard unsupple bodies and great clumsy claws? Concepts, half remembered or less than that, rushed through his mind: the Taj Mahal, the Gutenberg

Bible, the Sistine Chapel, the Madonna of the Rocks, the great window at Chartres. Could lobsters create those? Could squids? What a poor place this world must be, McCulloch thought sadly, how gray, how narrow, how tightly bounded by the ocean above and the endless sandy floor.

—*Tell me,* he said to his host. *Are there any fishes in this sea?*

The response was what he was coming to recognize as a sigh.

—*Fishes? That is another word without meaning.*

—*A form of marine life, with an internal bony structure—*

—*With its shell inside?*

—*That's one way of putting it,* said McCulloch.

—*There are no such creatures. Such creatures have never existed. There is no room for the shell within the soft parts of the body. I can barely comprehend such an arrangement: surely there is no need for it!*

—*It can be useful, I assure you. In the former world it was quite common.*

—*The world of human beings?*

—*Yes. My world,* McCulloch said.

—*Anything might have been possible in a former world, human McCulloch. Perhaps indeed before the world's last Molting shells were worn inside. And perhaps after the next one they will be worn there again. But in the world I know, human McCulloch, it is not the practice.*

—*Ah,* McCulloch said. *Then I am even farther from home than I thought.*

—*Yes,* said his host. *I think you are very far from home indeed. Does that cause you sorrow?*

—*Among other things.*

—*If it causes you sorrow, I grieve for your grief, because we are companions now.*

—*You are very kind,* said McCulloch to his host.

The lobster asked McCulloch if he was ready to begin their journey; and when McCulloch indicated that he was, his host serenely kicked itself free of the ledge with a single powerful stroke of its tail. For an instant it hung suspended; then it glided toward the sandy bottom as gracefully as though it were floating through air. When it landed, it was with all its many legs poised delicately *en pointe,* and it stood that way, motionless, a long moment.

Then it suddenly set out with great haste over the ocean floor, running so light-footedly that it scarcely raised a puff of sand wherever it touched down. More than once it ran right across some bottom-grubbing creature, some slug or scallop, without appearing to disturb it at all. McCulloch thought the lobster was capering in sheer exuberance, after its long internment in the cave; but some growing sense of awareness of his companion's mind told him after a time that this was no casual frolic, that the lobster was not in fact dancing but fleeing.

—*Is there an enemy?* McCulloch asked.

—*Yes. Above.*

The lobster's antennae stabbed upward at a sharp angle, and McCulloch, seeing through the other's eyes, perceived now a large looming cylindrical shape swimming in slow circles near the upper border of their range of vision. It might have been a shark, or even a whale. McCulloch felt deceived and betrayed; for the lobster had told this was an invertebrate world, and surely that creature above him—

—*No,* said the lobster, without slowing its manic sprint. *That animal has no shell of the sort you described within its body. It is only a bag of flesh. But it is very dangerous.*

—*How will we escape it?*

—*We will not escape it.*

The lobster sounded calm, but whether it was the calm of fatalism or mere expressionlessness, McCulloch could not say: the lobster had been calm even in the first moments of McCulloch's arrival in its mind, which must surely have been alarming and even terrifying to it.

It had begun to move now in ever-widening circles. This seemed not so much an evasive tactic as a ritualistic one, now, a dance indeed. A farewell to life? The swimming creature had descended until it was only a few lobster lengths above them, and McCulloch had a clear view of it. No, not a fish or a shark or any type of vertebrate at all, he realized, but an animal of a kind wholly unfamiliar to him, a kind of enormous wormlike thing whose meaty yellow body was reinforced externally by some sort of chitinous struts running its entire length. Fleshy vanelike fins rippled along its sides, but their purpose seemed to be more one of guidance than propulsion, for it appeared to move by guzzling in great quantities of water and expelling them through an anal siphon. Its mouth was vast, with a row of dim little green eyes ringing the scarlet lips. When the creature yawned, it revealed itself to be toothless, but capable of swallowing the lobster easily at a gulp.

Looking upward into that yawning mouth, McCulloch had a sudden image of himself elsewhere, spread-eagled under an inverted pyramid of shining machinery as the countdown reached its final moments, as the technicians made ready to—

—to hurl him—

—to hurl him forward in time—

Yes. An experiment. Definitely an experiment. He could remember it now. Bleier, Caldwell, Rodrigues, Mortenson. And all the others. Gathered around him, faces tight, forced smiles. The lights. The colors. The bizarre coils of equipment. And the volunteer. The volunteer. First human subject to be sent forward in time. The various rabbits and mice of the previous experiments, though they had apparently survived the round trip unharmed, had not been capable of delivering much of a report on their adventures. "I'm smarter than any rabbit," McCulloch had said. "Send me. I'll tell you what it's like up there." The volunteer. All that was coming back to him in great swatches now, as he crouched here within the mind of something much like a lobster, waiting for a vast yawning predator to pounce. The project, the controversies, his coworkers, the debate over risking a human mind under the machine, the drawing of lots. McCulloch had not been the only volunteer. He was just the lucky one. "Here you go, Jim-boy. A hundred years down the time line."

Or fifty, or eighty, or a hundred and twenty. They didn't have really precise trajectory control. They thought he might go as much as a hundred twenty years. But beyond much doubt they had overshot by a few hundred million. Was that within the permissible parameters of error?

He wondered what would happen to him if his host here were to perish. Would he die also? Would he find himself instantly transferred to some other being of this epoch? Or would he simply be hurled back instead to his own time? He was not ready to go back. He had just begun to observe, to understand, to explore—

McCulloch's host had halted its running now, and stood quite still in what was obviously a defensive mode, body cocked and upreared, claws extended, with the huge crusher claw erect and the long narrow cutting claw opening and closing in a steady rhythm. It was a threatening pose, but the swimming thing did not appear to be greatly troubled by it. Did the lobster mean to let itself be swallowed, and then to carve an exit for itself with those awesome weapons, before the alimentary juices could go to work on its armor?

"You choose your prey foolishly," said McCulloch's host to its enemy.

The swimming creature made a reply that was unintelligible to McCulloch: vague blurry words, the clotted outspew of a feeble intelligence. It continued its unhurried downward spiral.

"You are warned," said the lobster. "You are not selecting your victim wisely."

Again came a muddled response, sluggish and incoherent, the speech of an entity for whom verbal communication was a heavy, all-but-impossible effort.

Its enormous mouth gaped. Its fins rippled fiercely as it siphoned itself downward the last few yards to engulf the lobster. McCulloch prepared himself for transition to some new and even more unimaginable state when his host met its death. But suddenly the ocean floor was swarming with lobsters. They must have been arriving from all sides—summoned by his host's frantic dance? McCulloch wondered—while McCulloch, intent on the descent of the swimmer, had not noticed. Ten, twenty, possibly fifty of them arrayed themselves now beside McCulloch's host, and as the swimmer, tail on high, mouth wide, lowered itself like some gigantic suction hose toward them, the lobsters coolly and implacably seized its lips in their claws. Caught and helpless, it began at once to thrash, and from the pores through which it spoke came bleating incoherent cries of dismay and torment.

There was no mercy for it. It had been warned. It dangled tail upward while the pack of lobsters methodically devoured it from below, pausing occasionally to strip away and discard the rigid rods of chitin that formed its superstructure. Swiftly they reduced it to a faintly visible cloud of shreds oscillating in the water, and then small scavenging creatures came to fall upon those, and there was nothing at all left but the scattered rods of chitin on the sand.

The entire episode had taken only a few moments: the coming of the predator, the dance of McCulloch's host, the arrival of the other lobsters, the destruction of the enemy. Now the lobsters were gathered in a sort of convocation about McCulloch's host, wordlessly manifesting a commonality of spirit, a warmth of fellowship after feasting, that seemed quite comprehensible to McCulloch. For a short while they had been uninhibited savage carnivores consuming convenient meat; now once again they were courteous, refined, cultured—Japanese gentlemen, Oxford dons, gentle Benedictine monks.

McCulloch studied them closely. They were definitely more like lobsters than like any other creature he had ever seen, very much like lobsters, and yet there were differences. They were larger. How much larger, he could not tell, for he had no real way of judging distance and size in this undersea world; but he supposed they must be at least three feet long, and he doubted that lobsters of his time, even the biggest, were anything like that in length. Their bodies were wider than those of lobsters, and their heads were larger. The two largest claws looked like those of the lobsters he remembered, but the ones just behind them seemed more elaborate, as if adapted for more delicate procedures than mere rending of food and stuffing it into the mouth. There was an odd little hump, almost a dome, midway down the lobster's back—the center of the expanded nervous system, perhaps.

The lobsters clustered solemnly about McCulloch's host, and each lightly tapped its claws against those of the adjoining lobster in a sort of handshake, a process that seemed to take quite some time. McCulloch became aware also that a conversation was under way. What they were talking about, he realized, was him.

"It is not painful to have a McCulloch within one," his host was explaining. "It came upon me at molting time, and that gave me a moment of difficulty, molting being what it is. But it was only a moment. After that my only concern was for the McCulloch's comfort."

"And it is comfortable now?"

"It is becoming more comfortable."

"When will you show it to us?"

"Ah, that cannot be done. It has no real existence, and therefore I cannot bring it forth."

"What is it, then? A wanderer? A revenant?"

"A revenant, yes. So I think. And a wanderer. It says it is a human being."

"And what is that? Is a human being a kind of McCulloch?"

"I think a McCulloch is a kind of human being."

"Which is a revenant."

"Yes, I think so."

"This is an Omen!"

"Where is its world?"

"Its world is lost to it."

"Yes, definitely an Omen."

"It lived on dry land."

"It breathed air."

"It wore its shell within its body."

"What a strange revenant!"

"What a strange world its world must have been."

"It is the former world, would you not say?"

"So I surely believe. And therefore this is an Omen."

"Ah, we shall Molt. We shall Molt."

McCulloch was altogether lost. He was not even sure when his own host was the speaker.

"Is it the time?"

"We have an Omen, do we not?"

"The McCulloch surely was sent as a herald."

"There is no precedent."

"Each Molting, though, is without precedent. We cannot conceive what came before. We cannot imagine what comes after. We learn by learning. The McCulloch is the herald. The McCulloch is the Omen."

"I think not. I think it is unreal and unimportant."

"Unreal, yes. But not unimportant."

"The Time is not at hand. The Molting of the World is not yet due. The human is a wanderer and a revenant, but not a herald and certainly not an Omen."

"It comes from the former world."

"It says it does. Can we believe that?"

"It breathed air. In the former world, perhaps there were creatures that breathed air."

"It says it breathed air. I think it is neither herald nor Omen, neither wanderer nor revenant. I think it is a myth and a fugue. I think it betokens nothing. It is an accident. It is an interruption."

"That is an uncivil attitude. We have much to learn from the McCulloch. And if it is an Omen, we have immediate responsibilities that must be fulfilled."

"But how can we be certain of what it is?"

—*May I speak?* said McCulloch to his host.

—*Of course.*

—*How can I make myself heard?*

—*Speak through me.*

"The McCulloch wishes to be heard!"

"Hear it! Hear it!"

"Let it speak!"

McCulloch said, and the host spoke the words aloud for him, "I am a stranger here, and your guest, and so I ask you to forgive me if I give offense, for I have little understanding of your ways. Nor do I know if I am a herald or an Omen. But I tell you in all truth that I am a wanderer, and that I am sent from the former world, where there are many creatures of my kind, who breathe air and live upon the land and carry their—shells—inside their body."

"An Omen, certainly," said several of the lobsters at once. "A herald, beyond doubt."

McCulloch continued, "It was our hope to discover something of the worlds that are to come after ours. And therefore I was sent forward—"

"A herald—certainly a herald!"

"—to come to you, to go among you, to learn to know you, and then to return to my own people, the air people, the human people, and bring the word of what is to come. But I think that I am not the herald you expect. I carry no message for you. We could not have known that you were here. Out of the former world I bring you the blessing of those that have gone before, however, and when I go back to that world I will bear tidings of your life, of your thought, of your ways—"

"Then our kind is unknown to your world?"

McCulloch hesitated. "Creatures somewhat like you do exist in the seas of the former world. But they are smaller and simpler than you, and I think their civilization, if they have one, is not a great one."

"You have no discourse with them, then?" one of the lobsters asked.

"Very little," he said. A miserable evasion, cowardly, vile.

McCulloch shivered. He imagined himself crying out, "We eat them!" and the water turning black with their shocked outbursts and saw them instantly falling upon him, swiftly and efficiently slicing him to scraps with their claws. Through his mind ran monstrous images of lobsters in tanks, lobsters boiling alive, lobsters smothered in rich sauces, lobsters shelled, lobsters minced, lobsters rendered into bisques—he could not halt the torrent of dreadful visions. Such was our discourse with your ancestors. Such was our mode of inter-species communication. He felt himself drowning in guilt and shame and fear.

The spasm passed. The lobsters had not stirred. They continued to regard him with patience: impassive, unmoving, remote. McCulloch wondered if all that had passed through his mind just then had been transmitted to his host. Very likely; the host earlier had seemed to have access to all of his thoughts, though McCulloch did not have the same entrée to the host's. And if the host knew, did all the others? What then, what then?

Perhaps they did not even care. Lobsters, he recalled, were said to be callous cannibals, who might attack one another in the very tanks where they were awaiting their turns in the chef's pot. It was hard to view these detached and aloof beings, these dons, these monks, as having that sort of ferocity: but yet he had seen them go to work on that swimming mouth-creature without any show of embarrassment, and perhaps some atavistic echo of their ancestors' appetites lingered in them, so that they would think it only natural that McCullochs and other humans had fed on such things as lobsters. Why should they be shocked? Perhaps they thought that humans fed on humans, too. It was all in the former world, was it not? And in any event it was foolish to fear that they would exact some revenge on him for Lobster Thermidor, no matter how appalled they might be. He wasn't here. He was nothing more than a figment, a revenant, a wanderer, a set of intrusive neural networks within their companion's brain. The worst they could do to him, he supposed, was to exorcise him, and send him back to the former world.

Even so, he could not entirely shake the guilt and the shame. Or the fear.

Bleier said, "Of course, you aren't the only one who's going to be in jeopardy when we throw the switch. There's your host to consider. One entire human ego slamming into his mind out of nowhere like a brick falling off a building—what's it going to do to him?"

"Flip him out, is my guess," said Jake Ybarra. "You'll land on him and he'll announce he's Napoleon, or Joan of Arc, and they'll hustle him off to the nearest asylum. Are you prepared for the possibility, Jim, that you're going to spend your entire time in the future sitting in a loony bin undergoing therapy?"

"Or exorcism," Mortenson suggested. "If there's been some kind of reversion to barbarism. Christ, you might even get your host burned at the stake!"

"I don't think so," McCulloch said quietly. "I'm a lot more optimistic than you guys. I don't expect to land in a world of witch doctors and mumbo jumbo, and I don't expect to find myself in a place that locks people up in Bedlam because they suddenly start acting a little strange. The chances are that I *am* going to unsettle my host when I enter him, but that he'll simply get two sanity-stabilizer pills from his medicine chest and take them with a glass of water and feel better in five minutes. And then I'll explain what's happening to him."

"More than likely, no explanations will be necessary," said Maggie Caldwell. "By the time you arrive, time travel will have been a going proposition for three or four generations, after all. Having a traveler from the past turn up in your head will be old stuff to them. Your host will probably know exactly what's going on from the moment you hit him."

"Let's hope so," Bleier said. He looked across the laboratory to Rodrigues. "What's the count, Bob?"

"T minus eighteen minutes."

"I'm not worried about a thing," McCulloch said.

Caldwell took his hand in hers. "Neither am I, Jim."

"Then why is your hand so cold?" he asked.

"So I'm a *little* worried," she said.

McCulloch grinned. "So am I. A little. Only a little."

"You're human, Jim. No one's ever done this before."

"It'll be a can of corn!" Ybarra said.

Bleier looked at him blankly. "What the hell does that mean, Jake?"

Ybarra said, "Archaic twentieth-century slang. It means it's going to be a lot easier than we think."

"I told you," said McCulloch, "I'm not worried."

"I'm still worried about the impact on the host," said Bleier.

"All those Napoleons and Joans of Arc that have been cluttering the asylums for the last few hundred years," Maggie Caldwell said. "Could it be that they're really hosts for time travelers going backward in time?"

"You can't go backward," said Mortenson. "You know that. The round trip has to begin with a forward leap."

"Under present theory," Caldwell said. "But present theory's only five years old. It may turn out to be incomplete. We may have had all sorts of travelers out of the future jumping through history, and never even knew it. All the nuts, lunatics, inexplicable geniuses, idiots savants—"

"Save it, Maggie," Bleier said. "Let's stick to what we understand right now. "

"Oh? Do we understand anything?" McCulloch asked.

Bleier gave him a sour look. "I thought you said you weren't worried."

"I'm not. Not much. But I'd be a fool if I thought we really had a firm handle on what we're doing. We're shooting in the dark, and let's never kid ourselves about it."

"T minus fifteen," Rodrigues called.

"Try to make the landing easy on your host, Jim," Bleier said.

"I've got no reason not to want to," said McCulloch.

He realized that he had been wandering. Bleier, Maggie, Mortenson, Ybarra—for a moment they had been more real to him than the congregation of lobsters. He had heard their voices, he had seen their faces, Bleier plump and perspiring and serious, Ybarra dark and lean, Maggie with her crown of short upswept red hair blazing in the laboratory light—and yet they were all dead, a hundred million years dead, two hundred million, back there with the triceratops and the trilobite in the drowned former world, and here he was among the lobster people. How futile all those discussions of what the world of the early twenty-second century was going to be like! Those speculations on population density, religious belief, attitudes toward science, level of technological achievement, all those late-night sessions in the final months of the project, designed to prepare him for any eventuality he might encounter while he was visiting the future—what a waste, what a needless exercise. As was all that fretting about upsetting the mental stability of the person who would receive his transtemporalized consciousness. Such qualms, such moral delicacy—all unnecessary, McCulloch knew now.

But of course they had not anticipated sending him so eerily far across the dark abysm of time, into a world in which humankind and all its works were not even legendary memories, and the host who would receive him was a calm and thoughtful crustacean capable of taking him in with only the most mild and brief disruption of its serenity.

The lobsters, he noticed now, had reconfigured themselves while his mind had been drifting. They had broken up their circle and were arrayed in a long line stretching over the ocean floor, with his host at the end of the procession. The queue was a close one, each lobster so close to the one before it that it could touch it with the tips of its antennae, which from time to time they seemed to be doing; and they all were moving in a weird kind of quasi-military lockstep, every lobster swinging the same set of walking-legs forward at the same time.

—*Where are we going?* McCulloch asked his host.

—*The pilgrimage has begun.*

—*What pilgrimage is that?*

—*To the dry place,* said the host. *To the place of no water. To the land.*

—*Why?*

—*It is the custom. We have decided that the time of the Molting of the World is soon to come; and therefore we must make the pilgrimage. It is the end of all things. It is the coming of a newer world. You are the herald: so we have agreed.*

—*Will you explain? I have a thousand questions. I need to know more about all this,* McCulloch said.

—*Soon. Soon. This is not a time for explanations.*

McCulloch felt a firm and unequivocal closing of contact, an emphatic withdrawal. He sensed a hard ringing silence that was almost an absence of the host, and knew it would be inappropriate to transgress against it. That was painful, for he brimmed now with an overwhelming rush of curiosity. The Molting of the World? The end of all things? A pilgrimage to the land? What land? Where? But he did not ask. He could not ask. The host seemed to have vanished from him, disappearing utterly into this pilgrimage, this migration, moving in its lockstep way with total concentration and a kind of mystic intensity. McCulloch did not intrude. He felt as though he had been left alone in the body they shared.

As they marched, he concentrated on observing, since he could not interrogate. And there was much to see; for the longer he dwelled within his host, the more accustomed he grew to the lobster's sensory mechanisms. The compound eyes, for instance. Enough of his former life had returned to him now so that he remembered human eyes clearly, those two large gleaming ovals, so keen, so subtle of focus, set beneath protecting ridges of bone. His host's eyes were nothing like that: they were two clusters of tiny lenses rising on jointed, movable stalks, and what they showed was an intricately dissected view, a mosaic of isolated points of light. But he was learning somehow to translate those complex and baffling images into a single clear one, just as, no doubt, a creature accustomed to compound-lens vision would sooner or later learn to see through human eyes, if need be. And McCulloch found now that he could not only make more sense out of the views he received through his host's eyes, but that he was seeing farther, into quite distant dim recesses of this sunless undersea realm.

Not that the stalked eyes seemed to be a very important part of the lobster's perceptive apparatus. They provided nothing more than a certain crude awareness of the immediate terrain. But apparently the real work of perceiving was done mainly by the thousands of fine bristles, so minute that they were all but invisible, that sprouted on every surface of his host's body. These seemed to send a constant stream of messages to the lobster's brain: information on the texture and topography of the ocean floor, on tiny shifts in the flow and temperature of the water, of the proximity of obstacles, and much else. Some of the small hair-like filaments were sensitive to touch, and others, it appeared, to chemicals; for whenever the lobster approached some other life-form, it received data on its scent—or the underwater equivalent—long before the creature itself was within visual range. The quantity and richness of these inputs astonished McCulloch. At every moment came a torrent of data corresponding to the landslide senses he remembered, smell, taste, touch; and some central processing unit within the lobster's brain handled everything in the most effortless fashion.

But there was no sound. The ocean world appeared to be wholly silent. McCulloch knew that that was untrue, that sound waves propagated through water as persistently as through air, if somewhat more rapidly. Yet the lobster seemed neither to possess nor to need any sort of auditory equipment. The sensory bristles brought in all the data it required. The "speech" of these creatures, McCulloch had long ago realized, was effected not by voice but by means of spurts of chemicals released into the water, hormones, perhaps, or amino acids, something of a distinct and readily recognizable identity, emitted in some high-redundancy pattern that permitted easy recognition and decoding despite the difficulties caused by currents and eddies. It was, McCulloch thought, like trying to communicate by printing individual letters on scraps of paper and hurling them into the wind. But it did somehow seem to work, however clumsy a concept it might be, because of the extreme sensitivity of the lobster's myriad chemoreceptors.

The antennae played some significant role also. There were two sets of them, a pair of three-branched ones just behind the eyes and a much longer single-branched pair behind those. The long ones restlessly twitched and probed inquisitively, and most likely, he suspected, served as simple balancing and coordination devices much like the whiskers of a cat. The purpose of the smaller antennae eluded him, but it was his guess that they were involved in the process of communication between one lobster and another, either by some semaphore system or in a deeper communion beyond his still awkward comprehension.

McCulloch regretted not knowing more about the lobsters of his own era. But he had only a broad general knowledge of natural history, extensive, fairly deep, yet not good enough to tell him whether these elaborate sensory functions were characteristic of all lobsters or had evolved during the millions of years it had taken to create the water world. Probably some of each, he decided. Very likely even the lobsters of the former world had had much of this scanning equipment, enough to allow them to locate their prey, to find their way around in the dark suboceanic depths, to undertake their long and unerring migrations. But he found it hard to believe that they could have had much "speech" capacity, that they gathered in solemn sessions to discuss abstruse questions of theology and mythology, to argue gently about omens and heralds and the end of all things. That was something that the patient and ceaseless unfoldings of time must have wrought.

The lobsters marched without show of fatigue: not scampering in that dancelike way that his host had adopted while summoning its comrades to save it from the swimming creature, but moving nevertheless in an elegant and graceful fashion, barely touching the ground with the tips of their legs, going onward step by step by step steadily and fairly swiftly.

McCulloch noticed that new lobsters frequently joined the procession, cutting in from left or right just ahead of his host, who always remained at the rear of the line; that line now was so long, hundreds of lobsters long, that it was impossible to see its beginning. Now and again one would reach out with its bigger claw to seize some passing animal, a starfish or urchin or small crab, and without missing a step would shred and devour it, tossing the unwanted husk to the cloud of planktonic scavengers that always hovered nearby. This foraging on the march was done with utter lack of self-consciousness; it was almost by reflex that these creatures snatched and gobbled as they journeyed.

And yet all the same they did not seem like mere marauding mouths. From this long line of crustaceans there emanated, McCulloch realized, a mysterious sense of community, a wholeness of society, that he did not understand but quite sharply sensed. This was plainly not a mere migration but a true pilgrimage. He thought ruefully of his earlier condescending view of these people, incapable of achieving the Taj Mahal or the Sistine Chapel, and felt abashed: for he was beginning to see that they had other accomplishments of a less tangible sort that were only barely apparent to his displaced and struggling mind.

"When you come back," Maggie said, "you'll be someone else. There's no escaping that. It's the one thing I'm frightened of. Not that you'll die making the hop, or that you'll get into some sort of terrible trouble in the future, or that we won't be able to bring you back at all, or anything like that. But that you'll have become someone else."

"I feel pretty secure in my identity," McCulloch told her.

"I know you do. God knows, you're the most stable person in the group, and that's why you're going. But even so. Nobody's ever done anything like this before. It can't help but change you. When you return, you're going to be unique among the human race."

"That sounds very awesome. But I'm not sure it'll matter that much, Mag. I'm just taking a little trip. If I were going to Paris, or Istanbul, or even Antarctica, would I come back totally transformed? I'd have had some new experiences, but—"

"It isn't the same," she said. "It isn't even remotely the same." She came across the room to him and put her hands on his shoulders, and stared deep into his eyes, which sent a little chill through him, as it always did; for when she looked at him that way there was a sudden flow of energy between them, a powerful warm rapport rushing from her to him and from him to her as though through a huge conduit, that delighted and frightened him both at once. He could lose himself in her. He had never let himself feel that way about anyone before. And this was not the moment to begin. There was no room in him for such feelings, not now, not when he was within a couple of hours of leaping off into the most unknown of unknowns. When he returned—if he returned—he might risk allowing something at last to develop with Maggie. But not on the eve of departure, when everything in his universe was tentative and conditional. "Can I tell you a little story, Jim?" she asked.

"Sure."

"When my father was on the faculty at Cal, he was invited to a reception to meet a couple of the early astronauts, two of the Apollo men—I don't remember which ones, but they were from the second or third voyage to the Moon. When he showed up at the faculty club, there were two or three hundred people there, milling around having cocktails, and most of them were people he didn't know. He walked in and looked around and within ten seconds he had found the astronauts. He didn't have to be told. He just *knew.* And this is my father, remember, who doesn't believe in ESP or anything like that. But he said they were impossible to miss, even in that crowd. You could see it on their faces, you could feel the radiance coming from them, there was an aura, there was something about their eyes. Something that said, *I have walked on the Moon, I have been to that place which is not of our world and I have come back, and now I am someone else. I am who I was before, but I am someone else also.*"

"But they went to the *Moon,* Mag!"

"And you're going to the *future,* Jim. That's even weirder. You're going to a place that doesn't exist. And you may meet yourself there—ninety-nine years old, and waiting to shake hands with you—or you might meet me, or your grandson, or find out that everyone on Earth is dead, or that everyone has turned into a disembodied spirit, or that they're all immortal super-beings, or—or—Christ, I don't know. You'll see a world that nobody alive today is supposed to see. And when you come back, you'll have that aura. You'll be transformed."

"Is that so frightening?"

"To me it is," she said.

"Why is that?"

"Dummy," she said. "Dope. How explicit do I have to be, anyway? I thought I was being obvious enough."

He could not meet her eyes. "This isn't the best moment to talk about—"

"I know. I'm sorry, Jim. But you're important to me, and you're going somewhere and you're going to become someone else, and I'm scared. Selfish and scared."

"Are you telling me not to go?"

"Don't be absurd. You'd go no matter what I told you, and I'd despise you if you didn't. There's no turning back now."

"No."

"I shouldn't have dumped any of this on you today. You don't need it right this moment."

"It's okay," he said softly. He turned until he was looking straight at her, and for a long moment he simply stared into her eyes and did not speak, and then at last he said, "Listen, I'm going to take a big fantastic improbably insane voyage, and I'm going to be a witness to God knows what, and then I'm going to come back, and yes, I'll be changed—only an ox wouldn't be changed, or maybe only a block of stone—but I'll still be me, whoever *me* is. Don't worry, okay? I'll still be me. And we'll still be us."

"Whoever *us* is."

"Whoever. Jesus, I wish you were going with me, Mag!"

"That's the silliest schoolboy thing I've ever heard you say."

"True, though."

"Well, I can't go. Only one at a time can go, and it's you. I'm not even sure I'd want to go. I'm not as crazy as you are, I suspect. You go, Jim, and come back and tell me all about it."

"Yes."

"And then we'll see what there is to see about you and me."

"Yes," he said.

She smiled. "Let me show you a poem, okay? You must know it, because it's Eliot, and you know all the Eliot there is. But I was reading him last night—thinking of you, reading him—and I found this, and it seemed to be the right words, and I wrote them down. From one of the *Quartets.*"

"I think I know," he said:

> *"Time past and time future*
> *Allow but a little consciousness—"*

"That's a good one, too," Maggie said. "But it's not the one I had in mind." She unfolded a piece of paper. "It's this:

> *"We shall not cease from exploration*
> *And the end of all our exploring*
> *Will be to arrive where we started—"*

"*And know the place for the first time,*" he completed. "Yes. Exactly. To arrive where we started. And know the place for the first time."

THE LOBSTERS WERE SINGING AS they marched. That was the only word, McCulloch thought, that seemed to apply. The line of pilgrims now was immensely long—there must have been thousands in the procession by this time, and more were joining constantly—and from them arose an outpouring of chemical signals, within the narrowest of tonal ranges, that mingled in a close harmony and amounted to a kind of sustained chant on a few notes, swelling, filling all the ocean with its powerful and intense presence. Once again he had an image of them as monks, but not Benedictines now: these were Buddhist, rather, an endless line of yellow-robed holy men singing a great *om* as they made their way up some Tibetan slope. He was awed and humbled by it—by the intensity, and by the wholeheartedness of the devotion. It was getting hard for him to remember that these were crustaceans, no more than ragged claws scuttling across the floors of silent seas; he sensed minds all about him, whole and elaborate minds arising out of some rich cultural matrix, and it was coming to seem quite natural to him that these people should have armored exoskeletons and jointed eyestalks and a dozen busy legs.

His host had still not broken its silence, which must have extended now over a considerable period. Just how long a period, McCulloch had no idea, for there were no significant alternations of light and dark down here to indicate the passing of time, nor did the marchers ever seem to sleep, and they took their food, as he had seen, in a casual and random way without breaking step. But it seemed to McCulloch that he had been effectively alone in the host's body for many days.

He was not minded to try to reenter contact with the other just yet—not until he received some sort of signal from it. Plainly the host had withdrawn into some inner sanctuary to undertake a profound meditation; and McCulloch, now that the early bewilderment and anguish of his journey through time had begun to wear off, did not feel so dependent upon the host that he needed to blurt his queries constantly into his companion's consciousness. He would watch, and wait, and attempt to fathom the mysteries of this place unaided.

The landscape had undergone a great many changes since the beginning of the march. That gentle bottom of fine white sand had yielded to a terrain of rough dark gravel, and that to one of a pale sedimentary stuff made up of tiny shells, the mortal remains, no doubt, of vast hordes of diatoms and foraminifera, which rose like clouds of snowflakes at the lobsters' lightest steps. Then came a zone where a stratum of thick red clay spread in all directions. The clay held embedded in it an odd assortment of rounded rocks and clamshells and bits of chitin, so that it had the look of some complex paving material from a fashionable terrace. And after that they entered a region where slender spires of a sharp black stone, faceted like worked flint, sprouted stalagmite-fashion at their feet. Through all of this the lobster-pilgrims marched unperturbed, never halting, never breaking their file, moving in a straight line whenever possible and making only the slightest of deviations when compelled to it by the harshness of the topography.

Now they were in a district of coarse yellow sandy globules, out of which two types of coral grew: thin angular strands of deep jet, and supple, almost mobile fingers of a rich lovely salmon hue. McCulloch wondered where on Earth such stuff might be found, and chided himself at once for the foolishness of the thought: the seas he knew had been swallowed long ago in the great all-encompassing ocean that swathed the world, and the familiar continents, he supposed, had broken from their moorings and slipped to strange parts of the globe well before the rising of the waters. He had no landmarks. There was an equator somewhere, and there were two poles, but down here beyond the reach of direct sunlight, in this warm changeless uterine sea neither north nor south nor east held any meaning. He remembered other lines:

Sand-strewn caverns, cool and deep
Where the winds are all asleep;
Where the spent lights quiver and gleam;
Where the salt weed sways in the stream;
Where the sea-beasts rang'd all round
Feed in the ooze of their pasture-ground . . .

What was the next line? Something about great whales coming sailing by, sail and sail with unshut eye, round the world for ever and aye. Yes, but there were no great whales here, if he understood his host correctly, no dolphins, no sharks, no minnows; there were only these swarming lower creatures, mysteriously raised on high, lords of the world. And mankind? Birds and bats, horses and bears? Gone. Gone. And the valleys and meadows? The lakes and streams? Taken by the sea. The world lay before him like a land of dreams, transformed. But was it, as the poet had said, a place which hath really neither joy, nor love, nor light, nor certitude, nor peace, nor help for pain? It did not seem that way. For light there was merely that diffuse faint glow, so obscure it was close to nonexistent, that filtered down through unknown fathoms. But what was that lobster song, that ever-swelling crescendo, if not some hymn to love and certitude and peace, and help for pain? He was overwhelmed by peace, surprised by joy, and he did not understand what was happening to him. He was part of the march, that was all. He was a member of the pilgrimage.

HE HAD WANTED TO KNOW if there was any way he could signal to be pulled back home: a panic button, so to speak. Bleier was the one he asked, and the question seemed to drive the man into an agony of uneasiness. He scowled, he tugged at his jowls, he ran his hands through his sparse strands of hair.

"No," he said finally. "We weren't able to solve that one, Jim. There's simply no way of propagating a signal backward in time."

"I didn't think so," McCulloch said. "I just wondered."

"Since we're not actually sending your physical body, you shouldn't find yourself in any real trouble. Psychic discomfort, at the worst—disorientation, emotional upheaval, at the worst a sort of terminal homesickness. But I think you're strong enough to pull your way through any of that. And you'll always know that we're going to be yanking you back to us at the end of the experiment."

"How long am I going to be gone?"

"Elapsed time will be virtually nil. We'll throw the switch, off you'll go, you'll do your jaunt, we'll grab you back, and it'll seem like no time at all, perhaps a thousandth of a second. We aren't going to believe that you went anywhere at all, until you start telling us about it."

McCulloch sensed that Bleier was being deliberately evasive, not for the first time since McCulloch had been selected as the time traveler. "It'll seem like no time at all to the people watching in the lab," he said. "But what about for me?"

"Well, of course for you it'll be a little different, because you'll have had a subjective experience in another time frame."

"That's what I'm getting at. How long are you planning to leave me in the future? An hour? A week?"

"That's really hard to determine, Jim."

"What does that mean?"

"You know, we've sent only rabbits and stuff. They've come back okay, beyond much doubt—"

"Sure. They still munch on lettuce when they're hungry and they don't tie their ears together in knots before they hop. So I suppose they're none the worse for wear."

"Obviously we can't get much of a report from a rabbit."

"Obviously."

"You're sounding awfully goddamned hostile today, Jim. Are you sure you don't want us to scrub the mission and start training another volunteer?" Bleier asked.

"I'm just trying to elicit a little hard info," McCulloch said. "I'm not trying to back out. And if I sound hostile, it's only because you're dancing all around my questions, which is becoming a considerable pain in the ass."

Bleier looked squarely at him and glowered. "All right. I'll tell you anything you want to know that I'm capable of answering. Which is what I think I've been doing all along. When the rabbits come back, we test them and we observe no physiological changes, no trace of ill effects as a result of having separated the psyche from the body for the duration of a time jaunt. Christ, we can't even tell the rabbits *have* been on a time jaunt, except that our instruments indicate the right sort of thermodynamic drain and entropic reversal, and for all we know we're kidding ourselves about that, which is why we're risking our reputations and your neck to send a human being who can tell us what the fuck happens when we throw the switch. But you've seen the rabbits jaunting. You know as well as I do that they come back okay."

Patiently McCulloch said, "Yes. As okay as a rabbit ever is, I guess. But what I'm trying to find out from you, and what you seem unwilling to tell me, is how long I'm going to be up there in subjective time."

"We don't know, Jim," Bleier said.

"You don't *know*? What if it's ten years? What if it's a thousand? What if I'm going to live out an entire life span, or whatever is considered a life span a hundred years from now, and grow old and wise and wither away and die and then wake up a thousandth of a second later on your lab table?"

"We don't know. That's why we have to send a human subject."

"There's no way to measure subjective jaunt-time?"

"Our instruments are here. They aren't *there.* You're the only instrument we'll have there. For all we know, we're sending you off for a million years, and when you come back here you'll have turned into something out of H. G. Wells. Is that straightforward enough for you, Jim? But I don't think it's going to happen that way, and Mortenson doesn't think so either, or Ybarra for that matter. What we think is that you'll spend something between a day and a couple of months in the future, with the outside possibility of a year. And when we give you the hook, you'll be back here with virtually nil elapsed time. But to answer your first question again, there's no way you can instruct us to yank you back. You'll just have to sweat it out, however long it may be. I thought you knew that. The book, when it comes, will be virtually automatic, a function of the thermodynamic homeostasis, like the recoil of a gun. An equal and opposite reaction: or maybe more like the snapping back of a rubber band. Pick whatever metaphor you want. But if you don't like the way any of this sounds, it's not too late for you to back out, and nobody will say a word against you. It's never too late to back out. Remember that, Jim."

McCulloch shrugged. "Thanks for leveling with me. I appreciate that. And no, I don't want to drop out. The only thing I wonder about is whether my stay in the future is going to seem too long or too goddamned short. But I won't know that until I get there, will I? And then the time I have to wait before coming home is going to be entirely out of my hands. And out of yours, too, is how it seems. But that's all right. I'll take my chances. I just wondered what I'd do if I got there and found that I didn't much like it there."

"My bet is that you'll have the opposite problem," said Bleier. "You'll like it so much you won't want to come back."

AGAIN AND AGAIN, WHILE THE pilgrims traveled onward, McCulloch detected bright flares of intelligence gleaming like brilliant pinpoints of light in the darkness of the sea. Each creature seemed to have a characteristic emanation, a glow of neural energy. The simple ones—worms, urchins, starfish, sponges—emitted dim gentle signals; but there were others as dazzling as beacons. The lobster-folk were not the only sentient life-forms down here.

Occasionally he saw, as he had in the early muddled moments of the jaunt, isolated colonies of the giant sea anemones: great flowery-looking things, rising on thick pedestals. From them came a soft alluring lustful purr, a siren crooning calculated to bring unwary animals within reach of their swaying tentacles and the eager mouths hidden within the fleshy petals. Cemented to the floor on their swaying stalks, they seemed like somber philosophers, lost in the intervals between meals in deep reflections on the purpose of the cosmos. McCulloch longed to pause and try to speak with them, for their powerful emanation appeared plainly to indicate that they possessed a strong intelligence, but the lobsters moved past the anemones without halting.

The squid-like beings that frequently passed in flotillas overhead seemed even keener of mind: large animals, sleek and arrogant of motion, with long turquoise bodies that terminated in hawser-like arms, and enormous bulging eyes of a startling scarlet color. He found them ugly and repugnant, and did not quite know why. Perhaps it was some attitude of his host's that carried over subliminally to him; for there was an unmistakable chill among the lobsters whenever the squids appeared, and the chanting of the marchers grew more vehement, as though betokening a warning.

That some kind of frosty detente existed between the two kinds of life-forms was apparent from the regard they showed one another and from the distances they maintained. Never did the squids descend into the ocean-floor zone that was the chief domain of the lobsters, but for long spans of time they would soar above, in a kind of patient aerial surveillance, while the lobsters, striving ostentatiously to ignore them, betrayed discomfort by quickened movements of their antennae.

Still other kinds of high-order intelligence manifested themselves as the pilgrimage proceeded. In a zone of hard and rocky terrain McCulloch felt a new and distinctive mental pulsation, coming from some creature that he must not have encountered before. But he saw nothing unusual: merely a rough grayish landscape pockmarked by dense clumps of oysters and barnacles, some shaggy outcroppings of sponges and yellow seaweeds, a couple of torpid anemones. Yet out of the midst of all that unremarkable clutter came clear strong signals, produced by minds of considerable force. Whose? Not the oysters and barnacles, surely. The mystery intensified as the lobsters, without pausing in their march, interrupted their chant to utter words of greeting, and had greetings in return, drifting toward them from that tangle of marine underbrush.

"Why do you march?" the unseen speakers asked, in a voice that rose in the water like a deep slow groaning.

"We have had an Omen," answered the lobsters.

"Ah, is it the Time?"

"The Time will surely be here," the lobsters replied.

"Where is the herald, then?"

"The herald is within me," said McCulloch's host, breaking its long silence at last.

—To whom do you speak? McCulloch asked.

—Can you not see? There. Before us.

McCulloch saw only algae, barnacles, sponges, oysters.

—Where?

—In a moment you will see, said the host.

The column of pilgrims had continued all the while to move forward, until now it was within the thick groves of seaweed. And now McCulloch saw who the other speakers were. Huge crabs were crouched at the bases of many of the larger rock formations, creatures far greater in size than the largest of the lobsters, but they were camouflaged so well that they were virtually invisible except at the closest range. On their broad arching backs whole gardens grew: brilliantly-colored sponges, algae in somber reds and browns, fluffy many-branched crimson things, odd complex feathery growths, even a small anemone or two, all jammed together in such profusion that nothing of the underlying crab showed except beady long-stalked eyes and glinting claws. Why beings that signaled their presence with potent telepathic outputs should choose to cloak themselves in such elaborate concealments, McCulloch could not guess: perhaps it was to deceive a prey so simple that it was unable to detect the emanations of these crabs' minds.

As the lobsters approached, the crabs heaved themselves up a little way from the rocky bottom, and shifted themselves ponderously from side to side, causing the intricate streamers and filaments and branches of the creatures growing on them to stir and wave about. It was like a forest agitated by a sudden hard gust wind from the north.

"Why do you march, why do you march?" called the crabs. "Surely it is not yet the time. Surely!"

"Surely it is," the lobsters replied. "So we all agree. Will you march with us?"

"Show us your herald!" the crabs cried. "Let us see the Omen!"

—*Speak to them,* said McCulloch's host.

—*But what am I to say?*

—*The truth. What else can you say?*

—*I know nothing. Everything here is a mystery to me.*

—*I will explain all things afterward. Speak to them now.*

—*Without understanding?*

—*Tell them what you told us.*

Baffled, McCulloch said, speaking through the host, "I have come from the former world as an emissary. Whether I am a herald, whether I bring an Omen, is not for me to say. In my own world I breathed air and carried my shell within my body."

"Unmistakably a herald," said the lobsters.

To which the crabs replied, "That is not so unmistakable to us. We sense a wanderer and a revenant among you. But what does that mean? The Molting of the World is not a small thing, good friends. Shall we march, just because this strangeness is come upon you? It is not enough evidence. And to march is not a small thing either, at least for us."

"We have chosen to march," the lobsters said, and indeed they had not halted at all throughout this colloquy; the vanguard of their procession was far out of sight in a black-walled canyon, and McCulloch's host, still at the end of the line, was passing now through the last few crouching places of the great crabs. "If you mean to join us, come now."

From the crabs came a heavy outpouring of regret. "Alas, alas, we are large, we are slow, the way is long, the path is dangerous."

"Then we will leave you."

"If it is the Time, we know that you will perform the offices on our behalf. If it is not the Time, it is just as well that we do not make the pilgrimage. We are—not—certain. We—cannot—be—sure—it—is—an—Omen—"

McCulloch's host was far beyond the last of the crabs. Their words were faint and indistinct, and the final few were lost in the gentle surgings of the water.

—*They make a great error,* said McCulloch's host to him. *If it is truly the Time, and they do not join the march, it might happen that their souls will be lost. That is a severe risk: but they are a lazy folk. Well, we will perform the offices on their behalf.*

And to the crabs the host called, "We will do all that is required, have no fear!" But it was impossible, McCulloch thought, that the words could have reached the crabs across such a distance.

He and the host now were entering the mouth of the black canyon. With the host awake and talkative once again, McCulloch meant to seize the moment at last to have some answers to his questions.

—*Tell me now*—he began.

But before he could complete the thought, he felt the sea roil and surge about him as though he had been swept up in a monstrous wave. That could not be, not at this depth; but yet that irresistible force, booming toward him out of the dark canyon and catching him up, hurled him into a chaos as desperate as that of his moment of arrival. He sought to cling, to grasp, but there was no purchase; he was loose of his moorings; he was tossed and flung like a bubble on the winds.

—*Help me!* he called. *What's happening to us?*

—*To you, friend human McCulloch. To you alone. Can I aid you?*

What was that? Happening only to him? But certainly he and the lobster both were caught in this undersea tempest, both being thrown about, both whirled in the same maelstrom—

Faces danced around him. Charlie Bleier, pudgy, earnest-looking. Maggie, tender-eyed, troubled. Bleier had his hand on McCulloch's right wrist, Maggie on the other, and they were tugging, tugging—

But he had no wrists. He was a lobster.

"Come, Jim—"

"No! Not yet!"

"Jim—Jim—"

'Stop—pulling—you're hurting—"

"Jim—"

McCulloch struggled to free himself from their grasp. As he swung his arms in wild circles, Maggie and Bleier, still clinging to them, went whipping about like tethered balloons. "Let go," he shouted. "You aren't here! There's nothing for you to hold on to! You're just hallucinations! Let—go—!"

And then, as suddenly as they had come, they were gone.

THE SEA WAS CALM. HE was in his accustomed place, seated somewhere deep within his host's consciousness. The lobster was moving forward, steady as ever, into the black canyon, following the long line of its companions.

McCulloch was too stunned and dazed to attempt contact for a long while. Finally, when he felt some measure of composure return, he reached his mind into his host's:

—What happened?

—I cannot say. What did it seem like to you?

—The water grew wild and stormy. I saw faces out of the former world. Friends of mine. They were pulling at my arms. You felt nothing?

—Nothing, said the host, *except a sense of your own turmoil. We are deep here: beyond the reach of storms.*

—Evidently I'm not.

—Perhaps your homefaring time is coming. Your world is summoning you.

Of course! The faces, the pulling at his arms—the plausibility of the host's suggestion left McCulloch trembling with dismay. Homefaring time! Back there in the lost and inconceivable past, they had begun angling for him, casting their line into the vast gulf of time—

—*I'm not ready,* he protested. *I've only just arrived here! I know nothing yet! How can they call me so soon?*

—*Resist them, if you would remain.*

—*Will you help me?*

—*How would that be possible?*

—*I'm not sure,* McCulloch said. *But it's too early for me to go back. If they pull on me again, hold me! Can you?*

—*I can try, friend human McCulloch.*

—*And you have to keep your promise to me now.*

—*What promise is that?*

—*You said you would explain things to me. Why you've undertaken this pilgrimage. What it is I'm supposed to be the Omen of. What happens when the Time comes. The Molting of the World.*

—*Ah,* said the host.

But that was all it said. In silence it scrabbled with busy legs over a sharply creviced terrain. McCulloch felt a fierce impatience growing in him. What if they yanked him again, now, and this time they succeeded? There was so much yet to learn! But he hesitated to prod the host again, feeling abashed. Long moments passed. Two more squids appeared: the radiance of their probing minds was like twin searchlights overhead. The ocean floor sloped downward gradually but perceptibly here. The squids vanished, and another of the predatory big-mouthed swimming-things, looking as immense as a whale and, McCulloch supposed, filling the same ecological niche, came cruising down into the level where the lobsters marched, considered their numbers in what appeared to be some surprise, and swam slowly upward again and out of sight. Something else of great size, flapping enormous wings somewhat like those of a stingray but clearly just a boneless mass of chitin-strutted flesh, appeared next, surveyed the pilgrims with equally bland curiosity, and flew to the front of the line of lobsters, where McCulloch lost it in the darkness. While all of this was happening the host was quiet and inaccessible, and McCulloch did not dare attempt to penetrate its privacy. But then, as the pilgrims were moving through a region where huge, dim-witted scallops with great bright eyes nestled everywhere, waving gaudy pink and blue mantles, the host unexpectedly resumed the conversation as though there had been no interruption, saying:

—*What we call the Time of the Molting of the World is the time when the world undergoes a change of nature, and is purified and reborn. At such a time, we journey to the place of dry land, and perform certain holy rites.*

—*And these rites bring about the Molting of the World?* McCulloch asked.

—*Not at all. The Molting is an event wholly beyond our control. The rites are performed for our own sakes, not for the world's.*

—*I'm not sure I understand.*

—*We wish to survive the Molting, to travel onward into the world to come. For this reason, at a Time of Molting, we must make our observances, we must demonstrate our worth. It is the responsibility of my people. We bear the duty for all the peoples of the world.*

—*A priestly caste, is that it?* McCulloch said. *When this cataclysm comes, the lobsters go forth to say the prayers for everyone, so that everyone's soul will survive?*

The host was silent again: pondering McCulloch's terms, perhaps, translating them into more appropriate equivalents. Eventually it replied:

—*That is essentially correct.*

—*But other peoples can join the pilgrimage if they want. Those crabs. The anemones. The squids, even?*

—*We invite all to come. But we do not expect anyone but ourselves actually to do it.*

—*How often has there been such a ceremony?* McCulloch asked.

—*I cannot say. Never, perhaps.*

—*Never?*

—*The Molting of the World is not a common event. We think it has happened only twice since the beginning of time.*

In amazement McCulloch said:

—Twice since the world began, and you think it's going to happen again in your own lifetimes?

—Of course we cannot be sure of that. But we have had an Omen, or so we think, and we must abide by that. It was foretold that when the end is near, an emissary from the former world would come among us. And so it has come to pass. Is that not so?

—Indeed.

—Then we must make the pilgrimage, for if you have not brought the Omen we have merely wasted some effort, but if you are the true herald we will have forfeited all of eternity if we let your message go unheeded.

It sounded eerily familiar to McCulloch: a messianic prophecy, a cult of the millennium, an apocalyptic transfiguration. He felt for a moment as though he had landed in the tenth century instead of in some impossibly remote future epoch. And yet the host's tone was so calm and rational, the sense of spiritual obligation that the lobster conveyed was so profound, that McCulloch found nothing absurd in these beliefs. Perhaps the world *did* end from time to time, and the performing of certain rituals did in fact permit its inhabitants to transfer their souls onward into whatever unimaginable environment was to succeed the present one. Perhaps.

—Tell me, said McCulloch. *What were the former worlds like, and what will the next one be?*

—You should know more about the former worlds than I, friend human McCulloch. And as for the world to come, we may only speculate.

—But what are your traditions about those worlds?

—The first world, the lobster said, *was a world of fire.*

—You can understand fire, living in the sea?

—We have heard tales of it from those who have been to the dry place. Above the water there is air, and in the air there hangs a ball of fire, which gives the world warmth. Is this not the case?

McCulloch, hearing a creature of the ocean floor speak of things so far beyond its scope and comprehension, felt a warm burst of delight and admiration.

—Yes! We call that ball of fire the sun.

—Ah, so that is what you mean, when you think of the sun! The word was a mystery to me, when first you used it. But I understand you much better now, do you not agree?

—You amaze me, McCulloch said.

—The first world, so we think, was fire: it was like the sun. And when we dwelled upon that world, we were fire also. It is the fire that we carry within us to this day, that glow, that brightness, which is our life, and which goes from us when we die. After a span of time so long that we could never describe its length, the Time of the Molting came upon the fire world and it grew hard, and gathered a cloak of air about itself, and creatures lived upon the land and breathed the air. I find that harder to comprehend, in truth, than I do the fire world. But that was the first Molting, when the air world emerged: that world from which you have come to us. I hope you will tell me of your world, friend human McCulloch, when there is time.

—So I will, said McCulloch. *But there is so much more I need to hear from you first!*

—Ask it.

—The second Molting—the disappearance of my world, the coming of yours—

—The tradition is that the sea existed, even in the former world, and that it was not small. At the Time of the Molting it rose and devoured the land and all that was upon it, except for one place that was not devoured, which is sacred. And then all the world was covered by water, and that was the second Molting, which brought forth the third world.

—How long ago was that?

How can I speak of the passing of time? There is no way to speak of that. Time passes, and lives end, and worlds are transformed. But we have no words for that. If every grain of sand in the sea were one lifetime, then it would be as many lifetimes ago as there are grains of sand in the sea. But does that help you? Does that tell you anything? It happened. It was very long ago. And now our world's turn has come, or so we think.

—And the next world? What will that be like? McCulloch asked.

—There are those who claim to know such things, but I am not one of them. We will know the next world when we have entered it, and I am content to wait until then for the knowledge.

McCulloch had a sense then that the host had wearied of this sustained contact, and was withdrawing once again from it; and, though his own thirst for knowledge was far from sated, he chose once again not to attempt to resist that withdrawal.

All this while the pilgrims had continued down a gentle incline into the great bowl of a sunken valley. Once again now the ocean floor was level, but the water was notably deeper here, and the diffused light from above was so dim that only the most rugged of algae could grow, making the landscape bleak and sparse. There were no sponges here, and little coral, and the anemones were pale and small, giving little sign of the potent intelligence that infused their larger cousins in the shallower zones of the sea.

But there were other creatures at this level that McCulloch had not seen before. Platoons of alert, mobile oysters skipped over the bottom, leaping in agile bounds on columns of water that they squirted like jets from tubes in their dark green mantles: now and again they paused in mid-leap and their shells quickly opened and closed, snapping shut, no doubt, on some hapless larval thing of the plankton too small for McCulloch, via the lobster's imperfect vision, to detect. From these oysters came bright darting blurts of mental activity, sharp and probing: they must be as intelligent, he thought, as cats or dogs. Yet from time to time a lobster, swooping with an astonishingly swift claw, would seize one of these oysters and deftly, almost instantaneously, shuck and devour it. Appetite was no respecter of intelligence in this world of needful carnivores, McCulloch realized.

Intelligent, too, in their way, were the hordes of nearly invisible little crustaceans—shrimp of some sort, he imagined—that danced in shining clouds just above the line of march. They were ghostly things, perhaps an inch long, virtually transparent, colorless, lovely, graceful. Their heads bore two huge glistening black eyes; their intestines, glowing coils running the length of their bodies, were tinged with green; the tips of their tails were an elegant crimson. They swam with the aid of a horde of busy finlike legs, and seemed almost to be mocking their stolid, plodding cousins as they marched; but these sparkling little creatures also occasionally fell victim to the lobsters' inexorable claws, and each time it was like the extinguishing of a tiny brilliant candle.

An emanation of intelligence of a different sort came from bulky animals that McCulloch noticed roaming through the gravelly foothills flanking the line of march. These seemed at first glance to be another sort of lobster, larger even than McCulloch's companions: heavily armored things with many-segmented abdomens and thick paddle-shaped arms. But then, as one of them drew nearer, McCulloch saw the curved tapering tail with its sinister spike, and realized he was in the presence of the scorpions of the sea.

They gave off a deep, almost somnolent mental wave: slow thinkers but not light ones, Teutonic ponderers, grapplers with the abstruse. There were perhaps two dozen of them, who advanced upon the pilgrims and in quick one-sided struggles pounced, stung, slew. McCulloch watched in amazement as each of the scorpions dragged away a victim and, no more than a dozen feet from the line of march, began to gouge into its armor to draw forth tender chunks of pale flesh, without drawing the slightest response from the impassive, steadily marching column of lobsters.

They had not been so complacent when the great-mouthed swimming-thing had menaced McCulloch's host; then, the lobsters had come in hordes to tear the attacker apart. And whenever one of the big squids came by, the edgy hostility of the lobsters, their willingness to do battle if necessary, was manifest. But they seemed indifferent to the scorpions. The lobsters accepted their onslaught as placidly as though it were merely a toll they must pay in order to pass through this district. Perhaps it was. McCulloch was only beginning to perceive how dense and intricate a fabric of ritual bound this submarine world together.

The lobsters marched onward, chanting in unfailing rhythm as though nothing untoward had happened. The scorpions, their hungers evidently gratified, withdrew and congregated a short distance off, watching without much show of interest as the procession went by them. By the time McCulloch's host, bringing up the rear, had gone past the scorpions, they were fighting among themselves in a lazy, halfhearted way, like playful lions after a successful hunt. Their mental emanation, sluggishly booming through the water, grew steadily more blurred, more vague, more toneless.

And then it was overlaid and entirely masked by the pulsation of some new and awesome kind of mind ahead: one of enormous power, whose output beat upon the water with what was almost a physical force, like some massive metal chain being lashed against the surface of the ocean. Apparently the source of this gigantic output still lay at a considerable distance, for, strong as it was, it grew stronger still as the lobsters advanced toward it, until at last it was an overwhelming clangor, terrifying, bewildering. McCulloch could no longer remain quiescent under the impact of that monstrous sound. Breaking through to the sanctuary of his host, he cried:

—*What is it?*

—*We are approaching a god,* the lobster replied.

—*A god, did you say?*

—*A divine presence, yes. Did you think we were the rulers of this world?*

In fact McCulloch had, assuming automatically that his time jaunt had deposited him within the consciousness of some member of this world's highest species, just as he would have expected to have landed had he reached the twenty-second century as intended, in the consciousness of a human rather than in a frog or a horse. But obviously the division between humanity and all subsentient species in his own world did not have an exact parallel here; many races, perhaps all of them, had some sort of intelligence, and it was becoming clear that the lobsters, though a high life-form, were not the highest. He found that dismaying and even humbling; for the lobsters seemed quite adequately intelligent to him, quite the equals—for all his early condescension to them—of mankind itself. And now he was to meet one of their gods? How great a mind was a god likely to have?

The booming of that mind grew unbearably intense, nor was there any way to hide from it. McCulloch visualized himself doubled over in pain, pressing his hands to his ears, an image that drew a quizzical shaft of thought from his host. Still the lobsters pressed forward, but even they were responding now to the waves of mental energy that rippled outward from that unimaginable source. They had at last broken ranks, and were fanning out horizontally on the broad dark plain of the ocean floor, as though deploying themselves before a place of worship. Where was the god? McCulloch, striving with difficulty to see in this nearly lightless place, thought he made out some vast shape ahead, some dark entity, swollen and fearsome, that rose like a colossal boulder in the midst of the suddenly diminutive-looking lobsters. He saw eyes like bright yellow platters, gleaming furiously; he saw a huge frightful beak; he saw what he thought at first to be a nest of writhing serpents, and then realized to be tentacles, dozens of them, coiling and uncoiling with a terrible restless energy. To the host he said:

—Is that your god?

But he could not hear the reply, for an agonizing new force suddenly buffeted him, one even more powerful than that which was emanating from the giant creature that sat before him. It ripped upward through his soul like a spike. It cast him forth, and he tumbled over and over, helpless in some incomprehensible limbo, where nevertheless he could still hear the faint distant voice of his lobster host:

—Friend human McCulloch? Friend human McCulloch?

HE WAS DROWNING. HE HAD waded incautiously into the surf, deceived by the beauty of the transparent tropical water and the shimmering white sand below, and a wave had caught him and knocked him to his knees, and the next wave had come before he could rise, pulling him under. And now he tossed like a discarded doll in the suddenly turbulent sea, struggling to get his head above water and failing, failing, failing.

Maggie was standing on the shore, calling in panic to him, and somehow he could hear her words even through the tumult of the crashing waves: "This way, Jim, swim toward me! Oh, please, Jim, this way, this way!"

Bleier was there, too, Mortenson, Bob Rodrigues, the whole group, ten or fifteen people, running about worriedly, beckoning to him, calling his name. It was odd that he could see them, if he was under water. And he could hear them so clearly, too, Bleier telling him to stand up and walk ashore, the water wasn't deep at all, and Rodrigues saying to come in on hands and knees if he couldn't manage to get up, and Ybarra yelling that it was getting late, that they couldn't wait all the goddamned afternoon, that he had been swimming long enough. McCulloch wondered why they didn't come after him, if they were so eager to get him to shore. Obviously he was in trouble. Obviously he was unable to help himself.

"Look," he said, "I'm drowning, can't you see? Throw me a line, for Christ's sake!" Water rushed into his mouth as he spoke. It filled his lungs, it pressed against his brain.

"We can't hear you, Jim!"

"Throw me a line!" he cried again, and felt the torrents pouring through his body. "I'm drowning—drowning—"

And then he realized that he did not at all want them to rescue him, that it was worse to be rescued than to drown. He did not understand why he felt that way, but he made no attempt to question the feeling. All that concerned him now was preventing those people on the shore, those humans, from seizing him and taking him from the water. They were rushing about, assembling some kind of machine to pull him in, an arm at the end of a great boom. McCulloch signaled to them to leave him alone.

"I'm okay," he called. "I'm not drowning after all! I'm fine right where I am!"

But now they had their machine in operation, and its long metal arm was reaching out over the water toward him. He turned and dived, and swam as hard as he could away from the shore, but it was no use: the boom seemed to extend over an infinite distance, and no matter how fast he swam the boom moved faster, so that it hovered just above him now, and from its tip some sort of hook was descending—

"No—no—let me be! I don't want to go ashore!"

Then he felt a hand on his wrist: firm, reassuring, taking control. All right, he thought. They've caught me after all, they're going to pull me in. There's nothing I can do about it. They have me, and that's all there is to it. But he realized, after a moment, that he was heading not toward shore but out to sea, beyond the waves, into the calm warm depths. And the hand that was on his wrist was not a hand; it was a tentacle, thick as heavy cable, a strong sturdy tentacle lined on one side by rounded section cups that held him in an unbreakable grip.

That was all right. Anything to be away from that wild crashing surf. It was much more peaceful out here. He could rest, catch his breath, get his equilibrium. And all the while that powerful tentacle towed him steadily seaward. He could still hear the voices of his friends onshore, but they were as faint as the cries of distant seabirds now, and when he looked back he saw only tiny dots, like excited ants, moving along the beach. McCulloch waved at them. "See you some other time," he called. "I didn't want to come out of the water yet anyway." Better here. Much, much better. Peaceful. Warm. Like the womb. And that tentacle around his wrist: so reassuring, so steady.

—Friend human McCulloch? Friend human McCulloch?

—This is where I belong. Isn't it?

—Yes. This is where you belong. You are one of us, friend human McCulloch. You are one of us.

Gradually the turbulence subsided, and he found himself regaining his balance. He was still within the lobster; the whole horde of lobsters was gathered around him, thousands upon thousands of them, a gentle solicitous community, and right in front of him was the largest octopus imaginable, a creature that must have been fifteen or twenty feet in diameter, with tentacles that extended an implausible distance on all sides. Somehow he did not find the sight frightening.

"He is recovered now," his host announced.

—What happened to me? McCulloch asked.

—Your people called you again. But you did not want to make your homefaring, and you resisted them. And when we understood that you wanted to remain, the god aided you, and you broke free of their pull.

—The god?

His host indicated the great octopus.

—There.

It did not seem at all improbable to McCulloch now. The infinite fullness of time brings about everything, he thought: even intelligent lobsters, even a divine octopus. He still could feel the mighty telepathic output of the vast creature, but though it had lost none of its power, it no longer caused him discomfort; it was like the roaring thunder of some great waterfall, to which one becomes accustomed, and which, in time, one begins to love. The octopus sat motionless, its immense yellow eyes trained on McCulloch, its scarlet mantle rippling gently, its tentacles weaving in intricate patterns. McCulloch thought of an octopus he had once seen when he was diving in the West Indies: a small shy scuttling thing, hurrying to slither behind a gnarled coral head. He felt chastened and awed by this evidence of the magnifications wrought by the eons. A hundred million years? Half a billion? The numbers were without meaning. But that span of years had produced this creature. He sensed a serene intelligence of incomprehensible depth, benign, tranquil, all-penetrating: a god indeed. Yes. Truly a god. Why not?

The great cephalopod was partly sheltered by an overhanging wall of rock. Clustered about it were dozens of the scorpion-things, motionless, poised: plainly a guard force. Overhead swam a whole army of the big squids, doubtless guardians also, and for once the presence of those creatures did not trigger any emotion in the lobsters, as if they regarded squids in the service of the god as acceptable ones. The scene left McCulloch dazed with awe. He had never felt farther from home.

—*The god would speak with you,* said his host.

—*What shall I say?*

—*Listen, first.*

McCulloch's lobster moved forward until it stood virtually beneath the octopus's huge beak. From the octopus, then, came an outpouring of words that McCulloch did not immediately comprehend, but which, after a moment, he understood to be some kind of benediction that enfolded his soul like a warm blanket. And gradually he perceived that he was being spoken to.

"Can you tell us why you have come all this way, human McCulloch?"

"It was an error. They didn't mean to send me so far—only a hundred years or less, that was all we were trying to cross. But it was our first attempt. We didn't really know what we were doing. And I suppose I wound up halfway across time—a hundred million years, two hundred, maybe a billion—who knows?"

"It is a great distance. Do you feel no fear?"

"At the beginning I did. But not any longer. This world is alien to me, but not frightening."

"Do you prefer it to your own?"

"I don't understand," McCulloch said.

"Your people summoned you. You refused to go. You appealed to us for aid, and we aided you in resisting your homecalling, because it was what you seemed to require from us."

"I'm—not ready to go home yet," he said. "There's so much I haven't seen yet, and that I want to see. I want to see everything. I'll never have an opportunity like this again. Perhaps no one ever will. Besides, I have services to perform here. I'm the herald; I bring the Omen; I'm part of this pilgrimage. I think I ought to stay until the rites have been performed. I want to stay until then."

"Those rites will not be performed," said the octopus quietly.

"Not performed?"

"You are not the herald. You carry no Omen. The Time is not at hand."

McCulloch did not know what to reply. Confusion swirled within him. No Omen? Not the Time?

—*It is so,* said the host. *We were in error. The god has shown us that we came to our conclusion too quickly. The Time of the Molting may be near, but it is not yet upon us. You have many of the outer signs of a herald, but there is no Omen upon you. You are merely a visitor. An accident.*

McCulloch was assailed by a startlingly keen pang of disappointment. It was absurd; but for a time he had been the central figure in some apocalyptic ritual of immense significance, or at least had been thought to be, and all that suddenly was gone from him, and he felt strangely diminished, irrelevant, bereft of his bewildering grandeur. A visitor. An accident.

—*In that case I feel great shame and sorrow,* he said. *To have caused so much trouble for you. To have sent you off on this pointless pilgrimage.*

—*No blame attaches to you,* said the host. *We acted of our free choice, after considering the evidence.*

"Nor was the pilgrimage pointless," the octopus declared. "There are no pointless pilgrimages. And this one will continue."

"But if there's no Omen—if this is not the Time—"

"There are other needs to consider," replied the octopus, "and other observances to carry out. We must visit the dry place ourselves, from time to time, so that we may prepare ourselves for the world that is to succeed ours, for it will be very different from ours. It is time now for such a visit, and well past time. And also we must bring you to the dry place, for only there can we properly make you one of us."

"I don't understand," said McCulloch.

"You have asked to stay among us; and if you stay, you must become one of us, for your sake, and for ours. And that can best be done at the dry place. It is not necessary that you understand that now, human McCulloch."

—*Make no further reply,* said McCulloch's host. *The god has spoken. We must proceed.*

Shortly the lobsters resumed their march, chanting as before, though in a more subdued way, and, so it seemed to McCulloch, singing a different melody. From the context of his conversation with it, McCulloch had supposed that the octopus now would accompany them, which puzzled him, for the huge unwieldy creature did not seem capable of any extensive journey. That proved to be the case: the octopus did not go along, though the vast booming resonances of its mental output followed the procession for what must have been hundreds of miles.

Once more the line was a single one, with McCulloch's host at the end of the file. A short while after departure it said:

—*I am glad, friend human McCulloch, that you chose to continue with us. I would be sorry to lose you now.*

—*Do you mean that? Isn't it an inconvenience for you, to carry me around inside your mind?*

—I have grown quite accustomed to it. You are part of me, friend human McCulloch. We are part of one another. At the place of the dry land we will celebrate our sharing of this body.

—I was lucky, said McCulloch, *to have landed like this in a mind that would make me welcome.*

—Any of us would have made you welcome, responded the host.

McCulloch pondered that. Was it merely a courteous turn of phrase, or did the lobster mean him to take the answer literally? Most likely the latter: the host's words seemed always to have only a single level of meaning, a straightforwardly literal one. So any of the lobsters would have taken him in uncomplainingly? Perhaps so. They appeared to be virtually interchangeable beings, without distinctive individual personalities, without names, even. The host had remained silent when McCulloch had asked him its name, and had not seemed to understand what kind of a label McCulloch's own name was. So powerful was their sense of community, then, that they must have little sense of private identity. He had never cared much for that sort of hive mentality, where he had observed it in human society. But here it seemed not only appropriate but admirable.

—How much longer will it be, McCulloch asked, *before we reach the place of dry land?*

—Long.

—Can you tell me where it is?

—It is in the place where the world grows narrower, said the host.

McCulloch had realized, the moment he asked the question, that it was meaningless: what useful answer could the lobster possibly give? The old continents were gone and their names long forgotten. But the answer he had received was meaningless, too: where, on a round planet, is the place where the world grows narrower? He wondered what sort of geography the lobsters understood. If I live among them a hundred years, he thought, I will probably just begin to comprehend what their perceptions are like.

Where the world grows narrower. All right. Possibly the place of the dry land was some surviving outcropping of the former world, the summit of Mount Everest, perhaps, Kilimanjaro, whatever. Or perhaps not:

perhaps even those peaks had been ground down by time, and new ones had arisen—one of them, at least, tall enough to rise above the universal expanse of sea. It was folly to suppose that any shred at all of his world remained accessible: it was all down there beneath tons of water and millions of years of sediments, the old continents buried, hidden, rearranged by time like pieces scattered about a board.

The pulsations of the octopus's mind could no longer be felt. As the lobsters went tirelessly onward, moving always in that lithe skipping stride of theirs and never halting to rest or to feed, the terrain rose for a time and then began to dip again, slightly at first and then more than slightly. They entered into waters that were deeper and significantly darker, and somewhat cooler as well. In this somber zone, where vision seemed all but useless, the pilgrims grew silent for long spells for the first time, neither chanting nor speaking to one another, and McCulloch's host, who had become increasingly quiet, disappeared once more into its impenetrable inner domain and rarely emerged.

In the gloom and darkness there began to appear a strange red glow off to the left, as though someone had left a lantern hanging midway between the ocean floor and the surface of the sea. The lobsters, when that mysterious light came into view, at once changed the direction of their line of march to go veering off to the right; but at the same time they resumed their chanting, and kept one eye trained on the glowing place as they walked.

The water felt warmer here. A zone of unusual heat was spreading outward from the glow. And the taste of the water, and what McCulloch persisted in thinking of as its smell, were peculiar, with a harsh choking salty flavor. Brimstone? Ashes?

McCulloch realized that what he was seeing was an undersea volcano, belching forth a stream of red-hot lava that was turning the sea into a boiling bubbling caldron. The sight stirred him oddly. He felt that he was looking into the pulsing ancient care of the world, the primordial flame, the geological link that bound the otherwise vanished former worlds to this one. There awakened in him a powerful tide of awe, and a baffling unfocused yearning that he might have termed homesickness, except that it was not, for he was no longer sure where his true home lay.

—*Yes,* said the host. *It is a mountain on fire. We think it is a part of the older of the two former worlds that has endured both of the Moltings. It is a very sacred place.*

—*An object of pilgrimage?* McCulloch asked.

—*Only to those who wish to end their lives. The fire devours all who approach it.*

—*In my world we had many such fiery mountains,* McCulloch said. *They often did great destruction.*

—*How strange your world must have been!*

—*It was very beautiful,* said McCulloch.

—*Surely. But strange. The dry land, the fire in the air—the sun, I mean—the air-breathing creatures—yes, strange, very strange. I can scarcely believe it really existed.*

—*There are times, now, when I begin to feel the same way,* McCulloch said.

THE VOLCANO RECEDED IN THE distance; its warmth could no longer be felt; the water was dark again, and cold, and growing colder, and McCulloch could no longer detect any trace of that sulfurous aroma. It seemed to him that they were moving now down an endless incline, where scarcely any creatures dwelled.

And then he realized that the marchers ahead had halted, and were drawn up in a long row as they had been when they came to the place where the octopus held its court. Another god? No. There was only blackness ahead.

—*Where are we?* he asked.

—*It is the shore of the great abyss.*

Indeed what lay before them looked like the Pit itself: lightless, without landmark, an empty landscape. McCulloch understood now that they had been marching all this while across some sunken continent's coastal plain, and at last they had come to—what?—the graveyard where one of Earth's lost oceans lay buried in ocean?

—*Is it possible to continue?* he asked.

—*Of course,* said the host. *But now we must swim.*

Already the lobsters before them were kicking off from shore with vigorous strokes of their tails and vanishing into the open sea beyond. A moment later McCulloch's host joined them. Almost at once there was no sense of a bottom beneath them—only a dark and infinitely deep void. Swimming across this, McCulloch thought, is like falling through time—an endless descent and no safety net.

The lobsters, he knew, were not true swimming creatures: like the lobsters of his own era they were bottom-dwellers, who walked to get where they needed to go. But they could never cross this abyss that way, and so they were swimming now, moving steadily by flexing their huge abdominal muscles and their tails. Was it terrifying to them to be setting forth into a place without landmarks like this? His host remained utterly calm, as though this were no more than an afternoon stroll.

McCulloch lost what little perception of the passage of time that he had had. Heave, stroke, forward, heave, stroke, forward, that was all, endless repetition. Out of the depths there occasionally came an upwelling of cold water, like a dull, heavy river miraculously flowing upward through air, and in that strange surging from below rose a fountain of nourishment, tiny transparent struggling creatures and even smaller flecks of some substance that must have been edible, for the lobsters, without missing a stroke, sucked in all they could hold. And swam on and on. McCulloch had a sense of being involved in a trek of epic magnitude, a once-in-many-generations thing that would be legendary long after.

Enemies roved this open sea: the free-swimming creatures that had evolved out of God only knew which kinds of worms or slugs to become the contemporary equivalents of sharks and whales. Now and again one of these huge beasts dived through the horde of lobsters, harvesting it at will. But they could eat only so much; and the survivors kept going onward.

Until at last—months, years later?—the far shore came into view; the ocean floor, long invisible, reared up beneath them and afforded support; the swimmers at last put their legs down on the solid bottom, and with something that sounded much like gratitude in their voices began once again to chant in unison as they ascended the rising flank of a new continent.

THE FIRST RAYS OF THE sun, when they came into view an unknown span of time later, struck McCulloch with an astonishing, overwhelming impact. He perceived them first as a pale-greenish glow resting in the upper levels of the sea just ahead, striking downward like illuminated wands; he did not then know what he was seeing, but the sight engendered wonder in him all the same, and later, when that radiance diminished and was gone and in a short while returned, he understood that the pilgrims were coming up out of the sea. So they had reached their goal: the still point of the turning world, the one remaining unsubmerged scrap of the former Earth.

—*Yes,* said the host. *This is it.*

In that same instant McCulloch felt another tug from the past: a summons dizzying in its inoperative impact. He thought he could hear Maggie Caldwell's voice crying across the time winds: "Jim, Jim, come back to us!" And Bleier, grouchy, angered, muttering, "For Christ's sake, McCulloch, stop holding on up there! This is getting expensive!" Was it all his imagination, that fantasy of hands on his wrists, familiar faces hovering before his eyes?

"Leave me alone," he said. "I'm still not ready."

"Will you ever be?" That was Maggie. "Jim, you'll be marooned. You'll be stranded there if you don't let us pull you back now."

"I may be marooned already," he said, and brushed the voices out of his mind with surprising ease.

He returned his attention to his companions and saw that they had halted their trek a little way short of that zone of light that now was but a quick scramble ahead of them. Their linear formation was broken once again. Some of the lobsters, marching blindly forward, were piling up in confused-looking heaps in the shallows, forming mounds fifteen or twenty lobsters deep. Many of the others had begun a bizarre convulsive dance: a wild twitchy cavorting, rearing up on their back legs, waving their claws about, flicking their antennae in frantic circles.

—*What's happening?* McCulloch asked his host. *Is this the beginning of a rite?*

But the host did not reply. The host did not appear to be within their shared body at all. McCulloch felt a silence far deeper than the host's earlier withdrawals; this seemed not a withdrawal but an evacuation, leaving McCulloch in sole possession. That new solitude came rolling in upon him with a crushing force. He sent forth a tentative probe, found nothing, found less than nothing. Perhaps it's meant to be this way, he thought. Perhaps it was necessary for him to face his climactic initiation unaided, unaccompanied.

Then he noticed that what he had taken to be a weird jerky dance was actually the onset of a mass molting prodrome. Hundreds of the lobsters had been stricken simultaneously, he realized, with that strange painful sense of inner expansion, of volcanic upheaval and stress: that heaving and rearing about was the first stage of the splitting of the shell.

And all of the molters were females.

Until that instant McCulloch had not been aware of any division into sexes among the lobsters. He had barely been able to tell one from the next; they had no individual character, no shred of uniqueness. Now, suddenly, strangely, he knew without being told that half of his companions were females, and that they were molting now because they were fertile only when they had shed their old armor, and that the pilgrimage to the place of the dry land was the appropriate time to engender the young. He had asked no questions of anyone to learn that; the knowledge was simply within him; and, reflecting on that, he saw that the host was absent from him because the host was wholly fused with him; he was the host, the host was Jim McCulloch.

He approached a female, knowing precisely which one was the appropriate one, and sang to her, and she acknowledged his song with a song of her own, and raised her third pair of legs to him, and let him plant his gametes beside her oviducts. There was no apparent pleasure in it, as he remembered pleasure from his days as a human. Yet it brought him a subtle but unmistakable sense of fulfillment, of the completion of biological destiny, that had a kind of orgasmic finality about it, and left him calm and anchored at the absolute dead center of his soul: yes, truly the still point of the turning world, he thought.

His mate moved away to begin her new Growing and the awaiting of her motherhood. And McCulloch, unbidden, began to ascend the slope that led to the land.

The bottom was fine sand here, soft, elegant. He barely touched it with his legs as he raced shoreward. Before him lay a world of light, radiant, heavenly, a bright irresistible beacon. He went on until the water, pearly pink and transparent, was only a foot or two deep, and the domed upper curve of his back was reaching into the air. He felt no fear. There was no danger in this. Serenely he went forward—the leader, now, of the trek—and climbed out into the hot sunlight.

It was an island, low and sandy, so small that he imagined he could cross it in a day. The sky was intensely blue, and the sun, hanging close to a noon position, looked swollen and fiery. A little grove of palm trees clustered a few hundred yards inland, but he saw nothing else, no birds, no insects, no animal life of any sort. Walking was difficult here—his breath was short, his shell seemed to be too tight, his stalked eyes were stinging in the air—but he pulled himself forward, almost to the trees. Other male lobsters, hundreds of them, thousands of them, were following. He felt himself linked to each of them: his people, his nation, his community, his brothers.

Now, at that moment of completion and communion, came one more call from the past.

There was no turbulence in it this time. No one was yanking at his wrists, no surf boiled and heaved in his mind and threatened to dash him on the reefs of the soul. The call was simple and clear: *This is the moment of coming back, Jim.*

Was it? Had he no choice? He belonged here. These were his people. This was where his loyalties lay.

And yet, and yet: he knew that he had been sent on a mission unique in human history, that he had been granted a vision beyond all dreams, that it was his duty to return and report on it. There was no ambiguity about that. He owed it to Bleier and Maggie and Ybarra and the rest to return, to tell them everything.

How clear it all was! He belonged *here,* and he belonged *there,* and an unbreakable net of loyalties and responsibilities held him to both places. It was a perfect equilibrium; and therefore he was tranquil and of ease. The pull was on him; he resisted nothing, for he was at last beyond all resistance to anything. The immense sun was a drumbeat in the heavens; the fiery warmth was a benediction; he had never known such peace.

"I must make my homefaring now," he said, and released himself, and let himself drift upward, light as a bubble, toward the sun.

STRANGE FIGURES SURROUNDED HIM, TALL and narrow-bodied, with odd fleshy faces and huge moist mouths and bulging staring eyes, and their kind of speech was a crude hubbub of sound waves that bashed and battered against his sensibilities with painful intensity. "We were afraid the signal wasn't reaching you, Jim," they said. "We tried again and again, but there was no contact, nothing. And then just as we were giving up, suddenly your eyes were opening, you were stirring, you stretched your arms—"

He felt air pouring into his body, and dryness all about him. It was a struggle to understand the speech of these creatures who were bending over him, and he hated the reek that came from their flesh and the booming vibrations that they made with their mouths. But gradually he found himself returning to himself, like one who has been lost in a dream so profound that it eclipses reality for the first few moments of wakefulness.

"How long was I gone?" he asked.

"Four minutes and eighteen seconds," Ybarra said.

McCulloch shook his head. "Four minutes? Eighteen seconds? It was more like forty months, to me. Longer. I don't know how long."

"Where did you go, Jim? What was it like?"

"Wait," someone else said. "He's not ready for debriefing yet. Can't you see he's about to collapse?"

McCulloch shrugged. "You sent me too far."

"How far? Five hundred years?" Maggie asked.

"Millions," he said.

Someone gasped.

"He's dazed," a voice said at his left ear.

"Millions of years," McCulloch said in a slow, steady, determinedly articulate voice. "*Millions.* The whole earth was covered by the sea, except for one little island. The people are lobsters. They have a society, a culture. They worship a giant octopus."

Maggie was crying. "Jim, oh, Jim—"

"No. It's true. I went on migration with them. Intelligent lobsters is what they are. And I wanted to stay with them forever. I felt you pulling at me, but I—didn't—want—to—go—"

"Give him a sedative, Doc," Bleier said.

"You think I'm crazy? You think I'm deranged? They were lobsters, fellows. *Lobsters.*"

AFTER HE HAD SLEPT AND showered and changed his clothes they came to see him again, and by that time he realized that he must have been behaving like a lunatic in the first moments of his return, blurting out his words, weeping, carrying on, crying out what surely had sounded like gibberish to them. Now he was rested, he was calm, he was at home in his own body once again.

He told them all that had befallen him, and from their faces he saw at first that they still thought he had gone around the bend: but as he kept speaking, quietly, straightforwardly, in rich detail, they began to acknowledge his report in subtle little ways, asking questions about the geography, about the ecological balance, in a manner that showed him they were not simply humoring him. And after that, as it sank in upon them that he really had dwelled for a period of many months at the far end of time, beyond the span of the present world, they came to look upon him—it was unmistakable—as someone who was now wholly unlike them. In particular he saw the cold, glassy stare in Maggie Caldwell's eyes.

Then they left him, for he was tiring again; and later Maggie came to see him alone, and took his hand and held it between hers, which were cold.

She said, "What do you want to do now, Jim?"

"To go back there."

"I thought you did."

"It's impossible, isn't it?" he said.

"We could try. But it couldn't ever work. We don't know what we're doing, yet, with that machine. We don't know where we'd send you. We might miss by a million years. By a billion."

"That's what I figured, too."

"But you want to go back?"

He nodded. "I can't explain it. It was like being a member of some Buddhist monastery, do you see? Feeling *absolutely sure* that this is where you belong, that everything fits together perfectly, that you're an integral part of it. I've never felt anything like that before. I never will again."

"I'll talk to Bleier, Jim, about sending you back."

"No. Don't. I can't possibly get there. And I don't want to land anywhere else. Let Ybarra take the next trip. I'll stay here."

"Will you be happy?"

He smiled. "I'll do my best," he said.

When the others understood what the problem was, they saw to it that he went into re-entry therapy—Bleier had already foreseen something like that, and made preparations for it—and after a while the pain went from him, that sense of having undergone a violent separation, of having been ripped untimely from the womb. He resumed his work in the group and gradually recovered his mental balance and took an active part in the second transmission, which sent a young anthropologist named Ludwig off for two minutes and eight seconds. Ludwig did not see lobsters, to McCulloch's intense disappointment. He went sixty years into the future and came back glowing with wondrous tales of atomic-fusion plants.

That was too bad, McCulloch thought. But soon he decided that it was just as well, that he preferred being the only one who had encountered the world beyond this world, probably the only human being who ever would.

He thought of that world with love, wondering about his mate and her millions of larvae, about the journey of his friends back across the great abyss, about the legends that were being spun about his visit in that unimaginably distant epoch. Sometimes the pain of separation returned, and Maggie found him crying in the night, and held him until he was whole again. And eventually the pain did not return. But still he did not forget, and in some part of his soul he longed to make his homefaring back to his true kind, and he rarely passed a day when he did not think he could hear the inaudible sound of delicate claws, scurrying over the sands of silent seas.

◆

WHAT WE LEARNED FROM THIS MORNING'S NEWSPAPER

And here we have a story built around one of the most familiar of all science fictional concepts, the supposed advantages to be had by getting an advance peek at tomorrow's news. In the olden days every pulpster in the business had a crack at writing the story that was usually called something like "The Man Who Saw Tomorrow," with results that usually were as predictable to the reader as they would have been to the protagonist, although in the hands of real masters the theme carried plenty of impact. (I think especially of C. M. Kornbluth's acidulous little story "Dominoes," and Philip K. Dick's novel The World Jones Made.*)*

Since playing games with time has long been one of my own obsessions as a storyteller, it's not surprising that I, too, have written "The Man Who Saw Tomorrow," not once, but a number of times. Here's one example. I feel no guilt whatsoever having offered the world yet another the-next-day's-newspaper story. My version of the theme has its own original touches, its own individual stylistic flourishes, its own properly Silverbergian ending, and so be it. Here it is, without apologies. I wrote it in January 1972, and the editor Bob Hoskins published it in the fourth volume of his anthology Infinity.

1.

I GOT HOME FROM THE office as usual at 6:47 this evening and discovered that our peaceful street has been in some sort of crazy uproar all day. The newsboy it seems came by today and delivered *The New York Times* for Wednesday December 1 to every house on Redbud Crescent. Since today is Monday November 22 it follows therefore that Wednesday, December 1 is the middle of next week. I said to my wife are you sure that this really happened? Because I looked at the newspaper myself before I went off to work this morning and it seemed quite all right to me.

At breakfast time the newspaper could be printed in Albanian and it would seem quite all right to you my wife replied. Here look at this. And she took the newspaper from the hall closet and handed it all folded up to me. It looked just like any other edition of *The New York Times* but I saw what I had failed to notice at breakfast time, that it said Wednesday December 1.

Is today the 22nd of November I asked? Monday?

It certainly is my wife told me. Yesterday was Sunday and tomorrow is going to be Tuesday and we haven't even come to Thanksgiving yet. Bill what are we going to do about this?

I glanced through the newspaper. The front page headlines were nothing remarkable I must admit, just the same old *New York Times* stuff that you get any day when there hasn't been some event of cosmic importance. NIXON, WITH WIFE, TO VISIT 3 CHINESE CITIES IN 7 DAYS. Yes. 10 HURT AS GUNMEN SHOOT WAY INTO AND OUT OF BANK. All right. GROUP OF 10, IN ROME, BEGINS NEGOTIATING REALIGNMENT OF CURRENCIES. Okay. The same old *New York Times* stuff and no surprises. But the paper was dated Wednesday December 1 and that was a surprise of sorts I guess.

This is only a joke I told my wife.

Who would do such a thing for a joke? To print up a whole newspaper? It's impossible Bill.

It's also impossible to get next week's newspaper delivered this week you know or hadn't you considered what I said?

She shrugged and I picked up the second section. I opened to page fifty which contained the obituary section and I admit I felt quite queasy for a moment since after all this might not be any joke and what would it be like to find my own name there? To my relief the people whose obituaries I saw were Harry Rogoff Terry Turner Dr. M. A. Feinstein and John Millis. I will not say that the deaths of these people gave me any pleasure but better them than me of course. I even looked at the death notices in small type but there was no listing for me. Next I turned to the sports section and saw KNICKS' STREAK ENDED, 110–109. We had been talking about going to get tickets for that game at the office and my first thought now was that it isn't worth bothering to see it. Then I remembered you can bet on basketball games and I knew who was going to win and that made me feel very strange. So also I felt odd to look at the bottom of page sixty-four where they had the results of the racing at Yonkers Raceway and then quickly flip flip flip I was on page sixty-nine and the financial section lay before my eyes. DOW INDEX RISES BY 1.61 TO 831.34 the headline said. National Cash Register was the most active stock closing at 27 off ¼. Then Eastman Kodak 88 down 1⅛. By this time I was starting to sweat very hard and I gave my wife the paper and took off my jacket and tie.

I said how many people have their newspaper?

Everybody on Redbud Crescent she said that's eleven houses altogether.

And nowhere beyond our street?

No the others got the ordinary paper today we've been checking on that.

Who's we I asked?

Marie and Cindy and I she said. Cindy was the one who noticed about the paper first and called me and then we all got together and talked about it. Bill what are we going to do? We have the stock market prices and everything Bill.

If it isn't a joke I told her. It looks like the real paper doesn't it Bill? I think I want a drink I said. My hands were shaking all of a sudden and the sweat was still coming. I had to laugh because it was just the other Saturday night some of us were talking about the utter predictable regularity of life out here in the suburbs the dull smooth sameness of it all. And now this. The newspaper from the middle of next week. It's like God was listening to us and laughed up His sleeve and said to Gabriel or whoever it's time to send those stuffed shirts on Redbud Crescent a little excitement.

2.

AFTER DINNER JERRY WESLEY CALLED and said we're having a meeting at our place tonight Bill can you and your lady come?

I asked him what the meeting was about and he said it's about the newspaper.

Oh yes I said. The newspaper. What about the newspaper?

Come to the meeting he said I really don't want to talk about this on the phone.

Of course we'll have to arrange a sitter Jerry.

No you won't we've already arranged it he told me. The three Fischer girls are going to look after all the kids on the block. So just come over around quarter to nine.

Jerry is an insurance broker very successful at that he has the best house on the Crescent, two-story Tudor style with almost an acre of land and a big paneled rumpus room in the basement. That's where the meeting took place. We were the seventh couple to arrive and soon after us the Maxwells the Bruces and the Thomasons came in. Folding chairs were set out and Cindy Wesley had done her usual great trays of canapés and such and there was a lot of liquor, self-service at the bar. Jerry stood up in front of everybody and grinned and said I guess you've all been wondering why I called you together this evening. He held up his copy of the newspaper. From where I was sitting I could make out only one headline clearly it was 10 HURT AS GUNMEN SHOOT WAY INTO AND OUT OF BANK but that was enough to enable me to recognize it as the newspaper.

Jerry said did all of you get a copy of this paper today? Everybody nodded. You know Jerry said that this paper gives us some extraordinary opportunities to improve our situation in life. I mean if we can accept it as the real December 1 edition and not some kind of fantastic hoax then I don't need to tell you what sort of benefits we can get from it, right?

Sure Bob Thomason said but what makes anybody think it isn't a hoax? I mean next week's newspaper who could believe that?

Jerry looked at Mike Nesbit. Mike teaches at Columbia Law and is more of an intellectual than most of us.

Mike said well of course the obvious conclusion is that somebody's playing a joke on us. But have you looked at the newspaper closely? Every one of those stories has been written in a perfectly legitimate way. There aren't any details that ring false. It isn't like one of those papers where the headlines have been cooked up but the body of the text is an old edition. So we have to consider the probabilities. Which sounds more fantastic? That someone would take the trouble of composing an entire fictional edition of the *Times* setting it in type printing it and having it delivered or that through some sort of fluke of the fourth dimension we've been allowed a peek at next week's newspaper? Personally I don't find either notion easy to believe but I can accept fourth-dimensional hocus-pocus more readily than I can the idea of a hoax. For one thing unless you've had a team the size of the *Times'* own staff working on this newspaper it would take months and months to prepare it and there's no way that anybody could have begun work on the paper more than a few days in advance because there are things in it that nobody could have possibly known as recently as a week ago. Like the Phase Two stuff and the fighting between India and Pakistan.

But how could we get next week's newspaper Bob Thomason still wanted to know?

I can't answer that said Mike Nesbit. I can only reply that I am willing to accept it as genuine. A miracle if you like.

So am I said Tim McDermott and a few others said the same. We can make a pile of money out of this thing said Dave Bruce. Everybody began to smile in a strange strained way. Obviously everybody had looked at the stock market stuff and the racetrack stuff and had come to the same conclusions.

Jerry said there's one important thing we ought to find out first. Has anybody here spoken about this newspaper to anybody who isn't currently in this room?

People said nope and uh-uh and not me.

Good said Jerry. I propose we keep it that way. We don't notify the *Times* and we don't tell Walter Cronkite and we don't even let our brother-in-law on Dogwood Lane know, right? We just put our newspapers away in a safe place and quietly do whatever we want to do about the information we've got. Okay? Let's put that to a vote. All in favor of stamping this newspaper top secret raise your right hand.

Twenty-two hands went up.

Good said Jerry. That includes the kids you realize. If you let the kids know anything they'll want to bring the paper to school for show and tell for Christ's sake. So cool it you hear?

Sid Fischer said are we going to work together on exploiting this thing or do we each act independently?

Independently said Dave Bruce. Right independently said Bud Maxwell. It went all around the room that way. The only one who wanted some sort of committee system was Charlie Harris. Charlie has bad luck in the stock market and I guess he was afraid to take any risks even with a sure thing like next week's paper. Jerry called for a vote and it came out ten to one in favor of individual enterprise. Of course if anybody wants to team up with anybody else I said there's nothing stopping anybody.

As we started to adjourn for refreshments Jerry said remember you only have a week to make use of what you've been handed. By the first of December this is going to be just another newspaper and a million other people will have copies of it. So move fast while you've got an advantage.

3.

THE TROUBLE IS WHEN THEY give you only next week's paper you don't ordinarily have a chance to make a big killing in the market. I mean stocks don't generally go up fifty per cent or eighty per cent in just a few trading sessions. The really broad swings take weeks or months to develop. Still and all I figured I could make out all right with the data I had. For one thing there evidently was going to be a pretty healthy rally over the next few days. According to the afternoon edition of the *Post* that I brought home with me the market had been off seven on the 22nd, closing with the Dow at 803.15, the lowest all year. But the December 1 *Times* mentioned "a stunning two-day advance" and the average finished at 831.34 on the 30th. Not bad. Then too I could work on margin and other kinds of leverage to boost my return. We're going to make a pile out of this I told my wife.

If you can trust that newspaper she said.

I told her not to worry. When we got home from Jerry's I spread out the *Post* and the *Times* in the den and started hunting for stocks that moved up at least ten percent between November 22 and November 30. This is the chart I made up:

STOCK	NOV 22 CLOSE	NOV 30 HIGH
Levitz Furniture	89½	103¾
Bausch & Lomb	133	149
Natomas	45¼	57
Disney	99	116¾
EG&G	19¼	23¾

Spread your risk Bill I told myself. Don't put all your eggs in one basket. Even if the newspaper was phony I couldn't get hurt too badly if I bought all five. So at half past nine the next morning I phoned my broker and told him I wanted to do some buying in the margin account at the opening. He said don't be in a hurry Bill the market's in lousy shape. Look at yesterday there were 201 new lows this market's going to be under 750 by Christmas. You can see from this that he's an unusual kind of broker since most of them will never try to discourage you from placing an order that'll bring them a commission. But I said no I'm playing a hunch I want to go all out on this and I put in buys on Levitz Bausch Natomas Disney and EG&G. I used the margin right up to the hilt and then some. Okay I told myself if this works out the way you hope it will you've just bought yourself a vacation in Europe and a new Chrysler and a mink for the wife and a lot of other goodies. And if not? If not you just lost yourself a hell of a lot of money Billy boy.

4.

Also I made some use out of the sports pages.

At the office I looked around for bets on the Knicks vs. the SuperSonics next Tuesday at the Garden. A couple of guys wondered why I was interested in action so far ahead but I didn't bother to answer and finally I got Eddie Martin to take the Knicks by eleven points. Also I got Marty Felks to take Milwaukee by eight over the Warriors that same night. Felks thinks Abdul-Jabbar is the best center the game ever had and he'll always bet the Bucks but my paper had it that the Warriors would cop it, 106–103. At lunch with the boys from Leclair & Anderson I put down $250 with Butch Hunter on St Louis over the Giants on Sunday. Next I stopped off at the friendly neighborhood Off-track Betting Office and entered a few wagers on the races at Aqueduct. My handy guide to the future told me that the Double paid $52.40 and the third Exacta paid $62.20, so I spread a little cash on each. Too bad there were no $2,500 payoffs that day but you can't be picky about your miracles can you?

5.

Tuesday night when I got home I had a drink and asked my wife what's new and she said everybody on the block had been talking about the newspaper all day and some of the girls had been placing bets and phoning their brokers. A lot of the women here play the market and even the horses though my wife is not like that, she leaves the male stuff strictly to me.

What stocks were they buying I asked?

Well she didn't know the names. But a little while later Joni Bruce called up for a recipe and my wife asked her about the market and Joni said she had bought Winnebago Xerox and Transamerica. I was relieved at that because I figured it might look really suspicious if everybody on Redbud Crescent suddenly phoned in orders the same day for Levitz Bausch Disney Natomas and EG&G. On the other hand what was I worrying about nobody would draw any conclusions and if anybody did we could always say we had organized a neighborhood investment club. In any case I don't think there's any law against people making stock market decisions on the basis of a peek at next week's newspaper. Still and all who needs publicity and I was glad we were all buying different stocks.

I got the paper out after dinner to check out Joni's stocks. Sure enough Winnebago moved up from 33¼ to 38, Xerox from 105¾ to 111, and Transamerica from 14 to 17. I thought it was dumb of Joni to bother with Xerox getting only a six percent rise since it's the percentages where you pay off but Winnebago was up better than ten percent and Transamerica close to twenty percent. I wished I had noticed Transamerica at least although no sense being greedy, my own choices would make out all right.

Something about the paper puzzled me. The print looked a little blurry in places and on some pages I could hardly read the words. I didn't remember any blurry pages. Also the paper it's printed on seemed a different color, darker gray, older-looking. I compared it with the newspaper that came this morning and the December I issue was definitely darker. A paper shouldn't get old-looking that fast, not in two days.

I wonder if something's happening to the paper I said to my wife. What do you mean? Like it's deteriorating or anyway starting to change. Anything can happen said my wife. It's like a dream you know and in dreams things change all the time without warning.

6.

Wednesday November 24. I guess we just have to sweat this thing out so far the market in general isn't doing much one way or the other. This afternoon's *Post* gives the closing prices there was a rally in the morning but it all faded by the close and the Dow is down to 798.63. However my own five stocks all have had decent upward moves Tues and Wed so maybe I shouldn't worry. I have four points profit in Bausch already two in Natomas five in Levitz two in Disney three-quarters in EG&G and even though that's a long way from the quotations in the Dec 1 newspaper it's better than having losses, also there's still that "stunning two-day advance" due at the end of the month. Maybe I'm going to make out all right. Winnebago Transamerica and Xerox are also up a little bit. Market's closed tomorrow on account of Thanksgiving.

7.

THANKSGIVING DAY. WE WENT TO the Nesbits in the afternoon. It used to be that people spent Thanksgiving with their own kin their aunts uncles grandparents cousins et cetera but you can't do that out here in a new suburb where everybody comes from someplace far away so we eat the turkey with neighbors instead. The Nesbits invited the Fischers the Harrises the Thomasons and us with all the kids of course too. A big noisy gathering. The Fischers came very late so late that we were worried and thinking of sending someone over to find out what was the matter. It was practically time for the turkey when they showed up and Edith Fischer's eyes were red and puffy from crying.

My God my God she said I just found out my older sister is dead.

We started to ask the usual meaningless consoling questions like was she a sick woman and where did she live and what did she die of? And Edith sobbed and said I don't mean she's dead yet I mean she's going to die next Tuesday.

Next Tuesday Tammy Nesbit asked? What do you mean I don't understand how you can know that now. And then she thought a moment and she did understand and so did all the rest of us. Oh Tammy said the newspaper.

The newspaper yes Edith said. Sobbing harder.

Edith was reading the death notices Sid Fischer explained God knows why she was bothering to look at them just curiosity I guess and all of a sudden she lets out this terrible cry and says she sees her sister's name. Sudden passing, a heart attack.

Her heart is weak Edith told us. She's had two or three bad attacks this year.

Lois Thomason went to Edith and put her arms around her the way Lois does so well and said there there Edith it's a terrible shock to you naturally but you know it must have been inevitable sooner or later and at least the poor woman isn't suffering any more.

But don't you see Edith cried. She's still alive right now maybe if I phone and say go to the hospital right away they can save her? They might put her under intensive care and get ready for the attack before it even comes. Only I can't say that can I? Because what can I tell her? That I read about her death in next week's newspaper? She'll think

I'm crazy and she'll laugh and she won't pay any attention to me. Or maybe she'll get very upset and drop dead right on the spot all on account of me. What can I do oh God what can I do?

You could say it was a premonition my wife suggested. A very vivid dream that had the ring of truth to you. If your sister puts any faith at all in things like that maybe she'll decide it can't hurt to see her doctor and then—

No Mike Nesbit broke in you mustn't do any such thing Edith. Because they can't save her. No way. They didn't save her when the time came.

The time hasn't come yet said Edith.

So far as we're concerned said Mike the time has already come because we have the newspapers that describe the events of November 30 in the past tense. So we know your sister is going to die and to all intents and purposes is already dead. It's absolutely certain because it's in the newspaper and if we accept the newspaper as authentic then it's a record of actual events beyond any hope of changing.

But my sister Edith said.

Your sister's name is already on the roll of the dead. If you interfere now it'll only bring unnecessary aggravation to her family and it won't change a thing.

How do you know it won't Mike?

The future mustn't be changed Mike said. For us the events of that one day in the future are as permanent as any event in the past. We don't dare play around with changing the future not when it's already signed sealed and delivered in that newspaper. For all we know the future's like a house of cards. If we pull one card out say your sister's life we might bring the whole house tumbling down. You've got to accept the decree of fate Edith. You've got to. Otherwise there's no telling what might happen.

My sister Edith said. My sister's going to die and you won't let me do anything to save her.

8.

Edith carrying on like that put a damper on the whole Thanksgiving celebration. After a while she pulled herself together more or less but she couldn't help behaving like a woman in mourning and it was hard for us to be very jolly and thankful with her there choking back the sobs. The

Fischers left right after dinner and we all hugged Edith and told her how sorry we were. Soon afterward the Thomasons and the Harrises left too.

Mike looked at my wife and me and said I hope you aren't going to run off also.

No I said not yet there's no hurry is there?

We sat around some while longer. Mike talked about Edith and her sister. The sister can't be saved he kept saying. And it might be very dangerous for everybody if Edith tries to interfere with fate.

To get the subject away from Edith we started talking about the stock market. Mike said he had bought Natomas Transamerica and Electronic Data Systems which he said was due to rise from 36¾ on November 22 to 47 by the 30th. I told him I had bought Natomas too and I told him my other stocks and pretty soon he had his copy of the December 1 paper out so we could check some of the quotations.

Looking over his shoulder I observed that the print was even blurrier than it had seemed to me Tuesday night which was the last occasion I had examined my paper and also the pages seemed very gray and rough.

What do you think is going on I said? The paper definitely seems to be deteriorating.

It's entropic creep he said.

Entropic creep?

Entropy you know is the natural tendency of everything in nature to come apart at the seams as time goes along. These newspapers must be subject to unusually strong entropic strains because of their anomalous position out of their proper place in time. I've been noticing how the print is getting harder to read and I wouldn't be surprised if it became completely illegible in another couple of days.

We hunted up the prices of my stocks in his paper and the first one we saw was Bausch & Lomb hitting a high of 149¾ on November 30. Wait a second I said I'm sure the high is supposed to be 149 even.

Mike thought it might be an effect of the general blurriness but no it was still quite clear on that page of stock market quotations and it said 149¾. I looked up Natomas and the high that was listed was 56. I said I'm positive it's 57. And so on with several other stocks. The figures didn't jibe with what I remembered. We had a friendly little discussion about that and then it became not so friendly as Mike implied my memory was faulty and in the end I jogged down the street to my place and got my own copy of the paper. We spread them both out side by side and compared the quotes. Sure enough the two were different. Hardly any quote in his paper matched those in mine, all of them off an eighth here, a quarter there. What was even worse the figures didn't quite match the ones I had noted down on the first day. My paper now gave the Bausch high for November 30 as 149½ and Natomas as 56½ and Disney as 117. Levitz 104, EG&G 23. Everything seemed to be sliding around.

It's a bad case of entropic creep Mike said.

I wonder if the newspapers were ever identical to each other I said. We should have compared them on the first day. Now we'll never know whether we all had the same starting point.

Let's check out the other pages Bill.

We compared things. The front page headlines were all the same but there were little differences in the writing. The classified ads had a lot of rearrangements. Some of the death notices were different. All in all the papers were similar but not anything like identical.

How can this be happening I asked? How can words on a printed page be different one day from another?

How can a newspaper from the future get delivered in the first place Mike asked?

9.

We phoned some of the others and asked about stock prices. Just trying to check something out we explained. Charlie Harris said Natomas was quoted at 56 and Jerry Wesley said it was 57¼ and Bob Thomason found that the whole stock market page was too blurry to read although he thought the Natomas quote was 57½. And so on. Everybody's paper slightly different.

Entropic creep. It's hitting hard. What can we trust? What's real?

10.

Saturday afternoon Bob Thomason came over very agitated. He had his newspaper under his arm. He showed it to me and said look at this Bill how can it be? The pages were practically falling apart and they were completely blank. You could make out little dirty traces where there once had been words but that was all. The paper looked about a million years old.

I got mine out of the closet. It was in bad shape but not that bad. The print was faint and murky yet I could still make some things out clearly. Natomas 56¼. Levitz Furniture 103½. Disney 117¼. New numbers all the time.

Meanwhile out in the real world the market has been rallying for a couple of days right on schedule and all my stocks are going up. I may go crazy but it looks at least like I'm not going to take a financial beating.

11.

MONDAY NIGHT NOVEMBER 29. ONE week since this whole thing started. Everybody's newspaper is falling apart. I can read patches of print on two or three pages of mine and the rest is pretty well shot. Dave Bruce says his paper is completely blank the way Bob's was on Saturday. Mike's is in better condition but it won't last long. They're all getting eaten up by entropy. The market rallied strongly again this afternoon. Yesterday the Giants got beaten by St. Louis and at lunch today I collected my winnings from Butch Hunter. Yesterday also Sid and Edith Fischer left suddenly for a vacation in Florida. That's where Edith's sister lives, the one who's supposed to die tomorrow.

12.

I CAN'T HELP WONDERING WHETHER Edith did something about her sister after all despite the things Mike said to her Thanksgiving.

13.

SO NOW IT'S TUESDAY NIGHT November 30 and I'm home with the *Post* and the closing stock prices. Unfortunately I can't compare them with the figures in my copy of tomorrow's *Times* because I don't have the paper any more it turned completely to dust and so did everybody else's but I still have the notes I took the first night when I was planning my market action. And I'm happy to say everything worked out perfectly despite the effects of entropic creep. The Dow Industrials closed at 831.34 today which is just what my record says. And look at this list of highs for the day where my broker sold me out on the nose:

Levitz Furniture	103¾
Bausch & Lomb	149
Natomas	57
Disney	116¾
EG&G	23¾

So whatever this week has cost me in nervous aggravation it's more than made up in profits.

Tomorrow is December 1 finally and it's going to be funny to see that newspaper again. With the headlines about Nixon going off to China and the people wounded in the bank robbery and the currency negotiations in Rome. Like an old friend coming home.

14.

I SUPPOSE EVERYTHING HAS TO balance out. This morning before breakfast I went outside as usual to get the paper and it was sitting there in the bushes but it wasn't the paper for Wednesday December 1 although this is in fact Wednesday December 1. What the newsboy gave me this morning was the paper for Monday November 22 which I never actually received the day of the first mix-up.

That in itself wouldn't be so bad. But this paper is full of stuff I don't remember from last Monday. As though somebody had reached into last week and switched everything around, making up a bunch of weird events. Even though I didn't get to see the *Times* that day I'm sure I would have heard about the assassination of the Governor of Missouri. And the earthquake in Peru that killed ten thousand people. And Mayor Lindsay resigning to become Nixon's new Secretary of State. Especially about Mayor Lindsay resigning to become Nixon's new Secretary of State. This paper *has* to be a joke.

But what about the one we got last week? How about those stock prices and the sports results?

When I get into the city this morning I'm going to stop off first thing at the New York Public Library and check the file copy of the November 22 *Times*. I want to see if the library's copy is anything like the one I just got.

What kind of newspaper am I going to get tomorrow?

15.

DON'T THINK I'M GOING TO get to work at all today. Went out after breakfast to get the car and drive to the station and the car wasn't there nothing was there just gray everything gray no lawn no shrubs no trees none of the other houses in sight just gray like a thick fog swallowing everything up at ground level. Stood there on the front step afraid to go into that gray. Went back into the house woke up my wife told her. What does it mean Bill she asked what does it mean why is it all gray? I don't know I said. Let's turn on the radio. But there was no sound out of the radio nothing on the TV not even a test pattern the phone line dead too everything dead and I don't know what's happening or where we are I don't understand any of this except that this must be a very bad case of entropic creep. All of time must have looped back on itself in some crazy way and I don't know anything I don't understand a thing.

Edith what have you done to us?

I don't want to live here anymore I want to cancel my newspaper subscription I want to see my house I want to get away from here back into the real world but how how I don't know it's all gray gray gray everything gray nothing out there just a lot of gray.

HUNTERS IN THE FOREST

One pleasant aspect of being a writer who dabbles in editing is that every once in a while you get to sell a story to yourself. Of course, I have to sell every *story I write to myself before I can sell it to anyone else—if I don't think much of it, after all, how can I offer it to someone for publication with a straight face?—but when I'm simultaneously both writer and editor I don't have to worry, at least, about all those silly little editorial quibbles that other editors often insist on inflicting on me before they'll publish something of mine.*

In this case, the well-known book packager Byron Preiss was assembling a majestic coffee table volume called The Ultimate Dinosaur, *a large volume offering a mixture of scientific essays, short stories, and color plates, and, dinosaurs having been a source of deep fascination for me since I was a small boy, I had gladly volunteered to serve as fiction editor for the book. I assembled a team of top-level science fictionists (Poul Anderson, L. Sprague de Camp, Gregory Benford, etc.) to write the stories, each of whom was matched in theme to one of the essays. And I grabbed the theme of "Dinosaur Predators" for myself and illustrated it with this nasty little item, in which, as often happens in my fiction, the most dangerous beast turns out to be something other than the obvious one.*

I wrote the story in November 1990. Omni *published it in magazine form in its October 1991 issue and* The Ultimate Dinosaur *appeared the following year.*

Twenty minutes into the voyage nothing more startling than a dragonfly the size of a hawk has come into view, fluttering for an eye-blink moment in front of the timemobile window and darting away, and Mallory decides it's time to exercise Option Two: abandon the secure cozy comforts of the timemobile capsule, take his chances on foot out there in the steamy mists, a futuristic pygmy roaming virtually unprotected among the dinosaurs of this fragrant Late Cretaceous forest. That has been his plan all along—to offer himself up to the available dangers of this place, to experience the thrill of the hunt without ever quite being sure whether he was the hunter or the hunted.

Option One is to sit tight inside the timemobile capsule for the full duration of the trip—he has signed up for twelve hours—and watch the passing show, if any, through the invulnerable window. Very safe, yes. But self-defeating, also, if you have come here for the sake of tasting a little excitement for once in your life. Option Three, the one nobody ever talks about except in whispers and which perhaps despite all rumors to the contrary no one has actually ever elected, is self-defeating in a different way: simply walk off into the forest and never look back. After a prearranged period, usually twelve hours, never more than twenty-four, the capsule will return to its starting point in the 23rd century whether or not you're aboard. But Mallory isn't out to do himself in, not really. All he wants is a little endocrine action, a hit of adrenaline to rev things up, the unfamiliar sensation of honest fear contracting his auricles and chilling his bowels: all that good old chancy stuff, damned well unattainable down the line in the modern era where risk is just about extinct. Back here in the Mesozoic, risk aplenty is available enough for those who can put up the price of admission. All he has to do is go outside and look for it. And so it's Option Two for him, then, a lively little walkabout, and then back to the capsule in plenty of time for the return trip.

With him he carries a laser rifle, a backpack medical kit, and lunch. He jacks a thinko into his waistband and clips a drinko to his shoulder. But no helmet, no potted air supply. He'll boldly expose his naked nostrils to the Cretaceous atmosphere. Nor does he avail himself of the one-size-fits-all body armor that the capsule is willing to provide. That's the true spirit of Option Two, all right: go forth unshielded into the Mesozoic dawn.

Open the hatch, now. Down the steps, hop skip jump. Booted feet bouncing on the spongy primordial forest floor.

There's a hovering dankness but a surprisingly pleasant breeze is blowing. Things feel tropical but not uncomfortably torrid. The air has an unusual smell. The mix of nitrogen and carbon dioxide is different from what he's accustomed to, he suspects, and certainly none of the impurities that six centuries of industrial development have poured into the atmosphere are present. There's something else, too, a strange subtext of an odor that seems both sweet and pungent: it must be the aroma of dinosaur farts, Mallory decides. Uncountable hordes of stupendous beasts simultaneously releasing vast roaring boomers for a hundred million years surely will have filled the prehistoric air with complex hydrocarbons that won't break down until the Oligocene at the earliest.

Scaly tree trunks thick as the columns of the Parthenon shoot heavenward all around him. At their summits, far overhead, whorls of stiff long leaves jut tensely outward. Smaller trees that look like palms, but probably aren't, fill in the spaces between them, and at ground level there are dense growths of awkward angular bushes. Some of them are in bloom, small furry pale-yellowish blossoms, very diffident-looking, as though they were so newly evolved that they were embarrassed to find themselves on display like this. All the vegetation big and little has a battered, shopworn look, trunks leaning this way and that, huge leaf-stalks bent and dangling, gnawed boughs hanging like broken arms. It is as though an army of enormous tanks passes through this forest every few days. In fact that isn't far from the truth, Mallory realizes.

But where are they? Twenty-five minutes gone already and he still hasn't seen a single dinosaur, and he's ready for some.

"All right," Mallory calls out. "Where are you, you big dopes?"

As though on cue the forest hurls a symphony of sounds back at him: strident honks and rumbling snorts and a myriad blatting snuffling wheezing skreeing noises. It's like a chorus of crocodiles getting warmed up for Handel's *Messiah*.

Mallory laughs. "Yes, I hear you, I hear you!"

He cocks his laser rifle. Steps forward, looking eagerly to right and left. This period is supposed to be the golden age of dinosaurs, the grand tumultuous climactic epoch just before the end, when bizarre new species popped out constantly with glorious evolutionary profligacy, and all manner of grotesque goliaths roamed the earth. The thinko has shown him pictures of them, spectacularly decadent in size and appearance, long-snouted duckbilled monsters as big as a house and huge lumbering ceratopsians with frilly baroque bony crests and toothy things with knobby horns on their elongated skulls and others with rows of bristling spikes along their high-ridged backs. He aches to see them. He wants them to scare him practically to death. Let them loom; let them glower; let their great jaws yawn. Through all his untroubled days in the orderly and carefully-regulated world of the 23rd century Mallory has never shivered with fear as much as once, never known a moment of terror or even real uneasiness, is not even sure he understands the concept; and he has paid a small fortune for the privilege of experiencing it now.

Forward. Forward.

Come on, you oversized bastards, get your asses out of the swamp and show yourselves!

There. Oh, yes, yes, *there*!

He sees the little spheroid of a head first, rising above the treetops like a grinning football attached to a long thick hose. Behind it is an enormous humped back, unthinkably high. He hears the piledriver sound of the behemoth's footfall and the crackle of huge tree trunks breaking as it smashes its way serenely toward him.

He doesn't need the murmured prompting of his thinko to know that this is a giant sauropod making its majestic passage through the forest—"one of the titanosaurs or perhaps an ultrasaur," the quiet voice says, admitting with just a hint of chagrin in its tone that it can't identify the particular species—but Mallory isn't really concerned with detail on that level. He is after the thrill of size. And he's getting size, all right. The thing is implausibly colossal. It emerges into the clearing where he stands and he is given the full view, and gasps. He can't even guess how big it is. Twenty meters high? Thirty? Its ponderous corrugated legs are thick as sequoias. Giraffes on tiptoe could go skittering between them without grazing the underside of its massive belly. Elephants would look like housecats beside it. Its tail, held out stiffly to the rear, decapitates sturdy trees with its slow steady lashing. A hundred million years of saurian evolution have produced this thing, Darwinianism gone crazy, excess building remorselessly on excess, irrepressible chromosomes gleefully reprogramming themselves through the millennia to engender thicker bones, longer legs, ever bulkier bodies, and the end result is this walking mountain, this absurdly overstated monument to reptilian hyperbole.

"Hey!" Mallory cries. "Look here! Can you see this far down? There's a human down here. *Homo sapiens.* I'm a mammal. Do you know what a mammal is? Do you know what my ancestors are going to do to your descendants?" He is practically alongside it, no more than a hundred meters away. Its musky stink makes him choke and cough. Its ancient leathery brown hide, as rigid as cast iron, is pocked with parasitic growths, scarlet and yellow and ultramarine, and criss-crossed with the gulleys and ravines of century-old wounds deep enough for him to hide in. With each step it takes Mallory feels an earthquake. He is nothing next to it, a flea, a gnat. It could crush him with a casual stride and never even know.

And yet he feels no fear. The sauropod is so big he can't make sense out of it, let alone be threatened by it.

Can you fear the Amazon River? The planet Jupiter? The pyramid of Cheops?

No, what he feels is anger, not terror. The sheer preposterous bulk of the monster infuriates him. The pointless superabundance of it inspires him with wrath.

"My name is Mallory," he yells. "I've come from the 23rd century to bring you your doom, you great stupid mass of meat. I'm personally going to make you extinct, do you hear me?"

He raises the laser rifle and centers its sight on the distant tiny head. The rifle hums its computations and modifications and the rainbow beam jumps skyward. For an instant the sauropod's head is engulfed in a dazzling fluorescent nimbus. Then the light dies away, and the animal moves on as though nothing has happened.

No brain up there? Mallory wonders.

Too dumb to die?

He moves up closer and fires again, carving a bright track along one hypertrophied haunch. Again, no effect. The sauropod moves along untroubled, munching on treetops as it goes. A third shot, too hasty, goes astray and cuts off the crown of a tree in the forest canopy. A fourth zings into the sauropod's gut but the dinosaur doesn't seem to care. Mallory is furious now at the unkillability of the thing. His thinko quietly reminds him that these giants supposedly had had their main nerve-centers at the base of their spines. Mallory runs around behind the creature and stares up at the galactic expanse of its rump, wondering where best to place his shot. Just then the great tail swings upward and to the left and a torrent of immense steaming green turds as big as boulders comes cascading down, striking the ground all around Mallory with thunderous impact. He leaps out of the way barely in time to keep from being entombed, and goes scrambling frantically away to avoid the choking fetor that rises from the sauropod's vast mound of excreta. In his haste he stumbles over a vine, loses his footing in the slippery mud, falls to hands and knees. Something that looks like a small blue dog with a scaly skin and a ring of sharp spines around its neck jumps up out of the muck, bouncing up and down and hissing and screeching and snapping at him. Its teeth are deadly-looking yellow fangs. There isn't room to fire the laser rifle. Mallory desperately rolls to one side and bashes the thing with the butt instead, hard, and it runs away growling. When he has a chance finally to catch his breath and look up again, he sees the great sauropod vanishing in the distance.

He gets up and takes a few limping steps further away from the reeking pile of ordure.

He has learned at last what it's like to have a brush with death. Two brushes, in fact, within the span of ten seconds. But where's the vaunted thrill of danger narrowly averted, the hot satisfaction of the *frisson*? He feels no pleasure, none of the hoped-for rush of keen endocrine delight.

Of course not. A pile of falling turds, a yapping little lizard with big teeth: what humiliating perils! During the frantic moments when he was defending himself against them he was too busy to notice what he was feeling, and now, muddy all over, his knee aching, his dignity dented, he is left merely with a residue of annoyance, frustration, and perhaps a little ironic self-deprecation, when what he had wanted was the white ecstasy of genuine terror followed by the post-orgasmic delight of successful escape recollected in tranquility.

Well, he still has plenty of time. He goes onward, deeper into the forest.

Now he is no longer able to see the timemobile capsule. That feels good, that sudden new sense of being cut off from the one zone of safety he has in this fierce environment. He tries to divert himself with fantasies of jeopardy. It isn't easy. His mind doesn't work that way; nobody's does, really, in the nice, tidy, menace-free society he lives in. But he works at it. Suppose, he thinks, I lose my way in the forest and can't get back to—no, no hope of that, the capsule sends out constant directional pulses that his thinko picks up by microwave transmission. What if the thinko breaks down, then? But they never do. If I take it off and toss it into a swamp? That's Option Three, though, self-damaging behavior designed to maroon him here. He doesn't do such things. He can barely even fantasize them.

Well, then, the sauropod comes back and steps on the capsule, crushing it beyond use—

Impossible. The capsule is strong enough to withstand submersion to 30-atmosphere pressures.

The sauropod pushes it into quicksand, and it sinks out of sight?

Mallory is pleased with himself for coming up with that one. It's good for a moment or two of interesting uneasiness. He imagines himself standing at the edge of some swamp, staring down forlornly as the final minutes tick away and the timemobile, functional as ever even though it's fifty fathoms down in gunk, sets out for home without him. But no, no good: the capsule moves just as effectively through space as through time, and it would simply activate its powerful engine and climb up onto terra firma again in plenty of time for his return trip.

What if, he thinks, a band of malevolent *intelligent* dinosaurs appears on the scene and forcibly prevents me from getting back into the capsule?

That's more like it. A little shiver that time. Good! Cut off, stranded in the Mesozoic! Living by his wits, eating God knows what, exposing himself to extinct bacteria. Getting sick, blazing with fever, groaning in unfamiliar pain. Yes! Yes! He piles it on. It becomes easier as he gets into the swing of it. He will lead a life of constant menace. He imagines himself taking out his own appendix. Setting a broken leg. And the unending hazards, day and night. Toothy enemies lurking behind every bush. Baleful eyes glowing in the darkness. A life spent forever on the run, never a moment's ease. Cowering under fern-fronds as the giant carnivores go lalloping by. Scorpions, snakes, gigantic venomous toads. Insects that sting. Everything that has been eliminated from life in the civilized world pursuing him here: and he flitting from one transitory hiding place to another, haggard, unshaven, bloodshot, brow shining with sweat, struggling unceasingly to survive, living a gallant life of desperate heroism in this nightmare world—

"Hello," he says suddenly. "Who the hell are you?"

In the midst of his imaginings a genuine horror has presented itself, emerging suddenly out of a grove of tree ferns. It is a towering bipedal creature with the powerful thighs and small dangling forearms of the familiar tyrannosaurus, but this one has an enormous bony crest like a warrior's helmet rising from its skull, with five diabolical horns radiating outward behind it and two horrendous incisors as long as tusks jutting from its cavernous mouth, and its huge lashing tail is equipped with a set of great spikes at the tip. Its mottled and furrowed skin is a bilious yellow and the huge crest on its head is fiery scarlet. It is everybody's bad dream of the reptilian killer-monster of the primeval dawn, the ghastly overspecialized end-product of the long saurian reign, shouting its own lethality from every bony excrescence, every razor-keen weapon on its long body.

The thinko scans it and tells him that it is a representative of an unknown species belonging to the saurischian order and it is almost certainly predatory.

"Thank you very much," Mallory replies.

He is astonished to discover that even now, facing this embodiment of death, he is not at all afraid. Fascinated, yes, by the sheer deadliness of the creature, by its excessive horrificality. Amused, almost, by its grotesqueries of form. And coolly aware that in three bounds and a swipe of its little dangling paw it could end his life, depriving him of the sure century of minimum expectancy that remains to him. Despite that threat he remains calm. If he dies, he dies; but he can't actually bring himself to believe that he will. He is beginning to see that the capacity for fear, for any sort of significant psychological distress, has been bred out of him. He is simply too stable. It is an unexpected drawback of the perfection of human society.

The saurischian predator of unknown species slavers and roars and glares. Its narrow yellow eyes are like beacons. Mallory unslings his laser rifle and gets into firing position. Perhaps this one will be easier to kill than the colossal sauropod.

Then a woman walks out of the jungle behind it and says, "You aren't going to try to shoot it, are you?"

Mallory stares at her. She is young, only fifty or so unless she's on her second or third retread, attractive, smiling. Long sleek legs, a fluffy burst of golden hair. She wears a stylish hunting outfit of black sprayon and carries no rifle, only a tiny laser pistol. A space of no more than a dozen meters separates her from the dinosaur's spiked tail, but that doesn't seem to trouble her.

He gestures with the rifle. "Step out of the way, will you?"

She doesn't move. "Shooting it isn't a smart idea."

"We're here to do a little hunting, aren't we?"

"Be sensible," she says. "This one's a real son of a bitch. You'll only annoy it if you try anything, and then we'll both be in a mess." She walks casually around the monster, which is standing quite still, studying them both in an odd perplexed way as though it actually wonders what they might be. Mallory has aimed the rifle now at the thing's left eye, but the woman coolly puts her hand to the barrel and pushes it aside.

"Let it be," she says. "It's just had its meal and now it's sleepy. I watched it gobble up something the size of a hippopotamus and then eat half of another one for dessert. You start sticking it with your little laser and you'll wake it up, and then it'll get nasty again. Mean-looking bastard, isn't it?" she says admiringly.

"Who are you?" Mallory asks in wonder. "What are you doing here?"

"Same thing as you, I figure. Cretaceous Tours?"

"Yes. They said I wouldn't run into any other—"

"They told me that too. Well, it sometimes happens. Jayne Hyland. New Chicago, 2281."

"Tom Mallory. New Chicago also. And also 2281."

"Small geological epoch, isn't it? What month did you leave from?"

"August."

"I'm September."

"Imagine that."

The dinosaur, far above them, utters a soft snorting sound and begins to drift away.

"We're boring it," she says.

"And it's boring us, too. Isn't that the truth? These enormous terrifying monsters crashing through the forest all around us and we're as blasé as if we're home watching the whole thing on the polyvid." Mallory raises his rifle again. The scarlet-frilled killer is almost out of sight. "I'm tempted to take a shot at it just to get some excitement going."

"Don't," she says. "Unless you're feeling suicidal. Are you?"

"Not at all."

"Then don't annoy it, okay?—I know where there's a bunch of ankylosaurs wallowing around. That's one really weird critter, believe me. Are you interested in having a peek?"

"Sure," says Mallory.

He finds himself very much taken by her brisk no-nonsense manner, her confident air. When we get back to New Chicago, he thinks, maybe I'll look her up. The September tour, she said. So he'll have to wait a while after his own return. I'll give her a call around the end of the month, he tells himself.

She leads the way unhesitatingly, through the tree-fern grove and around a stand of giant horsetails and across a swampy meadow of small plastic-looking plants with ugly little mud-colored daisyish flowers. On the far side they zig around a great pile of bloodied bones and zag around a treacherous bog with a sinisterly quivering surface. A couple of giant dragonflies whiz by, droning like airborne missiles. A crimson frog as big as a rabbit grins at them from a pond. They have been walking for close to an hour now and Mallory no longer has any idea where he is in relation to his timemobile capsule. But the thinko will find the way back for him eventually, he assumes.

"The ankylosaurs are only about a hundred meters further on," she says, as if reading his mind. She looks back and gives him a bright smile. "I saw a pack of troodons the day before yesterday out this way. You know what they are? Little agile guys, no bigger than you or me, smart as whips. Teeth like sawblades, funny knobs on their heads. I thought for a minute they were going to attack, but I stood my ground and finally they backed off. You want to shoot something, shoot one of those."

"The day before yesterday?" Mallory asks, after a moment. "How long have you been here?"

"About a week. Maybe two. I've lost count, really. Look, there are those ankylosaurs I was telling you about."

He ignores her pointing hand. "Wait a second. The longest available time tour lasts only—"

"I'm Option Three," she says.

He gapes at her as though she has just sprouted a scarlet bony crust with five spikes behind it.

"Are you serious?" he asks.

"As serious as anybody you ever met in the middle of the Cretaceous forest. I'm here for keeps, friend. I stood right next to my capsule when the twelve hours were up and watched it go sailing off into the ineffable future. And I've been having the time of my life ever since."

A tingle of awe spreads through him. It is the strongest emotion he has ever felt, he realizes.

She is actually living that gallant life of desperate heroism that he had fantasized. Avoiding the myriad menaces of this incomprehensible place for a whole week or possibly even two, managing to stay fed and healthy, in fact looking as trim and elegant as if she had just stepped out of her capsule a couple of hours ago. And never to go back to the nice safe orderly world of 2281. Never. Never. She will remain here until she dies—a month from now, a year, five years, whenever. Must remain. Must. By her own choice. An incredible adventure.

Her face is very close to his. Her breath is sweet and warm. Her eyes are bright, penetrating, ferocious. "I was sick of it all," she tells him. "Weren't you? The perfection of everything. The absolute predictability. You can't even stub your toe because there's some clever sensor watching out for you. The biomonitors. The automedics. The guides and proctors. I hated it."

"Yes. Of course."

Her intensity is frightening. For one foolish moment, Mallory realizes, he was actually thinking of offering to *rescue* her from the consequences of her rashness. Inviting her to come back with him in his own capsule when his twelve hours are up. They could probably both fit inside, if they stand very close to each other. A reprieve from Option Three, a new lease on life for her. But that isn't really possible, he knows. The mass has to balance in both directions of the trip within a very narrow tolerance; they are warned not to bring back even a twig, even a pebble, nothing aboard the capsule that wasn't aboard it before. And in any case being rescued is surely the last thing she wants. She'll simply laugh at him. Nothing could make her go back. She loves it here. She feels truly alive for the first time in her life. In a universe of security-craving dullards she's a woman running wild. And her wildness is contagious. Mallory trembles with sudden new excitement at the sheer proximity of her.

She sees it, too. Her glowing eyes flash with invitation.

"Stay here with me!" she says. "Let your capsule go home without you, the way I did."

"But the dangers—" he hears himself blurting inanely.

"Don't worry about them. I'm doing all right so far, aren't I? We can manage. We'll build a cabin. Plant fruits and vegetables. Catch lizards in traps. Hunt the dinos. They're so dumb they just stand there and let you shoot them. The laser charges won't ever run out. You and me, me and you, all alone in the Mesozoic! Like Adam and Eve, we'll be.

The Adam and Eve of the Late Cretaceous. And they can all go to hell back there in 2281."

His fingers are tingling. His throat is dry. His cheeks blaze with savage adrenal fires. His breath is coming in ragged gasps. He has never felt anything like this before in his life.

He moistens his lips.

"Well—"

She smiles gently. The pressure eases. "It's a big decision, I know. Think about it," she says. Her voice is soft now. The wild zeal of a moment before is gone from it. "How soon before your capsule leaves?"

He glances at his wrist. "Eight, nine more hours."

"Plenty of time to make up your mind."

"Yes. Yes."

Relief washes over him. She has dizzied him with the overpowering force of her revelation and the passionate frenzy of her invitation to join her in her escape from the world they have left behind. He isn't used to such things. He needs time now, time to absorb, to digest, to ponder. To decide. That he would even consider such a thing astonishes him. He has known her how long—an hour, an hour and a half?—and here he is thinking of giving up everything for her. Unbelievable. Unbelievable.

Shakily he turns away from her and stares at the ankylosaurs wallowing in the mudhole just in front of them.

Strange, strange, strange. Gigantic low-slung tubby things, squat as tanks, covered everywhere by armor. Vaguely triangular, expanding vastly toward the rear, terminating in armored tails with massive bony excrescences at the tips, like deadly clubs. Slowly snuffling forward in the muck, tiny heads down, busily grubbing away at soft green weeds. Jayne jumps down among them and dances across their armored backs, leaping from one to another. They don't even seem to notice. She laughs and calls to him. "Come on," she says, prancing like a she-devil.

They dance among the ankylosaurs until the game grows stale. Then she takes him by the hand and they run onward, through a field of scarlet mosses, down to a small clear lake fed by a swift-flowing stream. They strip and plunge in, heedless of risk. Afterward they embrace on the grassy bank. Some vast creature passes by, momentarily darkening the sky. Mallory doesn't bother even to look up.

Then it is on, on to spy on something with a long neck and a comic knobby head, and then to watch a pair of angry ceratopsians butting heads in slow motion, and then to applaud the elegant migration of a herd of towering duckbills across the horizon. There are dinosaurs everywhere, everywhere, everywhere, an astounding zoo of them. And the time ticks away.

It's fantastic beyond all comprehension. But even so—

Give up everything for this? he wonders.

The chalet in Gstaad, the weekend retreat aboard the L5 satellite, the hunting lodge in the veldt? The island home in the Seychelles, the plantation in New Caledonia, the pied-a-terre in the shadow of the Eiffel Tower?

For this? For a forest full of nightmare monsters, and a life of daily peril?

Yes. Yes. Yes. Yes.

He glances toward her. She knows what's on his mind, and she gives him a sizzling look. *Come live with me and be my love, and we will all the pleasures prove.* Yes. Yes. Yes. Yes.

A beeper goes off on his wrist and his thinko says, "It is time to return to the capsule. Shall I guide you?"

And suddenly it all collapses into a pile of ashes, the whole shimmering fantasy perishing in an instant.

"Where are you going?" she calls.

"Back," he says. He whispers the word hoarsely—croaks it, in fact.

"Tom!"

"Please. Please."

He can't bear to look at her. His defeat is total; his shame is cosmic. But he isn't going to stay here. He isn't. He isn't. He simply isn't. He slinks away, feeling her burning contemptuous glare drilling holes in his shoulder blades. The quiet voice of the thinko steadily instructs him, leading him around pitfalls and obstacles. After a time he looks back and can no longer see her.

On the way back to the capsule he passes a pair of sauropods mating, a tyrannosaur in full slather, another thing with talons like scythes, and half a dozen others. The thinko obligingly provides him with their names, but Mallory doesn't even give them a glance. The brutal fact of his own inescapable cowardice is the only thing that occupies his mind. *She* has had the courage to turn her back on the stagnant overperfect world where they live, regardless of all danger, whereas he—he—

"There is the capsule, sir," the thinko says triumphantly.

Last chance, Mallory.

No. No. No. He can't do it.

He climbs in. Waits. Something ghastly appears outside, all teeth and claws, and peers balefully at him through the window. Mallory peers back at it, nose to nose, hardly caring what happens to him now. The creature takes an experimental nibble at the capsule. The impervious metal resists. The dinosaur shrugs and waddles away.

A chime goes off. The Late Cretaceous turns blurry and disappears.

In mid-October, seven weeks after his return, he is telling the somewhat edited version of his adventure at a party for the fifteenth time that month when a woman to his left says, "There's someone in the other room who's just came back from the dinosaur tour too."

"Really," says Mallory, without enthusiasm.

"You and she would love to compare notes, I'll bet. Wait, and I'll get her. Jayne! Jayne, come in here for a moment!"

Mallory gasps. Color floods his face. His mind swirls in bewilderment and chagrin. Her eyes are as sparkling and alert as ever, her hair is a golden cloud.

"But you told me—"

"Yes," she says. "I did, didn't I?"

"Your capsule—you said it had gone back—"

"It was just on the far side of the ankylosaurs, behind the horsetails. I got to the Cretaceous about eight hours before you did. I had signed up for a 24-hour tour."

"And you let me believe—"

"Yes. So I did." She grins at him and says softly, "It was a lovely fantasy, don't you think?"

He comes close to her and gives her a cold, hard stare. "What would you have done if I had let my capsule go back without me and stranded myself there for the sake of your lovely fantasy? Or didn't you stop to think about that?"

"I don't know," she tells him. "I just don't know." And she laughs.

◆

JENNIFER'S LOVER

Through much of 1981 I was busy writing short stories for such high-paying slick magazines as Omni *and* Playboy, with the result that both magazines soon found themselves with enough of my work on hand to last them for quite a while. So *I began to look around for other markets of the same sort. My attention fastened on* Penthouse, *the chief competitor to* Playboy *in the field of slick-paper, male-oriented magazines, which had published a story of mine ("In the Group") in 1973. In what was, for me, the unusually active month of October 1981, I wrote to Kathy Green, the fiction editor of* Penthouse, *asking whether she'd be interested in seeing the occasional short story of the sort that I was currently writing for* Playboy *and* Omni. *She was, and, as has so often happened, yet another time travel idea immediately presented itself to me: a little tale of cross-generational incest. I wrote "Jennifer's Lover" a couple of weeks later and sent it to her. She promptly accepted it and used it in the May 1982 issue.*

FINCH HAD MARRIED VERY YOUNG—HE had been only twenty-three, and Jennifer even younger—and even so he hoped they would live happily ever after. Marriage had been back in fashion for a few years, then, but all the same it was unusual to do it so early, and friends and relatives warned them of the risks. Get out and live in the adult world for a while, they said. There's plenty of time later for settling down.

But marrying was more than a matter of fashion for Finch. He had since adolescence felt himself to be a basically married person. Like one of the primordial creatures of Plato's *Symposium* is how he saw himself—a twofold being that somehow had been divided and could not be happy until it had been reunited with its missing half. He searched diligently until he found Jennifer, who seemed to be that separated segment of himself; and then he quickly took care to join her securely to him once again. They settled in a sleek and snug Connecticut suburb. He sold portable computer terminals for a dynamic little hi-tech outfit in Bridgeport, and she worked for a publishing company in Greenwich, and before long they had a daughter named Samantha and a son named Jason, after which Jennifer quit her job and began doing some volunteer work at the local museum. Their parents, who had been pretty wild items in their own day, doing dope and marching for peace and trashing campuses, were amazed at the way everything had come around full circle in just one generation.

Finch was on the road a lot, making sales calls in a territory that stretched from Rhode Island to Delaware, and occasionally he wondered if Jennifer might someday amuse herself with a lover. But the idea was really too alien to make sense to him. Even when he was away from home three or four nights in a row, sleeping in drab motels in New Jersey or Pennsylvania, he saw no need to go outside his warm and secure marriage, and he imagined Jennifer felt the same way. He wondered if that was naive and decided it wasn't. As a couple they were complete, a single entity, a unity. Naturally the early raptures were only warm memories now, but the expectable cooling of passion had been followed by deep friendship. They were together even when they were apart; a lover would be a superfluity; Finch told himself that if he learned Jennifer had been unfaithful to him, he would not so much be jealous as merely mystified.

And of course there were the children to bind them always: Samantha was already beautiful at seven, a slim golden creature who was as apt to speak French as English. She awed them both, and they were immensely proud of her precocious elegance. Jason, not quite six, was of a different substance, a stolid and literal person whose toys were made of microprocessors and LEDs. He had his father's love of technology, and Finch saw in him a chance to create what he himself had not managed to be—a genuinely original scientific intellect rather than a peddler of other people's inventions. Whenever he returned from a long trip he brought gifts for everyone, a book or a record for Jennifer, something pretty for Samantha, and invariably a computer game or mechanical puzzle for Jason. They were splendid children, and he and Jennifer often congratulated one another on having produced them.

At a computer showroom in Philadelphia one rainy autumn afternoon, Finch bought a wonderful toy for Jason, a little synthesizer that played lively tunes when you tapped out signals in a binary code. Not only would it develop Jason's musical skills—and that side of the brain needed to be trained too, Finch thought—but it would sharpen his ability to count in binary. It was so expensive that he felt guilty and eased his conscience by getting the new supercassette of *Die Meistersinger* for Jennifer and a sweater of some glittering furry fabric for Samantha; but on the long drive home he thought only of Jason creating buoyant melodies out of skeins of binary digits.

Jason accepted it politely but seemed not very interested. He watched as Finch demonstrated it, and when it was his turn he generated a few fragmentary atonal squawks. Then a call from Jennifer's parents interrupted things, and afterward, Finch noticed, the child wandered off to his room without taking the synthesizer with him. That was disappointing, but Finch reminded himself that six-year-olds had a way of being preoccupied with one thing at a time, and possibly Jason's preoccupation of the moment was so compelling that even a wondrous new device could not gain much of a grip on his attention.

After dinner, feeling a little miffed, Finch took the synthesizer to Jason's room and found him hunched over an odd glowing thing the size of a large marble. When he saw Finch enter, the boy disingenuously pushed it into the clutter on his tabletop and pretended to be busy with his holographic viewer. "You left this in the living room," Finch said, giving him the synthesizer. Jason took it and obligingly hit the keys in his mild, obedient way, but he looked uncomfortable and impatient. Finch said, pointing at the little glowing thing, "What's that?"

"Nothing much."

"It's very pretty. Mind if I see it?"

Jason shrugged. He generated a jagged screeching tune. Finch picked up the sphere. Jason looked even more restless.

"What does it do?" Finch asked.

"You press it in places. It turns colors. You have to get it the same color all over."

"Rubik's Cube," Finch said. "An old idea brought up to date, I guess." He put his fingertips to the sphere and watched in surprise as colors of eerie indefinable hues came and went, blending, shifting. Touch it a certain way and there were stripes; another and there were triangular patterns; another and the surface of the sphere burst into thick, brilliant, throbbing patches of color, almost like a Van Gogh landscape. He had never seen anything like it. "Where'd you get it?" he asked. "Jennifer buy it for you?"

"No."

"Grandpa Finch send it?"

"No."

Finch felt himself growing annoyed. "Then who gave it to you?"

The child looked momentarily troubled, tugging at his lower lip, twisting his head at a peculiar angle. Then he began to contemplate the synthesizer, and the old serene Jason, imperturbable, studious, returned.

"Nort gave it to me," he said.

"Nort?"

"*You* know."

"I don't. Who's Nort?"

Jason was manipulating the synthesizer, quickly getting the hang of it, making something close to a tune emerge. He had dismissed Finch from his awareness as thoroughly as though Finch had been transported to Pluto. Gently Finch said, "You aren't answering me. Who's Nort?"

"He plays with me sometimes."

Finch decided to drop it. Jason would tell him about Nort in his own good time, he supposed. Meanwhile the boy was mastering the synthesizer with gratifying swiftness; no point distracting him from that. Finch picked up the sphere again, stroked it so that it went through a whole new series of color changes, and brought it almost to the single hue that apparently one was meant to achieve. But he did something wrong and kicked it into a geometrical pseudo-Mondrian pattern instead. A clever gadget, he thought, and went off to find Jennifer and to catch up on local gossip. The mysterious Nort quickly slipped from his mind, and he might never have thought of him again at all if Samantha had not remarked, when he was in her room to say good night to her, "I'm glad you're back. I don't like Nort, really. I hope he doesn't come here anymore."

Very calmly Finch said, "Oh, he was here again?"

"Two days, this time. Tell him not to come, will you?"

"I don't know if I can do that. You know who Nort is, after all, don't you?"

"Sure. *Maman's* nephew. A nephew is something like a brother, *n'est ce pas?*"

"A little bit," said Finch. He kissed her lightly. "I'll see what I can do about Nort, all right? And if he comes back when I'm gone, you tell me about it, sweet. I don't think I like him either. But let's not say anything about this to *maman,* okay? She's very fond of her nephew, you know, and it would upset her if she knew that you and I didn't like him."

He paused a moment in the hallway, pressing his forehead against the wall, catching his breath. *Maman's nephew.* Jennifer had no nephews. Finch was trembling. Visiting lovers usually claimed to be uncles, he thought. A nephew? *Jennifer's lover?* It was craziness, a phantasm, a melodrama of a tired mind. Jennifer had no lovers. Finch could visualize their marriage, that abstraction, as a solid concrete thing, a gleaming polished marble sphere rather like Jason's glowing toy, and in the perfection of that sphere there was neither need nor room for lovers. In his own way he would find out who Nort was, he resolved, but above all else he would stay calm. He poured himself a drink and rejoined Jennifer, studying her covertly as if looking for signs of adultery on her forehead, in her cheeks. She was playing *Meistersinger,* humming along with the jollier choruses. When they went to bed, he turned to her as he always did when he came home from a long trip, but he imagined that something strange had descended between them like a curtain of metal links, and he was unable to embrace her. The unknown Nort lay as a barrier in their bed. Finch ran his hands halfheartedly over her breasts and flanks but did nothing else. "You must be very tired," Jennifer whispered.

"I am. All that rain—the traffic skidding around—"

She kissed the tip of his nose. "Get a good night's rest," she said.

He had trouble sleeping. He felt her presence inches away as a pulsating vibration that made his fingers and toes tingle disagreeably. That she might have a lover frightened him, for it meant he held faulty assumptions about their relationship, that his evaluation of reality was defective. And he had to admit that he was upset on a much simpler level: a stranger was creeping into his bed, and he hated that as a violation of his rights. He found his reaction embarrassing. Mere jealousy, he thought, is ugly and stupid and very much beneath me. Nonetheless, beneath him or not, he felt what he felt, and it hurt him keenly.

Eventually he fell asleep, and when he woke to brilliant October sunlight streaming through the blazing leaves of the red maple outside their bedroom everything seemed normal again. Jason was using the synthesizer, getting it to play something that almost might have been *Three Blind Mice.* Finch was intensely pleased by that. At work that day he thought sometimes about Nort, but not in any very painful way—some neighborhood person, he supposed, an artist Jennifer had met at the museum, maybe, who drops around for a drink and some artistic chitchat, most likely gay, gentle, fond of children, harmless. He was much more interested in that peculiar glowing sphere. That night he went into Jason's room to examine it again. Ingenious, the play of colors, the tantalizing way it *almost* went one-toned as you handled it and then slipped away into patterns. He had no idea how it worked. Sensitive to skin-temperature fluctuations, perhaps, or possibly even pressure-sensitive, though it was solid as a marble. And what generated the changing colors and projected them to the surface? He was tempted to ask Jason to get a second sphere from Nort that he could try to take apart.

The week after next he was up in Boston for three days on his regular monthly trip. The first two went well; but on the evening of the third, as he returned to his motel after an overly winy dinner with a buyer from a Cambridge data-shop chain, the incandescent image of Jennifer getting into bed with Nort suddenly blazed in his soul. The Nort that Finch invented was older than he, perhaps thirty-seven, dark and muscular, with a dancer's supple body and an easy, self-assured manner. Finch bit his lip and tried to force the unwanted vision away, but it grew ever more vivid and ever more graphic, and the pain of it was astonishing. He thought seriously of driving home in the middle of the night. But that would be insane, he realized.

He came home on schedule with the usual gifts, and when he gave Jason his—a little screen on which he could draw with a light-pen—he feared the boy, still enthralled by some phenomenal incomprehensible thing that Nort had just brought him, might snub it. But Jason said nothing about Nort and was instantly fascinated by the screen. Finch felt a surge of relief until Samantha drew him aside, an hour later, to tell him, "He was here again."

"Nort?"

"Oui. Mardi et marcredi."

"Mercredi," he corrected automatically. Her French still had some flaws; but she was only seven. He turned away to hide his look of torment. Two nights, again. Tuesday, Wednesday. He had no idea what he was supposed to do. Confront her with his suspicions and demand an explanation? They had never even had a real quarrel. Swallow his agony and count himself grateful that there was someone here protecting his home and family while he was away? Sure. Sure. In a dull voice he said, "What do Nort and *maman* do when he's visiting her?"

"They have dinner after we go to sleep. Then they stay up late and talk. In the morning he asks us questions about school and things and tries to be nice to us."

In the morning. Finch winced.

He forced himself to make love with Jennifer that evening so she would not suspect that he suspected, but he was without desire and barely managed to enter her, which made it all even worse. Guilty herself, she would want to assume the worst in him, and this uncharacteristic failure of virility after three nights away from her probably would lead her to think he had been with women in Boston, which would encourage her to give herself even more flagrantly to her own lover, which—

In the two weeks before his next road trip he thought constantly of what would take place between Jennifer and Nort while he was away. He was jittery, remote, short-tempered, and morose; Jennifer seemed to be trying to please him, but whatever she did was counterproductive, and he was reduced to pleading business worries and headaches to keep from having to blurt out what was really on his mind. He wanted no confrontations with her. The love he bore her should be great enough to allow scope for a little discreet adultery, and if it did not, well, he would try to work on his attitudes.

But as he drove off toward Hartford under gray November skies, he imagined Nort's car gliding into the garage, Nort entering the house, Nort with his hands on her breasts, Nort leading her toward the bedroom. The absurd intensity of his obsession alarmed and dismayed him. But he could not control his feelings. In Hartford he checked into his motel and drifted like a man in a daze through his first three calls; he must have seemed in terrible shape, because everyone commented on the way he looked; he had two drinks before making his fourth call, which he never did, and then he canceled the call and returned to the motel. There he had another drink, ate a hamburger in the coffee-shop, and stared unseeingly at the television set until midnight, when he abruptly rose, dressed, stumbled outside, and grimly began to drive homeward. He knew that this was absolute madness. He would let himself into the house and catch them in bed together, and then the three of them would sit down and discuss things. And he had no idea what would happen after that.

Just before two in the morning he parked in front of his house and saw, with perverse satisfaction, that a lamp was lit in the bedroom.

Strangely calm, Finch peered through the garage window, but saw only Jennifer's station-wagon inside. So Nort *was* a neighborhood person, Finch thought. She phones him and he walks over here and she lets him in.

Noiselessly Finch unlocked the door, punched in his identity code on the burglar-alarm keyboard, slipped off his shoes, and tiptoed upstairs. His heart pounded with such startling force that he began to fear real damage to it. At the top of the stairs he paused, paralyzed with shame and misgivings. Leave them alone, he told himself. This is unquestionably the most stupid and reckless and self-defeating thing you've done in your life. He was quivering. He did not dare go forward.

"Dale?" Jennifer called from the bedroom. "Dale, is that you? It *better* be you!"

"Me," he croaked, and lurched into the room.

She was alone, sitting up in bed, looking frightened and surprised. Finch, ashen and shaking, still had the presence of mind to scan the room for spoor of Nort, an overlooked wristwatch, a stray sock. Nothing. Jennifer was naked. She slept that way with him, but she had once told him that she always wore pajamas when he was away, for warmth. Certainly Nort was still here. Nobody jumps out a second-floor window to escape an angry husband. In the closet? In the bathroom? Under the bed? Finch knew he had created a preposterous farce.

"I felt ill," he mumbled. "Dizzy—hot flashes—I couldn't be alone. I just climbed into the car and headed for home—to be with you—the kids—"

"Dale, what's the matter? What hurts you?" She was as tense and anguished as he was, but she seemed to be recovering her poise. She got out of bed—were those the red imprints of Nort's fingers on her breasts and thighs?—and pulled on her robe and came to him. "If you were so sick, you shouldn't have tried to drive all the way from Hartford. Why didn't you call first? Why didn't you try to have the motel get you a doctor?" He swayed. His legs felt like concrete. He leaned against her, sniffing for the other man's cologne or even the smell of his sweat, and let Jennifer ease him down to the bed. He wanted to ask her where she had hidden Nort. But the words would not come. She helped him undress and brought him aspirins, and turned the thermostat up because he was shivering so violently, and clasped him in her arms. Her body was so warm and yielding and tender against him that he nearly began to cry. He let himself relax in her embrace, and to his amazement his desires rose and he reached for her. She tried to quiet him, telling him she was too exhausted for any such thing, but there was no halting him and he took her quickly and with uncharacteristic force. Jennifer met his thrusts with a vigor he had not encountered in months. It must be because Nort's done all the foreplay for me, he thought bitterly, and came at once, with a sob, and collapsed against her breast. At once he was asleep, and in the morning it all seemed like a dreadful dream, nothing more. Finch insisted on going back to Hartford and making his rounds, and would hear no objection from Jennifer. But first he went into Samantha's room and, cutting short her expression of surprise at seeing her father return from his trip so soon, asked her bluntly whether Nort had come for dinner the night before.

"Yes," she said. "He was here when I got home from school. Is he still upstairs with *maman?*"

Finch asked himself, as he drove shakily back to Hartford, whether to seek the advice of friends, his parents, the local minister, a therapist. He had never done any of that. His life had always been an amiable progression toward deeper happiness. By the time he reached the motel, he knew he would consult no one, would take no action at all, would simply wait and see. He would let Jennifer make the next move.

But she said nothing and he said nothing and after his next trip, a brief one, he found Jason with another strange new toy, an arrangement of gleaming wires that crossed and recrossed and seemed to disappear at one juncture into a baffling uncharted dimension, visible only as a dazzling flicker of green light. Yes, the boy said, Nort had given it to him. Finch felt a surge of frantic anger. He was almost desperate now to bring this thing to some sort of resolution, for it was devouring him. Jennifer remained tender and loving and outwardly unchanged. Finch suffered. He could not push his fears and confusions below the threshold of awareness for more than an hour or two at a time; he was losing weight; everyone commented on his frayed and frazzled appearance. He was drowning in the silent turbulence of his altered life.

A second time he returned prematurely from a sales trip, hoping to catch them together. Again the light was on in the bedroom in the middle of the night. Again he stumbled in to find Jennifer flustered but alone. He explained that he was drunk and bewildered. "I think I'm having some sort of a breakdown," he told her, and this time he called in sick and took a week off, though the Christmas holidays were coming and it looked very bad to do that now. Impulsively he went with Jennifer to Bermuda for four days, leaving the children with his parents, and it was like a second honeymoon for them, the pink sandy shore, the palm trees. But the moment they came home his mind was full of Nort again. A few days before Christmas he had to go to Pittsburgh for a meeting, but when still at the airport he was consumed with the awareness that Nort was in his house, joking amiably with Jason and Samantha. Grimly Finch boarded his plane, sat in a cold funk of silence all the way and, in Pittsburgh, bought a ticket on the next flight back to JFK. A light snowfall had begun, and his car, sitting in the vast lot, looked dainty and virginal in its thin white mantle. He reached home at midnight. The bedroom light was on. Finch let himself in and took the stairs two at a time. Jennifer was sitting up in bed, naked at least to the waist, her bare breasts blazing at him like beacons, and next to her, relaxed, comfortable, his hands clasped behind his head, was a slender, naked young man, perhaps thirty at most, with cool green eyes and dense red hair that clung to his head in a curious cap-like way.

Finch felt a kind of relief. "You're Nort?"

"Yes. Is time we finally met, I think, Mr. Dale."

"Mr. *Finch.* Or Dale." Nort had some slight accent. Finch said, "I don't know what the protocol is in a thing like this. I suppose I should be furious and smash things and make threats. But I'm hollow inside by now. I've known about this a long time."

"We know," Jennifer said. "Why else would you have kept coming here trying to catch us in the middle of the night?"

"Twice," said Nort. "This be the third. I thought this time I stay and talk with you."

"You were here the other two times?"

"Certainly. But Jennifer wanted no face-to-face. So when the Dale-detector went off, I did the vanish. You follow?"

Finch stared wearily at his wife. "Jennifer, who is this man and how did he get into our lives?"

"He's my nephew," she said.

"You have no—"

"—eleven generations removed."

"What?"

"A remote descendant in my sister's line. He comes from AD 2215. He's here to do research."

Finch thought of the toys Nort had given Jason. His eyes glazed.

Nort said. "I make the field trip, you follow? I do genealogical research, visit the ancestors, family anecdotes. In my era is very important, knowing the history. I have made many journeys over a long span."

"He has my whole family tree," said Jennifer. "I never knew it, but I'm descended from Millard Fillmore and Johann Sebastian Bach and possibly John of Gaunt."

Finch nodded. "That's fascinating."

Nort said, "We do not interfere, you know. We move around like spies, doing our studies and never interacting with the past-folk, out of fear of consequences, of course. But this was an exception. I was captivated by Jennifer instantly."

"Captivated," said Finch bleakly.

"Captivated, yes. We became lovers. It is a kind of incest, I imagine, but is not very serious, outside the direct maternal line, yes? My studies suffer. Now I come only to this year. Jennifer is a wonderful woman. You know?"

"I know, yes." Finch looked toward Jennifer. "I haul my ass over eight states peddling primitive data-processing devices while you amuse yourself with a lover from the twenty-third century. That absolutely captivates me, Jennifer. I can't tell you how—"

"Dale, please. You know I love you. But—but—"

Nort looked troubled. "You are not accepting of this?"

"I am not accepting, no," Finch said.

"But this is the late twentieth century, a decadent time for the marriage custom, and you are sophisticated, educated, elite persons. It is my understanding that toleration of nonmarital sexual interpersonation is widespread in your cohort. You are displeased I love your wife?"

"Very," said Finch in a gray voice. He lowered himself into the chair by the window and said, "You're a hell of a guy for keeping a straight face, Nort. I have to admire that. Throughout this whole routine you've been very convincing. But I'm worn out, and I can't take any futuristic rigmarole any more. Please put your clothes on and go away and don't come back, and leave Jennifer and me to pick up the pieces of our marriage. Okay? Because if I catch you here again, I might do something violent, which is against my nature, and I'll probably have to divorce Jennifer, which is the last thing in the world I want to do even now."

"You doubt I am from a future time?"

"I doubt you are from a future time, yes."

Nort climbed out of the bed. Finch noticed a thin plastic band of some constantly oscillating greenish color around his left thigh. He touched it and disappeared, and when he reappeared, a moment later, he was in a different corner of the room, holding out a folded newspaper to Finch. Finch glanced at it: the New York *Times* for April 16, 2037. The main headline was something about Pope Sixtus performing Easter services on the moon. Finch made a little choking sound and started to scan the other stories, but Nort, with an apologetic smile, took the paper from him, vanished again, and reappeared without it, back in the bed. "I have sorrow," he said softly, "but I am forbidden to let you inspect the newspaper in detail. Shall I do other things? What would convince you I am genuine?"

Finch wanted to sob. He shook his head and said, "Don't bother. I don't need to know. You probably are what you say you are. Will you go away now? Go annoy Millard Fillmore."

"I am loving your wife."

"You *have loved* my wife. That's the correct grammar. It's over. Listen, I'm a ruthless late-twentieth-century man, and you're on dangerous ground. I have weapons. If you're killed while on a field trip, will you stay dead in 2215?"

Jennifer said, "Dale, stop talking that way."

"What do you want me to say? He flashes in here like something out of Buck Rogers, he screws my wife every time I look the other way, he upsets my daughter and alienates my son with his crazy future toys, and now I'm supposed to—"

"You mustn't threaten him, Dale. You're behaving *extremely* prehistorically. Haven't you ever had an affair?"

"Never. Not once."

"Those motels—"

"Not once. I suppose you've had plenty, though."

"Two before this one," she said, reddening a little. "I thought you knew. This isn't 1906, after all. They were both absolutely casual."

Finch thought of that polished perfect sphere that was his metaphor for the flawlessness of his relationship with Jennifer. He thought of the two-bodied male-female entities of Plato's *Symposium*. His face was leaden and his hands shook.

She said, "This is more serious, Dale. I'm terribly fond of Nort. I love you as much as ever, but he's shown me other aspects of life, things I never dreamed of, and I'm not talking about sex. I mean spiritual concepts, human potentialities, the—"

"All right," said Finch. "I won't try to compete. I won't shoot him and I won't punch him and I won't do anything else uncivilized. Why don't the two of you get the hell off to AD 2215 and carry on the rest of your affair there, okay? Go have a flying fuck in the century after next and let me alone. Okay? Okay? The two of you. *Let—me—*"

Nort disappeared. So did Jennifer.

"Alone," Finch finished weakly. "Jennifer? Jennifer? Where are you? Hey, I wasn't serious! Jennifer! Goddamn it, what kind of sadistic stunt is this? Where are you?"

The cruelty of their game astounded him. He waited for them to pop back into the room as Nort had done with the newspaper, but they did not, and as the minutes went by he began to suspect that they were not going to. Numb with disbelief, he prowled the house, searching closets for them. Suddenly horror-struck, he rushed to Jason's room, then to Samantha's, but the children were still there, Jason asleep, Samantha awake and troubled by the shouting she had heard. He picked her up and held her a long moment, and tears came to him. "It's all right," he murmured. "Go back to sleep." He returned to the bedroom and sat there until dawn, waiting for Jennifer.

In the morning he phoned the office to say that severe family problems had forced him to return from Pittsburgh suddenly and that he needed an indefinite leave of absence, with or without pay. His supervisor was wholly understanding, not at all skeptical, as if Finch's voice communicated precisely how stunned and bewildered he was. He managed to deliver the children to school, and then spent the morning by the telephone, hoping to hear from Jennifer. But no word came from her all day. In late afternoon he called his parents to say that Jennifer had gone off somewhere without warning and could they please come early for their holiday visit, because he wasn't sure he could handle all this domestic stuff alone. They arrived the next day and asked blessedly few questions. In their generation, he thought, it must have been the usual thing for marriages to break up without warning.

Jennifer did not come back. He felt like someone who had been given a single wish and had used it stupidly: now she was off in the inconceivable future with Nort. Was that possible? Was this not all some kind of bizarre dream? Apparently not, for on Christmas Eve a note from Jennifer materialized inexplicably on the living room table, dated 14 Oct 2215 and wishing him happy holidays and assuring him of her love and telling him not to expect her back. "Sometimes you simply have to follow your destiny," she concluded. "I had only a fraction of a second to make my decision and I made it, and maybe I'll regret it, but I did what I had to do. I miss you, darling. And you know how much I miss Samantha and Jason." Next to the note was a little package, with a tag marked Merry Christmas from Nort. It contained a tiny crystal ball that, when held close to his eye, showed him what looked like an Antarctic landscape, gales howling and placid penguins wandering around on an ice floe. He put it down, and when he picked it up a second time it displayed the Pyramids, with a long line of tourists milling about. Finch flung it against the wall and it cracked in half and turned cloudy. He wished he had not done that.

Getting through the holidays was even more of an ordeal than usual, but his parents were an immense help, and his friends, once they discovered that Jennifer was gone, came magnificently to his aid. He was scarcely alone the whole week, and he suspected that it would not have been hard for him to find company for the night, either, but of course that was out of the question. The children were perplexed by Jennifer's disappearance, but after some disorientation they appeared to adapt, which Finch found more than a little chilling. He hired a housekeeper early in January and, feeling like a sleepwalker, went back to work. Because of the change in his family circumstances, the company took him off the outlying routes, so that he would not have to spend nights away from home.

Some time in early spring he started genuinely to believe that Jennifer had skipped away into the future with her lover. Notes from her arrived now and then, always friendly, with regards for the children and reminders about oiling the furnace and taking the cars in for tune-ups. She said she was having a wonderful time but missed him terribly. There was never any mention of coming back. From time to time, also, little gifts appeared—gadgets, toys, knickknacks of the future. Perhaps they were meant for Jason, but Finch kept them himself, hoarding them in his closet and examining them at night with awe. He had always loved gadgets—computers, remote-control devices, wrist videos, and such—but these seemed more like miracles than gadgets to him, and he ceased to doubt that Nort was what he said he was. Finch hoped another of the crystal balls would turn up, but it never did. He did get something that appeared to tune in the music of the spheres, and another that could be programmed to give him the dreams he wanted, and one that displayed abstract color-fields of a serene unearthly kind.

When summer came, he drifted with surprising ease into a romance with Estelle, the company's PR consultant, and that carried him into late autumn. Gently she extricated herself from the relationship then, but he had learned how to meet and win women once again, and he ran through a lively bachelorhood in the months that followed. The first anniversary of Jennifer's disappearance passed. The notes from her and the gifts from Nort came less frequently and then not at all. He was quite competent at running a family without a wife by now, but he had never lost that old sense of himself as an innately married man, as half of a couple, and so, admitting that Jennifer was never coming back, he filed for divorce and won an uncontested decree. That was the strangest part thus far, the knowledge that he was no longer married to Jennifer. He looked for a new wife in his diligent, serious-minded way and, within six months, found one. Her name was Sharon and she was warm-hearted and lovely and rather like Jennifer, though her interests ran more to drama and poetry than to music and painting. She had had an unhappy marriage just after college and had a boy of four, Joshua, very bright. Joshua got along wonderfully with Jason and Samantha, they accepted Sharon readily as their new mother—Jennifer was only a hazy memory to them now—and everything seemed to have worked out for the best. Sometimes Finch called Sharon "Jennifer" when they made love, but she was very understanding about that. Sometimes, too, he woke up drenched with sweat, wondering where he had misplaced his one true wife, his sundered half; but whenever that happened, Sharon held him until he regained his grasp on reality. He moved up nicely in the firm, which was expanding at a remarkable rate, and stayed trim and agile all through his forties. Samantha and Jason turned out well, too: Jason went to Cal Tech, joined a West Coast company, and invented an information-encapsulating device that made him a stock-option millionaire by the time he was twenty-two. Samantha grew tall and radiant and even more beautiful, pursued her interest in French, and achieved splendid translations of Rabelais and Ronsard and married the French ambassador. Finch saw less and less of his children once they were grown, of course, but they always came home for a family reunion at Christmas. They were with him that afternoon twenty-three years after Jennifer's disappearance when Jennifer reappeared.

Finch did not know who she was, at first. She quite suddenly was *there* in the living room, a handsome, slender, full-breasted young woman of about thirty, with golden hair in tight waves against her scalp, who wore a clinging garment of metallic mesh. She blinked and looked about and gasped as she saw Finch, who was in his mid-fifties and reasonably youthful-looking for his age.

"Dale?" she said doubtfully.

He let his drink clatter to the floor. "No," he said. "It isn't possible. Christ, what are you doing here?"

"I had to come back. Oh, Dale, it's the wrong year, isn't it? I wanted to see the children again!"

"There they are," he said stonily. "Take a look."

"Where—which—"

Jason was there and Samantha, and also Joshua and some of their friends; and obviously Jennifer did not recognize her own. Finch pointed. The stocky broad-shouldered young man with the earnest myopic gaze was Jason. The long-legged, awesomely beautiful woman was Samantha. Jennifer's glossy poise seemed to shatter. She was trembling and close to tears. "I wanted to see the children," she whispered. "They were so small—he was six, she was seven—oh, Dale, I've set the timer wrong! I've made a mess of it, haven't I?"

Samantha, quick as always, was the only other one who understood. She went toward her mother and stared at her as though Jennifer were an intruder from some other planet. Finch had heard that Samantha often used her beauty as a weapon, but he had never before seen it. Jennifer appeared to shrivel before the sleek, dazzling woman she had helped to create. In a low husky voice Samantha said, "You don't belong here now, you know. This is a happy time for us, and we don't need you and we don't want you. Will you go away?"

"Wait," Finch muttered.

Too late. Jennifer, reddening, dismayed, nodded and said to Samantha, "I'm terribly sorry. I'm sorry for everything." She ran from the room. Finch raced after her, out to the hall, but of course she had disappeared. White-faced, Finch returned to the party. He looked toward Sharon, who was both smiling and frowning. He had never told her or anyone else exactly what had become of his first wife.

"Who was that?" Sharon asked amiably. "Some girlfriend of yours, Dale?" There was nothing like jealousy in her voice. She was only mildly curious.

"No—no, nothing like that—"

"I wonder how she got in here. Like coming out of thin air, almost. Strange. Why did she dash away like that?"

"She didn't belong here," Finch said hoarsely. He poured himself another drink. "She was in the wrong time, the wrong place." He glanced at his daughter, who was flushed with triumph. What power she had, what force! All the same, he was starting to regret that Samantha had driven her off so quickly. With a wobbly hand he raised his glass. "Merry Christmas, everybody! Merry, merry, merry Christmas!"

For a few years after that he found himself wondering, as the holiday season approached, whether Jennifer would make another appearance, like some ghost of marriages past coming round again. Had she tired of Nort and Nort's century? Did she yearn for all she had abandoned? Though there was no longer any room in Finch's life for her, he held no grudge after all this time; he was almost eager to go off and talk with her a little, to find out who she had become, this woman who had once been part of him. But she never again returned. Perhaps she spent her holidays with Millard Fillmore now, he thought. Or singing carols by the blazing Yule log at the fireside of great-great-great-grandpa Johann Sebastian Bach.

SAILING TO BYZANTIUM

Here's one in which a traveler goes into a very strange future indeed. It is, he has somehow learned, the fiftieth century—but the fiftieth century after what? The world he has entered is so unutterably transformed that it seems impossible that the transformation could have been achieved in a mere thirty centuries. But who knows what that phrase, "the fiftieth century," means to the people among whom he finds himself?

I myself was still in the twentieth century. It was the spring of 1984, in fact. I had just completed my historical/fantasy novel Gilgamesh the King, *set in ancient Sumer, and antiquity was very much on my mind when Shawna McCarthy, who had just begun her brief and brilliant career as editor of* Isaac Asimov's Science Fiction Magazine, *came to the San Francisco area, where I live, on holiday. I ran into her at a party and she asked me if I'd write a story for her. "I'd like to, yes." And, since the novella is my favorite form, I added, "a long one."*

"How long?"

"Long," I told her. "A novella."

"Good," she said. We did a little haggling over the price, and that was that. She went back to New York and I got going on Sailing to Byzantium *and by late summer it was done.*

It wasn't originally going to be called Sailing to Byzantium. *The used manila envelope on which I had jotted the kernel of the idea out of which* Sailing to Byzantium *grew—I always jot down my story ideas on the backs of old envelopes—bears the title,* The Hundred-Gated City. *That's a reference to ancient Thebes, in Egypt, and this was my original note:*

> Ancient Egypt has been re-created at the end of time, along with various other highlights of history—a sort of Disneyland. A twentieth-century man, through error, has been regenerated in Thebes, though he belongs in the replica of Los Angeles. The misplaced Egyptian has been sent to Troy, or maybe Knossos, and a Cretan has been displaced into a Brasilia-equivalent of the twenty-ninth century. They move about, attempting to return to their proper places.

It's a nice idea, but it's not quite the story I ultimately wrote, perhaps because I decided it might turn out to be nothing more than an updating of Murray Leinster's classic novella Sidewise in Time, *a story that was first published before I was born but which is still well remembered in certain quarters. I did use the "Hundred-Gated" tag in an entirely different story many years later—*Thebes of the Hundred Gates. *(I'm thrifty with titles as well as old envelopes.) But what emerged in the summer of 1984 is the story you are about to read, which quickly acquired the title it now bears as I came to understand the direction my original idea had begun to take.*

From the earliest pages I knew I was on to something special, and it remains one of my favorite stories, out of all the millions and millions of words of science fiction I've published in the past six decades. It was published first as an elegant limited edition book, now very hard to find, by the house of Underwood-Miller, and soon afterward it appeared in Asimov's Science Fiction *for February 1985. Immediate acclaim came from many sides, and that year it was chosen with wonderful editorial unanimity for all three of the best-science fiction-of-the-year anthologies, those edited by Donald A. Wollheim, Terry Carr, and Gardner Dozois. "A possible classic," is what Wollheim called it, praise that gave me great delight, because the crusty, sardonic Wollheim had been reading science fiction almost since the stuff was invented, and he was not one to throw such words around lightly. "Sailing to Byzantium" won me a Nebula award in 1986, and was nominated for a Hugo, but finished in second place, losing by four votes out of 800. Since then the story has been reprinted many times and translated into a dozen languages or more. It's a piece of which I'm extremely proud.*

At dawn he arose and stepped out onto the patio for his first look at Alexandria, the one city he had not yet seen. That year the five cities were Changan, Asgard, New Chicago, Timbuctoo, Alexandria: the usual mix of eras, cultures, realities. He and Gioia, making the long flight from Asgard in the distant north the night before, had arrived late, well after sundown, and had gone straight to bed. Now, by the gentle apricot-hued morning light, the fierce spires and battlements of Asgard seemed merely something he had dreamed.

The rumor was that Asgard's moment was finished anyway. In a little while, he had heard, they were going to tear it down and replace it, elsewhere, with Mohenjo-daro. Though there were never more than five cities, they changed constantly. He could remember a time when they had had Rome of the Caesars instead of Chang-an, and Rio de Janeiro rather than Alexandria. These people saw no point in keeping anything very long.

It was not easy for him to adjust to the sultry intensity of Alexandria after the frozen splendors of Asgard. The wind, coming off the water, was brisk and torrid both at once. Soft turquoise wavelets lapped at the jetties. Strong presences assailed his senses: the hot heavy sky, the stinging scent of the red lowland sand borne on the breeze, the sullen swampy aroma of the nearby sea. Everything trembled and glimmered in the early light. Their hotel was beautifully situated, high on the northern slope of the huge artificial mound known as the Paneium that was sacred to the goat-footed god. From here they had a total view of the city: the wide noble boulevards, the soaring obelisks and monuments, the palace of Hadrian just below the hill, the stately and awesome Library, the temple of Poseidon, the teeming marketplace, the royal lodge that Marc Antony had built after his defeat at Actium. And of course the Lighthouse, the wondrous many-windowed Lighthouse, the seventh wonder of the world, that immense pile of marble and limestone and reddish-purple Aswan granite rising in majesty at the end of its mile-long causeway. Black smoke from the beacon fire at its summit curled lazily into the sky. The city was awakening. Some temporaries in short white kilts appeared and began to trim the dense dark hedges that bordered the great public buildings. A few citizens wearing loose robes of vaguely Grecian style were strolling in the streets.

There were ghosts and chimeras and phantasies everywhere about. Two slim elegant centaurs, a male and a female, grazed on the hillside. A burly thick-thighed swordsman appeared on the porch of the temple of Poseidon holding a Gorgon's severed head and waved it in a wide arc, grinning broadly. In the street below the hotel gate three small pink sphinxes, no bigger than housecats, stretched and yawned and began to prowl the curbside. A larger one, lion-sized, watched warily from an alleyway: their mother, surely. Even at this distance he could hear her loud purring.

Shading his eyes, he peered far out past the Lighthouse and across the water. He hoped to see the dim shores of Crete or Cyprus to the north, or perhaps the great dark curve of Anatolia. Carry me toward that great Byzantium, he thought. Where all is ancient, singing at the oars. But he beheld only the endless empty sea, sun-bright and blinding though the morning was just beginning. Nothing was ever where he expected it to be. The continents did not seem to be in their proper places any longer. Gioia, taking him aloft long ago in her little flitterflitter, had shown him that. The tip of South America was canted far out into the Pacific; Africa was weirdly foreshortened; a broad tongue of ocean separated Europe and Asia. Australia did not appear to exist at all. Perhaps they had dug it up and used it for other things. There was no trace of the world he once had known. This was the fiftieth century. "The fiftieth century after what?" he had asked several times, but no one seemed to know, or else they did not care to say.

"Is Alexandria very beautiful?" Gioia called from within.

"Come out and see."

Naked and sleepy-looking, she padded out onto the white-tiled patio and nestled up beside him. She fit neatly under his arm. "Oh, yes, yes!" she said softly. "So very beautiful, isn't it? Look, there, the palaces, the Library, the Lighthouse! Where will we go first? The Lighthouse, I think. Yes? And then the marketplace—I want to see the Egyptian magicians—and the stadium, the races—will they be having races today, do you think? Oh, Charles, I want to see everything!"

"Everything? All on the first day?"

"All on the first day, yes," she said. "Everything."

"But we have plenty of time, Gioia."

"Do we?"

He smiled and drew her tight against his side.

"Time enough," he said gently.

He loved her for her impatience, for her bright bubbling eagerness. Gioia was not much like the rest in that regard, though she seemed identical in all other ways. She was short, supple, slender, dark-eyed, olive-skinned, narrow-hipped, with wide shoulders and flat muscles. They were all like that, each one indistinguishable from the rest, like a horde of millions of brothers and sisters—a world of small lithe childlike Mediterraneans, built for juggling, for bull-dancing, for sweet white wine at midday and rough red wine at night. They had the same slim bodies, the same broad mouths, the same great glossy eyes. He had never seen anyone who appeared to be younger than twelve or older than twenty. Gioia was somehow a little different, although he did not quite know how; but he knew that it was for that imperceptible but significant difference that he loved her. And probably that was why she loved him also.

He let his gaze drift from west to east, from the Gate of the Moon down broad Canopus Street and out to the harbor, and off to the tomb of Cleopatra at the tip of long slender Cape Lochias. Everything was here and all of it perfect, the obelisks, the statues and marble colonnades, the courtyards and shrines and groves, great Alexander himself in his coffin of crystal and gold: a splendid gleaming pagan city. But there were oddities—an unmistakable mosque near the public gardens, and what seemed to be a Christian church not far from the Library. And those ships in the harbor, with all those red sails and bristling masts—surely they were medieval, and late medieval at that. He had seen such anachronisms in other places before. Doubtless these people found them amusing. Life was a game for them. They played at it unceasingly. Rome, Alexandria, Timbuctoo—

why not? Create an Asgard of translucent bridges and shimmering ice-girt palaces, then grow weary of it and take it away? Replace it with Mohenjo-daro? Why not? It seemed to him a great pity to destroy those lofty Nordic feasting halls for the sake of building a squat brutal sun-baked city of brown brick; but these people did not look at things the way he did. Their cities were only temporary. Someone in Asgard had said that Timbuctoo would be the next to go, with Byzantium rising in its place. Well, why not? Why not? They could have anything they liked. This was the fiftieth century, after all. The only rule was that there could be no more than five cities at once. "Limits," Gioia had informed him solemnly when they first began to travel together, "are very important." But she did not know why, or did not care to say.

He stared out once more toward the sea.

He imagined a newborn city congealing suddenly out of mists, far across the water: shining towers, great domed palaces, golden mosaics. That would be no great effort for them. They could just summon it forth whole out of time, the Emperor on his throne and the Emperor's drunken soldiery roistering in the streets, the brazen clangor of the cathedral gong rolling through the Grand Bazaar, dolphins leaping beyond the shoreside pavilions. Why not? They had Timbuctoo. They had Alexandria. Do you crave Constantinople? Then behold Constantinople! Or Avalon, or Lyonesse, or Atlantis. They could have anything they liked. It is pure Schopenhauer here: the world as will and imagination. Yes! These slender dark-eyed people journeying tirelessly from miracle to miracle. Why not Byzantium next? Yes! Why not? That is no country for old men, he thought. The young in one another's arms, the birds in the trees—yes! Yes! Anything they liked. They even had him. Suddenly he felt frightened. Questions he had not asked for a long time burst through into his consciousness. Who am I? Why am I here? Who is this woman beside me?

"You're so quiet all of a sudden, Charles," said Gioia, who could not abide silence for very long. "Will you talk to me? I want you to talk to me. Tell me what you're looking for out there."

He shrugged. "Nothing."

"Nothing?"

"Nothing in particular."

"I could see you seeing something."

"Byzantium," he said. "I was imagining that I could look straight across the water to Byzantium. I was trying to get a glimpse of the walls of Constantinople."

"Oh, but you wouldn't be able to see as far as that from here. Not really."

"I know."

"And anyway Byzantium doesn't exist."

"Not yet. But it will. Its time comes later on."

"Does it?" she said. "Do you know that for a fact?"

"On good authority. I heard it in Asgard," he told her. "But even if I hadn't, Byzantium would be inevitable, don't you think? Its time would have to come. How could we not do Byzantium, Gioia? We certainly will do Byzantium, sooner or later. I know we will. It's only a matter of time. And we have all the time in the world."

A shadow crossed her face. "Do we? Do we?"

He knew very little about himself, but he knew that he was not one of them. That he knew. He knew that his name was Charles Phillips and that before he had come to live among these people he had lived in the year 1984, when there had been such things as computers and television sets and baseball and jet planes, and the world was full of cities, not merely five but thousands of them, New York and London and Johannesburg and Paris and Liverpool and Bangkok and San Francisco and Buenos Aires and a multitude of others, all at the same time. There had been four and a half billion people in the world then; now he doubted that there were as many as four and a half million. Nearly everything had changed beyond comprehension. The moon still seemed the same, and the sun; but at night he searched in vain for familiar constellations. He had no idea how they had brought him from then to now, or why. It did no good to ask. No one had any answers for him; no one so much as appeared to understand what it was that he was trying to learn. After a time he had stopped asking; after a time he had almost entirely ceased wanting to know.

He and Gioia were climbing the Lighthouse. She scampered ahead, in a hurry as always, and he came along behind her in his more stolid fashion. Scores of other tourists, mostly in groups of two or three, were making their way up the wide flagstone ramps, laughing, calling to one another. Some of them, seeing him, stopped a moment, stared, pointed. He was used to that. He was so much taller than any of them; he was plainly not one of them. When they pointed at him he smiled. Sometimes he nodded a little acknowledgment.

He could not find much of interest in the lowest level, a massive square structure two hundred feet high built of huge marble blocks: within its cool musty arcades were hundreds of small dark rooms, the offices of the Lighthouse's keepers and mechanics, the barracks of the garrison, the stables for the three hundred donkeys that carried the fuel to the lantern far above. None of that appeared inviting to him. He forged onward without halting until he emerged on the balcony that led to the next level. Here the Lighthouse grew narrower and became octagonal: its face, granite now and handsomely fluted, rose in a stunning sweep above him.

Gioia was waiting for him there. "This is for you," she said, holding out a nugget of meat on a wooden skewer. "Roast lamb. Absolutely delicious. I had one while I was waiting for you." She gave him a cup of some cool green sherbet also, and darted off to buy a pomegranate. Dozens of temporaries were roaming the balcony, selling refreshments of all kinds.

He nibbled at the meat. It was charred outside, nicely pink and moist within. While he ate, one of the temporaries came up to him and peered blandly into his face. It was a stocky swarthy male wearing nothing but a strip of red and yellow cloth about its waist. "I sell meat," it said. "Very fine roast lamb, only five drachmas."

Phillips indicated the piece he was eating. "I already have some," he said.

"It is excellent meat, very tender. It has been soaked for three days in the juices of—"

"Please," Phillips said. "I don't want to buy any meat. Do you mind moving along?"

The temporaries had confused and baffled him at first, and there was still much about them that was unclear to him. They were not machines—they looked like creatures of flesh and blood—but they did not seem to be human beings, either, and no one treated them as if they were. He supposed they were artificial constructs, products of a technology so consummate that it was invisible. Some appeared to be more intelligent than others, but all of them behaved as if they had no more autonomy than characters in a play, which was essentially what they were. There were untold numbers of them in each of the five cities, playing all manner of roles: shepherds and swineherds, street-sweepers, merchants, boatmen, vendors of grilled meats and cool drinks, hagglers in the marketplace, schoolchildren, charioteers, policemen, grooms, gladiators, monks, artisans, whores and cutpurses, sailors—whatever was needed to sustain the illusion of a thriving, populous urban center. The dark-eyed people, Gioia's people, never performed work. There were not enough of them to keep a city's functions going, and in any case they were strictly tourists, wandering with the wind, moving from city to city as the whim took them, Chang-an to New Chicago, New Chicago to Timbuctoo, Timbuctoo to Asgard, Asgard to Alexandria, onward, ever onward.

The temporary would not leave him alone. Phillips walked away and it followed him, cornering him against the balcony wall. When Gioia returned a few minutes later, lips prettily stained with pomegranate juice, the temporary was still hovering about him, trying with lunatic persistence to sell him a skewer of lamb. It stood much too close to him, almost nose to nose, great sad cowlike eyes peering intently into his as it extolled with mournful mooing urgency the quality of its wares. It seemed to him that he had had trouble like this with temporaries on one or two earlier occasions. Gioia touched the creature's elbow lightly and said, in a short sharp tone Phillips had never heard her use before, "He isn't interested. Get away from him." It went at once. To Phillips she said, "You have to be firm with them."

"I was trying. It wouldn't listen to me."

"You ordered it to go away, and it refused?"

"I asked it to go away. Politely. Too politely, maybe."

"Even so," she said. "It should have obeyed a human, regardless."

"Maybe it didn't think I was human," Phillips suggested. "Because of the way I look. My height, the color of my eyes. It might have thought I was some kind of temporary myself."

"No," Gioia said, frowning. "A temporary won't solicit another temporary. But it won't ever disobey a citizen, either. There's a very clear boundary. There isn't ever any confusion. I can't understand why it went on bothering you." He was surprised at how troubled she seemed: far more so, he thought, than the incident warranted. A stupid device, perhaps miscalibrated in some way, overenthusiastically pushing its wares—what of it? What of it? Gioia, after a moment, appeared to come to the same conclusion. Shrugging, she said, "It's defective, I suppose. Probably such things are more common than we suspect, don't you think?" There was something forced about her tone that bothered him. She smiled and handed him her pomegranate. "Here. Have a bite, Charles. It's wonderfully sweet. They used to be extinct, you know. Shall we go on upward?"

The octagonal midsection of the Lighthouse must have been several hundred feet in height, a grim claustrophobic tube almost entirely filled by the two broad spiraling ramps that wound around the huge building's central well. The ascent was slow: a donkey team was a little way ahead of them on the ramp, plodding along laden with bundles of kindling for the lantern. But at last, just as Phillips was growing winded and dizzy, he and Gioia came out onto the second balcony, the one marking the transition between the octagonal section and the Lighthouse's uppermost story, which was cylindrical and very slender.

She leaned far out over the balustrade. "Oh, Charles, look at the view! Look at it!"

It was amazing. From one side they could see the entire city, and swampy Lake Mareotis and the dusty Egyptian plain beyond it, and from the other they peered far out into the gray and choppy

Mediterranean. He gestured toward the innumerable reefs and shallows that infested the waters leading to the harbor entrance. "No wonder they needed a lighthouse here," he said. "Without some kind of gigantic landmark they'd never have found their way in from the open sea."

A blast of sound, a ferocious snort, erupted just above him. He looked up, startled. Immense statues of trumpet-wielding Tritons jutted from the corners of the Lighthouse at this level; that great blurting sound had come from the nearest of them. A signal, he thought. A warning to the ships negotiating that troubled passage. The sound was produced by some kind of steam-powered mechanism, he realized, operated by teams of sweating temporaries clustered about bonfires at the base of each Triton.

Once again he found himself swept by admiration for the clever way these people carried out their reproductions of antiquity. Or were they reproductions? he wondered. He still did not understand how they brought their cities into being. For all he knew, this place was the authentic Alexandria itself, pulled forward out of its proper time just as he himself had been. Perhaps this was the true and original Lighthouse, and not a copy. He had no idea which was the case, nor which would be the greater miracle.

"How do we get to the top?" Gioia asked.

"Over there, I think. That doorway."

The spiraling donkey-ramps ended here. The loads of lantern fuel went higher via a dumbwaiter in the central shaft. Visitors continued by way of a cramped staircase, so narrow at its upper end that it was impossible to turn around while climbing. Gioia, tireless, sprinted ahead. He clung to the rail and labored up and up, keeping count of the tiny window slits to ease the boredom of the ascent. The count was nearing a hundred when finally he stumbled into the vestibule of the beacon chamber. A dozen or so visitors were crowded into it. Gioia was at the far side, by the wall that was open to the sea.

It seemed to him he could feel the building swaying in the winds up here. How high were they? Five hundred feet, six hundred, seven? The beacon chamber was tall and narrow, divided by a catwalk into upper and lower sections. Down below, relays of temporaries carried wood from the dumbwaiter and tossed it on the blazing fire. He felt its intense heat from where he stood, at the rim of the platform on which the giant mirror of polished metal was hung. Tongues of flame leaped upward and danced before the mirror, which hurled its dazzling beam far out to sea. Smoke rose through a vent. At the very top was a colossal statue of Poseidon, austere, ferocious, looming above the lantern.

Gioia sidled along the catwalk until she was at his side. "The guide was talking before you came," she said, pointing. "Do you see that place over there, under the mirror? Someone standing there and looking into the mirror gets a view of ships at sea that can't be seen from here by the naked eye. The mirror magnifies things."

"Do you believe that?"

She nodded toward the guide. "It said so. And it also told us that if you look in a certain way, you can see right across the water into the city of Constantinople."

She is like a child, he thought. They all are. He said, "You told me yourself this very morning that it isn't possible to see that far. Besides, Constantinople doesn't exist right now."

"It will," she replied. "You said that to me, this very morning. And when it does, it'll be reflected in the Lighthouse mirror. That's the truth. I'm absolutely certain of it." She swung about abruptly toward the entrance of the beacon chamber. "Oh, look, Charles! Here come Nissandra and Aramayne! And there's Hawk! There's Stengard!" Gioia laughed and waved and called out names. "Oh, everyone's here! Everyone!"

They came jostling into the room, so many newcomers that some of those who had been there were forced to scramble down the steps on the far side. Gioia moved among them, hugging, kissing. Phillips could scarcely tell one from another—it was hard for him even to tell which were the men and which the women, dressed as they all were in the same sort of loose robes—but he recognized some of the names. These were her special friends, her set, with whom she had journeyed from city to city on an endless round of gaiety in the old days before he had come into her life. He had met a few of them before, in Asgard, in Rio, in Rome. The beacon-chamber guide, a squat wide-shouldered old temporary wearing a laurel wreath on its bald head, reappeared and began its potted speech, but no one listened to it; they were all too busy greeting one another, embracing, giggling. Some of them edged their way over to Phillips and reached up, standing on tiptoes, to touch their fingertips to his cheek in that odd hello of theirs. "Charles," they said gravely, making two syllables out of the name, as these people often did. "So good to see you again. Such a pleasure. You and Gioia—such a handsome couple. So well suited to each other."

Was that so? He supposed it was.

The chamber hummed with chatter. The guide could not be heard at all. Stengard and Nissandra had visited New Chicago for the water-dancing—Aramayne bore tales of a feast in Chang-an that had gone on for days—Hawk and Hekna had been to Timbuctoo to see the arrival of the salt caravan, and were going back there soon—a final party soon to celebrate the end of Asgard that absolutely should not be missed—the plans for the new city, Mohenjo-daro—we have reservations for the opening, we wouldn't pass it up for anything—and, yes, they were definitely going to do Constantinople after that, the planners were already deep into their Byzantium research—so good to see you, you look so beautiful all the time—have you been to the Library yet? The zoo? To the temple of Serapis?—

To Phillips they said, "What do you think of our Alexandria, Charles? Of course, you must have known it well in your day. Does it look the way you remember it?" They were always asking things like that. They did not seem to comprehend that the Alexandria of the Lighthouse and the Library was long lost and legendary by the time his twentieth century had been. To them, he suspected, all the places they had brought back into existence were more or less contemporary. Rome of the Caesars, Alexandria of the Ptolemies, Venice of the Doges, Chang-an of the T'angs, Asgard of the Aesir, none any less real than the next nor any less unreal, each one simply a facet of the distant past, the fantastic immemorial past, a plum plucked from that dark backward abysm of time. They had no contexts for separating one era from another. To them all the past was one borderless timeless realm. Why, then, should he not have seen the Lighthouse before, he who had leaped into this era from the New York of 1984? He had never been able to explain it to them. Julius Caesar and Hannibal, Helen of Troy and Charlemagne, Rome of the gladiators and New York of the Yankees and Mets, Gilgamesh and Tristan and Othello and Robin Hood and George Washington and Queen Victoria—to them, all equally real and unreal, none of them any more than bright figures moving about on a painted canvas. The past, the past, the elusive and fluid past—to them it was a single place of infinite accessibility and infinite connectivity. Of course, they would think he had seen the Lighthouse before. He knew better than to try again to explain things. "No," he said simply. "This is my first time in Alexandria."

THEY STAYED THERE ALL WINTER long, and possibly some of the spring. Alexandria was not a place where one was sharply aware of the change of seasons, nor did the passage of time itself make itself very evident when one was living one's entire life as a tourist.

During the day there was always something new to see. The zoological garden, for instance: a wondrous park, miraculously green and lush in this hot dry climate, where astounding animals roamed in enclosures so generous that they did not seem like enclosures at all. Here were camels, rhinoceroses, gazelles, ostriches, lions, wild asses; and here, too, casually adjacent to those familiar African beasts, were hippogriffs, unicorns, basilisks, and fire-snorting dragons with rainbow scales. Had the original zoo of Alexandria had dragons and unicorns? Phillips doubted it. But this one did; evidently it was no harder for the backstage craftsmen to manufacture mythic beasts than it was for them to turn out camels and gazelles. To Gioia and her friends all of them were equally mythical, anyway. They were just as awed by the rhinoceros as by the hippogriff. One was no more strange—or any less—than the other. So far as Phillips had been able to discover, none of the mammals or birds of his era had survived into this one except for a few cats and dogs, though many had been reconstructed.

And then the Library! All those lost treasures, reclaimed from the jaws of time! Stupendous columned marble walls, airy high-vaulted reading rooms, dark coiling stacks stretching away to infinity. The ivory handles of seven hundred thousand papyrus scrolls bristling on the shelves. Scholars and librarians gliding quietly about, smiling faint scholarly smiles but plainly preoccupied with serious matters of the mind. They were all temporaries, Phillips realized. Mere props, part of the illusion. But were the scrolls illusions, too? "Here we have the complete dramas of Sophocles," said the guide with a blithe wave of its hand, indicating shelf upon shelf of texts. Only seven of his hundred twenty-three plays had survived the successive burnings of the library in ancient times by Romans, Christians, Arabs: were the lost ones here, the Triptolemus, the Nausicaa, the Jason, and all the rest? And would he find here, too, miraculously restored to being, the other vanished treasures of ancient literature—the memoirs of Odysseus, Cato's history of Rome, Thucydides' life of Pericles, the missing volumes of Livy? But when he asked if he might explore the stacks, the guide smiled apologetically and said that all the librarians were busy just now. Another time, perhaps? Perhaps, said the guide. It made no difference, Phillips decided. Even if these people somehow had brought back those lost masterpieces of antiquity, how would he read them? He knew no Greek.

The life of the city buzzed and throbbed about him. It was a dazzlingly beautiful place: the vast bay thick with sails, the great avenues running rigidly east-west, north-south, the sunlight rebounding almost audibly from the bright walls of the palaces of kings and gods. They have done this very well, Phillips thought: very well indeed. In the marketplace hard-eyed traders squabbled in half a dozen mysterious languages over the price of ebony, Arabian incense, jade, panther skins. Gioia bought a dram of pale musky Egyptian perfume in a delicate tapering glass flask. Magicians and jugglers and scribes called out stridently to passersby, begging for a few moments of attention and a handful of coins for their labor. Strapping slaves, black and tawny and some that might have been Chinese, were put up for auction, made to flex their muscles, to bare their teeth, to bare their breasts and thighs to prospective buyers. In the gymnasium naked athletes hurled javelins and discuses, and wrestled with terrifying zeal. Gioia's friend Stengard came rushing up with a gift for her, a golden necklace that would not have embarrassed Cleopatra. An hour later she had lost it, or perhaps had given it away while Phillips was looking elsewhere. She bought another, even finer, the next day. Anyone could have all the money he wanted, simply by asking: it was as easy to come by as air for these people.

Being here was much like going to the movies, Phillips told himself. A different show every day: not much plot, but the special effects were magnificent and the detail work could hardly have been surpassed. A mega-movie, a vast entertainment that went on all the time and was being played out by the whole population of Earth. And it was all so effortless, so spontaneous: just as when he had gone to a movie he had never troubled to think about the myriad technicians behind the scenes, the cameramen and the costume designers and the set builders and the electricians and the model makers and the boom operators, so, too, here he chose not to question the means by which Alexandria had been set before him. It felt real. It was real. When he drank the strong red wine it gave him a pleasant buzz. If he leaped from the beacon chamber of the Lighthouse he suspected he would die, though perhaps he would not stay dead for long: doubtless they had some way of restoring him as often as was necessary. Death did not seem to be a factor in these people's lives.

By day they saw sights. By night he and Gioia went to parties, in their hotel, in seaside villas, in the palaces of the high nobility. The usual people were there all the time, Hawk and Hekna, Aramayne, Stengard and Shelimir, Nissandra, Asoka, Afonso, Protay. At the parties there were five or ten temporaries for every citizen, some as mere servants, others as entertainers or even surrogate guests, mingling freely and a little daringly. But everyone knew, all the time, who was a citizen and who just a temporary. Phillips began to think his own status lay somewhere between. Certainly they treated him with a courtesy that no one ever would give a temporary, and yet there was a condescension to their manner that told him not simply that he was not one of them but that he was someone or something of an altogether different order of existence. That he was Gioia's lover gave him some standing in their eyes, but not a great deal: obviously he was always going to be an outsider, a primitive, ancient and quaint. For that matter he noticed that Gioia herself, though unquestionably a member of the set, seemed to be regarded as something of an outsider, like a tradesman's great-granddaughter in a gathering of Plantagenets. She did not always find out about the best parties in time to attend; her friends did not always reciprocate her effusive greetings with the same degree of warmth; sometimes he noticed her straining to hear some bit of gossip that was not quite being shared with her. Was it because she had taken him for her lover? Or was it the other way around: that she had chosen to be his lover precisely because she was not a full member of their caste?

Being a primitive gave him, at least, something to talk about at their parties. "Tell us about war," they said. "Tell us about elections. About money. About disease." They wanted to know everything, though they did not seem to pay close attention: their eyes were quick to glaze. Still, they asked. He described traffic jams to them, and politics, and deodorants, and vitamin pills. He told them about cigarettes, newspapers, subways, telephone directories, credit cards, and basketball. "Which was your city?" they asked. New York, he told them. "And when was it? The seventh century, did you say?" The twentieth, he told them. They exchanged glances and nodded. "We will have to do it," they said. "The World Trade Center, the Empire State Building, the Citicorp Center, the Cathedral of St. John the Divine: how fascinating! Yankee Stadium. The Verrazano Bridge. We will do it all. But first must come Mohenjo-daro. And then, I think, Constantinople. Did your city have many people?" Seven million, he said. Just in the five boroughs alone. They nodded, smiling amiably, unfazed by the number. Seven million, seventy million—it was all the same to them, he sensed. They would just bring forth the temporaries in whatever quantity was required. He wondered how well they would carry the job off. He was no real judge of Alexandrias and Asgards, after all. Here they could have unicorns and hippogriffs in the zoo, and live sphinxes prowling in the gutters, and it did not trouble him. Their fanciful Alexandria was as good as history's, or better. But how sad, how disillusioning it would be, if the New York that they conjured up had Greenwich Village uptown and Times Square in the Bronx, and the New Yorkers, gentle and polite, spoke with the honeyed accents of Savannah or New Orleans. Well, that was nothing he needed to brood about just now. Very likely they were only being courteous when they spoke of doing his New York. They had all the vastness of the past to choose from: Nineveh, Memphis of the Pharaohs, the London of Victoria or Shakespeare or Richard the Third, Florence of the Medici, the Paris of Abelard and Heloise or the Paris of Louis XIV, Moctezuma's Tenochtitlan and Atahuallpa's Cuzco; Damascus, St. Petersburg, Babylon, Troy. And then there were all the cities like New Chicago, out of time that was time yet unborn to him but ancient history to them. In such richness, such an infinity of choices, even mighty New York might have to wait a long while for its turn. Would he still be among them by the time they got around to it? By then, perhaps, they might have become bored with him and returned him to his own proper era. Or possibly he would simply have grown old and died. Even here, he supposed, he would eventually die, though no one else ever seemed to. He did not know. He realized that in fact he did not know anything.

The north wind blew all day long. Vast flocks of ibises appeared over the city, fleeing the heat of the interior, and screeched across the sky with their black necks and scrawny legs extended. The sacred birds, descending by the thousands, scuttered about in every crossroad, pouncing on spiders and beetles, on mice, on the debris of the meat shops and the bakeries. They were beautiful but annoyingly ubiquitous, and they splashed their dung over the marble buildings; each morning squadrons of temporaries carefully washed it off. Gioia said little to him now. She seemed cool, withdrawn, depressed; and there was something almost intangible about her, as though she were gradually becoming transparent. He felt it would be an intrusion upon her privacy to ask her what was wrong. Perhaps it was only restlessness. She became religious, and presented costly offerings at the temples of Serapis, Isis, Poseidon, Pan. She went to the necropolis west of the city to lay wreaths on the tombs in the catacombs. In a single day she climbed the Lighthouse three times without any sign of fatigue. One afternoon he returned from a visit to the Library and found her naked on the patio; she had anointed herself all over with some aromatic green salve. Abruptly she said, "I think it's time to leave Alexandria, don't you?"

SHE WANTED TO GO TO Mohenjo-daro, but Mohenjo-daro was not yet ready for visitors. Instead they flew eastward to Chang-an, which they had not seen in years. It was Phillips's suggestion: he hoped that the cosmopolitan gaudiness of the old T'ang capital would lift her mood.

They were to be guests of the Emperor this time: an unusual privilege, which ordinarily had to be applied for far in advance, but Phillips had told some of Gioia's highly placed friends that she was unhappy, and they had quickly arranged everything. Three endlessly bowing functionaries in flowing yellow robes and purple sashes met them at the Gate of Brilliant Virtue in the city's south wall and conducted them to their pavilion, close by the imperial palace and the Forbidden Garden. It was a light, airy place, thin walls of plastered brick braced by graceful columns of some dark, aromatic wood. Fountains played on the roof of green and yellow tiles, creating an unending cool rainfall of recirculating water. The balustrades were of carved marble, the door fittings were of gold.

There was a suite of private rooms for him, and another for her, though they would share the handsome damask-draped bedroom at the heart of the pavilion. As soon as they arrived, Gioia announced that she must go to her rooms to bathe and dress. "There will be a formal reception for us at the palace tonight," she said. "They say the imperial receptions are splendid beyond anything you could imagine. I want to be at my best." The Emperor and all his ministers, she told him, would receive them in the Hall of the Supreme Ultimate; there would be a banquet for a thousand people; Persian dancers would perform, and the celebrated jugglers of Chung-nan. Afterward everyone would be conducted into the fantastic landscape of the Forbidden Garden to view the dragon races and the fireworks.

He went to his own rooms. Two delicate little maidservants undressed him and bathed him with fragrant sponges. The pavilion came equipped with eleven temporaries who were to be their servants: soft-voiced unobtrusive catlike Chinese, done with perfect verisimilitude, straight black hair, glowing skin, epicanthic folds. Phillips often wondered what happened to a city's temporaries when the city's time was over. Were the towering Norse heroes of Asgard being recycled at this moment into wiry dark-skinned Dravidians for Mohenjo-daro? When Timbuctoo's day was done, would its brightly robed black warriors be converted into supple Byzantines to stock the arcades of Constantinople? Or did they simply discard the old temporaries like so many excess props, stash them in warehouses somewhere, and turn out the appropriate quantities of the new model? He did not know; and once when he had asked Gioia about it she had grown uncomfortable and vague. She did not like him to probe for information, and he suspected it was because she had very little to give. These people did not seem to question the workings of their own world; his curiosities were very twentieth-century of him, he was frequently told, in that gently patronizing way of theirs. As his two little maids patted him with their sponges he thought of asking them where they had served before Chang-an. Rio? Rome? Haroun al-Raschid's Baghdad? But these fragile girls, he knew, would only giggle and retreat if he tried to question them. Interrogating temporaries was not only improper but pointless: it was like interrogating one's luggage.

When he was bathed and robed in rich red silks he wandered the pavilion for a little while, admiring the tinkling pendants of green jade dangling on the portico, the lustrous auburn pillars, the rainbow hues of the intricately interwoven girders and brackets that supported the roof. Then, wearying of his solitude, he approached the bamboo curtain at the entrance to Gioia's suite. A porter and one of the maids stood just within. They indicated that he should not enter; but he scowled at them and they melted from him like snowflakes. A trail of incense led him through the pavilion to Gioia's innermost dressing room. There he halted, just outside the door.

Gioia sat naked with her back to him at an ornate dressing table of some rare flame-colored wood inlaid with bands of orange and green porcelain. She was studying herself intently in a mirror of polished bronze held by one of her maids: picking through her scalp with her fingernails, as a woman might do who was searching out her gray hairs.

But that seemed strange. Gray hair, on Gioia? On a citizen? A temporary might display some appearance of aging, perhaps, but surely not a citizen. Citizens remained forever young. Gioia looked like a girl. Her face was smooth and unlined, her flesh was firm, her hair was dark: that was true of all of them, every citizen he had ever seen. And yet there was no mistaking what Gioia was doing. She found a hair, frowned, drew it taut, nodded, plucked it. Another. Another. She pressed the tip of her finger to her cheek as if testing it for resilience. She tugged at the skin below her eyes, pulling it downward. Such familiar little gestures of vanity; but so odd here, he thought, in this world of the perpetually young. Gioia, worried about growing old? Had he simply failed to notice the signs of age on her? Or was it that she worked hard behind his back at concealing them? Perhaps that was it. Was he wrong about the citizens, then? Did they age even as the people of less blessed eras had always done, but simply have better ways of hiding it? How old was she, anyway? Thirty? Sixty? Three hundred?

Gioia appeared satisfied now. She waved the mirror away; she rose; she beckoned for her banquet robes. Phillips, still standing unnoticed by the door, studied her with admiration: the small round buttocks, almost but not quite boyish, the elegant line of her spine, the surprising breadth of her shoulders. No, he thought, she is not aging at all. Her body is still like a girl's. She looks as young as on the day they first had met, however long ago that was—he could not say; it was hard to keep track of time here; but he was sure some years had passed since they had come together. Those gray hairs, those wrinkles and sags for which she had searched just now with such desperate intensity, must all be imaginary, mere artifacts of vanity. Even in this remote future epoch, then, vanity was not extinct. He wondered why she was so concerned with the fear of aging. An affectation? Did all these timeless people take some perverse pleasure in fretting over the possibility that they might be growing old? Or was it some private fear of Gioia's, another symptom of the mysterious depression that had come over her in Alexandria?

Not wanting her to think that he had been spying on her, when all he had really intended was to pay her a visit, he slipped silently away to dress for the evening. She came to him an hour later, gorgeously robed, swaddled from chin to ankles in a brocade of brilliant colors shot through with threads of gold, face painted, hair drawn up tightly and fastened with ivory combs: very much the lady of the court. His servants had made him splendid also, a lustrous black surplice embroidered with golden dragons over a sweeping floor-length gown of shining white silk, a necklace and pendant of red coral, a five-cornered gray felt hat that rose in tower upon tower like a ziggurat. Gioia, grinning, touched her fingertips to his cheek. "You look marvelous!" she told him. "Like a grand mandarin!"

"And you like an empress," he said. "Of some distant land: Persia, India. Here to pay a ceremonial visit on the Son of Heaven." An excess of love suffused his spirit, and, catching her lightly by the wrist, he drew her toward him, as close as he could manage it considering how elaborate their costumes were. But as he bent forward and downward, meaning to brush his lips lightly and affectionately against the tip of her nose, he perceived an unexpected strangeness, an anomaly: the coating of white paint that was her makeup seemed oddly to magnify rather than mask the contours of her skin, highlighting and revealing details he had never observed before. He saw a pattern of fine lines radiating from the corners of her eyes, and the unmistakable beginning of a quirk mark in her cheek just to the left of her mouth, and perhaps the faint indentation of frown lines in her flawless forehead. A shiver traveled along the nape of his neck. So it was not affectation, then, that had had her studying her mirror so fiercely. Age was in truth beginning to stake its claim on her, despite all that he had come to believe about these people's agelessness. But a moment later he was not so sure. Gioia turned and slid gently half a step back from him—she must have found his stare disturbing—and the lines he had thought he had seen were gone. He searched for them and saw only girlish smoothness once again. A trick of the light? A figment of an overwrought imagination? He was baffled.

"Come," she said. "We mustn't keep the Emperor waiting."

Five mustachioed warriors in armor of white quilting and seven musicians playing cymbals and pipes escorted them to the Hall of the Supreme Ultimate. There they found the full court arrayed: princes and ministers, high officials, yellow-robed monks, a swarm of imperial concubines. In a place of honor to the right of the royal thrones, which rose like gilded scaffolds high above all else, was a little group of stern-faced men in foreign costumes, the ambassadors of Rome and Byzantium, of Arabia and Syria, of Korea, Japan, Tibet, Turkestan. Incense smoldered in enameled braziers. A poet sang a delicate twanging melody, accompanying himself on a small harp. Then the Emperor and Empress entered: two tiny aged people, like waxen images, moving with infinite slowness, taking steps no greater than a child's. There was the sound of trumpets as they ascended their thrones. When the little Emperor was seated—he looked like a doll up there, ancient, faded, shrunken, yet still somehow a figure of extraordinary power—he stretched forth both his hands, and enormous gongs began to sound. It was a scene of astonishing splendor, grand and overpowering.

These are all temporaries, Phillips realized suddenly. He saw only a handful of citizens—eight, ten, possibly as many as a dozen—scattered here and there about the vast room. He knew them by their eyes, dark, liquid, knowing. They were watching not only the imperial spectacle but also Gioia and him; and Gioia, smiling secretly, nodding almost imperceptibly to them, was acknowledging their presence and their interest. But those few were the only ones in here who were autonomous living beings. All the rest—the entire splendid court, the great mandarins and paladins, the officials, the giggling concubines, the haughty and resplendent ambassadors, the aged Emperor and Empress themselves, were simply part of the scenery. Had the world ever seen entertainment on so grand a scale before? All this pomp, all this pageantry, conjured up each night for the amusement of a dozen or so viewers?

At the banquet the little group of citizens sat together at a table apart, a round onyx slab draped with translucent green silk. There turned out to be seventeen of them in all, including Gioia; Gioia appeared to know all of them, though none, so far as he could tell, was a member of her set that he had met before. She did not attempt introductions. Nor was conversation at all possible during the meal: there was a constant astounding roaring din in the room. Three orchestras played at once and there were troupes of strolling musicians also, and a steady stream of monks and their attendants marched back and forth between the tables loudly chanting sutras and waving censers to the deafening accompaniment of drums and gongs. The Emperor did not descend from his throne to join the banquet; he seemed to be asleep, though now and then he waved his hand in time to the music. Gigantic half-naked brown slaves with broad cheekbones and mouths like gaping pockets brought forth the food, peacock tongues and breast of phoenix heaped on mounds of glowing saffron-colored rice, served on frail alabaster plates. For chopsticks they were given slender rods of dark jade. The wine, served in glistening crystal beakers, was thick and sweet, with an aftertaste of raisins, and no beaker was allowed to remain empty for more than a moment. Phillips felt himself growing dizzy: when the Persian dancers emerged he could not tell whether there were five of them or fifty, and as they performed their intricate whirling routines it seemed to him that their slender muslin-veiled forms were blurring and merging one into another. He felt frightened by their proficiency, and wanted to look away, but he could not. The Chung-nan jugglers that followed them were equally skillful, equally alarming, filling the air with scythes, flaming torches, live animals, rare porcelain vases, pink jade hatchets, silver bells, gilded cups, wagon wheels, bronze vessels, and never missing a catch. The citizens applauded politely but did not seem impressed. After the jugglers, the dancers returned, performing this time on stilts; the waiters brought platters of steaming meat of a pale lavender color, unfamiliar in taste and texture: filet of camel, perhaps, or haunch of hippopotamus, or possibly some choice chop from a young dragon. There was more wine. Feebly Phillips tried to wave it away, but the servitors were implacable. This was a drier sort, greenish-gold, austere, sharp on the tongue. With it came a silver dish, chilled to a polar coldness, that held shaved ice flavored with some potent smoky-flavored brandy. The jugglers were doing a second turn, he noticed. He thought he was going to be ill. He looked helplessly toward Gioia, who seemed sober but fiercely animated, almost manic, her eyes blazing like rubies. She touched his cheek fondly. A cool draft blew through the hall: they had opened one entire wall, revealing the garden, the night, the stars. Just outside was a colossal wheel of oiled paper stretched on wooden struts. They must have erected it in the past hour: it stood a hundred fifty feet high or even more, and on it hung lanterns by the thousands, glimmering like giant fireflies. The guests began to leave the hall. Phillips let himself be swept along into the garden, where under a yellow moon strange crook-armed trees with dense black needles loomed ominously. Gioia slipped her arm through his. They went down to a lake of bubbling crimson fluid and watched scarlet flamingo-like birds ten feet tall fastidiously spearing angry-eyed turquoise eels. They stood in awe before a fat-bellied Buddha of gleaming blue tilework, seventy feet high. A horse with a golden mane came prancing by, striking showers of brilliant red sparks wherever its hooves touched the ground. In a grove of lemon trees that seemed to have the power to wave their slender limbs about, Phillips came upon the Emperor, standing by himself and rocking gently back and forth. The old man seized Phillips by the hand and pressed something into his palm, closing his fingers tight about it; when he opened his fist a few moments later he found his palm full of gray irregular pearls. Gioia took them from him and cast them into the air, and they burst like exploding firecrackers, giving off splashes of colored light. A little later, Phillips realized that he was no longer wearing his surplice or his white silken undergown. Gioia was naked, too, and she drew him gently down into a carpet of moist blue moss, where they made love until dawn, fiercely at first, then slowly, languidly, dreamily. At sunrise he looked at her tenderly and saw that something was wrong.

"Gioia?" he said doubtfully.

She smiled. "Ah, no. Gioia is with Fenimon tonight. I am Belilala."

"With—Fenimon?"

"They are old friends. She had not seen him in years."

"Ah. I see. And you are—?"

"Belilala," she said again, touching her fingertips to his cheek.

IT WAS NOT UNUSUAL, BELILALA said. It happened all the time; the only unusual thing was that it had not happened to him before now. Couples formed, traveled together for a while, drifted apart, eventually reunited. It did not mean that Gioia had left him forever. It meant only that just now she chose to be with Fenimon. Gioia would return. In the meanwhile he would not be alone. "You and I met in New Chicago," Belilala told him. "And then we saw each other again in Timbuctoo. Have you forgotten? Oh, yes, I see that you have forgotten!" She laughed prettily; she did not seem at all offended.

She looked enough like Gioia to be her sister. But, then, all the citizens looked more or less alike to him. And apart from their physical resemblance, so he quickly came to realize, Belilala and Gioia were not really very similar. There was a calmness, a deep reservoir of serenity, in Belilala, that Gioia, eager and volatile and ever impatient, did not seem to have. Strolling the swarming streets of Chang-an with Belilala, he did not perceive in her any of Gioia's restless feverish need always to know what lay beyond, and beyond, and beyond even that. When they toured the Hsing-ch'ing Palace, Belilala did not after five minutes begin—as Gioia surely would have done—to seek directions to the Fountain of Hsuan-tsung or the Wild Goose Pagoda. Curiosity did not consume Belilala as it did Gioia. Plainly she believed that there would always be enough time for her to see everything she cared to see. There were some days when Belilala chose not to go out at all, but was content merely to remain at their pavilion playing a solitary game with flat porcelain counters, or viewing the flowers of the garden.

He found, oddly, that he enjoyed the respite from Gioia's intense world-swallowing appetites; and yet he longed for her to return. Belilala—beautiful, gentle, tranquil, patient—was too perfect for him. She seemed unreal in her gleaming impeccability, much like one of those Sung celadon vases that appear too flawless to have been thrown and glazed by human hands. There was something a little soulless about her: an immaculate finish outside, emptiness within. Belilala might almost have been a temporary, he thought, though he knew she was not. He could explore the pavilions and palaces of Chang-an with her, he could make graceful conversation with her while they dined, he could certainly enjoy coupling with her; but he could not love her or even contemplate the possibility. It was hard to imagine Belilala worriedly studying herself in a mirror for wrinkles and gray hairs. Belilala would never be any older than she was at this moment; nor could Belilala ever have been any younger. Perfection does not move along an axis of time. But the perfection of Belilala's glossy surface made her inner being impenetrable to him. Gioia was more vulnerable, more obviously flawed—her restlessness, her moodiness, her vanity, her fears—and therefore she was more accessible to his own highly imperfect twentieth-century sensibility.

Occasionally he saw Gioia as he roamed the city, or thought he did. He had a glimpse of her among the miracle-vendors in the Persian Bazaar, and outside the Zoroastrian temple, and again by the goldfish pond in the Serpentine Park. But he was never quite sure that the woman he saw was really Gioia, and he never could get close enough to her to be certain: she had a way of vanishing as he approached, like some mysterious Lorelei luring him onward and onward in a hopeless chase. After a while he came to realize that he was not going to find her until she was ready to be found.

He lost track of time. Weeks, months, years? He had no idea. In this city of exotic luxury, mystery, and magic all was in constant flux and transition and the days had a fitful, unstable quality. Buildings and even whole streets were torn down of an afternoon and re-erected, within days, far away. Grand new pagodas sprouted like toadstools in the night. Citizens came in from Asgard, Alexandria, Timbuctoo, New Chicago, stayed for a time, disappeared, returned. There was a constant round of court receptions, banquets, theatrical events, each one much like the one before. The festivals in honor of past emperors and empresses might have given some form to the year, but they seemed to occur in a random way, the ceremony marking the death of T'ai Tsung coming around twice the same year, so it seemed to him, once in a season of snow and again in high summer, and the one honoring the ascension of the Empress Wu being held twice in a single season. Perhaps he had misunderstood something. But he knew it was no use asking anyone.

ONE DAY BELILALA SAID UNEXPECTEDLY, "Shall we go to Mohenjo-daro?"

"I didn't know it was ready for visitors," he replied.

"Oh, yes. For quite some time now"

He hesitated. This had caught him unprepared. Cautiously he said, "Gioia and I were going to go there together, you know."

Belilala smiled amiably, as though the topic under discussion were nothing more than the choice of that evening's restaurant.

"Were you?" she asked.

"It was all arranged while we were still in Alexandria. To go with you instead—I don't know what to tell you, Belilala." Phillips sensed that he was growing terribly flustered. "You know that I'd like to go. With you. But on the other hand I can't help feeling that I shouldn't go there until I'm back with Gioia again. If I ever am." How foolish this sounds, he thought. How clumsy, how adolescent. He found that he was having trouble looking straight at her. Uneasily he said, with a kind of desperation in his voice, "I did promise her—there was a commitment, you understand—a firm agreement that we would go to Mohenjo-daro together—"

"Oh, but Gioia's already there!" said Belilala in the most casual way.

He gaped as though she had punched him.

"What?"

"She was one of the first to go, after it opened. Months and months ago. You didn't know?" she asked, sounding surprised, but not very. "You really didn't know?"

That astonished him. He felt bewildered, betrayed, furious. His cheeks grew hot, his mouth gaped. He shook his head again and again, trying to clear it of confusion. It was a moment before he could speak. "Already there?" he said at last. "Without waiting for me? After we had talked about going there together—after we had agreed—"

Belilala laughed. "But how could she resist seeing the newest city? You know how impatient Gioia is!"

"Yes. Yes."

He was stunned. He could barely think.

"Just like all short-timers," Belilala said. "She rushes here, she rushes there. She must have it all, now, now, right away, at once, instantly. You ought never expect her to wait for you for anything for very long: the fit seizes her, and off she goes. Surely you must know that about her by now"

"A short-timer?" He had not heard that term before.

"Yes. You knew that. You must have known that." Belilala flashed her sweetest smile. She showed no sign of comprehending his distress. With a brisk wave of her hand she said, "Well, then, shall we go, you and I? To Mohenjo-daro?"

"Of course," Phillips said bleakly.

"When would you like to leave?"

"Tonight," he said. He paused a moment. "What's a short-timer, Belilala?"

Color came to her cheeks. "Isn't it obvious?" she asked.

HAD THERE EVER BEEN A more hideous place on the face of the earth than the city of Mohenjo-daro? Phillips found it difficult to imagine one. Nor could he understand why, out of all the cities that had ever been, these people had chosen to restore this one to existence. More than ever they seemed alien to him, unfathomable, incomprehensible.

From the terrace atop the many-towered citadel he peered down into grim claustrophobic Mohenjo-daro and shivered. The stark, bleak city looked like nothing so much as some prehistoric prison colony. In the manner of an uneasy tortoise it huddled, squat and compact, against the gray monotonous Indus River plain: miles of dark burnt-brick walls enclosing miles of terrifyingly orderly streets, laid out in an awesome, monstrous gridiron pattern of maniacal rigidity. The houses themselves were dismal and forbidding too, clusters of brick cells gathered about small airless courtyards. There were no windows, only small doors that opened not onto the main boulevards but onto the tiny mysterious lanes that ran between the buildings. Who had designed this horrifying metropolis? What harsh sour souls they must have had, these frightening and frightened folk, creating for themselves in the lush fertile plains of India such a Supreme Soviet of a city!

"How lovely it is," Belilala murmured. "How fascinating!"

He stared at her in amazement.

"Fascinating? Yes," he said. "I suppose so. The same way that the smile of a cobra is fascinating."

"What's a cobra?"

"Poisonous predatory serpent," Phillips told her. "Probably extinct. Or formerly extinct, more likely. It wouldn't surprise me if you people had recreated a few and turned them loose in Mohenjo to make things livelier."

"You sound angry, Charles."

"Do I? That's not how I feel."

"How do you feel, then?"

"I don't know," he said after a long moment's pause. He shrugged. "Lost, I suppose. Very far from home."

"Poor Charles."

"Standing here in this ghastly barracks of a city, listening to you tell me how beautiful it is, I've never felt more alone in my life."

"You miss Gioia very much, don't you?"

He gave her another startled look.

"Gioia has nothing to do with it. She's probably been having ecstasies over the loveliness of Mohenjo just like you. Just like all of you. I suppose I'm the only one who can't find the beauty, the charm. I'm the only one who looks out there and sees only horror, and then wonders why nobody else sees it, why in fact people would set up a place like this for entertainment, for pleasure—"

Her eyes were gleaming. "Oh, you are angry! You really are!"

"Does that fascinate you, too?" he snapped. "A demonstration of genuine primitive emotion? A typical quaint twentieth-century outburst?" He paced the rampart in short quick anguished steps. "Ah. Ah. I think I understand it now, Belilala. Of course: I'm part of your circus, the star of the sideshow. I'm the first experiment in setting up the next stage of it, in fact." Her eyes were wide. The sudden harshness and violence in his voice seemed to be alarming and exciting her at the same time. That angered him even more. Fiercely he went on, "Bringing whole cities back out of time was fun for a while, but it lacks a certain authenticity, eh? For some reason you couldn't bring the inhabitants, too; you couldn't just grab a few million prehistorics out of Egypt or Greece or India and dump them down in this era, I suppose because you might have too much trouble controlling them, or because you'd have the problem of disposing of them once you were bored with them. So you had to settle for creating temporaries to populate your ancient cities. But now you've got me. I'm something more real than a temporary, and that's a terrific novelty for you, and novelty is the thing you people crave more than anything else: maybe the only thing you crave. And here I am, complicated, unpredictable, edgy, capable of anger, fear, sadness, love, and all those other formerly extinct things. Why settle for picturesque architecture when you can observe picturesque emotion, too? What fun I must be for all of you! And if you decide that I was really interesting, maybe you'll ship me back where I came from and check out a few other ancient types—a Roman gladiator, maybe, or a Renaissance pope, or even a Neanderthal or two—"

"Charles," she said tenderly. "Oh, Charles, Charles, Charles, how lonely you must be, how lost, how troubled! Will you ever forgive me? Will you ever forgive us all?"

Once more he was astounded by her. She sounded entirely sincere, altogether sympathetic. Was she? Was she, really? He was not sure he had ever had a sign of genuine caring from any of them before, not even Gioia. Nor could he bring himself to trust Belilala now. He was afraid of her, afraid of all of them, of their brittleness, their slyness, their elegance. He wished he could go to her and have her take him in her arms; but he felt too much the shaggy prehistoric just now to be able to risk asking that comfort of her.

He turned away and began to walk around the rim of the citadel's massive wall.

"Charles?"

"Let me alone for a little while," he said.

He walked on. His forehead throbbed and there was a pounding in his chest. All stress systems going full blast, he thought: secret glands dumping gallons of inflammatory substances into his bloodstream. The heat, the inner confusion, the repellent look of this place—

Try to understand, he thought. Relax. Look about you. Try to enjoy your holiday in Mohenjo-daro.

He leaned warily outward, over the edge of the wall. He had never seen a wall like this; it must be forty feet thick at the base, he guessed, perhaps even more, and every brick perfectly shaped, meticulously set. Beyond the great rampart, marshes ran almost to the edge of the city, although close by the wall the swamps had been dammed and drained for agriculture. He saw lithe brown farmers down there, busy with their wheat and barley and peas. Cattle and buffaloes grazed a little farther out. The air was heavy, dank, humid. All was still. From somewhere close at hand came the sound of a droning, whining stringed instrument and a steady insistent chanting.

Gradually a sort of peace pervaded him. His anger subsided. He felt himself beginning to grow calm again. He looked back at the city, the rigid interlocking streets, the maze of inner lanes, the millions of courses of precise brickwork.

It is a miracle, he told himself, that this city is here in this place and at this time. And it is a miracle that I am here to see it.

Caught for a moment by the magic within the bleakness, he thought he began to understand Belilala's awe and delight, and he wished now that he had not spoken to her so sharply. The city was alive. Whether it was the actual Mohenjo-daro of thousands upon thousands of years ago, ripped from the past by some wondrous hook, or simply a cunning reproduction, did not matter at all. Real or not, this was the true Mohenjo-daro. It had been dead, and now, for the moment, it was alive again. These people, these citizens, might be trivial, but reconstructing Mohenjo-daro was no trivial achievement. And that the city that had been reconstructed was oppressive and sinister-looking was unimportant. No one was compelled to live in Mohenjo-daro anymore. Its time had come and gone, long ago; those little dark-skinned peasants and craftsmen and merchants down there were mere temporaries, mere inanimate things, conjured up like zombies to enhance the illusion. They did not need his pity. Nor did he need to pity himself. He knew that he should be grateful for the chance to behold these things. Someday, when this dream had ended and his hosts had returned him to the world of subways and computers and income tax and television networks, he would think of Mohenjo-daro as he had once beheld it, lofty walls of tightly woven dark brick under a heavy sky, and he would remember only its beauty.

Glancing back, he searched for Belilala and could not for a moment find her. Then he caught sight of her carefully descending a narrow staircase that angled down the inner face of the citadel wall.

"Belilala!" he called.

She paused and looked his way, shading her eyes from the sun with her hand. "Are you all right?"

"Where are you going?"

"To the baths," she said. "Do you want to come?"

He nodded. "Yes. Wait for me, will you? I'll be right there." He began to run toward her along the top of the wall.

THE BATHS WERE ATTACHED TO the citadel: a great open tank the size of a large swimming pool, lined with bricks set on edge in gypsum mortar and waterproofed with asphalt, and eight smaller tanks just north of it in a kind of covered arcade. He supposed that in ancient times the whole complex had had some ritual purpose, the large tank used by common folk and the small chambers set aside for the private ablutions of priests or nobles. Now the baths were maintained, it seemed, entirely for the pleasure of visiting citizens. As Phillips came up the passageway that led to the main bath he saw fifteen or twenty of them lolling in the water or padding languidly about, while temporaries of the dark-skinned Mohenjo-daro type served them drinks and pungent little morsels of spiced meat as though this were some sort of luxury resort. Which was, he realized, exactly what it was. The temporaries wore white cotton loincloths; the citizens were naked. In his former life he had encountered that sort of casual public nudity a few times on visits to California and the south of France, and it had made him mildly uneasy. But he was growing accustomed to it here.

The changing rooms were tiny brick cubicles connected by rows of closely placed steps to the courtyard that surrounded the central tank. They entered one and Belilala swiftly slipped out of the loose cotton robe that she had worn since their arrival that morning. With arms folded she stood leaning against the wall, waiting for him. After a moment he dropped his own robe and followed her outside. He felt a little giddy, sauntering around naked in the open like this.

On the way to the main bathing area they passed the private baths. None of them seemed to be occupied. They were elegantly constructed chambers, with finely jointed brick floors and carefully designed runnels to drain excess water into the passageway that led to the primary drain. Phillips was struck with admiration for the cleverness of the prehistoric engineers. He peered into this chamber and that to see how the conduits and ventilating ducts were arranged, and when he came to the last room in the sequence he was surprised and embarrassed to discover that it was in use. A brawny grinning man, big-muscled, deep-chested, with exuberantly flowing shoulder-length red hair and a flamboyant, sharply tapering beard was thrashing about merrily with two women in the small tank. Phillips had a quick glimpse of a lively tangle of arms, legs, breasts, buttocks.

"Sorry," he muttered. His cheeks reddened. Quickly he ducked out, blurting apologies as he went. "Didn't realize the room was occupied—no wish to intrude—"

Belilala had proceeded on down the passageway. Phillips hurried after her. From behind him came peals of cheerful raucous booming laughter and high-pitched giggling and the sound of splashing water. Probably they had not even noticed him.

He paused a moment, puzzled, playing back in his mind that one startling glimpse. Something was not right. Those women, he was fairly sure, were citizens: little slender elfin dark-haired girlish creatures, the standard model. But the man? That great curling sweep of red hair? Not a citizen. Citizens did not affect shoulder-length hair. And red? Nor had he ever seen a citizen so burly, so powerfully muscular. Or one with a beard. But he could hardly be a temporary, either. Phillips could conceive no reason why there would be so Anglo-Saxon-looking a temporary at Mohenjo-daro; and it was unthinkable for a temporary to be frolicking like that with citizens, anyway.

"Charles?"

He looked up ahead. Belilala stood at the end of the passageway, outlined in a nimbus of brilliant sunlight. "Charles?" she said again. "Did you lose your way?"

"I'm right here behind you," he said. "I'm coming."

"Who did you meet in there?"

"A man with a beard."

"With a what?"

"A beard," he said. "Red hair growing on his face. I wonder who he is."

"Nobody I know," said Belilala. "The only one I know with hair on his face is you. And yours is black, and you shave it off every day." She laughed. "Come along, now! I see some friends by the pool!"

He caught up with her, and they went hand in hand out into the courtyard. Immediately a waiter glided up to them, an obsequious little temporary with a tray of drinks. Phillips waved it away and headed for the pool. He felt terribly exposed: he imagined that the citizens disporting themselves here were staring intently at him, studying his hairy primitive body as though he were some mythical creature, a Minotaur, a werewolf, summoned up for their amusement. Belilala drifted off to talk to someone and he slipped into the water, grateful for the concealment it offered. It was deep, warm, comforting. With swift powerful strokes he breast-stroked from one end to the other.

A citizen perched elegantly on the pool's rim smiled at him. "Ah, so you've come at last, Charles!" Char-less. Two syllables. Someone from Gioia's set: Stengard, Hawk, Aramayne? He could not remember which one. They were all so much alike.

Phillips returned the man's smile in a halfhearted, tentative way. He searched for something to say and finally asked, "Have you been here long?"

"Weeks. Perhaps months. What a splendid achievement this city is, eh, Charles? Such utter unity of mood—such a total statement of a uniquely single-minded esthetic—"

"Yes. Single-minded is the word," Phillips said dryly.

"Gioia's word, actually. Gioia's phrase. I was merely quoting."

Gioia. He felt as if he had been stabbed.

"You've spoken to Gioia lately?" he said.

"Actually, no. It was Hekna who saw her. You do remember Hekna, eh?" He nodded toward two naked women standing on the brick platform that bordered the pool, chatting, delicately nibbling morsels of meat. They could have been twins. "There is Hekna, with your Belilala."

Hekna, yes. So this must be Hawk, Phillips thought, unless there has been some recent shift of couples. "How sweet she is, your Belilala," Hawk said. "Gioia chose very wisely when she picked her for you."

Another stab: a much deeper one. "Is that how it was?" he said. "Gioia picked Belilala for me?"

"Why, of course!" Hawk seemed surprised. It went without saying, evidently. "What did you think? That Gioia would merely go off and leave you to fend for yourself?"

"Hardly. Not Gioia."

"She's very tender, very gentle, isn't she?"

"You mean Belilala? Yes, very," said Phillips carefully. "A dear woman, a wonderful woman. But of course I hope to get together with Gioia again soon." He paused. "They say she's been in Mohenjo-daro almost since it opened."

"She was here, yes."

"Was?"

"Oh, you know Gioia," Hawk said lightly. "She's moved along by now, naturally."

Phillips leaned forward. "Naturally," he said. Tension thickened his voice. "Where has she gone this time?"

"Timbuctoo, I think. Or New Chicago. I forget which one it was. She was telling us that she hoped to be in Timbuctoo for the closing-down party. But then Fenimon had some pressing reason for going to New Chicago. I can't remember what they decided to do." Hawk gestured sadly. "Either way, a pity that she left Mohenjo before the new visitor came. She had such a rewarding time with you, after all: I'm sure she'd have found much to learn from him also."

The unfamiliar term twanged an alarm deep in Phillips's consciousness. "Visitor?" he said, angling his head sharply toward Hawk. "What visitor do you mean?"

"You haven't met him yet? Oh, of course, you've only just arrived."

Phillips moistened his lips. "I think I may have seen him. Long red hair? Beard like this?"

"That's the one! Willoughby, he's called. He's—what?—a Viking, a pirate, something like that. Tremendous vigor and force. Remarkable person. We should have many more visitors, I think. They're far superior to temporaries, everyone agrees. Talking with a temporary is a little like talking to one's self, wouldn't you say? They give you no significant illumination. But a visitor—someone like this Willoughby—or like you, Charles—a visitor can be truly enlightening, a visitor can transform one's view of reality—"

"Excuse me," Phillips said. A throbbing began behind his forehead. "Perhaps we can continue this conversation later, yes?" He put the flats of his hands against the hot brick of the platform and hoisted himself swiftly from the pool. "At dinner, maybe—or afterward—yes? All right?" He set off at a quick half-trot back toward the passageway that led to the private baths.

As HE ENTERED THE ROOFED part of the structure his throat grew dry, his breath suddenly came short. He padded quickly up the hall and peered into the little bath chamber. The bearded man was still there, sitting up in the tank, breast-high above the water, with one arm around each of the women. His eyes gleamed with fiery intensity in the dimness. He was grinning in marvelous self-satisfaction; he seemed to brim with intensity, confidence, gusto.

Let him be what I think he is, Phillips prayed. I have been alone among these people long enough.

"May I come in?" he asked.

"Aye, fellow!" cried the man in the tub thunderously. "By my troth, come ye in, and bring your lass as well! God's teeth, I wot there's room aplenty for more folk in this tub than we!"

At that great uproarious outcry Phillips felt a powerful surge of joy. What a joyous rowdy voice! How rich, how lusty, how totally uncitizenlike!

And those oddly archaic words! God's teeth? By my troth? What sort of talk was that? What else but the good pure sonorous Elizabethan diction! Certainly it had something of the roll and fervor of Shakespeare about it. And spoken with—an Irish brogue, was it? No, not quite: it was English, but English spoken in no manner Phillips had ever heard.

Citizens did not speak that way. But a visitor might.

So it was true. Relief flooded Phillips's soul. Not alone, then! Another relic of a former age—another wanderer—a companion in chaos, a brother in adversity—a fellow voyager, tossed even farther than he had been by the tempests of time—

The bearded man grinned heartily and beckoned to Phillips with a toss of his head. "Well, join us, join us, man! 'Tis good to see an English face again, amidst all these Moors and rogue Portugals! But what have ye done with thy lass? One can never have enough wenches, d'ye not agree?"

The force and vigor of him were extraordinary: almost too much so. He roared, he bellowed, he boomed. He was so very much what he ought to be that he seemed more a character out of some old pirate movie than anything else, so blustering, so real, that he seemed unreal. A stage Elizabethan, larger than life, a boisterous young Falstaff without the belly.

Hoarsely Phillips said, "Who are you?"

"Why, Ned Willoughby's son Francis am I, of Plymouth. Late of the service of Her Most Protestant Majesty, but most foully abducted by the powers of darkness and cast away among these blackamoor Hindus, or whatever they be. And thyself?"

"Charles Phillips." After a moment's uncertainty he added, "I'm from New York."

"New York? What place is that? In faith, man, I know it not!"

"A city in America."

"A city in America, forsooth! What a fine fancy that is! In America, you say, and not on the Moon, or perchance underneath the sea?" To the women Willoughby said, "D'ye hear him? He comes from a city in America! With the face of an Englishman, though not the manner of one, and not quite the proper sort of speech. A city in America! A city. God's blood, what will I hear next?"

Phillips trembled. Awe was beginning to take hold of him. This man had walked the streets of Shakespeare's London, perhaps. He had clinked canisters with Marlowe or Essex or Walter Raleigh; he had watched the ships of the Armada wallowing in the Channel. It strained Phillips's spirit to think of it. This strange dream in which he found himself was compounding its strangeness now. He felt like a weary swimmer assailed by heavy surf, winded, dazed. The hot close atmosphere of the baths was driving him toward vertigo. There could be no doubt of it any longer. He was not the only primitive—the only visitor—who was wandering loose in this fiftieth century. They were conducting other experiments as well. He gripped the sides of the door to steady himself and said, "When you speak of Her Most Protestant Majesty, it's Elizabeth the First you mean, is that not so?"

"Elizabeth, aye! As to the First, that is true enough, but why trouble to name her thus? There is but one. First and Last, I do trow, and God save her, there is no other!"

Phillips studied the other man warily. He knew that he must proceed with care. A misstep at this point and he would forfeit any chance that Willoughby would take him seriously. How much metaphysical bewilderment, after all, could this man absorb? What did he know, what had anyone of his time known, of past and present and future and the notion that one might somehow move from one to the other as readily as one would go from Surrey to Kent? That was a twentieth-century idea, late nineteenth at best, a fantastical speculation that very likely no one had even considered before Wells had sent his time traveler off to stare at the reddened sun of the earth's last twilight. Willoughby's world was a world of Protestants and Catholics, of kings and queens, of tiny sailing vessels, of swords at the hip and ox-carts on the road: that world seemed to Phillips far more alien and distant than was this world of citizens and temporaries. The risk that Willoughby would not begin to understand him was great.

But this man and he were natural allies against a world they had never made. Phillips chose to take the risk.

"Elizabeth the First is the queen you serve," he said. "There will be another of her name in England, in due time. Has already been, in fact."

Willoughby shook his head like a puzzled lion. "Another Elizabeth, d'ye say?"

"A second one, and not much like the first. Long after your Virgin Queen, this one. She will reign in what you think of as the days to come. That I know without doubt."

The Englishman peered at him and frowned. "You see the future? Are you a soothsayer, then? A necromancer, mayhap? Or one of the very demons that brought me to this place?"

"Not at all," Phillips said gently. "Only a lost soul, like yourself." He stepped into the little room and crouched by the side of the tank. The two citizen-women were staring at him in bland fascination. He ignored them. To Willoughby he said, "Do you have any idea where you are?"

THE ENGLISHMAN HAD GUESSED, RIGHTLY enough, that he was in India: "I do believe these little brown Moorish folk are of the Hindu sort," he said. But that was as far as his comprehension of what had befallen him could go.

It had not occurred to him that he was no longer living in the sixteenth century. And of course he did not begin to suspect that this strange and somber brick city in which he found himself was a wanderer out of an era even more remote than his own. Was there any way, Phillips wondered, of explaining that to him?

He had been here only three days. He thought it was devils that had carried him off. "While I slept did they come for me," he said. "Mephistophilis Sathanas, his henchmen seized me—God alone can say why—and swept me in a moment out to this torrid realm from England, where I had reposed among friends and family. For I was between one voyage and the next, you must understand, awaiting Drake and his ship—you know Drake, the glorious Francis? God's blood, there's a mariner for ye! We were to go to the Main again, he and I, but instead here I be in this other place—" Willoughby leaned close and said, "I ask you, soothsayer, how can it be, that a man go to sleep in Plymouth and wake up in India? It is passing strange, is it not?"

"That it is," Phillips said.

"But he that is in the dance must needs dance on, though he do but hop, eh? So do I believe." He gestured toward the two citizen-women.

"And therefore to console myself in this pagan land I have found me some sport among these little Portugal women—"

"Portugal?" said Phillips.

"Why, what else can they be, but Portugals? Is it not the Portugals who control all these coasts of India? See, the people are of two sorts here, the blackamoors and the others, the fair-skinned ones, the lords and masters who lie here in these baths. If they be not Hindus, and I think they are not, then Portugals is what they must be." He laughed and pulled the women against himself and rubbed his hands over their breasts as though they were fruits on a vine. "Is that not what you are, you little naked shameless Papist wenches? A pair of Portugals, eh?"

They giggled, but did not answer.

"No," Phillips said. "This is India, but not the India you think you know. And these women are not Portuguese."

"Not Portuguese?" Willoughby said, baffled.

"No more so than you. I'm quite certain of that."

Willoughby stroked his beard. "I do admit I found them very odd, for Portugals. I have heard not a syllable of their Portugee speech on their lips. And it is strange also that they run naked as Adam and Eve in these baths, and allow me free plunder of their women, which is not the way of Portugals at home, God wot. But I thought me, this is India, they choose to live in another fashion here—"

"No," Phillips said. "I tell you, these are not Portuguese, nor any other people of Europe who are known to you."

"Prithee, who are they, then?"

Do it delicately, now, Phillips warned himself. Delicately.

He said, "It is not far wrong to think of them as spirits of some kind—demons, even. Or sorcerers who have magicked us out of our proper places in the world." He paused, groping for some means to share with Willoughby, in a way that Willoughby might grasp, this mystery that had enfolded them. He drew a deep breath. "They've taken us not only across the sea," he said, "but across the years as well. We have both been hauled, you and I, far into the days that are to come."

Willoughby gave him a look of blank bewilderment.

"Days that are to come? Times yet unborn, d'ye mean? Why, I comprehend none of that!"

"Try to understand. We're both castaways in the same boat, man! But there's no way we can help each other if I can't make you see—"

Shaking his head, Willoughby muttered, "In faith, good friend, I find your words the merest folly. Today is today, and tomorrow is tomorrow, and how can a man step from one to t'other until tomorrow be turned into today?"

"I have no idea," said Phillips. Struggle was apparent on Willoughby's face; but plainly he could perceive no more than the haziest outline of what Phillips was driving at, if that much. "But this I know," he went on. "That your world and all that was in it is dead and gone. And so is mine, though I was born four hundred years after you, in the time of the second Elizabeth."

Willoughby snorted scornfully. "Four hundred—"

"You must believe me!"

"Nay! Nay!"

"It's the truth. Your time is only history to me. And mine and yours are history to them—ancient history. They call us visitors, but what we are is captives." Phillips felt himself quivering in the intensity of his effort. He was aware how insane this must sound to Willoughby. It was beginning to sound insane to him. "They've stolen us out of our proper times—seizing us like gypsies in the night—"

"Fie, man! You rave with lunacy!"

Phillips shook his head. He reached out and seized Willoughby tightly by the wrist. "I beg you, listen to me!" The citizen-women were watching closely, whispering to one another behind their hands, laughing. "Ask them!" Phillips cried. "Make them tell you what century this is! The sixteenth, do you think? Ask them!"

"What century could it be, but the sixteenth of our Lord?"

"They will tell you it is the fiftieth."

Willoughby looked at him pityingly. "Man, man, what a sorry thing thou art! The fiftieth, indeed!" He laughed. "Fellow, listen to me, now there is but one Elizabeth, safe upon her throne in Westminster. This is India. The year is Anno 1591. Come, let us you and I steal a ship from these Portugals, and make our way back to England, and peradventure you may get from there to your America—"

"There is no England."

"Ah, can you say that and not be mad?"

"The cities and nations we knew are gone. These people live like magicians, Francis." There was no use holding anything back now, Phillips thought leadenly. He knew that he had lost. "They conjure up places of long ago, and build them here and there to suit their fancy, and when they are bored with them they destroy them, and start anew. There is no England. Europe is empty, featureless, void. Do you know what cities there are? There are only five in all the world. There is Alexandria of Egypt. There is Timbuctoo in Africa. There is New Chicago in America. There is a great city in China—in Cathay, I suppose you would say. And there is this place, which they call Mohenjo-daro, and which is far more ancient than Greece, than Rome, than Babylon."

Quietly Willoughby said, "Nay. This is mere absurdity. You say we are in some far tomorrow, and then you tell me we are dwelling in some city of long ago."

"A conjuration, only," Phillips said in desperation. "A likeness of that city. Which these folk have fashioned somehow for their own amusement. Just as we are here, you and I: to amuse them. Only to amuse them."

"You are completely mad."

"Come with me, then. Talk with the citizens by the great pool. Ask them what year this is; ask them about England; ask them how you come to be here." Once again Phillips grasped Willoughby's wrist. "We should be allies. If we work together, perhaps we can discover some way to get ourselves out of this place, and—"

"Let me be, fellow."

"Please—"

"Let me be!" roared Willoughby, and pulled his arm free. His eyes were stark with rage. Rising in the tank, he looked about furiously as though searching for a weapon. The citizen-women shrank back away from him, though at the same time they seemed captivated by the big man's fierce outburst. "Go to, get you to Bedlam! Let me be, madman! Let me be!"

DISMALLY PHILLIPS ROAMED THE DUSTY unpaved streets of Mohenjo-daro alone for hours. His failure with Willoughby had left him bleak-spirited and somber: he had hoped to stand back to back with the Elizabethan against the citizens, but he saw now that that was not to be. He had bungled things; or, more likely, it had been impossible ever to bring Willoughby to see the truth of their predicament.

In the stifling heat he went at random through the confusing congested lanes of flat-roofed windowless houses and blank featureless walls until he emerged into a broad marketplace. The life of the city swirled madly around him: the pseudo-life, rather, the intricate interactions of the thousands of temporaries who were nothing more than windup dolls set in motion to provide the illusion that pre-Vedic India was still a going concern. Here vendors sold beautiful little carved stone seals portraying tigers and monkeys and strange humped cattle, and women bargained vociferously with craftsmen for ornaments of ivory, gold, copper, and bronze. Weary-looking women squatted behind immense mounds of newly made pottery, pinkish red with black designs. No one paid any attention to him. He was the outsider here, neither citizen nor temporary. They belonged.

He went on, passing the huge granaries where workmen ceaselessly unloaded carts of wheat and others pounded grain on great circular brick platforms. He drifted into a public restaurant thronging with joyless silent people standing elbow to elbow at small brick counters, and was given a flat round piece of bread, a sort of tortilla or chapatti, in which was stuffed some spiced mincemeat that stung his lips like fire. Then he moved onward down a wide shallow timbered staircase into the lower part of the city, where the peasantry lived in cell-like rooms packed together as though in hives.

It was an oppressive city, but not a squalid one. The intensity of the concern with sanitation amazed him: wells and fountains and public privies everywhere, and brick drains running from each building, leading to covered cesspools. There was none of the open sewage and pestilent gutters that he knew still could be found in the India of his own time. He wondered whether ancient Mohenjo-daro had in truth been so fastidious. Perhaps the citizens had redesigned the city to suit their own ideals of cleanliness. No: most likely what he saw was authentic, he decided, a function of the same obsessive discipline that had given the city its rigidity of form. If Mohenjo-daro had been a verminous filthy hole, the citizens probably would have re-created it in just that way, and loved it for its fascinating reeking filth.

Not that he had ever noticed an excessive concern with authenticity on the part of the citizens; and Mohenjo-daro, like all the other restored cities he had visited, was full of the usual casual anachronisms. Phillips saw images of Shiva and Krishna here and there on the walls of buildings he took to be temples, and the benign face of the mother-goddess Kali loomed in the plazas. Surely those deities had arisen in India long after the collapse of the Mohenjo-daro civilization. Were the citizens indifferent to such matters of chronology? Or did they take a certain naughty pleasure in mixing the eras—a mosque and a church in Greek Alexandria, Hindu gods in prehistoric Mohenjo-daro? Perhaps their records of the past had become contaminated with errors over the thousands of years. He would not have been surprised to see banners bearing portraits of Gandhi and Nehru being carried in procession through the streets. And there were phantasms and chimeras at large here again, too, as if the citizens were untroubled by the boundary between history and myth: little fat elephant-headed Ganeshas blithely plunging their trunks into water fountains, a six-armed three-headed woman sunning herself on a brick terrace. Why not? Surely that was the motto of these people: Why not, why not, why not? They could do as they pleased, and they did. Yet Gioia had said to him, long ago, "Limits are very important." In what, Phillips wondered, did they limit themselves, other than the number of their cities? Was there a quota, perhaps, on the number of "visitors" they allowed themselves to kidnap from the past? Until today he had thought he was the only one; now he knew there was at least one other; possibly there were more elsewhere, a step or two ahead or behind him, making the circuit with the citizens who traveled endlessly from New Chicago to Chang-an to Alexandria. We should join forces, he thought, and compel them to send us back to our rightful eras. Compel? How? File a class-action suit, maybe? Demonstrate in the streets? Sadly he thought of his failure to make common cause with Willoughby. We are natural allies, he thought. Together perhaps we might have won some compassion from these people. But to Willoughby it must be literally unthinkable that Good Queen Bess and her subjects were sealed away on the far side of a barrier hundreds of centuries thick. He would prefer to believe that England was just a few months' voyage away around the Cape of Good Hope, and that all he need do was commandeer a ship and set sail for home. Poor Willoughby: probably he would never see his home again.

The thought came to Phillips suddenly:

Neither will you.

And then, after it:

If you could go home, would you really want to?

One of the first things he had realized here was that he knew almost nothing substantial about his former existence. His mind was well stocked with details on life in twentieth-century New York, to be sure; but of himself he could say not much more than that he was Charles Phillips and had come from 1984. Profession? Age? Parents' names? Did he have a wife? Children? A cat, a dog, hobbies? No data: none. Possibly the citizens had stripped such things from him when they brought him here, to spare him from the pain of separation. They might be capable of that kindness. Knowing so little of what he had lost, could he truly say that he yearned for it? Willoughby seemed to remember much more of his former life, somehow, and longed for it all the more intensely. He was spared that. Why not stay here, and go on and on from city to city, sightseeing all of time past as the citizens conjured it back into being? Why not? Why not? The chances were that he had no choice about it, anyway.

He made his way back up toward the citadel and to the baths once more. He felt a little like a ghost, haunting a city of ghosts.

Belilala seemed unaware that he had been gone for most of the day. She sat by herself on the terrace of the baths, placidly sipping some thick milky beverage that had been sprinkled with a dark spice. He shook his head when she offered him some.

"Do you remember I mentioned that I saw a man with red hair and a beard this morning?" Phillips said. "He's a visitor. Hawk told me that."

"Is he?" Belilala asked.

"From a time about four hundred years before mine. I talked with him. He thinks he was brought here by demons." Phillips gave her a searching look. "I'm a visitor, too, isn't that so?"

"Of course, love."

"And how was I brought here? By demons also?"

Belilala smiled indifferently. "You'd have to ask someone else. Hawk, perhaps. I haven't looked into these things very deeply."

"I see. Are there many visitors here, do you know?"

A languid shrug. "Not many, no, not really. I've only heard of three or four besides you. There may be others by now, I suppose." She rested her hand lightly on his. "Are you having a good time in Mohenjo, Charles?"

He let her question pass as though he had not heard it.

"I asked Hawk about Gioia," he said.

"Oh?"

"He told me that she's no longer here, that she's gone on to Timbuctoo or New Chicago, he wasn't sure which."

"That's quite likely. As everybody knows, Gioia rarely stays in the same place very long."

Phillips nodded. "You said the other day that Gioia is a short-timer. That means she's going to grow old and die, doesn't it?"

"I thought you understood that, Charles."

"Whereas you will not age? Nor Hawk, nor Stengard, nor any of the rest of your set?"

"We will live as long as we wish," she said. "But we will not age, no."

"What makes a person a short-timer?"

"They're born that way, I think. Some missing gene, some extra gene—I don't actually know. It's extremely uncommon. Nothing can be done to help them. It's very slow, the aging. But it can't be halted."

Phillips nodded. “That must be very disagreeable,” he said. “To find yourself one of the few people growing old in a world where everyone stays young. No wonder Gioia is so impatient. No wonder she runs around from place to place. No wonder she attached herself so quickly to the barbaric hairy visitor from the twentieth century, who comes from a time when everybody was a short-timer. She and I have something in common, wouldn’t you say?”

“In a manner of speaking, yes.”

“We understand aging. We understand death. Tell me: is Gioia likely to die very soon, Belilala?”

“Soon? Soon?” She gave him a wide-eyed childlike stare. “What is soon? How can I say? What you think of as soon and what I think of as soon are not the same things, Charles.” Then her manner changed: she seemed to be hearing what he was saying for the first time. Softly she said, “No, no, Charles. I don’t think she will die very soon.”

“When she left me in Chang-an, was it because she had become bored with me?”

Belilala shook her head. “She was simply restless. It had nothing to do with you. She was never bored with you.”

“Then I’m going to go looking for her. Wherever she may be, Timbuctoo, New Chicago, I’ll find her. Gioia and I belong together.”

“Perhaps you do,” said Belilala. “Yes. Yes, I think you really do.” She sounded altogether unperturbed, unrejected, unbereft. “By all means, Charles. Go to her. Follow her. Find her. Wherever she may be.”

THEY HAD ALREADY BEGUN DISMANTLING Timbuctoo when Phillips got there. While he was still high overhead, his flitterflitter hovering above the dusty tawny plain where the River Niger met the sands of the Sahara, a surge of keen excitement rose in him as he looked down at the square gray flat-roofed mud brick buildings of the great desert capital. But when he landed he found gleaming metal-skinned robots swarming everywhere, a horde of them scuttling about like giant shining insects, pulling the place apart.

He had not known about the robots before. So that was how all these miracles were carried out, Phillips realized: an army of obliging machines. He imagined them bustling up out of the earth whenever their services were needed, emerging from some sterile subterranean storehouse to put together Venice or Thebes or Knossos or Houston or whatever place was required, down to the finest detail, and then at some later time returning to undo everything that they had fashioned. He watched them now, diligently pulling down the adobe walls, demolishing the heavy metal-studded gates, bulldozing the amazing labyrinth of alleyways and thoroughfares, sweeping away the market. On his last visit to Timbuctoo that market had been crowded with a horde of veiled Tuaregs and swaggering Moors, black Sudanese, shrewd-faced Syrian traders, all of them busily dickering for camels, horses, donkeys, slabs of salt, huge green melons, silver bracelets, splendid vellum Korans. They were all gone now, that picturesque crowd of swarthy temporaries. Nor were there any citizens to be seen. The dust of destruction choked the air. One of the robots came up to Phillips and said in a dry crackling insect-voice, "You ought not to be here. This city is closed."

He stared at the flashing, buzzing band of scanners and sensors across the creature's glittering tapered snout. "I'm trying to find someone, a citizen who may have been here recently. Her name is—"

"This city is closed," the robot repeated inexorably.

They would not let him stay as much as an hour. There is no food here, the robot said, no water, no shelter. This is not a place any longer. You may not stay. You may not stay. You may not stay.

This is not a place any longer.

Perhaps he could find her in New Chicago, then. He took to the air again, soaring northward and westward over the vast emptiness. The land below him curved away into the hazy horizon, bare, sterile. What had they done with the vestiges of the world that had gone before? Had they turned their gleaming metal beetles loose to clean everything away? Were there no ruins of genuine antiquity anywhere? No scrap of Rome, no shard of Jerusalem, no stump of Fifth Avenue? It was all so barren down there: an empty stage, waiting for its next set to be built. He flew on a great arc across the jutting hump of Africa and on into what he supposed was southern Europe: the little vehicle did all the work, leaving him to doze or stare as he wished. Now and again he saw another flitterflitter pass by, far away, a dark distant winged teardrop outlined against the hard clarity of the sky. He wished there was some way of making radio contact with them, but he had no idea how to go about it. Not that he had anything he wanted to say; he wanted only to hear a human voice. He was utterly isolated. He might just as well have been the last living man on Earth. He closed his eyes and thought of Gioia.

"Like this?" Phillips asked. In an ivory-paneled oval room sixty stories above the softly glowing streets of New Chicago he touched a small cool plastic canister to his upper lip and pressed the stud at its base. He heard a foaming sound; and then blue vapor rose to his nostrils.

"Yes," Cantilena said. "That's right."

He detected a faint aroma of cinnamon, cloves, and something that might almost have been broiled lobster. Then a spasm of dizziness hit him and visions rushed through his head: Gothic cathedrals, the Pyramids, Central Park under fresh snow, the harsh brick warrens of Mohenjo-daro, and fifty thousand other places all at once, a wild roller-coaster ride through space and time. It seemed to go on for centuries. But finally his head cleared and he looked about, blinking, realizing that the whole thing had taken only a moment. Cantilena still stood at his elbow. The other citizens in the room—fifteen, twenty of them—had scarcely moved. The strange little man with the celadon skin over by the far wall continued to stare at him.

"Well?" Cantilena asked. "What did you think?"

"Incredible."

"And very authentic. It's an actual New Chicagoan drug. The exact formula. Would you like another?"

"Not just yet," Phillips said uneasily. He swayed and had to struggle for his balance. Sniffing that stuff might not have been such a wise idea, he thought.

He had been in New Chicago a week, or perhaps it was two, and he was still suffering from the peculiar disorientation that that city always aroused in him. This was the fourth time that he had come here, and it had been the same every time. New Chicago was the only one of the reconstructed cities of this world that in its original incarnation had existed after his own era. To him it was an outpost of the incomprehensible future; to the citizens it was a quaint simulacrum of the archaeological past. That paradox left him aswirl with impossible confusions and tensions.

What had happened to old Chicago was of course impossible for him to discover. Vanished without a trace, that was clear: no Water Tower, no Marina City, no Hancock Center, no Tribune building, not a fragment, not an atom. But it was hopeless to ask any of the million-plus inhabitants of New Chicago about their city's predecessor. They were only temporaries; they knew no more than they had to know, and all that they had to know was how to go through the motions of whatever it was that they did by way of creating the illusion that this was a real city. They had no need of knowing ancient history.

Nor was he likely to find out anything from a citizen, of course. Citizens did not seem to bother much about scholarly matters. Phillips had no reason to think that the world was anything other than an amusement park to them. Somewhere, certainly, there had to be those who specialized in the serious study of the lost civilizations of the past—for how, otherwise, would these uncanny reconstructed cities be brought into being? "The planners," he had once heard Nissandra or Aramayne say, "are already deep into their Byzantium research." But who were the planners? He had no idea. For all he knew, they were the robots. Perhaps the robots were the real masters of this whole era, who created the cities not primarily for the sake of amusing the citizens but in their own diligent attempt to comprehend the life of the world that had passed away. A wild speculation, yes; but not without some plausibility, he thought.

He felt oppressed by the party gaiety all about him. "I need some air," he said to Cantilena, and headed toward the window. It was the merest crescent, but a breeze came through. He looked out at the strange city below.

New Chicago had nothing in common with the old one but its name. They had built it, at least, along the western shore of a large inland lake that might even be Lake Michigan, although when he had flown over it had seemed broader and less elongated than the lake he remembered. The city itself was a lacy fantasy of slender pastel-hued buildings rising at odd angles and linked by a webwork of gently undulating aerial bridges. The streets were long parentheses that touched the lake at their northern and southern ends and arched gracefully westward in the middle. Between each of the great boulevards ran a track for public transportation—sleek aquamarine bubble-vehicles gliding on soundless wheels—and flanking each of the tracks were lush strips of park. It was beautiful, astonishingly so, but insubstantial. The whole thing seemed to have been contrived from sunbeams and silk.

A soft voice beside him said, "Are you becoming ill?"

Phillips glanced around. The celadon man stood beside him: a compact, precise person, vaguely Oriental in appearance. His skin was of a curious gray-green hue like no skin Phillips had ever seen, and it was extraordinarily smooth in texture, as though he were made of fine porcelain.

He shook his head. "Just a little queasy," he said. "This city always scrambles me."

"I suppose it can be disconcerting," the little man replied. His tone was furry and veiled, the inflection strange. There was something feline about him. He seemed sinewy, unyielding, almost menacing. "Visitor, are you?"

Phillips studied him a moment. "Yes," he said.

"So am I, of course."

"Are you?"

"Indeed." The little man smiled. "What's your locus? Twentieth century? Twenty-first at the latest, I'd say."

"I'm from 1984. AD 1984."

Another smile, a self-satisfied one. "Not a bad guess, then." A brisk tilt of the head. "Y'ang-Yeovil."

"Pardon me?" Phillips said.

"Y'ang-Yeovil. It is my name. Formerly Colonel Y'ang-Yeovil of the Third Septentriad."

"Is that on some other planet?" asked Phillips, feeling a bit dazed.

"Oh, no, not at all," Y'ang-Yeovil said pleasantly. "This very world, I assure you. I am quite of human origin. Citizen of the Republic of Upper Han, native of the city of Port Ssu. And you—forgive me—your name—?"

"I'm sorry. Phillips. Charles Phillips. From New York City, once upon a time."

"Ah, New York!" Y'ang-Yeovil's face lit with a glimmer of recognition that quickly faded. "New York—New York—it was very famous, that I know—"

This is very strange, Phillips thought. He felt greater compassion for poor bewildered Francis Willoughby now. This man comes from a time so far beyond my own that he barely knows of New York—he must be a contemporary of the real New Chicago, in fact; I wonder whether he finds this version authentic—and yet to the citizens this Y'ang-Yeovil too is just a primitive, a curio out of antiquity—

"New York was the largest city of the United States of America," Phillips said.

"Of course. Yes. Very famous."

"But virtually forgotten by the time the Republic of Upper Han came into existence, I gather."

Y'ang-Yeovil said, looking uncomfortable, "There were disturbances between your time and mine. But by no means should you take from my words the impression that your city was—"

Sudden laughter resounded across the room. Five or six newcomers had arrived at the party. Phillips stared, gasped, gaped. Surely that was Stengard—and Aramayne beside him—and that other woman, half hidden behind them—

"If you'll pardon me a moment—" Phillips said, turning abruptly away from Y'ang-Yeovil. "Please excuse me. Someone just coming in—a person I've been trying to find ever since—"

He hurried toward her.

"Gioia?" he called. "Gioia, it's me! Wait! Wait!"

Stengard was in the way. Aramayne, turning to take a handful of the little vapor-sniffers from Cantilena, blocked him also. Phillips pushed through them as though they were not there. Gioia, halfway out the door, halted and looked toward him like a frightened deer.

"Don't go," he said. He took her hand in his.

He was startled by her appearance. How long had it been since their strange parting on that night of mysteries in Chang-an? A year? A year and a half? So he believed. Or had he lost all track of time? Were his perceptions of the passing of the months in this world that unreliable? She seemed at least ten or fifteen years older. Maybe she really was; maybe the years had been passing for him here as in a dream, and he had never known it. She looked strained, faded, worn. Out of a thinner and strangely altered face her eyes blazed at him almost defiantly, as though saying, See? See how ugly I have become?

He said, "I've been hunting for you for—I don't know how long it's been, Gioia. In Mohenjo, in Timbuctoo, now here. I want to be with you again."

"It isn't possible."

"Belilala explained everything to me in Mohenjo. I know that you're a short-timer—I know what that means, Gioia. But what of it? So you're beginning to age a little. So what? So you'll only have three or four hundred years, instead of forever. Don't you think I know what it means to be a short-timer? I'm just a simple ancient man of the twentieth century, remember? Sixty, seventy, eighty years is all we would get. You and I suffer from the same malady, Gioia. That's what drew you to me in the first place. I'm certain of that. That's why we belong with each other now. However much time we have, we can spend the rest of it together, don't you see?"

"You're the one who doesn't see, Charles," she said softly.

"Maybe. Maybe I still don't understand a damned thing about this place. Except that you and I—that I love you—that I think you love me—"

"I love you, yes. But you don't understand. It's precisely because I love you that you and I—you and I can't—"

With a despairing sigh she slid her hand free of his grasp. He reached for her again, but she shook him off and backed up quickly into the corridor.

"Gioia?"

"Please," she said. "No. I would never have come here if I knew you were here. Don't come after me. Please. Please."

She turned and fled.

He stood looking after her for a long moment. Cantilena and Aramayne appeared, and smiled at him as if nothing at all had happened. Cantilena offered him a vial of some sparkling amber fluid. He refused with a brusque gesture. Where do I go now? he wondered. What do I do? He wandered back into the party.

Y'ang-Yeovil glided to his side. "You are in great distress," the little man murmured.

Phillips glared. "Let me be."

"Perhaps I could be of some help."

"There's no help possible," said Phillips. He swung about and plucked one of the vials from a tray and gulped its contents. It made him feel as if there were two of him, standing on either side of Y'ang-Yeovil. He gulped another. Now there were four of him. "I'm in love with a citizen," he blurted. It seemed to him that he was speaking in chorus.

"Love. Ah. And does she love you?"

"So I thought. So I think. But she's a short-timer. Do you know what that means? She's not immortal like the others. She ages. She's beginning to look old. And so she's been running away from me. She doesn't want me to see her changing. She thinks it'll disgust me, I suppose. I tried to remind her just now that I'm not immortal either, that she and I could grow old together, but she—"

"Oh, no," Y'ang-Yeovil said quietly. "Why do you think you will age? Have you grown any older in all the time you have been here?"

Phillips was nonplussed. "Of course I have. I—I—"

"Have you?" Y'ang-Yeovil smiled. "Here. Look at yourself." He did something intricate with his fingers and a shimmering zone of mirror-like light appeared between them. Phillips stared at his reflection. A youthful face stared back at him. It was true, then. He had simply not thought about it. How many years had he spent in this world? The time had simply slipped by: a great deal of time, though he could not calculate how much. They did not seem to keep close count of it here, nor had he. But it must have been many years, he thought. All that endless travel up and down the globe—so many cities had come and gone—Rio, Rome, Asgard, those were the first three that came to mind—and there were others; he could hardly remember every one. Years. His face had not changed at all. Time had worked its harshness on Gioia, yes, but not on him.

"I don't understand," he said. "Why am I not aging?"

"Because you are not real," said Y'ang-Yeovil. "Are you unaware of that?"

Phillips blinked. "Not—real?"

"Did you think you were lifted bodily out of your own time?" the little man asked. "Ah, no, no, there is no way for them to do such a thing. We are not actual time travelers: not you, not I, not any of the visitors. I thought you were aware of that. But perhaps your era is too early for a proper understanding of these things. We are very cleverly done, my friend. We are ingenious constructs, marvelously stuffed with the thoughts and attitudes and events of our own times. We are their finest achievement, you know: far more complex even than one of these cities. We are a step beyond the temporaries—more than a step, a great deal more. They do only what they are instructed to do, and their range is very narrow. They are nothing but machines, really. Whereas we are autonomous. We move about by our own will; we think, we talk, we even, so it seems, fall in love. But we will not age. How could we age? We are not real. We are mere artificial webworks of mental responses. We are mere illusions, done so well that we deceive even ourselves. You did not know that? Indeed, you did not know?"

He was airborne, touching destination buttons at random. Somehow he found himself heading back toward Timbuctoo. This city is closed. This is not a place any longer. It did not matter to him. Why should anything matter?

Fury and a choking sense of despair rose within him. I am software, Phillips thought. I am nothing but software.

Not real. Very cleverly done. An ingenious construct. A mere illusion.

No trace of Timbuctoo was visible from the air. He landed anyway. The gray sandy earth was smooth, unturned, as though there had never been anything there. A few robots were still about, handling whatever final chores were required in the shutting-down of a city. Two of them scuttled up to him. Huge bland gleaming silver-skinned insects, not friendly.

"There is no city here," they said. "This is not a permissible place."

"Permissible by whom?"

"There is no reason for you to be here."

"There's no reason for me to be anywhere," Phillips said. The robots stirred, made uneasy humming sounds and ominous clicks, waved their antennae about. They seemed troubled, he thought. They seem to dislike my attitude. Perhaps I run some risk of being taken off to the home for unruly software for debugging. "I'm leaving now," he told them. "Thank you. Thank you very much." He backed away from them and climbed into his flitterflitter. He touched more destination buttons.

We move about by our own will. We think, we talk, we even fall in love.

He landed in Chang-an. This time there was no reception committee waiting for him at the Gate of Brilliant Virtue. The city seemed larger and more resplendent: new pagodas, new palaces. It felt like winter: a chilly cutting wind was blowing. The sky was cloudless and dazzlingly bright. At the steps of the Silver Terrace he encountered Francis Willoughby, a great hulking figure in magnificent brocaded robes, with two dainty little temporaries, pretty as jade statuettes, engulfed in his arms. "Miracles and wonders! The silly lunatic fellow is here, too!" Willoughby roared. "Look, look, we are come to far Cathay, you and I!"

We are nowhere, Phillips thought. We are mere illusions, done so well that we deceive even ourselves.

To Willoughby he said, "You look like an emperor in those robes, Francis."

"Aye, like Prester John!" Willoughby cried. "Like Tamburlaine himself! Aye, am I not majestic?" He slapped Phillips gaily on the shoulder, a rough playful poke that spun him halfway about, coughing and wheezing. "We flew in the air, as the eagles do, as the demons do, as the angels do! Soared like angels! Like angels!" He came close, looming over Phillips. "I would have gone to England, but the wench Belilala said there was an enchantment on me that would keep me from England just now; and so we voyaged to Cathay. Tell me this, fellow, will you go witness for me when we see England again? Swear that all that has befallen us did in truth befall? For I fear they will say I am as mad as Marco Polo, when I tell them of flying to Cathay."

"One madman backing another?" Phillips asked. "What can I tell you? You still think you'll reach England, do you?" Rage rose to the surface in him, bubbling hot. "Ah, Francis, Francis, do you know your Shakespeare? Did you go to the plays? We aren't real. We aren't real. We are such stuff as dreams are made on, the two of us. That's all we are. O brave new world! What England? Where? There's no England. There's no Francis Willoughby. There's no Charles Phillips. What we are is—"

"Let him be, Charles," a cool voice cut in.

He turned. Belilala, in the robes of an empress, coming down the steps of the Silver Terrace.

"I know the truth," he said bitterly. "Y'ang-Yeovil told me. The visitor from the twenty-fifth century. I saw him in New Chicago."

"Did you see Gioia there, too?" Belilala asked.

"Briefly. She looks much older."

"Yes. I know. She was here recently."

"And has gone on, I suppose?"

"To Mohenjo again, yes. Go after her, Charles. Leave poor Francis alone. I told her to wait for you. I told her that she needs you, and you need her."

"Very kind of you. But what good is it, Belilala? I don't even exist. And she's going to die."

"You exist. How can you doubt that you exist? You feel, don't you? You suffer. You love. You love Gioia: is that not so? And you are loved by Gioia. Would Gioia love what is not real?"

"You think she loves me?"

"I know she does. Go to her, Charles. Go. I told her to wait for you in Mohenjo."

Phillips nodded numbly. What was there to lose?

"Go to her," said Belilala again. "Now"

"Yes," Phillips said. "I'll go now." He turned to Willoughby. "If ever we meet in London, friend, I'll testify for you. Fear nothing. All will be well, Francis."

He left them and set his course for Mohenjo-daro, half expecting to find the robots already tearing it down. Mohenjo-daro was still there, no lovelier than before. He went to the baths, thinking he might find Gioia there. She was not; but he came upon Nissandra, Stengard, Fenimon. "She has gone to Alexandria," Fenimon told him. "She wants to see it one last time, before they close it."

"They're almost ready to open Constantinople," Stengard explained. "The capital of Byzantium, you know, the great city by the Golden Horn. They'll take Alexandria away, you understand, when Byzantium opens. They say it's going to be marvelous. We'll see you there for the opening, naturally?"

"Naturally," Phillips said.

He flew to Alexandria. He felt lost and weary. All this is hopeless folly, he told himself. I am nothing but a puppet jerking about on its strings. But somewhere above the shining breast of the Arabian Sea the deeper implications of something that Belilala had said to him started to sink in, and he felt his bitterness, his rage, his despair, all suddenly beginning to leave him. You exist. How can you doubt that you exist? Would Gioia love what is not real? Of course. Of course. Y'ang-Yeovil had been wrong: visitors were something more than mere illusions. Indeed, Y'ang-Yeovil had voiced the truth of their condition without understanding what he was really saying: We think, we talk, we fall in love. Yes. That was the heart of the situation. The visitors might be artificial, but they were not unreal. Belilala had been trying to tell him that just the other night. You suffer. You love. You love Gioia. Would Gioia love what is not real? Surely he was real, or at any rate real enough. What he was was something strange, something that would probably have been all but incomprehensible to the twentieth-century people whom he had been designed to simulate. But that did not mean that he was unreal. Did one have to be of woman born to be real? No. No. No. His kind of reality was a sufficient reality. He had no need to be ashamed of it. And, understanding that, he understood that Gioia did not need to grow old and die. There was a way by which she could be saved, if only she would embrace it. If only she would.

When he landed in Alexandria he went immediately to the hotel on the slopes of the Paneium where they had stayed on their first visit, so very long ago; and there she was, sitting quietly on a patio with a view of the harbor and the Lighthouse. There was something calm and resigned about the way she sat. She had given up. She did not even have the strength to flee from him any longer.

"Gioia," he said gently.

She looked older than she had in New Chicago. Her face was drawn and sallow and her eyes seemed sunken; and she was not even bothering these days to deal with the white strands that stood out in stark contrast against the darkness of her hair. He sat down beside her and put his hand over hers and looked out toward the obelisks, the palaces, the temples, the Lighthouse. At length he said, "I know what I really am now."

"Do you, Charles?" She sounded very far away.

"In my age we called it software. All I am is a set of commands, responses, cross-references, operating some sort of artificial body. It's infinitely better software then we could have imagined. But we were only just beginning to learn how, after all. They pumped me full of twentieth-century reflexes. The right moods, the right appetites, the right irrationalities, the right sort of combativeness. Somebody knows a lot about what it was like to be a twentieth-century man. They did a good job with Willoughby, too, all that Elizabethan rhetoric and swagger. And I suppose they got Y'ang-Yeovil right. He seems to think so: who better to judge? The twenty-fifth century, the Republic of Upper Han, people with gray-green skin, half Chinese and half Martian for all I know. Somebody knows. Somebody here is very good at programming, Gioia."

She was not looking at him.

"I feel frightened, Charles," she said in that same distant way.

"Of me? Of the things I'm saying?"

"No, not of you. Don't you see what has happened to me?"

"I see you. There are changes."

"I lived a long time wondering when the changes would begin. I thought maybe they wouldn't, not really. Who wants to believe they'll get old? But it started when we were in Alexandria that first time. In Chang-an it got much worse. And now—now—"

He said abruptly, "Stengard tells me they'll be opening Constantinople very soon."

"So?"

"Don't you want to be there when it opens?"

"I'm becoming old and ugly, Charles."

"We'll go to Constantinople together. We'll leave tomorrow, eh? What do you say? We'll charter a boat. It's a quick little hop, right across the Mediterranean. Sailing to Byzantium! There was a poem, you know, in my time. Not forgotten, I guess, because they've programmed it into me. All these thousands of years, and someone still remembers old Yeats. The young in one another's arms, birds in the trees. Come with me to Byzantium, Gioia."

She shrugged. "Looking like this? Getting more hideous every hour? While they stay young forever? While you—" She faltered; her voice cracked; she fell silent.

"Finish the sentence, Gioia."

"Please. Let me alone."

"You were going to say, 'While you stay young forever, too, Charles,' isn't that it? You knew all along that I was never going to change. I didn't know that, but you did."

"Yes. I knew. I pretended that it wasn't true—that as I aged, you'd age, too. It was very foolish of me. In Chang-an, when I first began to see the real signs of it—that was when I realized I couldn't stay with you any longer. Because I'd look at you, always young, always remaining the same age, and I'd look at myself, and—" She gestured, palms upward. "So I gave you to Belilala and ran away."

"All so unnecessary, Gioia."

"I didn't think it was."

"But you don't have to grow old. Not if you don't want to!"

"Don't be cruel, Charles," she said tonelessly. "There's no way of escaping what I have."

"But there is," he said.

"You know nothing about these things."

"Not very much, no," he said. "But I see how it can be done. Maybe it's a primitive simpleminded twentieth-century sort of solution, but I think it ought to work. I've been playing with the idea ever since I left Mohenjo. Tell me this, Gioia: Why can't you go to them, to the programmers, to the artificers, the planners, whoever they are, the ones who create the cities and the temporaries and the visitors. And have yourself made into something like me!"

She looked up, startled. "What are you saying?"

"They can cobble up a twentieth-century man out of nothing more than fragmentary records and make him plausible, can't they? Or an Elizabethan, or anyone else of any era at all, and he's authentic, he's convincing. So why couldn't they do an even better job with you? Produce a Gioia so real that even Gioia can't tell the difference? But a Gioia that will never age—a Gioia-construct, a Gioia-program, a visitor-Gioia! Why not? Tell me why not, Gioia."

She was trembling. "I've never heard of doing any such thing!"

"But don't you think it's possible?"

"How would I know?"

"Of course it's possible. If they can create visitors, they can take a citizen and duplicate her in such a way that—"

"It's never been done. I'm sure of it. I can't imagine any citizen agreeing to any such thing. To give up the body—to let yourself be turned into—into—"

She shook her head, but it seemed to be a gesture of astonishment as much as of negation.

He said, "Sure. To give up the body. Your natural body, your aging, shrinking, deteriorating short-timer body. What's so awful about that?"

She was very pale. "This is craziness, Charles. I don't want to talk about it anymore."

"It doesn't sound crazy to me."

"You can't possibly understand."

"Can't I? I can certainly understand being afraid to die. I don't have a lot of trouble understanding what it's like to be one of the few aging people in a world where nobody grows old. What I can't understand is why you aren't even willing to consider the possibility that—"

"No," she said. "I tell you, it's crazy. They'd laugh at me."

"Who?"

"All of my friends. Hawk, Stengard, Aramayne—" Once again she would not look at him. "They can be very cruel, without even realizing it. They despise anything that seems ungraceful to them, anything sweaty and desperate and cowardly. Citizens don't do sweaty things, Charles. And that's how this will seem. Assuming it can be done at all. They'll be terribly patronizing. Oh, they'll be sweet to me, yes, dear Gioia, how wonderful for you, Gioia, but when I turn my back they'll laugh. They'll say the most wicked things about me. I couldn't bear that."

"They can afford to laugh," Phillips said. "It's easy to be brave and cool about dying when you know you're going to live forever. How very fine for them: but why should you be the only one to grow old and die? And they won't laugh, anyway. They're not as cruel as you think. Shallow, maybe, but not cruel. They'll be glad that you've found a way to save yourself. At the very least, they won't have to feel guilty about you any longer, and that's bound to please them. You can—"

"Stop it," she said.

She rose, walked to the railing of the patio, stared out toward the sea. He came up behind her. Red sails in the harbor, sunlight glittering along the sides of the Lighthouse, the palaces of the Ptolemies stark white against the sky. Lightly he rested his hand on her shoulder. She twitched as if to pull away from him, but remained where she was.

"Then I have another idea," he said quietly. "If you won't go to the planners, I will. Reprogram me, I'll say. Fix things so that I start to age at the same rate you do. It'll be more authentic, anyway, if I'm supposed to be playing the part of a twentieth-century man. Over the years I'll very gradually get some lines in my face, my hair will turn gray, I'll walk a little more slowly—we'll grow old together, Gioia. To hell with your lovely immortal friends. We'll have each other. We won't need them."

She swung around. Her eyes were wide with horror.

"Are you serious, Charles?"

"Of course."

"No," she murmured. "No. Everything you've said to me today is monstrous nonsense. Don't you realize that?"

He reached for her hand and enclosed her fingertips in his. "All I'm trying to do is find some way for you and me to—"

"Don't say any more," she said. "Please." Quickly, as though drawing back from a suddenly flaring flame, she tugged her fingers free of his and put her hand behind her. Though his face was just inches from hers he felt an immense chasm opening between them. They stared at one another for a moment; then she moved deftly to his left, darted around him, and ran from the patio.

Stunned, he watched her go, down the long marble corridor and out of sight. It was folly to give pursuit, he thought. She was lost to him: that was clear, that was beyond any question. She was terrified of him. Why cause her even more anguish? But somehow he found himself running through the halls of the hotel, along the winding garden path, into the cool green groves of the Paneium. He thought he saw her on the portico of Hadrian's palace, but when he got there the echoing stone halls were empty. To a temporary that was sweeping the steps he said, "Did you see a woman come this way?" A blank sullen stare was his only answer.

Phillips cursed and turned away.

"Gioia?" he called. "Wait! Come back!"

Was that her, going into the Library? He rushed past the startled mumbling librarians and sped through the stacks, peering beyond the mounds of double-handled scrolls into the shadowy corridors. "Gioia? Gioia!" It was a desecration, bellowing like that in this quiet place. He scarcely cared.

Emerging by a side door, he loped down to the harbor. The Lighthouse! Terror enfolded him. She might already be a hundred steps up that ramp, heading for the parapet from which she meant to fling herself into the sea. Scattering citizens and temporaries as if they were straws, he ran within. Up he went, never pausing for breath, though his synthetic lungs were screaming for respite, his ingeniously designed heart was desperately pounding. On the first balcony he imagined he caught a glimpse of her, but he circled it without finding her. Onward, upward. He went to the top, to the beacon chamber itself: no Gioia. Had she jumped? Had she gone down one ramp while he was ascending the other? He clung to the rim and looked out, down, searching the base of the Lighthouse, the rocks offshore, the causeway. No Gioia. I will find her somewhere, he thought. I will keep going until I find her. He went running down the ramp, calling her name. He reached ground level and sprinted back toward the center of town. Where next? The temple of Poseidon? The tomb of Cleopatra?

He paused in the middle of Canopus Street, groggy and dazed.

"Charles?" she said.

"Where are you?"

"Right here. Beside you." She seemed to materialize from the air. Her face was unflushed, her robe bore no trace of perspiration. Had he been chasing a phantom through the city? She came to him and took his hand, and said, softly, tenderly, "Were you really serious, about having them make you age?"

"If there's no other way, yes."

"The other way is so frightening, Charles."

"Is it?"

"You can't understand how much."

"More frightening than growing old? Than dying?"

"I don't know," she said. "I suppose not. The only thing I'm sure of is that I don't want you to get old, Charles."

"But I won't have to. Will I?"

He stared at her.

"No," she said. "You won't have to. Neither of us will."

Phillips smiled. "We should get away from here," he said after a while. "Let's go across to Byzantium, yes, Gioia? We'll show up in Constantinople for the opening. Your friends will be there. We'll tell them what you've decided to do. They'll know how to arrange it. Someone will."

"It sounds so strange," said Gioia. "To turn myself into—into a visitor? A visitor in my own world?"

"That's what you've always been, though."

"I suppose. In a way. But at least I've been real up to now."

"Whereas I'm not?"

"Are you, Charles?"

"Yes. Just as real as you. I was angry at first, when I found out the truth about myself. But I came to accept it. Somewhere between Mohenjo and here, I came to see that it was all right to be what I am: that I perceive things, I form ideas, I draw conclusions. I am very well designed, Gioia. I can't tell the difference between being what I am and being completely alive, and to me that's being real enough. I think, I feel, I experience joy and pain. I'm as real as I need to be. And you will be, too. You'll never stop being Gioia, you know. It's only your body that you'll cast away, the body that played such a terrible joke on you anyway." He brushed her cheek with his hand. "It was all said for us before, long ago:"

> Once out of nature I shall never take
> My bodily form from any natural thing,
> But such a form as Grecian goldsmiths make
> Of hammered gold and gold enamelling
> To keep a drowsy Emperor awake—

"Is that the same poem?" she asked.

"The same poem, yes. The ancient poem that isn't quite forgotten yet."

"Finish it, Charles."

> —Or set upon a golden bough to sing
> To lords and ladies of Byzantium
> Of what is past, or passing, or to come.

"How beautiful. What does it mean?"

"That it isn't necessary to be mortal. That we can allow ourselves to be gathered into the artifice of eternity, that we can be transformed, that we can move on beyond the flesh. Yeats didn't mean it in quite the way I do—he wouldn't have begun to comprehend what we're talking about, not a word of it—and yet, and yet—the underlying truth is the same. Live, Gioia! With me!" He turned to her and saw color coming into her pallid cheeks. "It does make sense, what I'm suggesting, doesn't it? You'll attempt it, won't you? Whoever makes the visitors can be induced to remake you. Right? What do you think: can they, Gioia?"

She nodded in a barely perceptible way. "I think so," she said faintly. "It's very strange. But I think it ought to be possible. Why not, Charles? Why not?"

"Yes," he said. "Why not?"

IN THE MORNING THEY HIRED a vessel in the harbor, a low sleek pirogue with a blood-red sail, skippered by a rascally-looking temporary whose smile was irresistible. Phillips shaded his eyes and peered northward across the sea. He thought he could almost make out the shape of the great city sprawling on its seven hills, Constantine's New Rome beside the Golden Horn, the mighty dome of Hagia Sophia, the somber walls of the citadel, the palaces and churches, the Hippodrome, Christ in glory rising above all else in brilliant mosaic streaming with light.

"Byzantium," Phillips said. "Take us there the shortest and quickest way."

"It is my pleasure," said the boatman with unexpected grace.

Gioia smiled. He had not seen her looking so vibrantly alive since the night of the imperial feast in Chang-an. He reached for her hand—her slender fingers were quivering lightly—and helped her into the boat.

◆

BRECKENRIDGE AND THE CONTINUUM

I was a newly fledged Californian in September 1972, having abandoned my native city of New York less than a year before for a new life on the other coast. Everything was still an experiment for me as the first summer of my new California life went on and on, so it was not surprising that my fiction would take an experimental turn too. An editor named Roger Elwood had asked me to contribute to one of his many anthologies of new science fiction stories, and as soon as I got back from the wild and woolly World Science Fiction Convention in Los Angeles, I complied. This book was called Showcase, *and described as, "In the tradition of Damon Knight's* Orbit *and Robert Silverberg's* New Dimensions," *that is, an anthology without a theme, simply a collection of new stories, essentially a magazine in hardcover form.*

The early 1970s were, as you may have heard, a pretty freaky time in Western culture, especially in California, and when I wasn't writing or swimming I was investigating a lot of odd corners of intellectual life. Among them were the structuralist theories of the anthropologist Claude Lévi-Strauss, who was analyzing the classical myths by breaking them down into their component parts through the use of diagrams. Since science fiction lends itself readily to the creation of new myths, I decided to invent a myth of my own and apply Lévi-Strauss's structuralist principles to it, and the result was this wide-ranging tale—I suppose it would be called "edgy" today—complete with a Lévi-Straussian structural chart a few pages from the end. Where does it take place? When? Who knows?

THEN BRECKENRIDGE SAID, "I SUPPOSE I could tell you the story of Oedipus King of Thieves tonight."

The late afternoon sky was awful: gray, mottled, fierce. It resonated with a strange electricity. Breckenridge had never grown used to that sky. Day after day, as they crossed the desert, it transfixed him with the pain of incomprehensible loss.

"Oedipus King of Thieves," Scarp murmured. Arios nodded. Horn looked toward the sky. Militor frowned. "Oedipus," said Horn. "King of Thieves," Arios said.

Breckenridge and his four companions were camped in a ruined pavilion in the desert—a handsome place of granite pillars and black marble floors, constructed perhaps for some delicious paramour of some forgotten prince of the city-building folk. The pavilion lay only a short distance outside the walls of the great dead city that they would enter, at last, in the morning. Once, maybe, this place had been a summer resort, a place for sherbet and swimming, in that vanished time when this desert had bloomed and peacocks had strolled through fragrant gardens. A fantasy out of the Thousand and One Nights: long ago, long ago, thousands of years ago. How confusing it was for Breckenridge to remember that that mighty city, now withered by time, had been founded and had thrived and had perished all in an era far less ancient than his own. The bonds that bound the continuum had loosened. He flapped in the time-gales.

"Tell your story," Militor said.

They were restless, eager; they nodded their heads, they shifted positions. Scarp added fuel to the campfire. The sun was dropping behind the bare low hills that marked the desert's western edge; the day's smothering heat was suddenly rushing skyward, and a thin wind whistled through the colonnade of grooved gray pillars that surrounded the pavilion. Grains of pinkish sand danced in a steady stream across the floor of polished stone on which Breckenridge and those who traveled with him squatted. The lofty western wall of the nearby city was already sleeved in shadow.

Breckenridge drew his flimsy cloak closer around himself. He stared in turn at each of the four hooded figures facing him. He pressed his fingers against the cold smooth stone to anchor himself. In a low droning voice he said, "This Oedipus was monarch of the land of Thieves, and a bold and turbulent man. He conceived an illicit desire for Eurydice his mother. Forcing his passions upon her, he grew so violent that in their coupling she lost her life. Stricken with guilt and fearing that her kinsmen would exact reprisals, Oedipus escaped his kingdom through the air, having fashioned wings for himself under the guidance of the magician Prospero; but he flew too high and came within the ambit of the chariot of his father Apollo, god of the sun. Wrathful over this intrusion, Apollo engulfed Oedipus in heat, and the wax binding the feathers of his wings was melted. For a full day and a night Oedipus tumbled downward across the heavens, plummeting finally into the ocean, sinking through the sea's floor into the dark world below. There he dwells for all eternity, blind and lame, but each spring he reappears among men, and as he limps across the fields green grasses spring up in his tracks."

There was silence. Darkness was overtaking the sky. The four rounded fragments of the shattered old moon emerged and commenced their elegant, baffling saraband, spinning slowly, soaking one another in shifting patterns of cool white light. In the north the glittering violet and green bands of the aurora flickered with terrible abruptness, like the streaky glow of some monstrous searchlight. Breckenridge felt himself penetrated by gaudy ions, roasting him to the core. He waited, trembling.

"Is that all?" Militor said eventually. "Is that how it ends?"

"There's no more to the story," Breckenridge replied. "Are you disappointed?"

"The meaning is obscure. Why the incest? Why did he fly too high? Why was his father angry? Why does Oedipus reappear every spring? None of it makes sense. Am I too shallow to comprehend the relationships? I don't believe that I am."

"Oh, it's old stuff," said Scarp. "The tale of the eternal return. The dead king bringing the new year's fertility. Surely you recognize it, Militor." The aurora flashed with redoubled frenzy, a coded beacon, crying out, SPACE AND TIME, SPACE AND TIME, SPACE AND TIME. "You should have been able to follow the outline of the story," Scarp said. "We've heard it a thousand times in a thousand forms."

—SPACE AND TIME—

"Indeed we have," Militor said. "But the components of any satisfying tale have to have some logical necessity of sequence, some essential connection." —SPACE—" What we've just heard is a mass of random floating fragments. I see the semblance of myth but not the inner truth."

—TIME—

"A myth holds truth," Scarp insisted, "no matter how garbled its form, no matter how many irrelevant interpolations have entered it. The interpolations may even be one species of truth, and not the lowest species at that."

The Dow Jones Industrial Average, Breckenridge thought, closed today at 1100432.86—

"At any rate, he told it poorly," Arios observed. "No drama, no intensity, merely a bald outline of events. I've heard better from you on other nights, Breckenridge. Scheherazade and the Forty Giants—now, that was a story! Don Quixote and the Fountain of Youth, yes! But this—this—"

Scarp shook his head. "The strength of a myth lies in its content, not in the melody of its telling. I sense the inherent power of tonight's tale. I find it acceptable."

"Thank you," Breckenridge said quietly. He threw sour glares at Militor and Arios. It was hateful when they quibbled over the stories he told them. What gift did he have for these four strange beings, anyhow, except his stories? When they received that gift with poor grace they were denying him his sole claim to their fellowship.

A million years from nowhere—

SPACE—TIME—

Apollo—Jesus—Apollo—

THE WIND GREW CHILLIER. No one spoke. Beasts howled on the desert. Breckenridge lay back, feeling an ache in his shoulders, and wriggled against the cold stone floor.

Merry my wife, Cassandra my daughter, Noel my son—

Space—Time—

Space—

His eyes hurt from the aurora's frosty glow. He felt himself stretched across the cosmos, torn between then and now, breaking, breaking, ripping into fragments like the moon—

The stars had come out. He contemplated the early constellations. They were unfamiliar; no matter how often Scarp or Horn pointed out the patterns to him, he saw only random sprinklings of light. In his other life he had been able to identify at least the more conspicuous constellations, but they did not seem to be here. How long does it take to effect a complete redistribution of the heavens? A million years? Ten million? Thank God Mars and Jupiter still were visible, the orange dot and the brilliant white one, to tell him that this place was his own world, his own solar system. Images danced in his aching skull. He saw everything double, suddenly. There was Pegasus, there was Orion, there was Sagittarius. An overlay, a mass of realities superimposed on realities.

"Listen to this music," Horn said after a long while, producing a fragile device of wheels and spindles from beneath his cloak.

He caressed it and delicate sounds came forth: crystalline, comforting, the music of dreams, sliding into the range of audibility with no perceptible instant of attack. Shortly Scarp began a wordless song, and one by one the others joined him—first Horn, then Militor, and lastly, in a dry, buzzing monotone, Arios.

"What are you singing?" Breckenridge asked.

"The hymn of Oedipus King of Thieves," Scarp told him

Had it been such a bad life? He had been healthy, prosperous, and beloved. His father was managing partner of Falkner, Breckenridge & Company, one of the most stable of the Wall Street houses, and Breckenridge, after coming up through the ranks in the family tradition, putting in his time as a customer's man and his time in the bond department and his time as a floor trader, was a partner too, only ten years out of Dartmouth. What was wrong with that? His draw in 1972 was $83,500—not as much as he had hoped for out of a partnership, but not bad, not bad at all, and next year might be much better. He had a wife and two children, an apartment on East 73rd Street, a country cabin on Candlewood Lake, a fair-size schooner that he kept in the Gulf Coast marina, and a handsome young mistress in an apartment of her own on the Upper West Side. What was wrong with that? When he burst through the fabric of the continuum and found himself in an unimaginably altered world at the end of time, he was astonished not that such a thing might happen but that it had happened to someone as settled and well-established as himself.

While they slept, a corona of golden light sprang into being along the top of the city wall; the glow awakened Breckenridge, and he sat up quickly, thinking that the city was on fire. But the light seemed cool and supple, and appeared to be propagated in easy rippling waves, more like the aurora than like the raw blaze of flames. It sprang from the very rim of the wall and leaped high, casting blurred, rounded shadows at cross-angles to the sharp crisp shadows that the fragmented moon created. There seemed also to be a deep segment of blackness in the side of the wall; looking closely, Breckenridge saw that the huge gate on the wall's western face was standing open. Without telling the others he left the camp and crossed the flat sandy wasteland, coming to the gate after a brisk march of about an hour. Nothing prevented him from entering. Just within the wall was a wide cobbled plaza, and beyond that stretched broad avenues lined with buildings of a strange sort, rounded and rubbery, porous of texture, all humps and parapets. Black unfenced wells at the center of each major intersection plunged to infinite depths. Breckenridge had been told that the city was empty, that it had been uninhabited for centuries since the spoiling of the climate in this part of the world, so he was surprised to find it occupied; pale figures flitted silently about, moving like wraiths, as though there were empty space between their feet and the pavement. He approached one and another and a third, but when he tried to speak no words would leave his lips. He seized one of the city dwellers by the wrist, a slender black-haired girl in a soft gray robe, and held her tightly, hoping that contact would lead to contact. Her dark somber eyes studied him without show of fear and she made no effort to break away. I am Noel Breckenridge, he said—Noel III—and I was born in the town of Greenwich, Connecticut in the year of our lord 1940, my wife's name is Merry and my daughter is Cassandra and my son is Noel Breckenridge IV, and I am not as coarse or stupid as you may think me to be. She made no reply and showed no change of expression. He asked, Can you understand anything I'm saying to you? Her face remained totally blank. He asked, Can you even hear the sound of my voice? There was no response. He went on: What is your name? What is this city called? When was it abandoned? What year is this on any calendar that I can comprehend? What do you know about me that I need to know? She continued to regard him in an altogether neutral way. He pulled her against his body and gripped her thin shoulders with his fingertips and kissed her urgently, forcing his tongue between her teeth. An instant later he found himself sprawled not far from the campsite with his face in the sand and sand in his mouth. Only a dream, he thought wearily, only a dream.

He was having lunch with Harry Munsey at the Merchants and Shippers Club: sleek chrome-and-redwood premises, sixty stories above William Street in the heart of the financial district. Subdued light fixtures glowed like pulsing red suns; waiters moved past the tables like silent moons. The club was over a century old, although the skyscraper in which it occupied a penthouse suite had been erected only in 1968—its fourth home, or maybe its fifth. Membership was limited to white male Christians, sober and responsible, who had important positions in the New York securities industry. There was nothing in the club's written constitution that explicitly limited its membership to white male Christians, but all the same there had never been any members who had not been white, male, and Christian. No one with a firm grasp of reality thought there ever would be.

Harry Munsey, like Noel Breckenridge, was white, male, and Christian. They had gone to Dartmouth together and they had entered Wall Street together, Breckenridge going into his family's firm and Munsey into his, and they had lunch together almost every day and saw each other almost every Saturday night, and each had slept with the other's wife, though each believed that the other knew nothing about that.

On the third martini Munsey said, "What's bugging you today, Noel?"

A dozen years ago Munsey had been an all-Ivy halfback; he was a big, powerful man, bigger even than Breckenridge, who was not a small man. Munsey's face was pink and unlined and his eyes were alive and youthful, but he had lost all his hair before he turned thirty.

"Is something bugging me?"

"Something's bugging you, yes. Why else would you look so uptight after you've had two and a half martinis?"

Breckenridge had found it difficult to grow used to the sight of the massive bright dome that was Munsey's skull.

He said, "All right. So I'm bugged."

"Want to talk about it?"

"No."

"Okay," Munsey said.

Breckenridge finished his drink. "As a matter of fact, I'm oppressed by a sophomoric sense of the meaninglessness of life, if you have to know."

"Really?"

"Really."

"The meaninglessness of life?"

"Life is empty, dumb, and mechanical," Breckenridge said.

"*Your* life?"

"Life."

"I know a lot of people who'd like to live your life. They'd trade with you, even up, asset for asset, liability for liability, life for life."

Breckenridge shook his head. "They're fools, then."

"It's that bad?"

"It all seems so pointless, Harry. Everything. We have a good time and con ourselves into thinking it means something. But what is there, actually? The pursuit of money? I have enough money. After a certain point it's just a game. French restaurants? Trips to Europe? Drinking? Sex? Swimming pools? Jesus! We're born, we grow up, we do a lot of stuff, we grow old, we die. Is that all? Jesus, Harry, is that *all?*"

Munsey looked embarrassed. "Well, there's family," he suggested. "Marriage, fatherhood, knowing that you're linking yourself into the great chain of life. Bringing forth a new generation. Transmitting your ideas, your standards, your traditions, everything that distinguishes us from the apes we used to be. Doesn't that count?"

Shrugging, Breckenridge said, "All right. Having kids, you say. We bring them into the world, we wipe their noses, we teach them to be little men and women, we send them to the right schools and get them into the right clubs, and they grow up to be carbon copies of their parents, lawyers or brokers or clubwomen or whatever—"

The lights fluttering. The aurora: red, green, violet, red, green. The straining fabric—the moon, the broken moon—the aurora—the lights—the fire atop the walls—

"—or else they grow up and deliberately fashion themselves into the opposites of their parents, and somewhere along the way the parents die off, and the kids have kids, and the cycle starts around again. Around and around, generation after generation, Noel Breckenridge III, Noel Breckenridge IV, Noel Breckenridge XVI—"

Arios—Scarp—Militor—Horn—

The city—the gate—

"—making money, spending money, living high, building nothing real, just occupying space on the planet for a little while, and what for? What for? What does it all mean?"

The granite pillars—the aurora—SPACE AND TIME—

"You're on a bummer today, Noel," Munsey said.

"I know. Aren't you sorry you asked what was bugging me?"

"Not particularly. Everybody goes through a phase like this."

"When he's seventeen, yes."

"And later, too."

"It's more than a phase," Breckenridge said. "It's a sickness. If I had any guts, Harry, I'd drop out. Drop right out and try to work out some meanings in the privacy of my own head."

"Why don't you? You can afford it. Go on. Why not?"

"I don't know," said Breckenridge.

Such strange constellations. Such a terrible sky.

Such a cold wind blowing out of tomorrow.

"I think it may be time for another martini," Munsey said.

THEY HAD BEEN CROSSING THE desert for a long time now—forty days and forty nights, Breckenridge liked to tell himself, but probably it had been more than that—and they moved at an unsparing pace, marching from dawn to sunset with as few rest periods as possible. The air was thin. His lungs felt leathery. Because he was the biggest man in the group, he carried the heaviest pack. That didn't bother him.

What did bother him was how little he knew about his expedition, its purposes, its origin, even how he had come to be a part of it. But asking such questions seemed somehow naive and awkward, and he never did. He went along, doing his share—making camp, cleaning up in the mornings—and tried to keep his companions amused with his stories. They demanded stories from him every night. "Tell us your myths," they urged. "Tell us the legends and fables you learned in your childhood."

After weeks of sharing this trek with them he knew little more about the other four than he had at the outset. His favorite among them was Scarp, who was sympathetic and flexible. He liked the hostile, contemptuous Militor the least. Horn—dreamy, poetic, unworldly, aloof—was beyond his reach; Arios, the most dry and objective and scientific of the group, did not seem worth trying to reach. So far as Breckenridge could determine they were human, although their skins were oddly glossy and of a peculiar olive hue, something on the far side of swarthy. They had strange noses, narrow, high-bridged noses of a kind he had never seen before, extremely fragile, like the noses of purebred society women carried to the ultimate possibilities of their design.

The desert was beautiful. A gaudy desolation, all dunes and sandy ripples, streaked blue and red and gold and green with brilliant oxides.

Sometimes when the aurora was going full blast—SPACE! TIME! SPACE! TIME!—the desert seemed merely to be a mirror for the sky.

But in the morning, when the electronic furies of the aurora had died away, the sand still reverberated with its own inner pulses of bright color.

And the sun—pale, remorseless—Apollo's deathless fires—

I am Noel Breckenridge and I am nine years old and this is how I spent my summer vacation—

Oh Lord Jesus forgive me.

Scattered everywhere on the desert were outcroppings of ancient ruins—colonnades, halls of statuary, guard posts, summer pavilions, hunting lodges, the stumps of antique walls, and invariably the marchers made their camp beside one of these. They studied each ruin, measured its dimensions, recorded its salient details, poked at its sand-shrouded foundations. Around Scarp's neck hung a kind of mechanized map, a teardrop-shaped black instrument that could be made to emit—

PING!

—sounds which daily guided them toward the next ruin in the chain leading to the city. Scarp also carried a compact humming machine that generated sweet water from handfuls of sand. For solid food they subsisted on small yellow pellets, quite tasty.

PING!

At the beginning Breckenridge had felt constant fatigue, but under the grinding exertions of the march he had grown steadily in strength and endurance, and now he felt he could continue forever, never tiring, parading—

PING!

—endlessly back and forth across this desert which perhaps spanned the entire world. The dead city, though, was their destination, and finally it was in view. They were to remain there for an indefinite stay. He was not yet sure whether these four were archeologists or pilgrims. Perhaps both, he thought. Or maybe neither. Or maybe neither.

"HOW DO YOU THINK YOU can make your life more meaningful, then?" Munsey asked.

"I don't know. I don't have any idea what would work for me. But I do know who the people are whose lives do have meaning."

"Who?"

"The creators, Harry. The shapers, the makers, the begetters. Beethoven, Rembrandt. Dr. Salk, Einstein, Shakespeare, that bunch. It isn't enough just to live. It isn't even enough just to have a good mind, to think clear thoughts. You have to add something to the sum of humanity's accomplishments, something real, something valuable. You have to *give*. Mozart. Newton. Columbus. Those who are able to reach into the well of creation, into that hot boiling chaos of raw energy down there, and pull something out, shape it, make something unique and new out of it. Making money isn't enough. Making more Breckenridges or Munseys isn't enough, either. You know what I'm saying, Harry? The well of creation. The reservoir of life, which is God. Do you ever think you believe in God? Do you wake up in the middle of the night sometimes saying, yes, yes, there *is* Something after all, I believe, I believe! I'm not talking about churchgoing now, you understand. Churchgoing's nothing but a conditioned reflex these days, a twitch, a tic. I'm talking about faith. Belief. The state of enlightenment. I'm not talking about God as an old man with long white whiskers, either, Harry. I mean something abstract, a force, a power, a current, a reservoir of energy underlying everything and connecting everything. God is that reservoir. That reservoir is God. I think of that reservoir as being something like the sea of molten lava down beneath the earth's crust: it's there, it's full of heat and power, it's accessible for those who know the way. Plato was able to tap into the reservoir. Van Gogh. Joyce. Schubert. El Greco. A few lucky ones knew how to reach it. Most of us can't. Most of us can't. For those who can't, God is dead. Worse: for them, He never lived at all. Oh, Christ, how awful it is to be trapped in an era where everybody goes around like some sort of zombie, cut off from the energies of the spirit, ashamed even to admit there are such energies. I hate it. I hate the whole stinking twentieth century, do you know that? Am I making any sense? Do I seem terribly drunk? Am I embarrassing you, Harry? Harry? Harry?"

In the morning they struck camp and set out on the final leg of their journey toward the city. The sand here had a disturbing crusty quality: white saline outcroppings gave Breckenridge the feeling that they were crossing a tundra rather than a desert. The sky was clear and pale, and in its bleached cloudlessness it took on something of the quality of a shield, of a mirror, seizing the morning heat that rose from the ground and hurling it inexorably back, so that the five marchers felt themselves trapped in an infinite baffle of unendurable dry smothering warmth.

As they moved cityward Militor and Arios chattered compulsively, falling after a while into a quarrel over certain obscure and controversial points of historical theory. Breckenridge had heard them have their argument at least a dozen times in the last two weeks, and no doubt they had been battling it out for years. The main area of contention was the origin of the city. Who were its builders? Militor believed they were colonists from some other planet, strangers to earth, representatives of some alien species of immeasurable grandeur and nobility, who had crossed space thousands of years ago to build this gigantic monument on Asia's flank. Nonsense, retorted Arios: the city was plainly the work of human beings, unusually gifted and energetic but human nonetheless. Why multiply hypotheses needlessly? Here is the city; humans have built many cities nearly as great as this one in their long history; this city is only quantitatively superior to the others, merely a little bigger, merely a bit more daringly conceived; to invoke extraterrestrial architects is to dabble gratuitously in fantasy. But Militor maintained his position. Humans, he said, were plainly incapable of such immense constructions. Neither in this present decadent epoch, when any sort of effort is too great, nor at any time in the past could human resources have been equal to such a task as the building of this city must have been. Breckenridge had his doubts about that, having seen what the twentieth century had accomplished. He tended to side with Arios. But indeed the city was extraordinary, Breckenridge admitted: an ultimate urban glory, a supernal Babylon, a consummate Persepolis, the soul's own hymn in brick and stone. The wall that girdled it was at least two hundred feet high—why pour so much energy into a wall? were no better means of defense at hand, or was the wall mere exuberant decoration?—and, judging by the easy angle of its curve, it must be hundreds of miles in circumference. A city larger than New York, more sprawling even than Los Angeles, a giant antenna of turbulent consciousness set like a colossal gem into this vast plain, a throbbing antenna for all the radiance of the stars: yes, it was overwhelming, it was devastating to contemplate the planning and the building of it, it seemed almost to require the hypothesis of a superior alien race. And yet he refused to accept that hypothesis. Arios, he thought, I am with you.

The city was uninhabited, a hulk, a ruin. Why? What had happened here to turn this garden plain into a salt-crusted waste? The builders grew too proud, said Militor. They defied the gods, they overreached even their own powers, and stumbling, they fell headlong into decay. The life went out of the soil, the sky gave no rain, the spirit lost its energies; the city perished and was forgotten, and was whispered about by mythmakers, a city out of time, a city at the end of the world, a mighty mass of dead wonders, a habitation for jackals, a place where no one went. We are the first in centuries, said Scarp, to seek this city.

Halfway between dawn and noon they reached the wall and stood before the great gate. The gate alone was fifty feet high, a curving slab of burnished blue metal set smoothly into a recess in the tawny stucco of the wall. Breckenridge saw no way of opening it, no winch, no portcullis, no handles, no knobs. He feared that the impatient Militor would merely blow a hole in it. But, groping along the base of the gate, they found a small doorway, man-high and barely man-wide, near the left-hand edge. Ancient hinges yielded at a push. Scarp led the way inside.

The city was as Breckenridge remembered it from his dream: the cobbled plaza, the broad avenues, the humped and rubbery buildings. The fierce sunlight, deflected and refracted by the undulant roof lines, reverberated from every flat surface and rebounded in showers of brilliant energy. Breckenridge shaded his eyes. It was as though the sky were full of pulsars. His soul was frying on a cosmic griddle, cooking in a torrent of hard radiation.

The city was inhabited.

Faces were visible at windows. Elusive figures emerged at street corners, peered, withdrew. Scarp called to them; they shrank back into the hard-edged shadows.

"Well?" Arios demanded. "They're human, aren't they?"

"What of it?" said Militor. "Squatters, that's all. You saw how easy it was to push open that door. They've come in out of the desert to live in the ruins."

"Maybe not. Descendants of the builders, I'd say. Perhaps the city never really was abandoned." Arios looked at Scarp. "Don't you agree?"

"They might be anything," Scarp said. "Squatters, descendants, even synthetics, even servants without masters, living on, waiting, living on, waiting—"

"Or projections cast by ancient machines," Militor said. "No human hand built this city."

Arios snorted. They advanced quickly across the plaza and entered into the first of the grand avenues. The buildings flanking it were sealed. They proceeded to a major intersection, where they halted to inspect an open circular pit, fifteen feet in diameter, smooth-rimmed, descending into infinite darkness. Breckenridge had seen many such dark wells in his vision of the night before. He did not doubt now that he had left his sleeping body and had made an actual foray into the city last night.

Scarp flashed a light into the well. A copper-colored metal ladder was visible along one face.

"Shall we go down?" Breckenridge asked.

"Later," said Scarp.

THE FAMOUS ANTHROPOLOGIST HAD BEEN drinking steadily all through the dinner party—wine, only wine, but plenty of it—and his eyes seemed glazed, his face flushed; nevertheless he continued to talk with superb clarity of perception and elegant precision of phrase, hardly pausing at all to construct his concepts. Perhaps he's merely quoting his own latest book from memory, Breckenridge thought, as he strained to follow the flow of ideas. "—A comparison between myth and what appears to have largely replaced it in modern societies, namely, politics. When the historian refers to the French Revolution it is always as a sequence of past happenings, a nonreversible series of events the remote consequences of which may still be felt at present. But to the French politician, as well as to his followers, the French Revolution is both a sequence belonging to the past—as to the historian—and an everlasting pattern which can be detected in the present French social structure and which provides a clue for its interpretation, a lead from which to infer the future developments. See, for instance, Michelet, who was a politically minded historian. He describes the French Revolution thus: 'This day . . . everything was possible . . . future became present . . . that is, no more time, a glimpse of eternity.'" The great man reached decisively for another glass of claret. His hand wavered; the glass toppled; a dark red torrent stained the tablecloth. Breckenridge experienced a sudden terrifying moment of complete disorientation, as though the walls and floor were shifting places: he saw a parched desert plateau, four hooded figures, a blazing sky of strange constellations, a pulsating aurora sweeping the heavens with old fire. A mighty walled city dominated the plain, and its frosty shadow, knifeblade-sharp, cut across Breckenridge's path. He shivered. The woman on Breckenridge's right laughed lightly and began to recite:

> I saw Eternity the other night
> Like a great ring of pure and endless light.
> All calm, as it was bright;
> And round beneath it, Time in hours, days, years,
> Driv'n by the spheres
> Like a vast shadow mov'd; in which the world
> And all her train were hurl'd.

"Excuse me," Breckenridge said. "I think I'm unwell." He rushed from the dining room. In the hallway he turned toward the washroom and found himself staring into a steaming tropical marsh, all ferns and horsetails and giant insects. Dragonflies the size of pigeons whirred past him. The sleek rump of a brontosaurus rose like a bubbling aneurysm from the black surface of the swamp. Breckenridge recoiled and staggered away. On the other side of the hall lay the desert under the lash of a frightful noonday sun. He gripped the frame of a door and held himself upright, trembling, as his soul oscillated wildly across the hallucinatory eons. "I am Scarp," said a quiet voice within him. "You have come to the place where all times are one, where all errors can be unmade, where past and future are fluid and subject to redefinition." Breckenridge felt powerful arms encircling and supporting him. "Noel? Noel? Here, sit down." Harry Munsey. Shiny pink skull, searching blue eyes. "Jesus, Noel, you look like you're having some kind of bad trip. Merry sent me after you to find out—"

"It's okay," Breckenridge said hoarsely. "I'll be all right."

"You want me to get her?"

"I'll be *all right.* Just let me steady myself a second." He rose uncertainly. "Okay. Let's go back inside."

The anthropologist was still talking. A napkin covered the wine stain and he held a fresh glass aloft like a sacramental chalice. "The key to everything, I think, lies in an idea that Franz Boas offered in 1898: 'It would seem that mythological worlds have been built up only to be shattered again, and that new worlds were built from the fragments.'"

Breckenridge said, "The first men lived underground and there was no such thing as private property. One day there was an earthquake and the earth was rent apart. The light of day flooded the subterranean cavern where mankind dwelled. Clumsily, for the light dazzled their eyes, they came upward into the world of brightness and learned how to see. Seven days later they divided the fields among themselves and began to build the first walls as boundaries marking the limits of their land."

By midday the city dwellers were losing their fear of the five intruders. Gradually, in twos and threes, they left their hiding places and gathered around the visitors until a substantial group had collected. They were dressed simply, in light robes, and they said nothing to the strangers, though they whispered frequently to one another. Among the group was the slender, dark-haired girl of Breckenridge's dream. "Do you remember me?" he asked. She smiled and shrugged and answered softly in a liquid, incomprehensible language. Arios questioned her in six or seven tongues, but she shook her head to everything. Then she took Breckenridge by the hand and led him a few paces away, toward one of the street-wells. Pointing into it, she smiled. She pointed to Breckenridge, pointed to herself, to the surrounding buildings. She made a sweeping gesture taking in all the sky. She pointed again into the well. "What are you trying to tell me?" he asked her. She answered in her own language. Breckenridge shook his head apologetically. She did a simple pantomime: eyes closed, head lolling against pressed-together hands. An image of sleep, certainly. She pointed to him. To herself. To the well. "You want me to sleep with you?" he blurted. "Down there?" He had to laugh at his own foolishness. It was ridiculous to assume the persistence of a cowardly, euphemistic metaphor like that across so many millennia. He gaped stupidly at her. She laughed—a silvery, tinkling laugh—and danced away from him, back toward her own people.

THEIR FIRST NIGHT IN THE city they made camp in one of the great plazas. It was an octagonal space surrounded by low green buildings, sharp-angled, each faced on its plaza side with mirror-bright stone. About a hundred of the city dwellers crouched in the shadows of the plaza's periphery, watching them. Scarp sprinkled fuel pellets and kindled a fire; Militor distributed dinner; Horn played music as they ate; Arios, sitting apart, dictated a commentary into a recording device he carried, the size and texture of a large pearl. Afterward they asked Breckenridge to tell a story, as usual, and he told them the tale of how Death Came to the World.

"Once upon a time," he began, "there were only a few people in the world and they lived in a green and fertile valley where winter never came and gardens bloomed all the year round. They spent their days laughing and swimming and lying in the sun, and in the evenings they feasted and sang and made love, and this went on without change, year in, year out, and no one ever fell ill or suffered from hunger, and no one ever died. Despite the serenity of this existence, one man in the village was unhappy. His name was Faust, and he was a restless, intelligent man with intense, burning eyes and a lean, unsmiling face. Faust felt that life must consist of something more than swimming and making love and plucking ripe fruit off vines. 'There is something else to life,' Faust insisted, 'something unknown to us, something that eludes our grasp, something the lack of which keeps us from being truly happy. We are incomplete.' The others listened to him and at first they were puzzled, for they had not known they were unhappy or incomplete, they had mistaken the ease and placidity of their existence for happiness. But after a while they started to believe that Faust might be right. They had not known how vacant their lives were until Faust had pointed it out. What can we do? they asked. How can we learn what the thing is that we lack? A wise old man suggested that they might ask the gods. So they elected Faust to visit the god Prometheus, who was said to be a friend to mankind, and ask him. Faust crossed hill and dale, mountain and river, and came at last to Prometheus on the storm-swept summit where he dwelled. He explained the situation and said, 'Tell me, O Prometheus, why we feel so incomplete.' The god replied, 'It is because you do not have the use of fire. Without fire there can be no civilization; you are uncivilized, and your barbarism makes you unhappy. With fire you can cook your food and enjoy many interesting new flavors. With fire you can work metals, and create effective weapons and other tools.' Faust considered this and said, 'But where can we obtain fire? What is it? How is it used?'

"'I will bring fire to you,' Prometheus answered.

"Prometheus then went to Zeus, the greatest of the gods, and said, 'Zeus, the humans desire fire, and I seek your permission to bestow it upon them.' But Zeus was hard of hearing and Prometheus lisped badly and in the language of the gods the words for fire and for death were very similar, and Zeus misunderstood and said, 'How odd of them to desire such a thing, but I am a benevolent god, and deny my creatures nothing that they crave.' So Zeus created a woman named Pandora and put death inside her and gave her to Prometheus, who took her back to the valley where mankind lived. 'Here is Pandora,' said Prometheus. 'She will give you fire.'

"As soon as Prometheus took his leave Faust came forward and embraced Pandora and lay with her. Her body was hot as flame, and as he held her in his arms death came forth from her and entered him, and he shivered and grew feverish, and cried out in ecstasy, 'This is fire! I have mastered fire!' Within the hour death began to consume him so that he grew weak and thin, and his skin became parched and yellowish, and he trembled like a leaf in a breeze. 'Go!' he cried to the others. 'Embrace her—she is the bringer of fire!' And he staggered off into the wilderness beyond the valley's edge, murmuring, 'Thanks be to Prometheus for this gift.' He lay down beneath a huge tree, and there he died, and it was the first time that death had visited a human being. And the tree died also.

"Then the other men of the village embraced Pandora, one after another, and death entered into them too, and they went from her to their own women and embraced them, so that soon all the men and women of the village were ablaze with death, and one by one their lives reached an end. Death remained in the village, passing into all who lived and into all who were born from their loins, and this is how death came to the world. Afterward, during a storm, lightning struck the tree that had died when Faust had died, and set it ablaze, and a man whose name is forgotten thrust a dry branch into the blaze and lit it, and learned how to build a fire and how to keep the fire alive, and after that time men cooked their food and used fire to work metal into weapons, and so it was that civilization began."

It was time to investigate one of the wells. Scarp, Arios, and Breckenridge would make the descent, with Militor and Horn remaining on the surface to cope with contingencies. They chose a well half a day's march from their campsite, deep into the city, a big one, broader and deeper than most they had seen. At its rim Scarp mounted a spherical fist-size light that cast a dazzling blue-white beam into the opening. Then, lightly swinging himself out onto the metal ladder, he began to climb down, shrouded in a nimbus of molten brightness. Breckenridge peered after him. Scarp's head and shoulders remained visible for a long while, dwindling until he was only a point of darkness in motion deep within the cone of light, and then he could no longer be seen. "Scarp?" Breckenridge called. After a moment came a muffled reply out of the depths. Scarp had reached bottom, somewhere beyond the range of the beam, and wanted them to join him.

Breckenridge followed. The descent seemed infinite. There was a stiffness in his left knee. He became a mere automaton, mechanically seizing the rungs; they were warm in his hands. His eyes, fixed on the pocked gray skin of the well's wall inches from his nose, grew glassy and unfocused. He passed through the zone of light as though sliding through the face of a mirror and moved downward in darkness without a change of pace until his boot slammed unexpectedly into a solid floor where he had thought to encounter the next rung. The left boot; his knee, jamming, protested. Scarp lightly touched his shoulder. "Step back here next to me," he said. "Take sliding steps and make sure you have a footing. For all we know, we're on some sort of ledge with a steep drop on all sides."

They waited while Arios came down. His footfalls were like thunder in the well: boom, boom, boom, transmitted and amplified by the rungs. Then the men at the surface lowered the light, fixed to the end of a long cord, and at last they could look around.

They were in a kind of catacomb. The floor of the well was a platform of neatly dressed stone slabs which gave access to horizontal tunnels several times a man's height, stretching away to right and left, to fore and aft. The mouth of the well was a dim dot of light far above. Scarp, after inspecting the perimeter of the platform, flashed the beam into one of the tunnels, stared a moment, and cautiously entered. Breckenridge heard him cough. "Dusty in here," Scarp muttered. Then he said, "You told us a story once about the King of the Dead Lands, Breckenridge. What was his name?"

"Thanatos."

"Thanatos, yes. This must be his kingdom. Come and look."

Arios and Breckenridge exchanged shrugs. Breckenridge stepped into the tunnel. The walls on both sides were lined from floor to ceiling with tiers of coffins, stacked eight or ten high and extending as far as the beam of light reached. The coffins were glass faced and covered over with dense films of dust. Scarp drew his fingers through the dust over one coffin and left deep tracks; clouds rose up, sending Breckenridge back, coughing and choking, to stumble into Arios. When the dust cleared they could see a figure within, seemingly asleep, the nude figure of a young man lying on his back. His expression was one of great serenity. Breckenridge shivered. Death's kingdom, yes, the place of Thanatos, the house of Pluto. He walked down the row, wiping coffin after coffin. An old man. A child. A young woman. An older woman. A whole population lay embalmed here. I died long ago, he thought, and I don't even sleep. I walk about beneath the earth. The silence was frightening here. "The people of the city?" Scarp asked. "The ancient inhabitants?"

"Very likely," said Arios. His voice was as crisp as ever. He alone was not trembling. "Slain in some inconceivable massacre? But what? But how?"

"They appear to have died natural deaths," Breckenridge pointed out. "Their bodies look whole and healthy. As though they were lying here asleep. Not dead, only sleeping."

"A plague?" Scarp wondered. "A sudden cloud of deadly gas? A taint of poison in their water supply?"

"If it had been sudden," said Breckenridge, "how would they have had time to build all these coffins? This whole tunnel—catacomb upon catacomb—" A network of passageways spanning the city's entire subterrane. Thousands of coffins. Millions. Breckenridge felt dazed by the presence of death on such a scale. The skeleton with the scythe, moving briskly about its work. Severed heads and hands and feet scattered like dandelions in the springtime meadow. The reign of Thanatos, King of Swords, Knight of Wands.

Thunder sounded behind them. Footfalls in the well.

Scarp scowled. "I told them to wait up there. That fool Militor—"

Arios said, "Militor should see this. Undoubtedly it's the resting place of the city dwellers. Undoubtedly these are human beings. Do you know what I imagine? A mass suicide. A unanimous decision to abandon the world of life. Years of preparation. The construction of tunnels, of machines for killing, a whole vast apparatus of immolation. And then the day appointed—long lines waiting to be processed—millions of men and women and children passing through the machines, gladly giving up their lives, going willingly to the coffins that await them—"

"And then," Scarp said, "there must have been only a few left and no one to process them. Living on, caretakers for the dead, perhaps, maintaining the machinery that preserves these millions of bodies—"

"Preserves them for what?" Arios asked.

"The day of resurrection," said Breckenridge.

The footfalls in the well grew louder. Scarp glanced toward the tunnel's mouth. "Militor?" he called. "Horn?" He sounded angry. He walked toward the well. "You were supposed to wait for us up—"

Breckenridge heard a grinding sound and whirled to see Arios tugging at the lid of a coffin—the one that held the serene young man. Instinctively he moved to halt the desecration, but he was too slow; the glass plate rose as Arios broke the seals, and, with a quick whooshing sound, a burst of greenish vapor rushed from the coffin. It hovered a moment in midair, speared by Arios's beam of light; then it congealed into a yellow precipitant and broke in a miniature rainstorm that stained the tunnel's stone floor. To Breckenridge's horror the young man's body jerked convulsively: muscles tightened into knots and almost instantly relaxed. "He's alive!" Breckenridge cried.

"Was," said Scarp.

Yes. The figure in the glass case was motionless. It changed color and texture, turning black and withered. Scarp shoved Arios aside and slammed the lid closed, but that could do no good now. A dreadful new motion commenced within the coffin. In moments something shriveled and twisted lay before them.

"Suspended animation," said Arios. "The city builders—they lie here, as human as we are, sleeping, not dead, sleeping. Sleeping! Militor! Militor, come quickly!"

FEINGOLD SAID, "LET ME SEE if I have it straight. After the public offering our group will continue to hold eighty-three percent of the Class B stock and thirty-four percent of the voting common, which constitutes a controlling block. We'll let you have 100,000 five-year warrants and we'll agree to a conversion privilege on the 1992 6½ percent debentures, plus we allow you the stipulated underwriting fee, providing your Argentinian friend takes up the agreed-upon allotment of debentures and follows through on his deal with us in Colorado. Okay? Now, then, assuming the SEC has no objections, I'd like to outline the proposed interlocking directorates with Heitmark A.G. in Liechtenstein and Hellaphon S.A. in Athens, after which—"

The high, clear, rapid voice went on and on. Breckenridge toyed with his lunch, smiled frequently, nodded whenever he felt it was appropriate, and otherwise remained disconnected, listening only with the automatic-recorder part of his mind. They were sitting on the terrace of an open-air restaurant in Tiberias, at the edge of the Sea of Galilee, looking across to the bleak, brown Syrian hills on the far side. The December air was mild, the sun bright. Last week Breckenridge had visited Monaco, Zurich, and Milan. Yesterday Tel Aviv, tomorrow Haifa, next Tuesday Istanbul. Then on to Nairobi, Johannesburg, Peking, Singapore. Finally San Francisco and then home. Zap! Zap! A crazy round-the-world scramble in twenty days, cleaning up a lot of international business for the firm. It could all have been handled by telephone, or else some of these foreign tycoons could have come to New York, but Breckenridge had volunteered to do the junket. Why? Why? Sitting here ten thousand miles from home having lunch with a man whose office was down the street from his own. Crazy. Why all this running, Noel? Where do you think you'll get?

"Some more wine?" Feingold asked. "What do you think of this Israeli stuff, anyway?"

"It goes well with the fish." Breckenridge reached for Feingold's copy of the agreement. "Here, let me initial all that."

"Don't you want to check it over first?"

"Not necessary. I have faith in you, Sid."

"Well, I wouldn't cheat you, that's true. But I could have made a mistake. I'm capable of making mistakes."

"I don't think so," Breckenridge said. He grinned. Feingold grinned. Behind the grin there was something chilly. Breckenridge looked away. You think I'm bending over backward to treat you like a gentleman, he thought, because you know what people like me are really supposed to think about Jews, and I know you know, and you know I know you know, and—and—well, screw it, Sid. Do I trust you? Maybe I do. Maybe I don't. But the basic fact is I just don't care. Stack the deck any way you like, Feingold. I just don't care. I wish I was on Mars. Or Pluto. Or the year Two Billion. Zap! Right across the whole continuum! Noel Breckenridge, freaking out! He heard himself say, "Do you want to know my secret fantasy, Sid? I dream of waking up Jewish one day. It's so damned boring being a gentile, do you know that? I feel so bland, so straight, so sunny. I envy you all that feverish kinky complexity of soul. All that history. Ghettos, persecutions, escapes, schemes for survival and revenge, a sense of tribal unity born out of shared pain. It's so hard for a goy to develop some honest paranoia, you know? Let alone a little schiziness." Feingold was still grinning. He filled Breckenridge's wineglass again. He showed no sign of having heard anything that might offend him. Maybe I didn't say anything, Breckenridge thought.

Feingold said, "When you get back to New York, Noel, I'd like you out to our place for dinner. You and your wife. A weekend, maybe. Logs on the fire, thick steaks, plenty of good wine. You'll love our place." Three Israeli jets roared low over Tiberias and vanished in the direction of Lebanon. "Will you come? Can you fit it into your schedule?"

Some possible structural hypotheses:

His audience was getting larger every night. They came from all parts of the city, silently arriving, drawn at sundown to the place where the visitors camped. Hundreds, now, squatting beyond the glow of the campfire. They listened intently, nodded, seemed to comprehend, murmured occasional comments to one another. How strange: they seemed to comprehend.

"The story of Samson and Odysseus," Breckenridge announced.

"Samson is blind but mighty. His woman is known as Delilah. To them comes the wily chieftain Odysseus, making his way homeward from the land of Ithaca. He penetrates the maze in which Samson and

Delilah live and hires himself to them as bondservant, giving his name as No Man. Delilah entices him to carry her off, and he abducts her. Samson is aware of the abduction but is unable to find them in the maze; he cries out in pain and rage, 'No Man steals my wife! No Man steals my wife!' His servants are baffled by this and take no action. In fury Samson brings the maze crashing down on himself and dies, while Odysseus carries Delilah off to Sparta, where she is seduced by Paris, Prince of Troy. Odysseus thus loses her and by way of gaining revenge he seduces Helen, the Queen of Troy, and the Trojan War begins."

And then he told the story of how mankind was created:

"In the beginning there was only a field of white sand. Lightning struck it, and where the lightning hit the sand it coagulated into a vessel of glass, and rainwater ran into the vessel and brought it to life, and from the vessel a she-wolf was born. Thunder entered her womb and fertilized her and she gave birth to twins, and they were not wolves but a human boy and a human girl. The wolf suckled the twins until they reached adulthood. Then they copulated and engendered children of their own. Because they were ashamed of their nakedness they killed the old wolf and made garments from her hide."

And then he told them the myth of the Wandering Jew, who scoffed at God and was condemned to drift through time until he himself was able to become God.

And he told them of the Golden Age and the Iron Age and the Age of Uranium.

And he told them how the waters and winds came into being, and the seasons, the months, day and night.

And he told them how art was born:

"Out of a hole in space pours a stream of life force. Many men and women attempted to seize the flow, but they were burned to ashes by its intensity. At last, however, a man devised a way. He hollowed himself out until there was nothing at all inside his body, and had himself dragged by a faithful dog to the place where the stream of energy descended from the heavens. Then the life force entered him and filled him, and instead of destroying him it took possession of him and restored him to life. But the force overflowed within him, brimming over, and the only way he could deal with that was to fashion stories and sculptures and songs, for otherwise the force would engulf him and drown him. His name was Gilgamesh and he was the first of the artists of mankind."

THE CITY DWELLERS CAME BY the thousands now. They listened and wept at Breckenridge's words.

HYPOTHESIS OF STRUCTURAL RESOLUTION:

Gradually the outlines of a master myth took place: the creation, the creation of man, the origin of private property, the origin of death, the loss of faith, the end of the world, the coming of a redeemer to start the cycle anew. Soon the structure would be complete. When it was, Breckenridge thought, perhaps rains would fall on the desert, perhaps the world would be reborn.

BRECKENRIDGE SLEPT. SLEEPING, HE EXPERIENCED an inward glow of golden light. The girl he had encountered before came to him and took his hand and led him through the city. They walked for hours, it seemed, until they came to a well different from all the others, rectangular rather than circular and surrounded at street level by a low railing of bright metal mesh. "Go down into this one," she told him. "When you reach the bottom, keep walking until you reach the room where the mechanisms of awakening are located." He looked at her in amazement, realizing that her words had been comprehensible. "Are you speaking my language," he asked, "or am I speaking yours?" She answered by smiling and pointing toward the well.

He stepped over the railing and began his descent. The well was deeper than the other one; the air in its depths was stale and dry. The golden glow lit his way for him to the bottom and thence along a low passageway with a rounded vault of a ceiling. After a long time he came to a large, brightly lit room filled with sleek gray machinery. It was much like the computer room at any large bank. Mounted on the walls were control panels, labeled in an unknown language but also clearly marked with sequential symbols:

I II III IIII IIIII IIIIII

While he studied these he became aware of a sliding, hissing sound from the corridor beyond. He thought of sturdy metal cables passing one against the other; but then into the control room slowly came a creature something like a scorpion in form, considerably greater than a man in size. Its curved tubular thorax was dark and of a waxen texture; a dense mat of brown bristles, thick as straws, sprouted on its abdomen; its many eyes were bright, alert, and malevolent. Breckenridge snatched up a steel bar that lay near his feet and tried to wield it like a lance as the monster approached. From its jaws, though, there looped a sudden lasso of newly spun silken thread that caught the end of the bar and jerked it from Breckenridge's grasp. Then a second loop, entangling his arms and shoulders. Struggle was useless. He was caught. The creature pulled him closer. Breckenridge saw fangs, powerful palpi, a scythe of a tail in which a dripping stinger had become erect. Breckenridge writhed in the monster's grip. He felt neither surprise nor fear; this seemed a necessary working out of some ancient foreordained pattern.

A cool, silent voice within his skull said, "Who are you?"

"Noel Breckenridge of New York City, born A.D. 1940."

"Why do you intrude here?"

"I was summoned. If you want to know why, ask someone else."

"Is it your purpose to awaken the sleepers?"

"Very possibly," Breckenridge said.

"So the time has come?"

"Maybe it has," said Breckenridge. All was still for a long moment. The monster made no hostile move. Breckenridge grew impatient. "Well, what's the arrangement?" he said finally.

"The arrangement?"

"The terms under which I get my freedom. Am I supposed to tell you a lot of diverting stories? Will I have to serve you six months out of the year, forevermore? Is there some precious object I'm obliged to bring you from the bottom of the sea? Maybe you have a riddle that I'm supposed to answer."

The monster made no reply.

"Is that it?" Breckenridge demanded. "A riddle?"

"Do you want it to be a riddle?"

"A riddle, yes."

There was another endless pause. Breckenridge met the beady gaze steadily. At last the voice said, "A riddle. A riddle. Very well. Tell me the answer to this. What goes on four legs in the morning, on two legs in the afternoon, on three legs in the evening."

Breckenridge repeated it. He pondered. He frowned. He coughed. Then he laughed. "A baby," he said, "crawls on all fours. A grown man walks upright. An old man requires the assistance of a cane. Therefore the answer to your riddle is—"

He left the sentence unfinished. The gleam went out of the monster's eyes; the silken loop binding Breckenridge dissolved; the creature began slowly and sadly to back away, withdrawing into the corridor from which it came. Its hissing, rustling sound persisted for a time, growing ever more faint.

Breckenridge turned and without hesitation pulled the switch marked I.

THE AURORA NO LONGER APPEARS in the night sky. A light rain has been falling frequently for some days, and the desert is turning green. The sleepers are awakening, millions of them, called forth from their coffins by the workings of automatic mechanisms. Breckenridge stands in the central plaza of the city, arms outspread, and the city dwellers, as they emerge from the subterranean sleeping places, make their way toward him. I am the resurrection and the life, he thinks. I am Orpheus the sweet singer. I am Homer the blind. I am Noel Breckenridge. He looks across the eons to Harry Munsey. "I was wrong," he says. "There's meaning everywhere, Harry.

For Sam Smith as well as for Beethoven. For Noel Breckenridge as well as for Michelangelo. Dawn after dawn, simply being alive, being part of it all, part of the cosmic dance of life—that's the meaning, Harry. Look! Look!" The sun is high now—not a cruel sun but a mild, gentle one, its heat softened by a humid haze. This is the dream-time, when all mistakes are unmade, when all things become one. The city folk surround him. They come closer. Closer yet. They reach toward him. He experiences a delicious flash of white light. The world disappears.

"JFK AIRPORT," HE TOLD THE taxi driver. The cab zoomed away. From the front seat came the voice of the radio with today's closing Dow Jones Industrials: 948.72, down 6.11. He reached the airport by half past five, and at seven he boarded a Pan Am flight for London. The next morning at nine, London time, he cabled his wife to say that he was well and planned to head south for the winter. Then he reported to the Air France counter for the nonstop flight to Morocco. Over the next week he cabled home from Rabat, Marrakech, and Timbuktu in Mali. The third cable said:

> guess what stop i'm really in timbuktu stop have rented jeep stop i set out into sahara tomorrow stop am very happy stop yes stop very happy stop very very happy stop stop stop.

It was the last message he sent. The night it arrived in New York there was a spectacular celestial display, an aurora that brought thousands of people out into Central Park. There was rain in the southeastern Sahara four days later, the first recorded precipitation there in eight years and seven months. An earthquake was reported in southern Sicily, but it did little damage. Things were much quieter after that for everybody.

◆

THE MAN WHO FLOATED IN TIME

The 1980s were an era of odd-concept science fiction anthologies, and one of the oddest concepts of all was the book called Speculations, *which a writer named Laura Haywood (who wrote and edited under the pseudonym of Alice Laurance) was doing in collaboration with Isaac Asimov. The idea was to commission short stories from a group of well-known science fiction writers and identify them only in code, so that their names were nowhere visible on the outside of the book and a complex decoding process was necessary in order to figure out who had written what. This didn't strike me as a particularly fruitful way to present a science fiction anthology, since readers often like to know whose work is contained in the book before they buy it, but I went along with the project anyway. So did Jack Williamson, Gene Wolfe, R. A. Lafferty, Alan Dean Foster, and a bunch of others, including Asimov himself.*

To make it easy for those who didn't want to bother solving the puzzle, I chose a theme that I have been identified with throughout much of my career—time travel—and wrote the story, in January 1981, in as Silverbergian-sounding style as I could manage. It was published the following year in the Laurance-Asimov anthology under a code name 35 digits long, beginning with "411332IIII323." In retrospect, I see that I played the game the wrong way: I should have written something that no one could possibly have recognized as my work by its style and content alone. If anyone ever asks me to write for such an anthology again, that's what I'll do. But I doubt that the opportunity is going to arise.

There was something shady and sly about him. For one thing he was small and slightly built, and I have an instinctive mistrust of men who stand less than five feet five: they seem too agile and unpredictable, shifty little Napoleons who are apt to come at you from three directions at once. Then, too, his narrow glittery gray eyes, though they did actually make contact with mine, never seemed to be aimed directly at me but rather, somehow, sent a beam of vision hooking around a sharply banked curve even when his face looked at me right square on. I didn't like that. He was about sixty, sixty-five, lean and trim, not well dressed, his gray hair cropped very short and gone at the crown.

"What I do," he said, "is travel in time. I float freely back to other eras."

"Really," I said. "Never forward?"

"Oh, no, never. That's quite impossible. The future doesn't exist. The past is there, solid and real, a *place,* you know, like Des Moines or Wichita. One can go to Wichita if one makes the proper connection. But one can't go to a city that's never been built. It isn't conceivable. Well, perhaps it's conceivable, but it isn't *doable,* do you follow me? I go to the past, though. I've seen Attila the Hun. I've seen Julius Caesar. I wish I could say I went to bed with Catherine the Great, but I didn't, although I had a few vodkas with someone who did. She smelled of garlic, he said, and she took forever to come. You don't believe any of what I'm saying, do you?"

"You're asking me to swallow quite a lot," I said mildly.

He leaned forward in a conspiratorial way. "You're not the kind of man who's easily convinced of the unusual. I can tell. No ancient astronaut stuff for you, no UFO contact stories, no psychic spoon-bendings. That's good. I don't want an easy believer. I want a skeptic to hear me out and test my words and arrive at his own acceptance of the truth his own way. That's all I ask of you, that you don't scoff, that you don't write me off instantly as a crackpot. All right?"

"I'll try."

"Now: what do you feel when I tell you I've traveled in time?"

"Instinctive resistance. An immediate sense that I've got myself mixed up with a crackpot or at best a charming liar."

"Fine. I wouldn't have come to you if I thought you'd react any other way."

"What do you want from me, then?"

"That you listen to me and suspend your disbelief at least now and then and ask me a question or two, probe me, test me, give me the benefit of the doubt long enough to let me get through to you. And then that you help me get my experiences down on paper. I'm old and I'm sick and I'm not going to be here much longer, and I want to leave a memoir, a record, do you see? And I need someone like you to help me."

"Why not write it yourself?" I asked.

"Easy enough to say. But I'm no writer. I don't have the gift. I can't even do letters without freezing up."

"Doing a memoir doesn't require a gift. You simply put down your story on paper, just as though you were telling it to me. Writing's not as hard as nonwriters like to think it is."

"Writing is easy for you," he said, "and time traveling is easy for me. And I'm about as capable of writing as you are of traveling in time. Do you see?" He put his hand on my wrist, a gesture of premature intimacy that sent a quick, and quickly suppressed, quiver through my entire arm. "Help me to get my story down, will you? You think I'm a crazy old drunk, and you wish you had never given me minute one of your time, but I ask you to put those feelings aside and accept just for the moment the possibility that this isn't just a mess of lies and fantasies. Can you do that?"

"Go on," I said. "Tell me about yourself."

He said his time traveling had begun when he was a boy. The technique by which he claimed to be able to unhitch himself from the bonds of the continuum and drift back along the time-line was apparently one that he developed spontaneously, a sort of applied meditation that amounted to artfully channeled fantasizing. Through this process, which he refined and perfected between the ages of eight and eleven, he achieved what I suppose must be called out-of-the-body experiences, in which his psyche, his consciousness, his walking intelligence, vanished into the past while his body remained here, ostensibly asleep.

On his first voyage he found himself in an American city of the colonial era. He had no idea where he was when he was older, working from his searingly vivid memories of the journey, he was able to identify it as Charleston, South Carolina—but he knew at once, from his third-grade studies, that the powdered wigs and three-cornered hats must mean the eighteenth century. He was there for three days, fascinated at first, then frightened and confused and terribly hungry—

"Hungry?" I said. "A wandering psyche with an appetite?"

"You don't perceive yourself as disembodied," he replied, looking pleased that I had raised an objection. "You feel that you have been quite literally transplanted to the other era. You need to eat, to sleep, to perform bodily functions. I was a small boy lost in a prerevolutionary city. The first night I slept in a forest. In the morning I returned to the city where some people found me, dirty and lost, and took me to a mansion where I was bathed and fed—"

"And given clothes? You must have been in your pajamas."

"No, you are always clothed in the clothing of the era when you arrive," he said. "And equipped with the language of the region and a certain amount of local currency."

"How very convenient. What providential force takes care of those little details?"

He smiled. "Those are part of the illusion. Plainly I have no real coins with me, and of course I haven't magically learned new languages. But the aspect of me that makes the journey has the capacity to lead others to feel that they are receiving true coinage from me; and as my soul makes contact with theirs, they imagine that it is their own language I speak. What I do is not actual bodily travel, you understand. It is astral projection, to use a phrase that I know will arouse hostility in you. My real body, in its pajamas, remained snug in my bed; but the questing *anima,* the roving spirit, arrived fully equipped. Of course the money is dream-money and melts away the moment I go farther from it than a certain range. In my travels I have left angry innkeepers and cheated peddlers and even a few swindled harlots all over the world, I'm afraid. But for the moment what I give them passes as honest coin."

"Yet the astral body must be fed with real food?"

"Indeed. And I think that if the astral body is injured, the sleeping real body feels the pain."

"How can you be sure of that?"

"Because," he said, "I have fallen headlong down temple steps in the Babylon of Hammurabi and awakened to find bruises on my thigh and shoulder. I have slashed myself on vines in the jungles of ancient Cambodia and awakened to see the cuts. I have stood in the snows of Pleistocene Europe shivering with the Neanderthals and awakened with frostbite in July."

There is an Italian saying: *Se non è vero, è ben trovato.* "If it is not true, it is well invented." There was in his eyes and on his thin gray-stubbled face at that moment a look of such passionate conviction, such absolute sincerity, that I began to tremble, hearing him talk of feeling the bite of Pleistocene winds, and for the first time I began to allow myself the possibility of thinking that this man could be something other than a boozy old scamp with a vivid imagination. But I was far from converted.

I said, "Then if through some mischance you were killed when traveling, your real body would perish also?"

"I have every reason to think so," he replied quietly.

He traveled through vast reaches of space and time when he was still a child. Most of the places he visited were bewilderingly alien to him, and he had little idea of where or when he was, but he learned to observe keenly, to note salient details, to bring back with him data that sooner or later would help him to determine what he had experienced. He was a bookish child anyway, and so it caused no amazement when he burrowed feverishly through the *National Geographic* or the *Britannica* or dusty volumes of history. As he grew older and his education deepened, it became easier for him to learn the identity of his destinations; and when he was still older, fully grown, it was not at all difficult for him simply to ask those about him, What is the name of this city? Who is the king here? What is the event of the day?

exactly as though he were a traveler newly arrived from a far-off land. For although he had journeyed in the form of a boy at first, his astral self always mirrored his true self, and as he aged, the projection that he sent to the past kept pace with him.

So, then, he visited while still a child the London of the Tudors, where rivers of muck ran in the streets, and he stood at the gates of Peking to watch the triumphal entry of the Great Khan Kublai, and he crept cautiously through the forests of the Dordogne to spy on the encampments of Neolithic huntsmen, and he tiptoed along the brutal brick battlements of a terrifying city of windowless buildings that proved to be Mohenjo-daro on the Indus, and he slipped with awe through the boulevards and plazas of majestic Tenochtitlan of the Aztecs, his pale skin growing sunburned under the heat of the pre-Columbian sun. And when he was older he stood in the frenzied crowd before the bloody guillotine of the Terror, and saw virgins hurled into the sacred well of Chichen Itza, and wandered through the smoldering ruins of Atlanta a week after General Sherman had put it to the torch, and drank thick red wine in a lovely town on the slopes of Vesuvius that may have been Pompeii. The stories rolled from him in wondrous profusion, and I listened to the charming old crank hour after hour, telling me sly tales of a history not to be found in books. Julius Caesar, he said, was a mincing dandy who reeked of vile perfume, and Cleopatra was squat and thick-lipped, and the Israelites of King David's time were brawling, conniving primitives no holier than the desert folk the next tribe over, and the Great Wall of China had been mostly a slovenly rampart of mud, decaying as fast as it was slapped together, and Socrates had never lived at all but was only a convenient pedagogical invention of Plato's, and Plato had charged an enormous fee even for mere conversation. As for the Crusaders, they were more feared by Christians than Saracens, for they raped and stole and sacked mercilessly as they trekked across Europe to the Holy Land; and Alexander the Great had rarely been sober enough to stand upright after the age of twenty-three; and the orchestras of Mozart's time played mostly out of tune on feeble, screechy instruments. All this poured from him in long disjointed monologues, which I interrupted less and less frequently for clarifications and amplifications. He spoke with utter conviction and with total disregard for my disbelief: I was invited to accept his tales as whatever I pleased, gospel revelations or amusing fraud, so long as I listened.

At our fifth or sixth meeting, after he had told me about his adventures among the bare-breasted wenches of Minoan Crete—the maze, he said, was nothing much, just some alleyways and gutters—and in the Constantinople of Justinian and in the vast unpeopled bison-herd lands of ancient North America, I said to him, "Is there any time or place you haven't visited?"

"Atlantis," he said. "I kept hoping to identify the unmistakable Atlantis, but never, never once—"

"Everywhere else, and every era?"

"Hardly. I've had only one lifetime."

"I wondered. I haven't been keeping a tally, but it seems to me it must have taken you eighty or ninety years to see all that you've seen. A week here, a month there—it adds up, doesn't it?"

"Yes."

"And while you're gone, you remain asleep here for weeks or months at a time?"

"Oh, no," he said. "You've misunderstood. Time spent *there* has no relation to elapsed time *here*. I can be gone for many days, and no more than an instant will have passed here. At most, an hour or two. Why, I've taken off on journeys even while I was sitting here talking with you!"

"What?"

"Yesterday, as we spoke of the San Francisco earthquake—between one eye-blink and the next, I spent eighteen hours in some German principality of the fourteenth century."

"And never said a word about it when you returned?"

He shrugged. "You were prickly and unreceptive yesterday, and I was having trouble keeping your sympathies. I felt it would be too stagy to tell you, Oh, by way, I've just been in Augsburg or Reutlingen or Ulm or whichever it was. Besides, it was a boring trip. I found it so dreary I didn't even trouble to ask the name of the place."

"Then why did you stay for so long?"

"Why, I have no control over that," he said.

"No control?"

"None. I drift away and I stay away however long I must and then I come back. It's been like that from the start. I can't choose my destination, either. I can best compare it to getting into a plane and being spirited off for a vacation of unknown length in an unknown land and not having a word to say about any of it. There have been times when I thought I wouldn't ever come back."

"Did that frighten you?"

"Only when I didn't like where I happened to be," he said. "The idea of spending the rest of my life in some mudhole in the middle of Mongolia or in an igloo in Greenland or—well, you get the idea." He pursed his lips. "Another thing—it happens automatically to me."

"I thought there was a ritual, a meditative process—"

"When I was a child, yes. But in time I internalized it so well that it happens of its own accord. Which is terrifying, because it can come over me anywhere, anytime, like a fit. Did you think there were no drawbacks to this? Did you think it was a lifelong picnic, roving space and time? I've had two or three uncontrolled departures a year since I was twenty. It's been my, luck that I haven't fallen down unconscious in the street, or anything like that. Though there have been some great embarrassments."

"How have your explained them?"

"With lies," he said. "You are the first to whom I've told the truth about myself."

"Should I believe that?"

"You are the first," he said with intense conviction. "And that because my time is almost over and I need at last to share my story with someone. Eh? Is that plausible? Do you still think I've fabricated it all?"

Indeed, I had no idea. To treat his story as lies or fantasy was easy enough to do; but for all his shiftiness of expression, there was an odd ring of truth even to his most enormous whoppers. And the wealth of information, the outpouring of circumstantial detail—I suppose a solitary life spent over history books could have explained that, but nevertheless, nevertheless—

And if it was true? What good had it all been? He had written nothing, no anecdotes of his adventures, no revisionist historical essays, no setting down of the philosophical insights that must have grown out of his exploration of thirty thousand years of human history. He had lived a strange and fitful and fragmentary life, flickering in and out of what we call the reality of the everyday world as though he were going to the movies, and bizarre movies they were, a week in Byzantium and a month in old Sumer and an hour among the Pharaohs. A life spent alone, a loveless life by the sound of it, a weird zigzagging chaos of a life such as has been granted no other human being—

If it was true.

And if not? *Se non è vero, è ben trovato.* I listened enraptured. I continued to probe for details of the mechanics of it. His journeys took him anywhere on earth? Anywhere, he said. Once he had arrived in a wasteland of glaciers that he believed from the strangeness of the constellations to have been Antarctica, though it might have been any icy land at a time when the stars were in other places in the sky. Happily that voyage had lasted less than an hour or he would have perished. But there seemed no limits—he might turn up on any continent, he said, and at any time. Or *almost* any time, for I queried him about dinosaurs and the era of the trilobites and the chance that he might find himself some day plunged into the primordial planetary soup of creation, but no, he had never gone back further than the Pleistocene, so far as he could tell, and he did not know why. I wondered also how he had seen so many of the great figures of history, Caesar and Cleopatra and Lincoln and Dante and the rest, when we who live only in today rarely encounter presidents and kings and movie stars in the course of our comings and goings, but he had an answer to that, too, saying that the world had been much smaller in earlier times, cities being deemed great if they had fifty or a hundred thousand people, and the mighty were far more accessible, going out into the marketplace and letting themselves be seen; besides, he had made it his business to seek them out, for what is the point of finding oneself miraculously transported to imperial Rome and coming away without at least a squint at Augustus or Caligula?

So I listened to it all and was caught up in it, and though I will not say that I ever came to believe the literal truth of his claims, I also did not quite disbelieve, and through his rambling discourses I felt the past return to life in an astonishing way. I made time for his visits, cleared all other priorities out of the way when he called to tell me he was coming and, beyond doubt, grew almost dependent on his tales, as though they were a drug, some potent hallucinogen that carried me off into gaudy realms of antiquity.

And in what proved to be his last conversation with me he said, "I could show you how it's done."

The simple words hung between us in the air like dancing swords.

I gaped at him and made no reply.

He said, "It would take perhaps three months of training. For me it was easy, natural, no challenge, but of course I was a child and I had no barriers to overcome. You, with your skepticism, your sophistication, your aloofness—it would be hard for you to master the technique, but I could show you and train you, and eventually you would succeed. Would you like that?"

I thought of watching Caesar's chariot rolling down the Via Flaminia. I thought of clinking canisters with Chaucer in some tavern just outside Canterbury. I thought of penetrating the caves of Lascaux to stare at the freshly painted bulls.

And then I thought of my quiet, orderly life, and how it would be to fall into a narcoleptic trance at unpredictable moments and swing off into the darkness of space and time, and land perhaps in the middle of some hideous massacre or in a season of plague or in a desolate land where no human foot had ever walked. I thought of pain and discomfort and risk, and possible sudden death, and the disruption of patterns of habit, and I looked into his eyes and saw the strangeness there, a strangeness that I did not want to share, and in simple cowardice I said, "I think I would rather not."

A flicker of something like disappointment passed across his features. But then he smiled and stood up and said, "I'm not surprised. But thank you for hearing me out. You were more open-minded than I expected."

He took my hand briefly in his. Then he was gone, and I never saw him again. A few weeks later, I learned of his death, and I heard his soft voice saying "I could show you how it's done," and a great sadness came over me, for although I knew he was a fraud, I knew also that there was a chance that he was not, and if so, I had foreclosed the possibility of infinite wonders for myself. How sad to have refused, I told myself, how pale and gray a thing to have done, how contemptible, really. Yes, contemptible to have refused him out of hand, without even attempting it, without offering him that final bit of credence. For several days I was deeply depressed; and then I went on to other things, as one does, and put him from my mind.

A few weeks after his death one of the big midtown banks called me. They mentioned his name and said they were executors of his estate and told me that he had left something for me, an envelope to be opened only after his death. If I could satisfactorily identify myself, the envelope would be shipped to my bank. So I went through the routine, sending a letter to my bank, which authenticated the signature and forwarded it to *his* bank, and in time my bank informed me that a parcel had come, and I went down to claim it. It was a fairly bulky manila envelope. I had the sudden wild notion that it contained some irrefutable proof of his voyages in time, something like a photograph of Jesus on the cross or a personal letter to my friend from William the Conqueror, but of course that was impossible; he had made it clear that nothing traveled in time except his intangible essence, no possessions, no artifacts. Yet my hand shook as I opened the envelope.

It contained a thick manuscript and a covering note that explained that he had decided, after all, to share with me the secrets of his technique. Without his guidance it might take me much longer to learn the knack, a year or more of diligent application, perhaps, but if I persevered, if I genuinely sought to achieve—

A wondrous dizziness came over me, as though I hung over an infinite abyss by the frailest of fraying threads and was being asked to choose between drab safety and the splendor of the unknown plunge. I felt the temptation.

And for the second time I refused the cup.

I did not read the manuscript. I was too timid for that. Nor did I destroy it, though the idea crossed my mind; but I was too cowardly even for that, I must admit, for I had no wish to bear the responsibility for having cast into oblivion so potent a secret, if potent it really was. I put the sheaf of papers—over which he must have labored with intense dedication, writing being so painfully difficult a thing for him—back into their envelope and sealed it again and put it in my vault, deep down below the bankbooks and the insurance policies and the stock certificates and the other symbols of the barricades I have thrown about myself to make my life secure.

Perhaps the manuscript, like everything else he told me, is mere fantastic nonsense. Perhaps not.

Someday, when life grows too drab for me, when the pleasures of the predictable and safe begin to pall, I will take that envelope from the vault and study its lessons, and if nothing then happens, so be it. But if I feel the power beginning to come to life in me, if I find myself once again swaying above that abyss with the choices within my reach, I hope I will find the courage to sever the thread, to loose all ties and restraints, to say farewell to order and routine, and to send myself soaring into that great uncharted infinite gulf of time.

◆

GIANNI

For many years I had wanted to sell a story to Playboy, *a magazine famous for its naked lady photographs but also noted for its fiction. It had run stories by such people as John Updike, Vladimir Nabokov, Bernard Malamud, and Jorge Luis Borges—but also it had made a sub-specialty of science fiction by many of the top people in the field: Ray Bradbury, Arthur C. Clarke, J. G. Ballard, Philip K. Dick, and others on that level, paying for them at a rate far beyond what the orthodox science fiction magazines paid.*

But until 1980 I simply watched from afar as the work of my friends and colleagues appeared there. I did nothing about offering a story to Playboy *until I finally bestirred myself and sent one to Alice K. Turner,* Playboy's *fiction editor. That one didn't bring a sale, but it resulted in a fascinating correspondence with her—Alice wanted to buy a story of mine, it turned out, as much as I wanted to sell one to her. She told me that she would visit the San Francisco area in the spring of 1981 and suggested we meet for dinner. I wanted to offer a new story to her before she arrived. So I wrote "Gianni" that February—a time travel story, of course; in facing a tough challenge one should always lead with one's strong suit. I sent it to her just before her visit, and a few weeks later came a three-page letter from Alice, which began by telling me that we were booked for dinner at the famous Chez Panisse restaurant, and went on to an extensive discussion of the revisions she wanted on "Gianni," which she was going to publish. She simply wanted a few small revisions, and she was so confident that I'd do them to her satisfaction that she enclosed a check in payment for the story—quite a large check.*

Her letter raised a number of interesting points. Some I agreed with, some I didn't; and I made notations in the margin indicating my reaction to the various changes she wanted. "Yes," I said to one, and "maybe" to another, and "no" to several. But there was one request that seemed absolutely impossible for me to comply with. "Gianni" was a first-person story, narrated by Dave Leavis, the scientist in charge of the time travel experiment. Alice wanted me to switch the story around so that a different character—Sam Hoaglund, the publicity agent—would be the narrator. I didn't see how that was possible. How could I rewrite a first-person story so that it now would be told by a different narrator, short of completely reconstructing the whole story? I had envisioned it all along as Leavis's story to tell. I couldn't imagine rethinking it so that it would be told by Hoaglund. But it appeared from her letter that Alice would insist on the change. If she did, it would kill the sale. So when I met her for dinner that night at Chez Panisse, I had Playboy*'s nice, big check in my coat pocket, ready to hand back to her at the end of our discussion.*

Eventually the conversation came around to "Gianni." I mentioned that I had a little problem with changing the narrator. And then Alice produced one of the biggest editorial surprises I have ever experienced in my long writing career.

She had anticipated my resistance to that particular change. So she had brought a copy of the story with her that she had marked in pencil to show me how easy it would be to do. She handed it to me and I leafed through it in amazement. She had done the impossible. With a few small strokes she had transferred the narrative center from Leavis to Hoagland—a technical stunt that astonished me, and I have been a close and careful student of the technical side of writing fiction for many decades.

So I said nothing about the check in my coat pocket, and I agreed to do the revisions, and I went home and started making them. On April 7, 1981, I sent it back to her, having made the viewpoint switch and having also accepted some (not all) of her other suggestions for changing the story. Playboy *published it in the February 1982 issue.*

That was the start of a long and wonderful editor-author relationship that would see me write fifteen or twenty more stories for Playboy *and become embroiled in some marvelous arguments with Alice about most of those stories before she was satisfied with them. Many years later, when we were looking back at the "Gianni" event, I told her that I had come to dinner that night prepared to give her back the check if she had insisted on having her way about the viewpoint switch—but hadn't done it, because she had been able to convince me that the switch was possible.*

"What would you have done," I asked, "if I had returned the check?"

"I would have published the story the way you wrote it, with Leavis as the narrator," she replied, and we both had a good laugh.

Since then, whenever I have had an opportunity to bring "Gianni" back into print in some anthology or a collection of my own short stories, I have used the Leavis-narrator version. When Alice reprinted the story herself in The Playboy Book of Science Fiction, *she used the version published in the magazine, with Hoaglund as the narrator. Which version of the story is the more effective one? I have no idea.*

"BUT WHY NOT MOZART?" HOAGLUND said, shaking his head. "Schubert, even? Or you could have brought back Bix Beiderbecke, for Christ's sake, if you wanted to resurrect a great musician."

"Beiderbecke was jazz," I said. "I'm not interested in jazz. Nobody's interested in jazz except you."

"And people are still interested in Pergolesi in the year 2008?"

"*I* am."

"Mozart would have been better publicity. You'll need more funding sooner or later. You tell the world you've got Mozart sitting in the back room cranking out a new opera, you can write your own ticket. But what good is Pergolesi? Pergolesi's totally forgotten."

"Only by the proletariat, Sam. Besides, why give Mozart a second chance? Maybe he died young, but it wasn't all *that* young, and he did his work, a ton of work. Gianni died at twenty-six, you know. He might have been greater than Mozart if he'd had another dozen years."

"Johnny?"

"Gianni. Giovanni Battista. Pergolesi. He calls himself Gianni. Come meet him."

"Mozart, Dave. You should have done Mozart."

"Stop being an idiot," I said. "When you've met him, you'll know I did the right thing. Mozart would have been a pain in the neck, anyway. The stories I've heard about Mozart's private life would uncurl your wig. Come on with me."

I led him down the long hallway from the office past the hardware room and the timescoop cage to the airlock separating us from the semidetached motel unit out back where Gianni had been living since we scooped him. We halted in the airlock to be sprayed. Sam frowned and I explained, "Infectious microorganisms have mutated a lot since the eighteenth century. Until we've got his resistance levels higher, we're keeping him in a pretty sterile environment. When we first brought him back, he was vulnerable to anything—a case of the sniffles would have killed him, most likely. Plus he was a dying man when we got him, one lung lousy with TB and the other one going."

"Hey," Hoaglund said.

I laughed. "You won't catch anything from him. It's in remission now, Sam. We didn't bring him back at colossal expense just to watch him die."

The lock opened and we stepped into the monitoring vestibule, glittering like a movie set with bank upon bank of telemetering instruments. The day nurse, Claudia, was checking diagnostic readouts. "He's expecting you, Dr. Leavis," she said. "He's very frisky this morning."

"Frisky?"

"Playful. You know."

Yes. Tacked to the door of Gianni's room was a card that hadn't been there yesterday, flamboyantly lettered in gaudy, free-flowing baroque script:

> ***Giovanni Battista Pergolesi***
>
> Jesi, January 3 1710—Pozzuoli, March 17 1736
> Los Angeles, Dec. 20 2007—.
> *Genuis At Work!!!!*
> *Per Piacere, Knock Before You enter!*

"He speaks English?" Hoaglund asked.

"Now he does," I said. "We gave him tapesleep the first week. He picks things up fast, anyway." I grinned. "Genius at work, eh? Or *genuis.* That's the sort of sign I would have expected Mozart to put up."

"They're all alike, these talents," Hoaglund said.

I knocked.

"Chi va là?" Gianni called.

"Dave Leavis."

"Avanti, dottore illustrissimo!"

"I thought you said he speaks English," Hoaglund murmured.

"He's frisky today, Claudia said, remember?"

We went in. As usual he had the blinds tightly drawn, shutting out the brilliant January sunlight, the yellow blaze of acacia blossoms just outside the window, the enormous scarlet bougainvillea, the sweeping hilltop vista of the valley and the mountains beyond. Maybe scenery didn't interest him—or, more likely, he preferred to keep his room a tightly sealed little cell, an island out of time. He had had to absorb a lot of psychic trauma in the past few weeks: it must give you a hell of a case of jet-lag to jump 271 years into the future.

But he looked lively, almost impish—a small man, graceful, delicate, with sharp, busy eyes, quick, elegant gestures, a brisk, confident manner. How much he had changed in just a few weeks! When we fished him out of the eighteenth century, he was a woeful sight, face lined and haggard, hair already gray at twenty-six, body gaunt, bowed, quivering. He looked like what he was, a shattered consumptive a couple of weeks from the grave. His hair was still gray, but he had gained ten pounds; the veils were gone from his eyes; there was color in his cheeks.

I said, "Gianni, I want you to meet Sam Hoaglund. He's going to handle publicity and promotion for our project. *Capisce?* He will make you known to the world and give you a new audience for your music."

He flashed a brilliant smile. "*Bene.* Listen to this."

The room was an electronic jungle, festooned with gadgetry: a synthesizer, a telescreen, a megabuck audio library, five sorts of data terminals and all manner of other things perfectly suited to your basic eighteenth-century Italian drawing room. Gianni loved it all and was mastering the equipment with astonishing, even frightening, ease. He swung around to the synthesizer, jacked it into harpsichord mode and touched the keyboard. From the cloud of floating mini speakers came the opening theme of a sonata, lovely, lyrical, to my ear unmistakably

Pergolesian in its melodiousness, and yet somehow weird. For all its beauty there was a strained, awkward, *suspended* aspect to it, like a ballet performed by dancers in galoshes. The longer he played, the more uncomfortable I felt. Finally he turned to us and said, "You like it?"

"What is it? Something of yours?"

"Mine, yes. My new style. I am under the influence of Beethoven today. Haydn yesterday, tomorrow Chopin. I try everything, no? By Easter I get to the ugly composers. Mahler, Berg, Debussy—those men were *crazy,* do you know? Crazy music, so ugly. But I will learn."

"Debussy ugly?" Hoaglund said quietly to me.

"Bach is modern music to him," I said. "Haydn is the voice of the future."

Gianni said, "I will be very famous."

"Yes. Sam will make you the most famous man in the world."

"I was very famous after I—died." He tapped one of the terminals. "I have read about me. I was so famous that everybody forged my music, and it was published as Pergolesi, do you know that? I have played it, too, this 'Pergolesi.' *Merda,* most of it. Not all. The *concerti armonici,* not bad—not mine, but not bad. Most of the rest, trash." He winked. "But you will make me famous while I live, eh? Good. Very good." He came closer to us and in a lower voice said, "Will you tell Claudia that the gonorrhea, it is all cured?"

"What?"

"She would not believe me. I said, 'The doctor swears it,' but she said, 'No, it is not safe; you must keep your hands off me; you must keep everything else off me.'"

"Gianni, have you been molesting your nurse?"

"I am becoming a healthy man, *dottore.* I am no monk. They sent me to live with the *cappuccini* in the monastery at Pozzuoli, yes, but it was only so the good air there could heal my consumption, not to make me a monk. I am no monk now and I am no longer sick. Could you go without a woman for three hundred years?" He put his face close to Hoaglund's, gave him a bright-eyed stare, leered outrageously. "You will make me very famous. And then there will be women again, yes? And you must tell them that the gonorrhea, it is entirely cured. This age of miracles!"

Afterward Hoaglund said to me, "And you thought Mozart was going to be too much trouble?"

When we first got him, there was no snappy talk out of him of women or fame or marvelous new compositions. Then he was a wreck, a dazed wraith, hollow, burned out. He wasn't sure whether he had awakened in heaven or in hell, but whichever it was left him alternately stunned and depressed. He was barely clinging to life, and we began to wonder if we had waited too long to get him. Perhaps it might be wiser, some of us thought, to toss him back and pick him up from an earlier point, maybe summer of 1735, when he wasn't so close to the grave. But we had no budget for making a second scoop, and also we were bound by our own rigid self-imposed rules. We had the power to yank anybody we liked out of the past—Napoleon, Genghis Khan, Jesus, Henry the Eighth—but we had no way of knowing what effects it might have on the course of history if we scooped up Lenin while he was still in exile in Switzerland, say, or collected Hitler while he was still a paperhanger. So we decided *a priori* to scoop only someone whose life and accomplishments were entirely behind him, and who was so close to the time of his natural death that his disappearance would not be likely to unsettle the fabric of the universe. For months I lobbied to scoop Pergolesi, and I got my way, and we took him out of the monastery eighteen days before his official date of death. Once we had him, it was no great trick to substitute a synthetic cadaver, who was duly discovered and buried, and so far as we have been able to tell, no calamities have resulted to history because one consumptive Italian was put in his grave two weeks earlier than the encyclopedia used to say he had been.

Yet it was touch and go at first, keeping him alive. Those were the worst days of my life, the first few after the scooping. To have planned for years, to have expended so many gigabucks on the project, and then to have our first human scoopee die on us anyway—

He didn't, though. The same vitality that had pulled sixteen operas and a dozen cantatas and uncountable symphonies and concerti and masses and sonatas out of him in a twenty-six-year lifespan pulled him back from the edge of the grave now, once the resources of modern medicine were put to work rebuilding his lungs and curing his assorted venereal diseases. From hour to hour we could see him gaining strength. Within days he was wholly transformed. It was almost magical, even to us. And it showed us vividly how many lives were needlessly lost in those archaic days for want of the things that are routine to us antibiotics, transplant technology, micro-surgery, regeneration therapy.

For me those were wondrous days. The pallid, feeble young man struggling for his life in the back unit was surrounded by a radiant aura of accumulated fame and legend built up over centuries: he was *Pergolesi,* the miraculous boy, the fountain of melody, the composer of the awesome *Stabat Mater* and the rollicking *Serva Padrona,* who in the decades after his early death was ranked with Bach, with Mozart, with Haydn, and whose most trivial works inspired the whole genre of light opera. But his own view of himself was different: he was a weary, sick, dying young man, poor pathetic Gianni, the failure, the washout, unknown beyond Rome and Naples and poorly treated there, his serious operas neglected cruelly, his masses and cantatas praised but rarely performed, only the comic operas that he dashed off so carelessly winning him any acclaim at all—poor Gianni, burned out at twenty-five, destroyed as much by disappointment as by tuberculosis and venereal disease, creeping off to the Capuchin monastery to die in miserable poverty. How could he have known he was to be famous? But we showed him. We played him recordings of his music, both the true works and those that had been constructed in his name by the unscrupulous to cash in on his posthumous glory. We let him read the biographies and critical studies and even the novels that had been published about him. Indeed, for him it must have been precisely like dying and going to heaven, and from day to day he gained strength and poise, he waxed and flourished, he came to glow with vigor and passion and confidence. He knew now that no magic had been worked on him, that he had been snatched into the unimaginable future and restored to health by ordinary human beings, and he accepted that and quickly ceased to question it. All that concerned him now was music. In the second and third weeks we gave him a crash course in post-Baroque musical history. Bach first, then the shift away from polyphony—*"Naturalmente,"* he said, "it was inevitable, I would have achieved it myself if I had lived"—and he spent hours with Mozart and Haydn and Johann Christian Bach, soaking up their complete works and entering a kind of ecstatic state. His nimble, agile mind swiftly began plotting its own directions. One morning I found him red-eyed with weeping. He had been up all night listening to *Don Giovanni* and *Marriage of Figaro.* "This Mozart," he said. "You bring him back, too?"

"Maybe someday we will," I said.

"I kill him! You bring him back, I strangle him, I trample him!" His eyes blazed. He laughed wildly. "He is wonder! He is angel! He is too good! Send me to his time, I kill him then! No one should compose like that! Except Pergolesi. He would have done it."

"I believe that."

"Yes! This *Figaro*—1786—I could have done it twenty years earlier! Thirty! If only I get the chance. Why this Mozart so lucky? I die, he live—why? Why, *dottore?*"

His love-hate relationship with Mozart lasted six or seven days. Then he moved on to Beethoven, who I think was a little too much for him, overwhelming, massive, crushing, and then the romantics, who amused him—"Berlioz, Tchaikovsky, Wagner, all lunatics, *dementi, pazzi,* but they are wonderful. I think I see what they are trying to do. Madmen! Marvelous madmen!" and quickly on to the twentieth century, Mahler, Schoenberg, Stravinsky, Bartok, not spending much time with any of them, finding them all either ugly or terrifying or simply incomprehensibly bizarre. More recent composers, Webern and the serialists, Penderecki, Stockhausen, Xenakis, Ligeti, the various electronicists and all that came after, he dismissed with a quick shrug, as though he barely recognized what they were doing as music. Their fundamental assumptions were too alien to him. Genius though he was, he could not assimilate their ideas, any more than Brillat-Savarin or Escoffier could have found much pleasure in the cuisine of another planet. After completing his frenzied survey of everything that had happened in music after his time, he returned to Bach and Mozart and gave them his full attention.

I mean *full* attention. Gianni was utterly incurious about the world outside his bedroom window. We told him he was in America, in California, and showed him a map. He nodded casually. We turned on the telescreen and let him look at the landscape of the early twenty-first century. His eyes glazed. We spoke of automobiles, planes, flights to Mars. Yes, he said, *meraviglioso, miracoloso,* and went back to the Brandenburg concerti. I realize now that the lack of interest he showed in the modern world was a sign neither of fear nor of shallowness, but rather only a mark of priorities. What Mozart had accomplished was stranger and more interesting to him than the entire technological revolution. Technology was only a means to an end, for Gianni—push a button, you get a symphony orchestra in your bedroom: *miracoloso!*—and he took it entirely for granted. That the *basso continuo* had become obsolete thirty years after his death, that the diatonic scales would be demoted from sacred constants to inconvenient anachronisms a century or so later, was more significant to him than the fusion reactor, the interplanetary spaceship, or even the machine that had yanked him from his deathbed into this brave new world.

In the fourth week he said he wanted to compose again. He asked for a harpsichord. Instead we gave him a synthesizer. He loved it.

In the sixth week he began asking questions about the outside world, and I realized that the tricky part of our experiment was about to begin.

HOAGLUND SAID, "PRETTY SOON WE have to reveal him. It's incredible we've been able to keep it quiet this long."

He had an elaborate plan. The problem was twofold: letting Gianni experience the world, and letting the world perceive that time travel as a practical matter involving real human beings—no more frogs and kittens hoisted from last month to this—had finally arrived. There was going to be a whole business of press conferences, media tours of our lab, interviews with Gianni, a festival of Pergolesi music at the Hollywood Bowl with the premiere of a symphony in the mode of Beethoven that he said would be ready by April, et cetera, et cetera, et cetera. But at the same time we would be taking Gianni on private tours of the L.A. area, gradually exposing him to the society into which he had been so unilaterally hauled. The medics said it was safe to let him encounter twenty-first-century microorganisms now. But would it be safe to let him encounter twenty-first-century civilization? He, with his windows sealed and his blinds drawn, his eighteenth-century mind wholly engrossed in the revelations that Bach and Mozart and Beethoven were pouring into it—what would he make of the world of spaceways and slice-houses and overload bands and freebase teams when he could no longer hide from it?

"Leave it all to me," said Hoaglund. "That's what you're paying me for, right?"

On a mild and rainy February afternoon Sam and I and the main physician, Nella Brandon, took him on his first drive through his new reality. Down the hill the back way, along Ventura Boulevard a few miles, onto the freeway, out to Topanga, back around through the landslide zone to what had been Santa Monica, and then straight up Wilshire across the entire heart of Los Angeles—a good stiff jolt of modernity. Dr. Brandon carried her full armamentarium of sedatives and tranks ready in case Gianni freaked out. But he didn't freak out.

He loved it—swinging round and round in the bubbletop car, gaping at everything. I tried to view L.A. through the eyes of someone whose entire life had been spent amid the splendors of Renaissance and Baroque architecture, and it came up hideous on all counts. But not to Gianni. "Beautiful," he sighed. "Wondrous! Miraculous! Marvelous!" The traffic, the freeways themselves, the fast-food joints, the peeling plastic facades, the great fire scar in Topanga, the houses hanging by spider-cables from the hillsides, the occasional superjet floating overhead on its way into LAX—everything lit him up. It was wonderland to him. None of those dull old cathedrals and *palazzi* and marble fountains here—no, everything here was brighter and larger and glitzier than life, and he loved it. The only part he couldn't handle was the beach at Topanga. By the time we got there the sun was out and so were the sunbathers, and the sight of eight thousand naked bodies cavorting on the damp sand almost gave him a stroke." What is this?" he demanded. "The market for slaves? The pleasure house of the king?"

"Blood pressure rising fast," Nella Brandon said softly, eyeing her wrist-monitors. "Adrenalin levels going up. Shall I cool him out?"

I shook my head.

"Slavery is unlawful," I told him. "There is no king. These are ordinary citizens amusing themselves."

"Nudo! Assolutamente nudo!"

"We long ago outgrew feeling ashamed of our bodies," I said. "The laws allow us to go nude in places like this."

"Straordinario! Incredibile!" He gaped in total astonishment. Then he erupted with questions, a torrent of Italian first, his English returning only with an effort. Did husbands allow their wives to come here? Did fathers permit daughters? Were there rapes on the beach? Duels? If the body had lost its mystery, how did sexual desire survive? If a man somehow did become excited, was it shameful to let it show? And on and on and on, until I had to signal Nella to give him a mild needle. Calmer now, Gianni digested the notion of mass public nudity in a more reflective way; but it had amazed him more than Beethoven, that was plain.

We let him stare for another ten minutes. As we started to return to the car, Gianni pointed to a lush brunette trudging along by the tide-pools and said, "I want her. Get her."

"Gianni, we can't do that!"

"You think I am eunuch? You think I can see these bodies and not remember breasts in my hands, tongue touching tongue?" He caught my wrist. "Get her for me."

"Not yet. You aren't well enough yet. And we can't just get her for you. Things aren't done that way here."

"She goes naked. She belongs to anyone."

"No," I said. "You still don't really understand, do you?" I nodded to Nella Brandon. She gave him another needle. We drove on, and he subsided. Soon we came to the barrier marking where the coast road had fallen into the sea, and we swung inland through the place where Santa Monica had been. I explained about the earthquake and the landslide. Gianni grinned.

"Ah, *il terremoto,* you have it here too? A few years ago there was great earthquake in Napoli. You have understood? And then they ask me to write a Mass of Thanksgiving afterward because not everything is destroyed. It is very famous mass for a time. You know it? No? You must hear it." He turned and seized my wrist. With an intensity greater than the brunette had aroused in him, he said, "I will compose a new famous mass, yes? I will be very famous again. And I will be rich. Yes? I was famous and then I was forgotten and then I died and now I live again and now I will be famous again. And rich. Yes? Yes?"

Sam Hoaglund looked over at him and said, "In another couple of weeks, Gianni, you're going to be the most famous man in the world."

Casually Sam poked the button turning on the radio. The car was well equipped for overload and out of the many speakers came the familiar pulsing tingling sounds of Wilkes Booth John doing *Membrane.* The subsonics were terrific. Gianni sat up straight as the music hit him. "What is that?" he demanded.

"Overload," Sam said. "Wilkes Booth John."

"Overload? This means nothing to me. It is a music? Of when?"

"The music of right now," said Nella Brandon.

As we zoomed along Wilshire Sam keyed in the colors and lights too, and the whole interior of the car began to throb and flash and sizzle. Wonderland for Gianni again. He blinked, he pressed his hands to his cheeks, he shook his head. "It is like the music of dreams," he said. "The composer? Who is?"

"Not a composer," said Sam. "A group. Wilkes Booth John, it calls itself. This isn't classical music, it's pop. Popular. Pop doesn't have a composer."

"It makes itself, this music?"

"No," I said. "The whole group composes it. And plays it."

"The orchestra. It is pop and the orchestra composes." He looked lost, as bewildered as he had been since the moment of his awakening, naked and frail, in the scoop cage. "Pop. Such strange music. So simple. It goes over and over again, the same thing, loud, no shape. Yet I think I like it. Who listens to this music? *Imbecili? Infanti?*"

"Everyone," Sam said.

THE FIRST OUTING IN Los Angeles not only told us Gianni could handle exposure to the modern world but also transformed his life among us in several significant ways. For one thing, there was no keeping him chaste any longer after Topanga Beach. He was healthy, he was lusty, he was vigorously heterosexual—an old biography of him I had seen blamed his ill health and early demise on "his notorious profligacy"—and we could hardly go on treating him like a prisoner or a zoo animal. Sam fixed him up with one of his secretaries, Melissa Burke, a willing volunteer.

Then, too, Gianni had been confronted for the first time with the split between classical and popular music, with the whole modernist cleavage between high art and lowbrow entertainment. That was new to him and baffling at first. "This *pop,*" he said, "it is the music of the peasants?" But gradually he grasped the idea of simple rhythmic music that everyone listened to, distinguished from "serious" music that belonged only to an elite and was played merely on formal occasions. "But *my* music," he protested, "it had tunes, people could whistle it. It was everybody's music." It fascinated him that composers had abandoned melody and made themselves inaccessible to most of the people. We told him that something like that had happened in all of the arts. "You poor crazy *futuruomini,*" he said gently.

Suddenly he began to turn himself into a connoisseur of overload groups. We rigged an imposing unit in his room, and he and Melissa spent hours plugged in, soaking up the waveforms let loose by Scissors and Ultrafoam and Wilkes Booth John and the other top bands. When I asked him how the new symphony was coming along, he gave me a peculiar look.

He began to make other little inroads into modern life. Sam and Melissa took him shopping for clothing on Figueroa Street, and in the *cholo* boutiques he acquired a flashy new wardrobe of the latest Aztec gear to replace the lab clothes he had worn since his awakening. He had his prematurely gray hair dyed red. He acquired jewelry that went flash, clang, zzz, and pop when the mood-actuated sensoria came into play. In a few days he was utterly transformed: he became the perfect young Angeleno, slim, dapper, stylish, complete with the slight foreign accent and exotic grammar.

"Tonight Melissa and I go to The Quonch," Gianni announced.

"The Quonch," I murmured, mystified.

"Overload palace," Hoaglund explained. "In Pomona. All the big groups play there."

"We have Philharmonic tickets tonight," I said feebly.

Gianni's eyes were implacable. "The Quonch," he said.

So we went to The Quonch. Gianni, Melissa, Sam, Sam's slice-junkie livewith, Oreo, and I. Gianni and Melissa had wanted to go alone, but I wasn't having that. I felt a little like an overprotective mother whose little boy wanted to try a bit of freebasing. No chaperones, no Quonch, I said. The Quonch was a gigantic geodesic dome in Pomona Downlevel, far underground. The stage whirled on antigrav gyros, the ceiling was a mist of floating speakers, the seats had pluggie intensifiers, and the audience, median age about fourteen, was sliced out of its mind. The groups performing that night were Thug, Holy Ghosts, Shining Orgasm Revival and Ultrafoam. For this I had spent untold multi-kilogelt to bring the composer of the *Stabat Mater* and *La Serva Padrona* back to life? The kids screamed, the great hall filled with dense, tangible, oppressive sound, colors and lights throbbed and pulsed, minds were blown. In the midst of the madness sat Giovanni Battista Pergolesi (1710–1736), graduate of the Conservatorio dei Poveri, organist of the royal chapel at Naples, *maestro di capella* to the Prince of Stigliano—plugged in, turned on, radiant, ecstatic, transcendent.

Whatever else The Quonch may have been, it didn't seem dangerous, so the next night I let Gianni go there just with Melissa. And the next. It was healthy for both of us to let him move out on his own a little. But I was starting to worry. It wouldn't be long until we broke the news to the public that we had a genuine eighteenth-century genius among us. But where were the new symphonies? Where were the heaven-sent sonatas? He wasn't producing anything visible. He was just doing a lot of overload. I hadn't brought him back here to be a member of the audience, especially *that* audience.

"Relax," Sam Hoaglund said. "He's going through a phase. He's dazzled by the novelty of everything, and also he's having fun for maybe the first time in his life. But sooner or later he'll get back to composing. Nobody steps out of character forever. The real Pergolesi will take control."

Then Gianni disappeared.

Came the frantic call at three in the afternoon on a crazy hot Saturday with Santa Anas blowing and a fire raging in Tujunga. Dr. Brandon had gone to Gianni's room to give him his regular checkup, and no Gianni. I went whistling across town from my house near the beach. Hoaglund, who had come running in from Santa Barbara, was there already. "I phoned Melissa," he said. "He's not with her. But she's got a theory."

"Tell."

"They've been going backstage the last few nights. He's met some of the kids from Ultrafoam and one of the other groups. She figures he's off jamming with them."

"If that's all, then hallelujah. But how do we track him?"

"She's getting addresses. We're making calls. Quit worrying, Dave."

Easy to say. I imagined him held for ransom in some East L.A. dive. I imagined swaggering machos sending me his fingers, one a day, waiting for fifty megabucks' payoff. I paced for half a dreadful hour, grabbing up phones as if they were magic wands, and then came word that they had found him working out with Shining Orgasm Revival in a studio in West Covina. We were there in half the legal time and to hell with the California Highway Patrol.

The place was a miniature Quonch, electronic gear everywhere, the special apparatus of overload rigged up, and Gianni sitting in the midst of six practically naked young uglies whose bodies were draped with readout tape and sonic gadgetry. So was his. He looked blissful and sweaty. "It is so beautiful, this music," he sighed when I collared him. "It is the music of my second birth. I love it beyond everything."

"Bach," I said. "Beethoven. Mozart."

"This is other. This is miracle. The total effect—the surround, the engulf—"

"Gianni, don't ever go off again without telling someone."

"You were afraid?"

"We have a major investment in you. We don't want you getting hurt or into trouble or—"

"Am I a child?"

"There are dangers in this city that you couldn't possibly understand yet. You want to jam with these musicians, jam with them, but don't just disappear. Understood?"

He nodded.

Then he said, "We will not hold the press conference for a while. I am learning this music. I will make my debut next month, maybe. If we can get booking at The Quonch as main attraction."

"This is what you want to be? An overload star?"

"Music is music."

"And you are Giovanni Battista Pergo—" An awful thought struck me. I looked sidewise at Shining Orgasm Revival. "Gianni, you didn't tell them who you—"

"No. I am still secret."

"Thank God." I put my hand on his arm. "Look, if this stuff amuses you, listen to it, play it, do what you want. But the Lord gave you a genius for real music."

"This is real music."

"Complex music. Serious music."

"I starved to death composing that music."

"You were ahead of your time. You wouldn't starve now. You will have a tremendous audience for your music."

"Because I am a freak, yes. And in two months I am forgotten again. *Grazie,* no, Dave. No more sonatas. No more cantatas. Is not the music of this world. I give myself to overload."

"I forbid it, Gianni!"

He glared. I saw something steely behind his delicate and foppish exterior.

"You do not own me, Dr. Leavis."

"I gave you life."

"So did my father and mother. They didn't own me either."

"Please, Gianni. Let's not fight. I'm only begging you not to turn your back on your genius, not to renounce the gift God gave you for—"

"I renounce nothing. I merely transform." He leaned up and put his nose almost against mine. "Let me free. I will not be a court composer for you. I will not give you masses and symphonies. No one wants such things today, not new ones, only a few people who want the old ones. Not good enough. I want to be famous, *capisce?* I want to be rich. Did you think I'd live the rest of my life as a curiosity, a museum piece? Or that I would learn to write the kind of noise they call modern music? Fame is what I want. I died poor and hungry, the books say. *You* die poor and hungry and find out what it is like, and then talk to me about writing cantatas. I will never be poor again." He laughed. "Next year, after I am revealed to the world, I will start my own overload group. We will wear wigs, eighteenth-century clothes, everything. We will call ourselves Pergolesi. All right? All right, Dave?"

He insisted on working out with Shining Orgasm Revival every afternoon. Okay. He went to overload concerts just about every night. Okay. He talked about going on stage next month. Even that was okay. He did no composing, stopped listening to any music but overload. Okay. He is going through a phase, Sam Hoaglund had said. Okay. You do not own me, Gianni had said.

Okay. Okay.

I let him have his way. I asked him who his overload playmates thought he was, why they had let him join the group so readily. "I say I am rich Italian Playboy," he replied. "I give them the old charm, you understand? Remember I am accustomed to winning the favors of kings, princes, cardinals. It is how we musicians earned our living. I charm them, they listen to me play, they see right away I am genius. The rest is simple. I will be very rich."

About three weeks into Gianni's overload phase, Nella Brandon came to me and said, "Dave, he's doing slice."

I don't know why I was surprised. I was.

"Are you sure?"

She nodded. "It's showing up in his blood, his urine, his metabolic charts. He probably does it every time he goes to play with that band. He's losing weight, corpuscle formation dropping off, resistance weakening. You've got to talk to him."

I went to him and said, "Gianni, I've stopped giving a damn what kind of music you write, but when it comes to drugs, I draw the line.

You're still not completely sound physically. Remember, you were at the edge of *death* just a few months ago, body-time. I don't want you killing yourself."

"You do not own me." Again, sullenly.

"I have some claim on you. I want you to go on living."

"Slice will not kill me."

"It's killed plenty already."

"Not Pergolesi!" he snapped. Then he smiled, took my hand, gave me the full treatment. "Dave, Dave, you listen. I die once. I am not interested in an encore. But the slice, it is essential. Do you know? It divides one moment from the next. You have taken it? No? Then, you cannot understand. It puts spaces in time. It allows me to comprehend the most intricate rhythms, because with slice there is time for everything, the world slows down, the mind accelerates. *Capisce?* I need it for my music."

"You managed to write the *Stabat Mater* without slice."

"Different music. For this, I need it." He patted my hand. "You do not worry, eh? I look after myself."

What could I say? I grumbled, I muttered, I shrugged. I told Nella to keep a very close eye on his readouts. I told Melissa to spend as much time as possible with him and keep him off the drug if she could manage it.

At the end of the month Gianni announced he would make his debut at The Quonch on the following Saturday. A big bill—five overload bands, Shining Orgasm Revival playing fourth, with Wilkes Booth John, no less, as the big group of the night. The kids in the audience would skull out completely if they knew that one of the Orgasms was three hundred years old, but of course they weren't going to find that out, so they'd just figure he was a new side-man and pay no attention. Later on Gianni would declare himself to be Pergolesi. He and Sam were already working on the altered PR program. I felt left out, off on another track. But it was beyond my control. Gianni now was like a force of nature, a hurricane of a man, frail and wan though he might be.

We all went to The Quonch for Gianni's overload debut.

There we sat, a dozen or more alleged adults, in that mob of screaming kids. Fumes, lights, colors, the buzzing of gadgetized clothes and jewels, people passing out, people coupling in the aisles, the whole crazy bit, like Babylon right before the end, and we sat through it. Kids selling slice, dole, coke, you name it, slipped among us. I wasn't buying but I think some of my people were. I closed my eyes and let it all wash over me, the rhythms and subliminals and ultrasonics of one group after another, Toad Star, then Bubblemilk, then Holy Ghosts, though I couldn't tell one from the next, and finally, after many hours, Shining Orgasm Revival was supposed to go on for its set.

A long intermission dragged on and on. And on.

The kids, zonked and crazed, didn't mind at first. But after maybe half an hour they began to boo and throw things and pound on the walls. I looked at Sam, Sam looked at me, Nella Brandon murmured little worried things.

Then Melissa appeared from somewhere, tugged at my arm and whispered, "Dr. Leavis, you'd better come backstage. Mr. Hoaglund. Dr. Brandon."

They say that if you fear the worst, you keep the worst at bay. As we made our way through the bowels of The Quonch to the performers' territory, I imagined Gianni sprawled backstage, wired with full gear, eyes rigid, tongue sticking out—dead of a slice overdose. And all our fabulous project ruined in a crazy moment. So we went backstage and there were the members of Shining Orgasm Revival running in circles, and a cluster of Quonch personnel conferring urgently, and kids in full war-paint peering in the back way and trying to get through the cordon. And there was Gianni, wired with full overload gear, sprawled on the floor, shirtless, skin shiny with sweat, mottled with dull purplish spots, eyes rigid, tongue sticking out. Nella Brandon pushed everyone away and dropped down beside him. One of the Orgasms said to no one in particular, "He was real nervous, man, he kept slicing off more and more, we couldn't stop him, you know—"

Nella looked up at me. Her face was bleak.

"OD?" I said.

She nodded. She had the snout of an ultrahypo against Gianni's limp arm and she was giving him some kind of shot to try to bring him around. But even in A.D. 2008, dead is dead is dead.

It was Melissa who said afterward through tears, "It was his karma to die young, don't you see? If he couldn't die in 1736, he was going to die fast here. He had no choice."

And I thought of the biography that had said of him long ago, "His ill health was probably due to his notorious profligacy." And I heard Sam Hoaglund's voice in my mind saying, "Nobody steps out of character forever. The real Pergolesi will take control." Yes. Gianni had always been on a collision course with death, I saw now; by scooping him from his own era we had only delayed things a few months. Self-destructive is as self-destructive does, and a change of scenery doesn't alter the case.

If that is so—if, as Melissa says, karma governs all—should we bother to try again? Do we reach into yesterday's yesterday for some other young genius dead too soon, Poe or Rimbaud or Caravaggio or Keats, and give him the second chance we had hoped to give Gianni? And watch him recapitulate his destiny, going down a second time? Mozart, as Sam once suggested? Benvenuto Cellini? Our net is wide and deep. All of the past is ours. But if we bring back another, and he willfully and heedlessly sends himself down the same old karmic chute, what have we gained, what have we achieved, what have we done to ourselves and to him? I think of Gianni, looking to be rich and famous at last, lying purpled on that floor. Would Shelley drown again? Would Van Gogh cut off the other ear before our eyes?

Perhaps someone more mature would be safer, eh? El Greco, Cervantes, Shakespeare? But then we might behold Shakespeare signing up in Hollywood, El Greco operating out of some trendy gallery, Cervantes sitting down with his agent to figure tax-shelter angles. Yes? No. I look at the scoop. The scoop looks at me. It is very very late to consider these matters, my friends. Years of our lives consumed, billions of dollars spent, the seals of time ripped open, a young genius's strange odyssey ending on the floor backstage at The Quonch, and for what, for what, for what? We can't simply abandon the project now, can we?

Can we?

I look at the scoop. The scoop looks at me.

◆

THE FAR SIDE OF THE BELL-SHAPED CURVE

During the late 1970s I took a substantial vacation from writing fiction—I cheerfully stayed off the job for nearly five years—but eventually one thing and another got me back to working again, and early in 1980 my old friend Robert Sheckley, who was working as the fiction editor of the new slick magazine Omni, *managed to coax a short story out of me and quickly suggested that I try another one for him. It just happened that an idea for a fairly complex time travel story had wandered into my head, and, since time travel was, of course, one of my favorite science fiction themes, I set about immediately sketching it out.*

It turned out to be the most ambitious story I had done in ten years or so, involving not only a very tricky plot but also a lot of historical and geographical research. (Sarajevo, where the story opens, would be all over the front pages of the newspapers a decade later when the former Yugoslavia collapsed into civil war, but this was 1980, remember, and the only thing anyone knew about Sarajevo then was that it was the place where the Austrian archduke Franz Ferdinand was assassinated in 1914, touching off the First World War.)

So I worked hard and long, with much revising along the way (a big deal, in those pre-computer days), and on August 16, 1980 I mailed it to Sheckley with a note that said, "Somehow I finished the story despite such distractions as the death of my cat and a visit from my mother and a lot of other headaches, some of which I'll tell you about as we sit sobbing into our drinks at the Boston convention and some of which I hope to have forgotten by then."

Though I was now writing regularly again—this was my fourth short story in eight months—I had not yet returned to full creative confidence, and, though I thought "Bell-Shaped Curve" was a fine story, I wasn't completely sure that Sheckley would agree. When we met two weeks later in Boston, though, he told me at once that he was going to publish it. But he hoped I'd take a second look at it and clean up some logical flaws.

"Sure," I said. "Just give me a list of them."

But Bob Sheckley, sweet man that he was, was not that sort of editor. He didn't have any list of the story's logical flaws—he simply felt sure there must be some. I was on my own. So after the Boston trip I went back to the story, giving it a very rigorous reading indeed, and, sure enough, there were places where the time travel logic didn't make sense. That came as no surprise to me, because time travel logic never does make sense, but I did see some ways of concealing, if not removing, the illogicalities. I revised the story and sent it back to him on September 23, telling him this in my accompanying letter:

"I have reworked 'Bell-Shaped Curve' to handle most of the obvious problems, without pretending that I have made time travel into anything as plausible as the internal combustion engine. Aside from a bunch of tiny cosmetic changes, the main revision has been to eliminate the discussion between Reichenbach and Ilsabet about being wary of duplication; they now speak in much more general terms of paradox problems. But in fact they don't understand any more about time travel than I do about what's under the hood of my car. . . .

"And remember that a story that may contain logical flaws is a story that will give the readers something to exercise their wits about. That will be pleasing to them. If they can come away from the issue feeling mentally superior to Robert Silverberg and the entire editorial staff of Omni, *haven't they thereby had their two dollars' worth of gratification?"*

Omni *published the story in its March 1982 issue.*

SARAJEVO WAS LOVELY ON THAT early summer day. The air sparkled, the breeze off the mountains was strong and pungent, the whitewashed villas glittered in the morning sunlight. Reichenbach, enchanted by the beauty of the place and spurred by a sense of impending excitement, stepped buoyantly out of a dark cobbled alley and made his way in quick virile strides toward the river's right embankment. It was nearly 10:30.

A crowd of silent, sullen Bosnian burghers lined the embankment. The black-and-gold Hapsburg banners fluttered from every lamppost and balcony. In a little while the archduke Franz Ferdinand, the emperor's nephew and heir, would come this way with his duchess in their open-topped car. Venturing into dangerous territory, they were, into a province of disaffected and reluctant citizens.

The townsfolk stirred faintly. The townsfolk muttered. Like puddings, Reichenbach thought, they awaited in a dull, dutiful way their future monarch. But he knew they must be seething with revolutionary fervor inside.

Reichenbach looked about him for dark taut youths with the peculiar bright-eyed look of assassins. No one nearby seemed to fit the pattern. He let his gaze wander up the hills to the dense cypress groves, the ancient wooden houses, the old Turkish mosques topped by slender, splendid minarets and back down toward the river to the crowd again. And—

Who is she?

He noticed her for the first time, no more than a dozen meters to his left, in front of the Bank of Austria-Hungary building: a tall auburn-haired woman of striking presence and aura, who in this mob of coarse, rough folk radiated such supreme alertness and force that Reichenbach knew at once she must be of his sort. Yes! He had come here alone, certain he would find an appropriate companion, and that confidence now was affirmed.

He began to move toward her.

His eyes met hers and she nodded and smiled in recognition and acknowledgment.

"Have you just arrived?" Reichenbach asked in German.

She answered in Serbian. "Three days ago."

Smoothly he shifted languages. "How did I fail to see you?"

"You were looking everywhere else. I saw you at once. You came this morning?"

"Fifteen minutes ago."

"Does it please you so far?"

"Very much," he said. "Such a picturesque place. Like a medieval fantasy. Time stands still here."

Her eyes were mischievous. "Time stands still everywhere," she said, moving on into English.

Reichenbach smiled. Again he matched her change of language. "I take your meaning. And I think you take mine. This charming architecture, the little river, the ethnic costumes—it's hard to believe, that a vast and hideous war is going to spring from so quaint a place."

"A nice irony, yes. And it's for ironies that we make these journeys, *n'est ce pas?*"

"Vraiment."

They were standing quite close now. He felt a current flowing between them, a pulsating, almost tangible force.

"Join me later for a drink?" he said.

"Certainly. I am Ilsabet."

"Reichenbach."

He longed to ask her when she had come from. But of course that was taboo.

"Look," she said. "The archduke and duchess."

The royal car, inching forward, had reached them. Franz Ferdinand, red-faced and tense in preposterous comic-opera uniform, waved halfheartedly to the bleakly staring crowd. Drab, plump Sophie beside him, absurdly overdressed, forced a smile. They were meaty-looking, florid people, rigid and nervous, all but clinging to each other in their nervousness.

"Now it starts," he said.

"Yes. The foreplay." She slipped her arm through his.

Not far away a tall, young, sallow-faced man appeared as if he had sprung from the pavement—wild hyperthyroid eyes, bobbing Adam's-apple, a sure desperado—and hurled something. It landed just behind the royal car. An odd popping sound—the detonator—and then Reichenbach heard a loud bang. There was a blurt of black smoke and the car behind the archduke's lurched and crumpled, dumping aides-de-camp into the street. The cortege halted abruptly. The imperial couple, unharmed, sat weirdly upright as if their survival depended on keeping their spines straight. A functionary riding with them said in a clear voice, "A bomb has gone off, your highness." And Franz Ferdinand, calm, disgusted: "I rather expected something like that. Look after the injured, will you?"

Ilsabet's hand tightened on Reichenbach's forearm as the bizarre comedy unfolded: the cars motionless, archduke and duchess still in plain view, the assassin wildly vaulting a parapet and plunging into the shallow river, police pursuing, pouncing, beating him with the flats of their swords, the crowd milling in confusion. At last the damaged car was pushed to the side of the road and the remaining vehicles rapidly drove off.

"End of act one," Ilsabet said, laughing.

"And forty minutes until act two. That drink, now?"

"I know a sidewalk café near here."

Under a broad turquoise umbrella Reichenbach had a slivovitz, Ilsabet a mug of dark beer. The stolid citizens at the surrounding tables talked more of hunting and fishing than of the bungled assassination. Reichenbach, pretending to be casual, studied Ilsabet hungrily. A cool, keen intelligence gleamed in her penetrating green eyes. Everything about her was sleek, self-possessed, sure. She was so much like him that he almost feared her, and that was a new feeling for him. What he feared most of all was that he would blunder here at the outset and lose her; but he knew, deep beneath all doubts, that he would not. They were meant for each other. He liked to believe that she came from his moment, and that there would be a chance to continue in realtime, when they had returned from displacement, whatever they began on this jaunt. Of course, one did not speak of such things.

Instead he said, "Where do you go next?"

"The burning of Rome. And you?"

"A drink with Shakespeare at the Mermaid Tavern."

"How splendid. I never thought of doing that."

He drew a deep breath and said, "We could do it together," and hesitated, watching her expression. She did not look displeased. "After we've heard Nero play his concerto. Eh?"

She seemed amused. "I like that idea."

He raised his glass. *"Prosit."*

"Zdravlje."

They snaked wrists, clinked glasses.

For a few minutes more they talked—lightly, playfully. He studied her gestures, her sentence structure, her use of idiom, seeking in the subtlest turns of her style some clue that might tell him that they were co-temporals, but she gave him nothing: a shrewd game player, this one. At length he said, "It's nearly time for the rest of the show."

Ilsabet nodded. He scattered some coins on the table and they returned to the embankment, walked up to the Latin Bridge, turned right into Franz Joseph Street. Shortly the royal motorcade, returning from a city-hall reception, came rolling along. There appeared to be some disagreement over the route: chauffeurs and aides-de-camp engaged in a noisy dispute and suddenly the royal car stopped. The chauffeur seemed to be trying to put the car into reverse. There was a clashing of gears. A gaunt boy emerged from a coffeehouse not three meters from the car, less than ten from Reichenbach and Ilsabet. He looked dazed, like a sleepwalker, as if astounded to find himself so close to the imperial heir. This is Gavrilo Princip, Reichenbach thought, the second and true assassin; but he felt little interest in what was about to happen. The gun was out, the boy was taking aim. But Reichenbach watched Ilsabet, more concerned with the quality of her reactions than with the deaths of two trivial people in fancy costumes. Thus he missed seeing the fatal shot through Franz Ferdinand's pouter-pigeon chest, though he observed Ilsabet's quick, frosty smile of satisfaction. When he glanced back at the royal car he saw the archduke sitting upright, stunned, tunic and lips stained with red, and the boy firing at the duchess. There was consternation among the aides-de-camp. The car sped away. It was 11:15.

"So," said Ilsabet. "Now the war begins, the dynasties topple, a civilization crumbles. Did you enjoy it?"

"Not as much as I enjoyed the way you smiled when the archduke was shot."

"Silly."

"The slaughter of a pair of overstuffed simpletons is ultimately less important to me than your smile."

It was risky: too strong too soon, maybe? But it got through to her the right way, producing a faint quirking of her lip that told him she was pleased.

"Come," she said, and took him by the hand.

Her hotel was an old gray stone building on the other side of the river. She had an elegant balconied room on the third floor, river view, ornate gas chandeliers, heavy damask draperies, capacious canopied bed. This era's style was certainly admirable, Reichenbach thought—lavish, slow, rich; even in a little provincial town like this, everything was deluxe. He shed his tight and heavy clothing with relief. She wore her timer high, a pale taut band just beneath her breasts. Her eyes glittered as she reached for him and drew him down beneath the canopy. At this moment at the other end of town, Franz Ferdinand and Sophie were dying. Soon there would be exchanges of stiff diplomatic notes, declarations of war by Austria-Hungary against Serbia, Germany against Russia and France, Europe engulfed in flames, the battle of the Marne, Ypres, Verdun, the Somme, the flight of the Kaiser, the armistice, the transformation of the monarchies—he had studied it all with such keen intensity, and now, having seen the celebrated assassinations that triggered everything, he was unmoved. Ilsabet had eclipsed the Great War for him.

No matter. There would be other epochal events to savor. They had all history to wander.

"To Rome, now," he said huskily.

THEY ROSE, BATHED, EMBRACED, WINKED conspiratorially. They were off to a good start. Hastily they gathered their 1914 gear, waistcoats and petticoats and boots and all that, within the prescribed two-meter radius. They synchronized their timers and embraced again, naked, laughing, bodies pressed tight together, and went soaring across the centuries.

At the halfway house outside imperial Rome, they underwent their preparations, receiving their Roman hairstyles and clothing, their hypnocourses in Latin, their purses of denarii and sestertii, their plague inoculations, their new temporary names. He was Quintus Junius Veranius, she was Flavia Julia Lepida.

Nero's Rome was smaller and far less grand than he expected—the Colosseum was still in the future, there was no Arch of Titus, even the Forum seemed sparsely built. But the city was scarcely mean. The first day, they strolled vast gardens and dense, crowded markets, stared in awe at crazy Caligula's bridge from the Palatine to the Capitoline, went to the baths, gorged themselves at their inn on capon and truffled boar. On the next, they attended the gladiatorial games and afterward made love with frantic energy in a chamber they had hired near the Campus Martius. There was a wonderful frenzy about the city that Reichenbach found intoxicating, and Ilsabet, he knew, shared his fervor: her eyes were aglow, her face gleamed. They could hardly bear to sleep, but explored the narrow winding streets from dark to dawn.

They knew, of course, that the fire would break out in the Circus Maximus where it adjoined the Palatine and Caelian hills, and took care to situate themselves safely atop the Aventine, where they had a fine view. There they watched the fierce blaze sweeping through the Circus, climbing the hills, dipping to ravage the lower ground. No one seemed to be fighting the fire; indeed, Reichenbach thought he could detect subsidiary fires flaring up in the outlying districts, as though arson were the sport of the hour, and soon those fires joined with the main one. The sky rained black soot; the stifling summer air was thick and almost impossible to breathe. For the first two days the destruction had a kind of fascinating beauty, as temples and mansions and arcades melted away, the Rome of centuries being unbuilt before their eyes. But then the discomfort, the danger, the monotony, began to pall on him. "Shall we go?" he said.

"Wait," Ilsabet replied. The conflagration seemed to have an almost sexual impact on her: she glistened with sweat, she trembled with some strange joy as the flames leaped from district to district. She could not get enough. And she clung to him in tight feverish embrace. "Not yet," she murmured, "not so soon. I want to see the emperor."

Yes. And here was Nero now, returning to town from holiday. In grand procession he crossed the charred city, descending from his litter now and then to inspect some ruined shrine or palace. They caught a glimpse of him as he entered the Gardens of Maecenas—thick-necked, paunchy, spindle-shanked, foul of complexion. "Oh, look," Ilsabet whispered. "He's *beautiful!* But where's the fiddle?" The emperor carried no fiddle, but he was grotesquely garbed in some kind of theatrical costume and his cheeks were daubed with paint. He waved and flung coins to the crowd and ascended the garden tower. For a better view, no doubt. Ilsabet pressed herself close to Reichenbach. "My throat is on fire," she said. "My lungs are choked with ashes. Take me to London. Show me Shakespeare."

THERE WAS SMOKE IN THE dark Cheapside alehouse too, thick sweet smoke curling up from sputtering logs on a dank February day. They sat in a cobwebbed corner playing word games while waiting for the actors to arrive. She was quick and clever, just as clever as he. Reichenbach took joy in that. He loved her for her agility and strength of soul. "Not many could be carrying off this tour," he told her. "Only special ones like us."

She grinned. "We who occupy the far side of the bell-shaped curve."

"Yes. Yes. It's horrible of us to have such good opinions of ourselves, isn't it?"

"Probably. But they're well earned, my dear."

He covered her hand with his, and squeezed, and she squeezed back. Reichenbach had never known anyone like her. Deeper and deeper was she drawing him, and his delight was tempered only by the knowledge that when they returned to realtime, to that iron world beyond the terminator where all paradoxes canceled out and the delicious freedoms of the jaunter did not apply, he must of necessity lose her. But there was no hurry about returning.

Voices, now: laughter, shouts, a company of men entering the tavern, actors, poets perhaps, Burbage, maybe, Heminges, Allen, Condell, Kemp, Ben Jonson possibly, and who was that, slender, high forehead, those eyes like lamps in the dark? Who else could it be? Plainly Shagspere, Chaxper, Shackspire, however they spelled it, surely Sweet Will here among these men calling for sack and malmsey, and behind that broad forehead Hamlet and Mercutio must be teeming, Othello,

Hotspur, Prospero, Macbeth. The sight of him excited Reichenbach as Nero had Ilsabet. He inclined his head, hoping to hear scraps of dazzling table-talk, some bit of newborn verse, some talk of a play taking form; but at this distance everything blurred. "I have to go to him," Reichenbach muttered.

"The regulations?"

"*Je m'en fous* the regulations. I'll be quick. People of our kind don't need to worry about the regulations. I promise you, I'll be quick."

She winked and blew him a kiss. She looked gorgeously sluttish in her low-fronted gown.

Reichenbach felt a strange quivering in his calves as he crossed the straw-strewn floor to the far-off crowded table.

"Master Shakespeare!" he cried.

Heads turned. Cold eyes glared out of silent faces. Reichenbach forced himself to be bold. From his purse he took two slender, crude shilling-pieces and put them in front of Shakespeare. "I would stand you a flagon or two of the best sack," he said loudly, "in the name of good Sir John."

"Sir John?" said Shakespeare, blank-faced. He frowned and shook his head. "Sir John Woodcocke, d'ye mean? Sir John Holcombe? I know not your Sir John, fellow."

Reichenbach's cheeks blazed. He felt like a fool.

A burly man beside Shakespeare said, with a rough nudge, "Me-thinks he speaks of Falstaff, Will. Eh? You recall your Falstaff?"

"Yes," Reichenbach said. "In truth I mean no other."

"Falstaff," Shakespeare said in a distant way. He looked displeased, uncomfortable. "I recall the name, yes. Friend, I thank you, but take back your shillings. It is bad custom for me to drink of strangers' sack."

Reichenbach protested, but only fitfully, and quickly he withdrew lest the moment grow ugly: plainly these folk had no use for his wine or for him, and to be wounded in a tavern brawl here in A.D. 1604 would bring monstrous consequences in realtime. He made a courtly bow and retreated. Ilsabet, watching, wore a cat-grin. He went slinking back to her, upset, bitterly aware he had bungled his cherished meeting with Shakespeare and, worse, had looked bumptious in front of her.

"We should go," he said. "We're unwelcome here."

"Poor dear one. You look so miserable."

"The contempt in his eyes—"

"No," she said. "The man is probably bothered by strangers all the time. And he was, you know, with his friends in the sanctuary of his own tavern. He meant no personal rebuke."

"I expected him to be different—to be one of *us,* to reach out toward me and draw me to him, to—to—"

"No," said Ilsabet gently. "He has his life, his wife, his pains, his problems. Don't confuse him with your fantasy of him. Come, now. You look so glum, my dear. Find yourself again!"

"Somewhen else."

"Yes. Somewhen else."

UNDER HER DEFT CONSOLATIONS THE sting of his oafishness at the Mermaid Tavern eased, and his mood brightened as they went onward. Few words passed between them: a look, a smile, the merest of contacts, and they communicated. Attending the trial of Socrates, they touched fingertips lightly, secretly, and it was the deepest of communions. Afterward they made love beneath the clear, bright winter sky of Athens on a gray-green hillside rich with lavender and myrtle, and emerged from shivering ecstasies to find themselves with an audience of mournful scruffy goats—a perfect leap of context and metaphor, and for days thereafter they made one another laugh with only the most delicate pantomimed reminder of the scene. Onward they went to see grim, limping, austere old Magellan sail off around the world with his five little ships from the mouth of the Guadalquivir, and at a whim they leaped to India, staining their skins and playing at Hindus as they viewed the expedition of Vasco da Gama come sailing into harbor at Calicut, and then it seemed proper to go on to Spain in dry, hot summer to drink sour white wine and watch ruddy freckled-faced Columbus get his pitiful little fleet out to sea.

Of course, they took other lovers from time to time. That was part of the game, too tasty a treat to forswear. In Byzantium, on the eve of the Frankish conquest, he passed a night with a dark-eyed voluptuous Greek who oiled her breasts with musky mysterious unguents, and Ilsabet with a towering garlicky Swede of the imperial guard, and when they found each other the next day, just as the Venetian armada burst into the Bosporus, they described to one another in the most flamboyant of detail the strangenesses of their night's sport—the tireless Norseman's toneless bellowing of sagas in his hottest moments: the Byzantine's startling, convulsive, climactic fit, almost epileptic in style, and, as she had admitted playfully at dawn, mostly a counterfeit. In Cleopatra's Egypt, while waiting for glimpses of the queen and Antony, they diverted themselves with a dark-eyed Coptic pair, brother and sister, no more than children and blithely interchangeable in bed. At the crowning of Charlemagne she found herself a Frankish merchant who offered her an estate along the Rhine, and he a mysteriously elliptical dusky woman who claimed to be a Catalonian Moor, but who—Reichenbach suddenly realized a few days later—must almost certainly have been a jaunter like himself, playing elegant games with him.

All this lent spice to their love and did no harm. These separate but shared adventures only enhanced the intensity of the relationship they were welding. He prayed the jaunt would never end, for Ilsabet was the perfect companion, his utter match, and so long as they sprinted together through the aeons, she was his, though he knew that would end when realtime reclaimed him. Nevertheless, that sad moment still was far away, and he hoped before then to find some way around the inexorable rules, some scheme for locating her and continuing with her in his own true time. Small chance of that, he knew. In the world beyond the terminator there was no time-jaunting; jaunting could be done only in the fluid realm of "history," and history was arbitrarily defined as everything that had happened before the terminator year of 2187. The rest was realtime, rigid and immutable, and what if her realtime were fifty years ahead of his, or fifty behind? There was no bridging that by jaunting. He did not know her realtime locus, and he did not dare ask. Deep as the love between them had come to be, Reichenbach still feared offending her through some unpardonable breach of their special etiquette.

With all the world to choose from, they sometimes took brief solo jaunts. That was Ilsabet's idea, holidays within their holiday, so that they would not grow stale with one another. It made sense to him. Thereupon he vaulted to the Paris of the 1920s to sip Pernod on the Boulevard Saint-Germain and peer at Picasso and Hemingway and Joyce, she in epicanthic mask of old Cathay to see Kublai Khan ride in triumph through the Great Wall, he to Cape Kennedy to watch the great Apollo rocket roaring moonward, she to London for King Charles's beheading. But these were brief adventures, and they reunited quickly, gladly, and went on hand in hand to their next together, to the fall of Troy and the diamond jubilee of Queen Victoria and the assassination of Lincoln and the sack of Carthage. Always when they returned from separate exploits, they regaled each other with extensive narratives of what had befallen them, the sights, the tastes, the ironies and perceptions, and, of course, the amorous interludes. By now Reichenbach and Ilsabet had accumulated an elaborate fabric of shared experience, a richness of joint history that gave them virtually a private language of evocative recollection, so that the slightest of cues—a goat on a hill, the taste of burned toast, the sight of a lop-eared beggar—sprang them into an intimate realm that no one else could ever penetrate: their unique place, furnished with their own things, the artifacts of love, the treasures of memory. And even that which they did separately became interwoven in that fabric, as of the telling of events as they lay in each other's arms had transformed those events into communal possessions.

Yet gradually Reichenbach realized that something was beginning to go wrong.

From a solo jaunt to Paris in 1794, where she toured the Reign of Terror, Ilsabet returned strangely evasive. She spoke in brilliant detail of the death of Robespierre and the sad despoliation of Notre Dame, but what she reported was mere journalism, with no inner meaning. He had to fish for information. Where had she lodged? Had she feared for her safety? Had she had interesting conversations with the Parisians? Shrugs, deflections. Had she taken a lover? Yes, yes, a fleeting liaison, nothing worth talking about; and then it was back to an account of the mobs, the tumbrels, the sound of the guillotine. At first Reichenbach accepted that without demur, though her vaguenesses violated their custom. But she remained moody and oblique while they were visiting the Crucifixion, and as they were about to depart for the Black Death she begged off, saying she needed another day to herself, and would go to Prague for the premiere of *Don Giovanni.* That too failed to trouble him—he was not musical—and he spent the day observing Waterloo from the hills behind Wellington's troops. When Ilsabet rejoined him in the late spring of 1349 for the Black Death in London, though, she seemed even more preoccupied and remote, and told him little of her night at the opera. He began to feel dismay, for they had been marvelously close and now she was obviously voyaging on some other plane. The plague-smitten city seemed to bore her. Her only flicker of animation came toward evening, in a Southwark hostelry, when as they dined on gristly lamb a stranger entered, a tall, gaunt, sharp-bearded man with the obvious aura of a jaunter. Reichenbach did not fail to notice the rebirth of light in Ilsabet's eyes, and the barely perceptible inclining-forward of her body as the stranger approached their table was amply perceptible to him. The newcomer knew them for what they were, naturally, and invited himself to join them. His name was Stavanger; he had been on his jaunt just a few days; he meant to see everything, *everything,* before his time was up. Not for many years had Reichenbach felt such jealousy. He was wise in these things, and it was not difficult to detect the current flowing from Ilsabet to Stavanger even as he sat there between them. Now he understood why she had no casual amours to report of her jaunts to Paris and Prague. This one was far from casual and would bear no retelling.

In the morning she said, "I still feel operatic. I'll go to Bayreuth tonight—the premiere of *Götterdämmerung.*"

Despising himself, he said, "A capital idea. I'll accompany you."

She looked disconcerted. "But music bores you!"

"A flaw in my character. Time I began to remedy it."

The fitful panic in Ilsabet's eyes gave way to cool and chilling calmness. "Another time, dear love. I prize my solitude. I'll make this little trip without you."

It was all plain to him. Gone now the open sharing; now there were secret rendezvous and an unwanted third player of their game. He could not bear it. In anguish he made his own arrangements and jaunted to Bayreuth in thick red wig and curling beard, and there she was, seated beside Stavanger in the Festspielhaus as the subterranean orchestra launched into the first notes. Reichenbach did not remain for the performance.

STAVANGER NOW CROSSED THEIR PATH openly and with great frequency. They met him at the siege of Constantinople, at the San Francisco earthquake, and at a fete at Versailles. This was more than coincidence, and Reichenbach said so to Ilsabet. "I suggested he follow some of our itinerary," she admitted. "He's a lonely man, jaunting alone. And quite charming. But of course if you dislike him, we can simply vanish without telling him where we're going, and he'll never find us again."

A disarming tactic, Reichenbach thought. It was impossible for her to admit to him that she and Stavanger were lovers, for there was too much substance to their affair; so instead she pretended he was a pitiful forlorn wanderer in need of company. Reichenbach was outraged. Fidelity was not part of his unspoken compact with her, and she was free to slip off to any era she chose for a tryst with Stavanger. But that she chose to conceal what was going on was deplorable, and that she was finding pretexts to drag Stavanger along on their travels, puncturing the privacy of their own rapport for the sake of a few smug stolen glances, was impermissible. Reichenbach was convinced now that Ilsabet and Stavanger were co-temporals, though he knew he had no rational basis for that idea; it simply seemed right to him, a final torment, the two of them now laying the groundwork for a realtime relationship that excluded him. Whether or not that was true, it was unbearable. Reichenbach was astounded by the intensity of his jealous fury. Yet it was a true emotion and one he would not attempt to repress. The joy he had known with Ilsabet had been unique, and Stavanger had tainted it.

He found himself searching for ways to dispose of his rival.

Merely whirling Ilsabet off elsewhen would achieve nothing. She would find ways of catching up with her paramour somewhen along the line. And if Ilsabet and Stavanger were co-temporal, and she and Reichenbach were not—no, no, Stavanger had to be expunged. Reichenbach, a stable and temperate man, had never imagined himself capable of such criminality; a bit of elitist regulation-bending was all he had ever allowed himself. But he had never been faced with the loss of an Ilsabet before, either.

In Borgia, Italy, Reichenbach hired a Florentine prisoner to do Stavanger in with a dram of nightshade. But the villain pocketed Reichenbach's down payment and disappeared without a care for the ducats due him on completion of the job. In the chaotic aftermath of the Ides of March, Reichenbach attempted to finger Stavanger as one of Caesar's murderers, but no one paid attention. Nor did he have luck denouncing him to the Inquisition one afternoon in 1485 in Torquemada's Castile, though even the most perfunctory questioning would have given sufficient proof of Stavanger's alliance with diabolical powers. Perhaps it would be necessary, Reichenbach concluded morosely, to deal with Stavanger with his own hands, repellent though that alternative was.

Not only was it repellent, it could be dangerous. He was without experience at serious crime, and Stavanger, cold-eyed and suave, promised to be a formidable adversary: Reichenbach needed an ally, an adviser, a collaborator. But who? While he and Ilsabet were making the circuit of the Seven Wonders, he puzzled over it, from Ephesus to Halicarnassus, to Gizeh, and as they stood in the shadow of the Colossus of Rhodes, the answer came to him. There was only one person he could trust sufficiently, and that person was himself.

To Ilsabet he said, "Do you know where I want to go next?"

"We still have the Hanging Gardens of Babylon, the Lighthouse of Alexandria, the Statue of Zeus at—"

"No, I'm not talking about the Seven Wonders tour. I want to go back to Sarajevo, Ilsabet."

"Sarajevo? Whatever for?"

"A sentimental pilgrimage, love, to the place of our first meeting."

"But Sarajevo was a bore. And—"

"We could make it exciting. Consider: our earlier selves would already be there. We would watch them meet, find each other well matched, become lovers. Here for months we've been touring the great events of history, when we're neglecting a chance to witness our own personal greatest event." He smiled wickedly. "And there are other possibilities. We could introduce ourselves to them. Hint at the joys that lie ahead of them. Perhaps even seduce them, eh? A nice kinky quirky business that would be. And—"

"No," she said. "I don't like it."

"You find the idea improper? Morally offensive?"

"Don't be an idiot. I find it dangerous."

"How so?"

"We aren't supposed to reenter a time-span where we're already present. There must be some good reason for that. The rules—"

"The rules," he said, "are made by timid old sods who've never moved beyond the terminator in their lives. The rules are meant to guide us, not to control us. The rules are meant to be broken by those who are smart enough to avoid the consequences."

She stared somberly at him a long while. "And are you?"

"I think I am."

"Yes. A shrewd man, a superior man, a member of the elite corps that lives on the far side of society's bell-shaped curve. Eh? Doing as you please throughout life. Holding yourself above all restraints. Rich enough and lucky enough to be able to jaunt anywhen you like and behave like a little god."

"You live the same way, I believe."

"In general, yes. But I still won't go with you to Sarajevo."

"Why not?"

"Because I don't know what will happen to me if I do. Kinky and quirky it may be to pile into bed with our other selves, but something about the idea troubles me, and I dislike needless risk. Do you believe you understand paradox theory fully?"

"Does anybody?"

"Exactly. It isn't smart to—"

"Paradoxes are much overrated, don't you think? We're in the fluid zone, Ilsabet. Anything goes, this side of the terminator. If I were you I wouldn't worry about—"

"*I* am me. I worry. If I were you, I'd worry more. Take your Sarajevo trip without me."

He saw she was adamant, and dropped the issue. Indeed, he saw it would be much simpler to make the journey alone. They went on from Rhodes to the Babylon of Nebuchadnezzar, where they spent four happy days untroubled by the shadow of Stavanger; it was the finest time they had had together since Carthage. Then Ilsabet announced she felt the need for another brief solo musicological jaunt—to Mantua in 1607 for Monteverdi's *Orfeo*. Reichenbach offered no objection. The instant she was gone, he set his timer for the twenty-eighth of June, 1914, Sarajevo in Bosnia, 10:27 A.M.

In his Babylonian costume he knew he looked ridiculous or even insane, but it was too chancy to have gone to the halfway house for proper preparation, and he planned to stay here only a few minutes. Moments after he materialized in the narrow cobble-paved alleyway, his younger self appeared, decked out elegantly in natty Edwardian finery. He registered only the most brief quiver of amazement at the sight of another Reichenbach already there.

Reichenbach said, "I have to speak quickly. You will go out there and near the Bank of Austria-Hungary you'll meet the most wonderful woman you've ever known, and you'll share with her the greatest joy you've ever tasted. And just as your love for her reaches its deepest strength, you'll lose her to a rival—unless you cooperate with me to rid us of him before they can ever meet."

The eyes of the other Reichenbach narrowed. "Murder?"

"Removal. We'll put him in the way of harm, and harm will come to him."

"Is the woman such a marvel that the risks are worth it?"

"I swear it. I tell you, you'll suffer pain beyond belief if he isn't eliminated. Trust me. My welfare is your welfare, is this not so?"

"Of course." But the other Reichenbach looked unconvinced. "Still, why must there be two of us in this? It's not yet my affair, after all."

"It will be. He's too slippery to tackle without help. I need you. And ultimately you'll be grateful to me for this. Take it on faith."

"And what if this is some elaborate game, and I the victim?"

"Damn it, *this is no game!* Our happiness is at stake—Yours, mine. We're both in this together. We're closer than any twins could ever be, don't you realize? You and me, different phases of the same person's time-line, following the same path? Our destinies are linked. Help me now or live forever with the torment of the consequences. Please help. *Please.*"

The other was wavering. "You ask a great deal."

"I offer a great deal," Reichenbach said. "Look, there's no more time for talking now. You have to get out there and meet Ilsabet before the archduke's assassination. Meet me in Paris, noon on the twenty-fifth of June, 1794, in the rue de Rivoli outside the Hôtel de Ville." He grasped the other's arm and stared at him with all the intensity and conviction at his command. "Agreed?"

A last moment of hesitation.

"Agreed."

Reichenbach touched his timer and disappeared.

In Babylon again he gathered his possessions and jaunted to the halfway house for the French Revolution. Momentarily he dreaded running into his other self there, a malfeasance that would be hard to justify, but the place was too big for that; the Revolution and Terror spanned five years and an immense service facility was needed to handle the tourist demand. Outfitted in the simple countryfolk clothes appropriate to the revolutionary period, equipped with freshly implanted linguistic skills and proper revolutionary rhetoric, altogether disguised to blend with the citizenry, Reichenbach descended into the terrible heat of that bloody Parisian summer and quickly effected his rendezvous with himself.

The face he beheld was clearly his, and yet unfamiliar, for he was accustomed to his mirror image; but a mirror image is a reversed one, and now he saw himself as others saw him and nothing looked quite right. This is what it must be like to have a twin, he thought. In a low, hoarse voice he said, "She's coming tomorrow to hear Robespierre's final speech and then to see his execution. Our enemy is in Paris already, with rooms at the Hôtel Brittanique in the rue Guénégaud. I'll track him down while your make contact with the Committee of Public Safety. I'll bring him here; you arrange the trap and the denunciation; with any luck he'll be hauled away in the same tumbrel that takes Robespierre to the guillotine. *D'accord?*"

"D'accord." A radiance came into the other's eyes. Softly he said, "You were right about Ilsabet. For such a woman even this is justifiable."

Reichenbach felt an unexpected pang. But to be jealous of himself was an absurdity. "Where have you been with her?"

"After Sarajevo, Nero's Rome. She's asleep there now, our third night: I intend to be gone only an instant. We go next to Shakespeare's time, and then—"

"Yes, I know. Socrates, Magellan, Vasco da Gama. All the best still lies ahead for you. But first there's work to do."

Without great difficulty he found his way to the Hôtel Brittanique, a modest place not far from the Pont Neuf. The concierge, a palsied woman with a thin-lipped mouth fixed in an unchanging scowl, offered little aid until Reichenbach spoke of the committee, the Law of Suspects, the dangers of refusing to cooperate with the revolutionary tribunal; then she was quick enough to admit that a dark man of great height with a beard of just the sort that M'sieu described was living on the fifth floor, a certain M. Stavanger. Reichenbach rented the adjoining room. He waited there an hour, until he heard the footsteps in the hallway, sounds next door.

He went out and knocked.

Stavanger peered blankly at him. "Yes?"

He has not yet met her, Reichenbach thought. He has not yet spoken with her, he has not yet touched her body, they have not yet gone to their damned operas together. And never will.

He said, "This is a wonderful place for a jaunt, isn't it."

"Who are you?"

"Reichenbach is my name. My friend and I saw you in the street and she sent me up to speak with you." He made a little self-deprecating gesture. "I often act as her—ah—go-between. She wishes to know if you'll meet her this afternoon and perhaps enjoy a day or two of French history with her. Her name is Ilsabet, and I can testify that you'll find her charming. Her particular interests are assassinations, architecture, and the first performances of great operas."

Stavanger showed sudden alertness. "Opera is a great passion of mine," he said. "Ordinarily I keep to myself when jaunting, but in this case—the possibilities—is she downstairs? Can you bring her to me?"

"Ah, no. She's waiting in front of the Hôtel de Ville."

"And wants me to come to her?"

Reichenbach nodded. "Certain protocols are important to her."

Stavanger, after a moment's consideration, said, "Take me to your Ilsabet, then. But I make no promises. Is that understood?"

"Of course," said Reichenbach.

The streets were almost empty at this hour. The miasma of the atmosphere in this heavy heat must be a factor in that, Reichenbach thought, and also that it was midday and the Parisians were at their *déjeuner;* but beyond that it seemed that the city was suffering a desolation of the spirit, a paralysis of energy under the impact of the monstrous bloodletting of recent months.

He walked quickly, struggling to keep up with Stavanger's long strides. As they approached the Hôtel de Ville, Reichenbach caught sight of his other self, and with him two or three men in revolutionary costume. Good. Good. The other Reichenbach nodded. Everything was arranged. The challenge now was to keep Stavanger from going for his timer the moment he sensed he was in jeopardy.

"Where is she?" Stavanger asked.

"I left her speaking with that group of men," said Reichenbach. The other Reichenbach stood with his face turned aside—a wise move. Now, though they had not rehearsed it, they moved as if parts of a single organism, the other Reichenbach pivoting, pointing, crying out, "I accuse that man of crimes against liberty," while in the same instant Reichenbach stepped behind Stavanger, thrust his arms up past those of the taller man, reached into Stavanger's loose tunic to wrench his timer into ruin with one quick twist, and held him firmly. Stavanger bellowed and tried to break free, but in a moment the street was full of men who seized and overpowered him and dragged him away. Reichenbach, panting, sweating, looked in triumph toward his other self.

"That one, too," said the other Reichenbach.

Reichenbach blinked. "What?"

Too late. They had his arms; the other Reichenbach was groping for his timer, seizing, tearing. Reichenbach fought ferociously, but they bore him to the ground and knelt on his chest.

Through a haze of fear and pain he heard the other saying, "This man is the proscribed aristocrat Charles Evremonde, called Darnay, enemy of the Republic, member of a family of tyrants. I denounce him for having used his privileges in the oppression of the people."

"He will face the tribunal tonight," said the one kneeling on Reichenbach.

Reichenbach said in a shocked voice, "What are you doing?"

The other crouched close to him and replied in English. "We have been duplicated, you see. Why do you think there are rules against entering a time where one is already present? There's room for only one of us back in realtime, is that not so? So, then, how can we both return?"

Reichenbach said, with a gasp, "But that isn't true!"

"Isn't it? Are you sure? Do you really comprehend all the paradoxes?"

"Do *you?* How can you do this to me, when I—when I'm—"

"You disappoint me, not seeing these intricacies. I would have expected more from one of us. But you must have been too muddled by jealousy to think straight. Do you imagine I dare run the risk of letting you jaunt around on the loose? Which of us is to have Ilsabet, after all?"

Already Reichenbach felt the blade hurtling toward his neck.

"Wait—wait—" he cried. "Look at him! His face is mine! We are brothers, twins! If I'm an aristocrat, what is he? I denounce him too! Seize him and try him with me!"

"There is indeed a strange resemblance between you two," said one of those holding Reichenbach.

The other smiled. "We have often been taken for brothers. But there is no kinship between us. He is the aristocrat Evrémonde, citizens. And I, I am only poor Sydney Carton, a person of no consequence or significance whatever, happy to have been of service to the people." He bowed and walked away, and in a moment was gone.

Safe beside Ilsabet in Nero's Rome, Reichenbach thought bitterly.

"Come. Up with him and bring him to trial," someone called. "The tribunal has no time to waste these days."

◆

DANCERS IN THE TIME-FLUX

Long ago, in what almost seems to me now another geological epoch, I wrote a novel called Son of Man. *The year was 1969, when the world was new and strange and psychedelic, and* Son of Man *was my attempt to reproduce in prose form some of the visionary aspects of life in that heady era and pass the result off as a portrait of the world of the far, far future. The results were very bizarre indeed, but to me, at least, exciting and rewarding; and over the years* Son of Man *has retained a small but passionate audience. It's the sort of book that polarizes readers in an extremely sharp way: some find themselves unable to get past page three, others read it over and over again. (I read it now and then myself, as a matter of fact.)*

Writing Son of Man *had been such an extraordinarily exhilarating experience that when I began writing again in 1980 after my long period of retirement, I found myself tempting to dip into the world of that novel again, possibly for a short story or two, perhaps even for a whole new book. But I gave the idea no serious thought until July of 1981, when the Pacific Northwest writer and editor Jessica Amanda Salmonson asked me to write a story for an anthology called* Heroic Visions *that she was assembling. (At that time Jessica dated all her letters "9981." I haven't heard from her lately, so I don't know whether she still regards herself as living in the hundredth century.)* Heroic Visions *was intended as an anthology of new stories of "high fantasy and heroic fantasy," according to Jessica's prospectus. High fantasy—Eddison, Dunsany, Charles Williams, William Morris—is something I read occasionally with pleasure, but have never intentionally written. Heroic fantasy—exemplified by such characters as Robert E. Howard's Conan, Fritz Leiber's Fafhrd and the Gray Mouser, and Michael Moorcock's Elric—is something that holds less interest for me as a reader, and though I suppose I could fake it as a writer if I saw some reason to do so, I have no true natural aptitude for it. So I really didn't belong in Jessica's book. Nor was the financial aspect of the project especially enticing. But I was just rediscovering writing again that year and was willing to do almost anything just then. I jotted at the bottom of the prospectus, "World of* Son of Man. *Two figures from the remote past are swept into the time-flux—a woman of 20th century, a man of—where? Ancient China? Sumer?" and dropped Jessica a card saying I might possibly send her a story a few months from then, when I had finished the project—the story collection known as* Majipoor Chronicles *that I was working on at the time.*

She was surprised and, I suppose, skeptical, justifiably so; I went on to other things and forgot all about Heroic Visions. *But on December 19, "9981," she tried again, asking me if there was any hope of getting the story. I replied that I'd do it, provided she could see a* Son of Man *spinoff as appropriate to her theme. She had read the book and knew it well. Back came her enthusiastic okay, and on January 9, 1982, I sent "Dancers in the Time-Flux" to her.*

As you'll see, it departs considerably from the scrawled original note of the previous July. The twentieth-century woman disappears from the plot—I tried without success to return to her later on, in a sequel that I never finished writing—and the man of ancient China or Sumer is transmogrified into the sixteenth-century Dutch circumnavigator Olivier van Noort, an actual historical figure about whom I had written at length years before in a nonfiction book called The Longest Voyage. *I do think the story recaptures the tone of* Son of Man *to a considerable extent, but whether it has the headlong wildness of that book is not so clear to me. It may be that years like 1969 come around only once in a lifetime. Which is, perhaps, a good thing.*

UNDER A WARM GOLDEN WIND from the west, Bhengarn the Traveler moves steadily onward toward distant Crystal Pond, his appointed place of metamorphosis. The season is late. The swollen scarlet sun clings close to the southern hills. Bhengarn's body—a compact silvery tube supported by a dozen pairs of sturdy three-jointed legs—throbs with the need for transformation. And yet the Traveler is unhurried. He has been bound on this journey for many hundreds of years. He has traced across the face of the world a glistening trail that zigzags from zone to zone, from continent to continent, and even now still glimmers behind him with a cold brilliance like a thread of bright metal stitching the planet's haunches. For the past decade he has patiently circled Crystal Pond at the outer end of a radial arm one-tenth the diameter of the Earth in length; now, at the prompting of some interior signal, he has begun to spiral inward upon it.

The path immediately before him is bleak. To his left is a district covered by furry green fog; to his right is a region of pale crimson grass sharp as spikes and sputtering with a sinister hostile hiss; straight ahead a roadbed of black clinkers and ashen crusts leads down a shallow slope to the Plain of Teeth, where menacing porcelaneous outcroppings make the wayfarer's task a taxing one. But such obstacles mean little to Bhengarn. He is a Traveler, after all. His body is superbly designed to carry him through all difficulties. And in his journeys he has been in places far worse than this.

Elegantly he descends the pathway of slag and cinders. His many feet are tough as annealed metal, sensitive as the most alert antennae. He tests each point in the road for stability and support, and scans the thick layer of ashes for concealed enemies. In this way he moves easily and swiftly toward the plain, holding his long abdomen safely above the cutting edges of the cold volcanic matter over which he walks.

As he enters the Plain of Teeth he sees a new annoyance: an Eater commands the gateway to the plain. Of all the forms of human life—and the Traveler has encountered virtually all of them in his wanderings, Eaters, Destroyers, Skimmers, Interceders, and the others—Eaters seem to him the most tiresome, mere noisy monsters. Whatever philosophical underpinnings form the rationale of their bizarre way of life are of no interest to him. He is wearied by their bluster and offended by their gross appetites.

All the same, he must get past this one to reach his destination. The huge creature stands straddling the path with one great meaty leg at each edge and the thick fleshy tail propping it from behind. Its steely claws are exposed, its fangs gleam, driblets of blood from recent victims stain its hard reptilian hide. Its chilly inquisitive eyes, glowing with demonic intelligence, track Bhengarn as the Traveler draws near.

The Eater emits a boastful roar and brandishes its many teeth.

"You block my way," Bhengarn declares.

"You state the obvious," the Eater replies.

"I have no desire for an encounter with you. But my destiny draws me toward Crystal Pond, which lies beyond you."

"For you," says the Eater, "nothing lies beyond me. Your destiny has brought you to a termination today. We will collaborate, you and I, in the transformation of your component molecules."

From the spiracles along his sides the Traveler releases a thick blue sigh of boredom. "The only transformation that waits for me is the one I will undertake at Crystal Pond. You and I have no transaction. Stand aside."

The Eater roars again. He rocks slightly on his gigantic claws and swishes his vast saurian tail from side to side. These are the preliminaries to an attack, but in a kind of ponderous courtesy he seems to be offering Bhengarn the opportunity to scuttle back up the ash-strewn slope.

Bhengarn says, "Will you yield place?"

"I am an instrument of destiny"

"You are a disagreeable boastful ignoramus," says Bhengarn calmly, and consumes half a week's energy driving the scimitars of his spirit to the roots of the world. It is not a wasted expense of soul, for the ground trembles, the sky grows dark, the hill behind him creaks and groans, the wind turns purplish and frosty. There is a chill droning sound that the Traveler knows is the song of the time-flux, an unpredictable force that often is liberated at such moments. Despite that, Bhengarn will not relent. Beneath the Eater's splayed claws the fabric of the road ripples. Sour smells rise from sudden crevasses. The enormous beast utters a yipping cry of rage and lashes his tail vehemently against the ground. He sways; he nearly topples; he calls out to Bhengam to cease his onslaught, but the Traveler knows better than to settle for a half-measure. Even more fiercely he presses against the Eater's bulky form.

"This is unfair," the Eater wheezes. "My goal is the same as yours: to serve the forces of necessity."

"Serve them by eating someone else today," answers Bhengarn curtly, and with a final expenditure of force shoves the Eater to an awkward untenable position that causes it to crash down onto its side. The downed beast, moaning, rakes the air with his claws but does not arise, and as Bhengarn moves briskly past the Eater he observes that fine transparent threads, implacable as stone, have shot forth from a patch of swamp beside the road and are rapidly binding the fallen Eater in an unbreakable net. The Eater howls. Glancing back, Bhengarn notices the threads already cutting their way through the Eater's thick scales like tiny streams of acid. "So, then," Bhengarn says, without malice, "the forces of necessity will be gratified today after all, but not by me. The Eater is to be eaten. It seems that this day *I* prove to be the instrument of destiny." And without another backward look he passes quickly onward into the plain. The sky regains its ruddy color, the wind becomes mild once more, the Earth is still. But a release of the time-flux is never without consequences, and as the Traveler trundles forward he perceives some new creature of unfamiliar form staggering through the nests ahead, confused and lost, lurching between the shining lethal formations of the Plain of Teeth in seeming ignorance of the perils they hold. The creature is upright, two-legged, hairy, of archaic appearance. Bhengarn, approaching it, recognizes it finally as a primordial human, swept millions of years past its own true moment.

"Have some care," Bhengarn calls. "Those teeth can bite!"

"Who spoke?" the archaic creature demands, whirling about in alarm.

"I am Bhengarn the Traveler. I suspect I am responsible for your presence here."

"Where are you? I see no one! Are you a devil?"

"I am a Traveler, and I am right in front of your nose."

The ancient human notices Bhengarn, apparently for the first time, and leaps back, gasping. "Serpent!" he cries. "Serpent with legs!

Worm! Devil!" Wildly he seizes rocks and hurls them at the Traveler, who deflects them easily enough, turning each into a rhythmic juncture of gold and green that hovers, twanging softly, along an arc between the other and himself. The archaic one lifts an immense boulder, but as he hoists it to drop it on Bhengarn he overbalances and his arm flies backward, grazing one of the sleek teeth behind him. At once the tooth releases a turquoise flare and the man's arm vanishes to the elbow. He sinks to his knees, whimpering, staring bewilderedly at the stump and at the Traveler before him.

Bhengarn says, "You are in the Plain of Teeth, and any contact with these mineral formations is likely to be unfortunate, as I attempted to warn you." He slides himself into the other's soul for an instant, pushing his way past thick encrusted stalagmites and stalactites of anger, fear, outraged pride, pain, disorientation, and arrogance, and discovers himself to be in the presence of one Olivier van Noort of Utrecht, former tavernkeeper at Rotterdam, commander of the voyage of circumnavigation that set forth from Holland on the second day of July 1598 and traveled the entire belly of the world, a man of exceedingly strong stomach and bold temperament, who has experienced much, having gorged on the meat of penguins at Cape Virgines and the isle called Pantagoms, having hunted beasts not unlike stags and buffaloes and ostriches in the cold lands by Magellan's Strait, having encountered whales and parrots and trees whose bark had the bite of pepper, having had strife with the noisome Portugals in Guinea and Brazil, having entered into the South Sea on a day of diverse storms, thunders, and lightnings, having taken ships of the Spaniards in Valparaiso and slain many Indians, having voyaged thence to the Isles of Ladrones or Thieves, where the natives bartered bananas, coconuts, and roots for old pieces of iron, overturning their canoes in their greed for metal, having suffered a bloody flux in Manila of eating palms, having captured vessels of China laden with rice and lead, having traded with folk on a ship of the Japans, whose men make themselves bald except a tuft left in the hinder part of the head, and wield swords that would, with one stroke cut through three men, having traded also with the bare-breasted women of Borneo, bold and impudent and shrewd, who carry iron-pointed javelins and sharp darts, and having after great privation and the loss of three of his four ships and all but forty-five of his 248 men, many of them executed by him or marooned on remote islands for their mutinies but a good number murdered by the treacheries of savage enemies, come again to Rotterdam on the twenty-sixth of August in 1601, bearing little in the way of salable goods to show for his hardships and calamities. None of this has any meaning to Bhengarn the Traveler except in the broadest, which is to say that he recognizes in Olivier van Noort a stubborn and difficult man who has conceived and executed a journey of mingled heroism and foolishness that spanned vast distances, and so they are brothers, of a sort, however millions of years apart. As a fraternal gesture Bhengarn restores the newcomer's arm. That appears to be as bewildering to the other as was its sudden loss. He squeezes it, moves it cautiously back and forth, scoops up a handful of pebbles with it. "This is Hell, then," he mutters, "and you are a demon of Satan."

"I am Bhengarn the Traveler, bound toward Crystal Pond, and I think that I conjured you by accident out of your proper place in time while seeking to thwart that monster." Bhengarn indicates the fallen Eater, now half dissolved. The other, who evidently had not looked that way before, makes a harsh choking sound at the sight of the giant creature, which still struggles sluggishly. Bhengarn says, "The time flux has seized you and taken you far from home, and there will be no going back for you. I offer regrets."

"You offer regrets? A worm with legs offers regrets! Do I dream this, or am I truly dead and gone to Hell?"

"Neither one."

"In all my sailing round the world I never saw a place so strange as this, or the likes of you, or of that creature over yonder. Am I to be tortured, demon?"

"You are not where you think you are."

"Is this not Hell?"

"This is the world of reality."

"How far are we, then, from Holland?"

"I am unable to calculate it," Bhengarn answers. "A long way, that's certain. Will you accompany me toward Crystal Pond, or shall we part here?"

Noort is silent a moment. Then he says, "Better the company of demons than none at all, in such a place. Tell me straight, demon: am I to be punished here? I see hellfire on the horizon. I will find the rivers of fire, snow, toads, and black water, will I not? And the place where sinners are pronged on hooks jutting from blazing wheels? The ladders of red-hot iron, eh? The wicked broiling on coals? And the Arch-Traitor himself, sunk in ice to his chest—he must be near, is he not?" Noort shivers. "The fountains of poison. The wild boars of Lucifer. The aloes biting bare flesh, the dry winds of the abyss—when will I see them?"

"Look here," says Bhengarn. Beyond the Plain of Teeth a column of black flame rises into the heavens, and in it dance creatures of a hundred sorts, melting, swirling, coupling, fading. A chain of staring lidless eyes spans the sky. Looping whorls of green light writhe on the mountaintops. "Is that what you expect? You will find whatever you expect here."

"And yet you say this is not Hell?"

"I tell you again, it is the true world, the same into which you were born long ago."

"And is this Brazil, or the Indies, or some part of Africa?"

"Those names mean little to me."

"Then we are in the Terra Australis," says Noort. "It must be. A land where worms have legs and speak good Dutch, and rocks can bite, and arms once lost can sprout anew—yes, it must surely be the Terra Australis, or else the land of Prester John. Eh? Is Prester John your king?" Noort laughs. He seems to be emerging from his bewilderment. "Tell me the name of this land, creature, so I may claim it for the United Provinces, if ever I see Holland again."

"It has no name."

"No name! No name! What foolishness! I never found a place whose folk had no name for it, not even in the endless South Sea. But I will name it, then. Let this province be called New Utrecht, eh? And all this land, from here to the shores of the South Sea, I annex hereby to the United Provinces in the name of the States-General. You be my witness, creature. Later I will draw up documents. You say I am not dead?"

"Not dead, not dead at all. But far from home. Come, walk beside me, and touch nothing. This is troublesome territory."

"This is strange and ghostly territory," says Noort. "I would paint it, if I could, and then let Mynheer Brueghel look to his fame, and old Bosch as well. Such sights! Were you a prince before you were transformed?"

"I have not yet been transformed," says Bhengarn. "That awaits me at Crystal Pond." The road through the plain now trends slightly uphill; they are advancing into the farther side of the basin. A pale-yellow tint comes into the sky. The path here is prickly with little many-faceted insects whose hard sharp bodies assail the Dutchman's bare tender feet. Cursing, he hops in wild leaps, bringing him dangerously close to outcroppings of teeth, and Bhengarn, in sympathy, fashions stout gray boots for him. Noort grins. He gestures toward his bare middle, and Bhengarn clothes him in a shapeless gray robe.

"Like a monk, is how I look!" Noort cries. "Well, well, a monk in Hell! But you say this is not Hell. And what kind of creature are you, creature?"

"A human being," says Bhengarn, "of the Traveler sort."

"A human being!" Noort booms. He leaps across a brook of sparkling bubbling violet-hued water and waits on the far side as Bhengarn trudges through it. "A human under an enchantment, I would venture."

"This is my natural form. Humankind has not worn your guise since long before the falling of the Moon. The Eater you saw was human. Do you see, on yonder eastern hill, a company of Destroyers turning the forest to rubble? They are human."

"The wolves on two legs up there?"

"Those, yes. And there are others you will see. Awaiters, Breathers, Skimmers—"

"These are mere noises to me, creature. What is human? A Dutchman is human! A Portugal is human! Even a Chinese, a black, a Japonder with a shaven head. But those beasts on yon hill? Or a creature with more legs than I have whiskers. No, Traveler, no! You flatter yourself. Do you happen to know, Traveler, how it is that I am here? I was in Amsterdam, to speak before the Lords Seventeen and the Company in general, to ask for ships to bring pepper from the Moluccas, but they said they would choose Joris van Spilbergen in my place—do you know Spilbergen? I think him much overpraised—and then all went dizzy, as though I had taken too much beer with my gin—and then—then—ah, this is a dream, is it not, Traveler? At this moment I sleep in Amsterdam. I am too old for such drinking. Yet never have I had a dream so real as this, and so strange. Tell me: when you walk, do you move the legs on the right side first, or the left?" Noort does not wait for a reply. "If you are human, Traveler, are you also a Christian, then?"

Bhengarn searches in Noort's mind for the meaning of that, finds something approximate, and says, "I make no such claim."

"Good. Good. There are limits to my credulity. How far is this Crystal Pond?"

"We have covered most of the distance. If I proceed at a steady pace I will come shortly to the land of smoking holes, and not far beyond that is the approach to the Wall of Ice, which will demand a difficult but not impossible ascent, and just on the far side of that I will find the vale that contains Crystal Pond, where the beginning of the next phase of my life will occur." They are walking now through a zone of sparkling rubbery cones of a bright vermilion color, from which small green Stangarones emerge in quick succession to chant their one-note melodies. The flavor of a heavy musk hangs in the air. Night is beginning to fall. Bhengarn says, "Are you tired?"

"Just a little."

"It is not my custom to travel by night. Does this campsite suit you?" Bhengarn indicates a broad circular depression bordered by tiny volcanic fumaroles. The ground here is warm and spongy, moist, bare of vegetation. Bhengarn extends an excavator claw and pulls free a strip of it, which he hands to Noort, indicating that he should eat. Noort tentatively nibbles. Bhengarn helps himself to some also. Noort, kneeling, presses his knuckles against the ground, makes it yield, mutters to himself, shakes his head, rips off another strip and chews it in wonder. Bhengarn says, "You find the world much changed, do you not?"

"Beyond all understanding, in fact."

"Our finest artists have worked on it since time immemorial, making it more lively, more diverting. We think it is a great success. Do you agree?"

Noort does not answer. He is staring bleakly at the sky, suddenly dark and jeweled with blazing stars. Bhengarn realizes that he is searching for patterns, navigators' signs. Noort frowns, turns round and round to take in the full circuit of the heavens, bites his lip, finally lets out a low groaning sigh and says, "I recognize nothing. Nothing. This is not the northern sky, this is not the southern sky, this is not any sky I can understand." Quietly he begins to weep. After a time he says somberly, "I was not the most adept of navigators, but I knew something, at least. And I look at this sky and I feel like a helpless babe. All the stars have changed places. Now I see how lost I am, how far from anything I ever knew, and once it gave me great pleasure to sail under strange skies, but not now, not here, because these skies frighten me and this land of demons offers me no peace. I have never wept, do you know that, creature, never, not once in my life! But Holland—my house, my tavern, my church, my sons, my pipe—where is Holland? Where is everything I knew? The skies above Magellan's Strait were not the thousandth part so strange as this." A harsh heavy sob escapes him, and he turns away, huddling into himself.

Compassion floods Bhengarn for this miserable wanderer. To ease Noort's pain he summons fantasies for him, dredging images from the reservoirs of the ancient man's spirit and hurling them against the sky, building a cathedral of fire in the heavens, and a royal palace, and a great armada of ships with bellying sails and the Dutch flag fluttering, and the watery boulevards of busy Amsterdam and the quiet streets of little Haarlem, and more. He paints for Noort the stars in their former courses, the Centaur, the Swan, the Bear, the Twins. He restores the fallen Moon to its place and by its cold light creates a landscape of time lost and gone, with avenues of heavy-boughed oaks and maples, and drifts of brilliant red and yellow tulips blaring beneath them, and golden roses arching in great bowers over the thick, newly mowed lawn. He creates fields of ripe wheat, and haystacks high as barns, and harvesters toiling in the hot sultry afternoon. He gives Noort the aroma of the Sunday feast and the scent of good Dutch gin and the sweet dense fumes of his long clay pipe. Noort nods and murmurs and clasps his hands, and gradually his sorrow ebbs and his weeping ceases, and he drifts off into a deep and easy slumber. The images fade. Bhengarn, who rarely sleeps, keeps watch until first light comes and a flock of fingerwinged birds passes overhead, shouting shrilly, jesting and swooping.

Noort is calm and quiet in the morning. He feeds again on the spongy soil and drinks from a clear emerald rivulet and they move onward toward Crystal Pond. Bhengarn is pleased to have his company. There is something crude and coarse about the Dutchman, perhaps even more so than another of his era might be, but Bhengarn finds that unimportant. He has always preferred companions of any sort to the solitary march, in his centuries of going to and fro upon the Earth. He has traveled with Skimmers and Destroyers, and once a ponderous Ruminant, and even on several occasions visitors from other worlds who have come to sample the wonders of Earth. At least twice Bhengarn has had as his traveling companion a castaway of the time-flux from some prehistoric era, though not so prehistoric as Noort's. And now it has befallen him that he will go to the end of his journey with this rough hairy being from the dawn of humanity's day. So be it. So be it.

Noort says, breaking a long silence as they cross a plateau of quivering gelatinous stuff, "Were you a man or a woman before the sorcery gave you this present shape?"

"I have always had this form."

"No. Impossible. You say you are human, you speak my language—"

"Actually, you speak *my* language," says Bhengarn.

"As you wish. If you are human you must once have looked like me. Can it be otherwise? Were you born a thing of silvery scales and many legs? I will not believe that."

"Born?" says Bhengarn, puzzled.

"Is this word unknown to you?"

"Born," the Traveler repeats. "I think I see the concept. To *begin,* to *enter,* to *acquire one's shape—*"

"Born," says Noort in exasperation. "To come from the womb. To hatch, to out, to drop. Everything alive has to be born!"

"No," Bhengarn says mildly. "Not any longer."

"You talk nonsense," Noort snaps, and scours his throat angrily and spits. His spittle strikes a node of assonance and blossoms into a dazzling mound of green and scarlet jewels. "Rubies," he murmurs. "Emeralds. I could puke pearls, I suppose." He kicks at the pile of gems and scatters them; they dissolve into spurts of moist pink air. The Dutchman gives himself over to a sullen brooding. Bhengarn does not transgress on the other's taciturnity; he is content to march forward in his steady plodding way, saying nothing.

Three Skimmers appear, prancing, leaping. They are heading to the south. The slender golden-green creatures salute the wayfarers with pulsations of their great red eyes. Noort, halting, glares at them and says hoarsely to Bhengarn, "These are human beings, too?"

"Indeed."

"Natives of this realm?"

"Natives of this era," says Bhengarn. "The latest form, the newest thing, graceful, supple, purposeless." The Skimmers laugh and transform themselves into shining streaks of light and soar aloft like a trio of auroral rays. Bhengarn says, "Do they seem beautiful to you?"

"They seem like minions of Satan," says the Dutchman sourly. He scowls. "When I awaken I pray I remember none of this. For if I do, I will tell the tale to Willem and Jan and Piet, and they will think I have lost my senses, and mock me. Tell me I dream, creature. Tell me I lie drunk in an inn in Amsterdam."

"It is not so," Bhengarn says gently.

"Very well. Very well. I have come to a land where every living thing is a demon or a monster. That is no worse, I suppose, than a land where everyone speaks Japanese and worships stones. It is a world of wonders, and I have seen more than my share. Tell me, creature, do you have cities in this land?"

"Not for millions of years."

"Then where do the people live?"

"Why, they live where they find themselves! Last night we lived where the ground was food. Tonight we will settle by the Wall of Ice. And tomorrow—"

"Tomorrow," Noort says, "we will have dinner with the Grand Diabolus and dance in the Witches' Sabbath. I am prepared, just as I was prepared to sup with the penguin-eating folk of the Cape, that stood six cubits high. I will be surprised by nothing." He laughs. "I am hungry, creature. Shall I tear up the earth again and stuff it down?"

"Not here. Try those fruits."

Luminous spheres dangle from a tree of golden limbs. Noort plucks one, tries it unhesitatingly, claps his hands, takes three more. Then he pulls a whole cluster free, and offers one to Bhengarn, who refuses.

"Not hungry?" the Dutchman asks.

"I take my food in other ways."

"Yes, you breathe it in from flowers as you crawl along, eh? Tell me, Traveler: to what end is your journey? To discover new lands? To fulfill some pledge? To confound your enemies? I doubt it is any of these."

"I travel out of simple necessity, because it is what my kind does, and for no special purpose."

"A humble wanderer, then, like the mendicant monks who serve the Lord by taking to the highways?"

"Something like that."

"Do you ever cease your wanderings?"

"Never yet. But cessation is coming. At Crystal Pond I will become my utter opposite, and enter the Awaiter tribe, and be made immobile and contemplative. I will root myself like a vegetable, after my metamorphosis."

Noort offers no comment on that. After a time he says, "I knew a man of your kind once. Jan Huyghen van Linschoten of Haarlem, who roamed the world because the world was there to roam, and spent his years in the India of the Portugals and wrote it all down in a great vast book, and when he had done that went off to Novaya

Zemlya with Barents to find the chilly way to the Indies, and I think would have sailed to the Moon if he could find the pilot to guide him. I spoke with him once. My own travels took me farther than Linschoten, do you know? I saw Borneo and Java and the world's hinder side, and the thick Sargasso Sea. But I went with a purpose other than my own amusement or the gathering of strange lore, which was to buy pepper and cloves, and gather Spanish gold, and win my fame and comfort. Was that so wrong, Traveler? Was I so unworthy?" Noort chuckles. "Perhaps I was, for I brought home neither spices nor gold nor most of my men, but only the fame of having sailed around the world. I think I understand you, Traveler. The spices go into a cask of meat and are eaten and gone; the gold is only yellow metal; but so long as there are Dutchmen, no one will forget that Olivier van Noort, the tavern-keeper of Rotterdam, strung a line around the middle of the world. So long as there are Dutchmen." He laughs. "It is folly to travel for profit. I will travel for wisdom from now on. What do you say, Traveler? Do you applaud me?"

"I think you are already on the proper path," says Bhengarn. "But look, look there: the Wall of Ice."

Noort gasps. They have come around a low headland and are confronted abruptly by a barrier of pure white light, as radiant as a mirror at noon, that spans the horizon from east to west and rises skyward like an enormous palisade filling half the heavens. Bhengarn studies it with respect and admiration. He has known for hundreds of years that he must ascend this wall if he is to reach Crystal Pond, and that the wall is formidable; but he has seen no need before now to contemplate the actualities of the problem, and now he sees that they are significant.

"Are we to ascend that?" Noort asks.

"I must. But here, I think, we shall have to part company."

"The throne of Lucifer must lie beyond that icy rampart."

"I know nothing of that," says Bhengarn, "but certainly Crystal Pond is on the farther side, and there is no other way to reach it but to climb the wall. We will camp tonight at its base, and in the morning I will begin my climb."

"Is such a climb possible?"

"It will have to be," Bhengarn replies.

"Ah. You will turn yourself to a puff of light like those others we met, and shoot over the top like some meteor. Eh?"

"I must climb," says Bhengarn, "using one limb after another, and taking care not to lose my grip. There is no magical way of making this ascent." He sweeps aside fallen branches of a glowing blue-limbed shrub to make a campsite for them. To Noort he says, "Before I begin the ascent tomorrow I will instruct you in the perils of the world, for your protection on your future wanderings. I hold myself responsible for your presence here, and I would not have you harmed once you have left my side."

Noort says, "I am not yet planning to leave your side. I mean to climb that wall alongside you, Traveler."

"It will not be possible for you."

"I will make it possible. That wall excites my spirit. I will conquer it as I conquered the storms of the Strait and the fevers of the Sargasso. I feel I should go with you to Crystal Pond, and pay my farewells to you there, for it will bring me luck to mark the beginning of my solitary journey by witnessing the end of yours. What do you say?"

"I say wait until the morning," Bhengarn answers, "and see the wall at close range, before you commit yourself to such mighty resolutions."

During the night a silent lightstorm plays overhead; twisting turbulent spears of blue and green and violet radiance clash in the throbbing sky, and an undulation of the atmosphere sends alternating waves of hot and cool air racing down from the Wall of Ice. The time-flux blows, and frantic figures out of forgotten eras are swept by now far aloft, limbs churning desperately, eyes rigid with astonishment. Noort sleeps through it all, though from time to time he stirs and mutters and clenches his fists. Bhengarn ponders his obligations to the Dutchman, and by the coming of the sharp blood-hued dawn he has arrived at an idea. Together they advance to the edge of the Wall; together they stare upward at that vast vertical field of shining whiteness, smooth as stone. Hesitantly Noort touches it with his fingertip, and hisses at the coldness of it. He turns his back to it, paces, folds and unfolds his arms.

He says finally, "No man or woman born could achieve the summit of that wall. But is there not some magic you could work, Traveler, that would enable me to make the ascent?"

"There is one. But I think you would not like it."

"Speak."

"I could transform you—for a short time, only a short time, no longer than the time it takes to climb the wall—into a being of the Traveler form. Thus we could ascend together."

Noort's eyes travel quickly over Bhengarn's body—the long tubular serpentine thorax, the tapering tail, the multitude of powerful little legs—and a look of shock and dismay and loathing comes over his face for an instant, but just an instant. He frowns. He tugs at his heavy lower lip.

Bhengarn says, "I will take no offense if you refuse."

"Do it."

"You may be displeased."

"Do it! The morning is growing old. We have much climbing to do. Change me, Traveler. Change me quickly." A shadow of doubt crosses Noort's features. "You will change me back, once we reach the top?"

"It will happen of its own accord. I have no power to make a permanent transformation."

"Then do what you can, and do it now!"

"Very well," says Bhengarn, and the Traveler, summoning his fullest force, drains metamorphic energies from the planets and the stars and a passing comet, and focuses them and hurls them at the Dutchman, and there is a buzzing and a droning and a shimmering and when it is done a second Traveler stands at the foot of the Wall of Ice.

Noort seems thunderstruck. He says nothing; he does not move; only after a long time does he carefully lift his frontmost left limb and swing it forward a short way and put it down. Then the one opposite it; then several of the middle limbs; then, growing more adept, he manages to move his entire body, adopting a curious wriggling style, and in another moment he appears to be in control. "This is passing strange," he remarks at length. "And yet it is almost like being in my own body, except that everything has been changed. You are a mighty wizard, Traveler. Can you show me now how to make the ascent?"

"Are you ready so soon?"

"I am ready," Noort says.

So Bhengarn demonstrates, approaching the wall, bringing his penetrator claws into play, driving them like pitons into the ice, hauling himself up a short distance, extending his claws, driving them in, pulling upward. He has never climbed ice before, though he has faced all other difficulties the world has to offer, but the climb, though strenuous, seems manageable enough. He halts after a few minutes and watches as Noort, clumsy but determined in his altered body, imitates him, scratching and scraping at the ice as he pulls himself up the face until they are side by side. "It is easy," Noort says.

And so it is, for a time, and then it is less easy, for now they hang high above the valley and the midday sun has melted the surface of the wall just enough to make it slick and slippery, and a terrible cold from within the mass of ice seeps outward into the climbers, and even though a Traveler's body is a wondrous machine fit to endure anything, this is close to the limit. Once Bhengarn loses his purchase, but Noort deftly claps a claw to the middle of his spine to hold him firmly until he has dug in again; and not much later the same happens to Noort, and Bhengarn grasps him. As the day wanes they are so far above the ground that they can barely make out the treetops below, and yet the top of the wall is too high to see. Together they excavate a ledge, burrowing inward to rest in a chilly nook, and at dawn they begin again, Bhengarn's sinuous body winding upward over the rim of their little cave and Noort following with less agility. Upward and upward they climb, never pausing and saying little, through a day of warmth and soft perfumed breezes and through a night of storms and falling stars, and then through a day of turquoise rain, and through another day and a night and a day and then they are at the top, looking out across the broad unending field of ferns and bright blossoms that covers the summit's flat surface, and as they move inward from the rim Noort lets out a cry and stumbles forward, for he has resumed his ancient form. He drops to his knees and sits there panting, stunned, looking in confusion at his fingernails, at his knuckles, at the hair on the backs of his hands, as though he has never seen such things before. "Passing strange," he says softly.

"You are a born Traveler," Bhengarn tells him.

They rest a time, feeding on the sparkling four-winged fruits that sprout in that garden above the ice. Bhengarn feels an immense calmness now that the climax of his peregrination is upon him. Never had he questioned the purpose of being a Traveler, nor has he had regret that destiny gave him that form, but now he is quite willing to yield it up.

"How far to Crystal Pond?" Noort asks.

"It is just over there," says Bhengarn.

"Shall we go to it now?"

"Approach it with great care," the Traveler warns. "It is a place of extraordinary power."

They go forward; a path opens for them in the swaying grasses and low fleshy-leaved plants; within minutes they stand at the edge of a perfectly circular body of water of unfathomable depth and of a clarity so complete that the reflections of the sun can plainly be seen on the white sands of its infinitely distant bed. Bhengarn moves to the edge and peers in, and is pervaded by a sense of fulfillment and finality.

Noort says, "What will become of you here?"

"Observe," says Bhengarn.

He enters Crystal Pond and swims serenely toward the farther shore, an enterprise quickly enough accomplished. But before he has reached the midpoint of the pond a tolling sound is heard in the air, as of bells of the most pure quality, striking notes without harmonic overtones. Sudden ecstasy engulfs him as he becomes aware of the beginning of his transformation: his body flows and streams in the flux of life, his limbs fuse, his soul expands. By the time he comes forth on the edge of the pond he has become something else, a great cone of passive flesh, which is able to drag itself no more than five or six times its own length from the water, and then sinks down on the sandy surface of the ground and begins the process of digging itself in. Here the Awaiter Bhengarn will settle, and here he will live for centuries of centuries, motionless, all but timeless, considering the primary truths of being. Already he is gliding into the Earth.

Noort gapes at him from the other side of the pond.

"Is this what you sought?" the Dutchman asks.

"Yes. Absolutely."

"I wish you farewell and Godspeed, then!" Noort cries.

"And you—what will become of you?"

Noort laughs. "Have no fears for me! I see my destiny unfolding!"

Bhengarn, nestled now deep in the ground, enwombed by the earth, immobile, established already in his new life, watches as Noort strides boldly to the water's edge. Only slowly, for an Awaiter's mind is less agile than a Traveler's, does Bhengarn comprehend what is to happen.

Noort says, "I've found my vocation again. But if I'm to travel, I must be equipped for traveling!"

He enters the pond, swimming in broad awkward splashing strokes, and once again the pure tolling sound is evoked, a delicate carillon of crystalline transparent tone, and there is sudden brilliance in the pond as Noort sprouts the shining scales of a Traveler, and the jointed limbs, and the strong thick tail. He scuttles out on the far side wholly transformed.

"Farewell!" Noort cries joyously.

"Farewell," murmurs Bhengarn the Awaiter, peering out from the place of his long repose as Olivier van Noort, all his legs ablaze with new energy, strides away vigorously to begin his second circumnavigation of the globe.

◆

HAWKSBILL STATION

Now and then over the course of my career I have given up the writing of science fiction for an extended period, sometimes because I wanted to do other things, sometimes simply because of fatigue. One of those periods was the winter of 1958–59, after four or five years of frenzied activity in which I had written enough of the stuff to fill three or four average careers. Still only in my mid-twenties, puzzled about my place in a genre that I loved deeply but seemed unable to serve well, I turned away and wandered for a few years in a morass of hackwork that still gives me the creeps when I look at the titles of the things I was writing then—"I Was Eaten by Monster Crabs," "World of Living Corpses," "The Syndicate Moves In," and much god-awful more.

And then came a wonderful offer I couldn't refuse from Frederik Pohl, the editor of the top-ranked science fiction magazine, Galaxy, *who promised to buy anything I would write for him, so long as I maintained a high level of quality. By freeing me from the risk of having stories rejected he teased me back into science fiction, at least on a now-and-then basis. I did a few short stories for him at a rate of about one every six months, and then the "Blue Fire" series of novelettes that became the book* To Open the Sky, *and by then—it was now 1965—I was hooked on writing SF all over again. Only this time, because Pohl had given me the space to write the stories exactly as I felt they ought to be written, because I was no longer (as I had been doing from 1955 to 1958) tailoring my product to some editor's notion of what was acceptable, I was far more satisfied with what I was writing: at last, stories which I as a critical reader would have been interested in reading.*

And so began the second phase of my career, the so-called "new Silverberg" that elicited so much surprised comment in the mid-1960s. After the "Blue Fire" stories came The Time Hoppers, *the novel for Doubleday that I expanded out of one of my earliest short stories, which I finished in March of 1966. Then, in mid-April, I wrote to Pohl about another ambitious project that had grown out of my own deep interest in paleontology and my almost obsessive fascination with the idea of traveling in time. What I told him was: "I'm thinking in very science fictional terms these days and I want to get these stories written while the fit is still on me. This one would be a novella—15,000 words, 20,000, somewhere within that range. I have it roughed out, though not solidly enough for me to want to talk much about the plot, except to say that the story takes place in a camp for political prisoners on Earth approximately two and a half billion years ago. If you can find room for a Silverberg story of this length, I'd like to write it sometime in the next month."*

Fred gave me the go-ahead; I set to work immediately, and wrote the story in one white-hot week, 20,000 words, mailing it to him on May 5. By May 11 I had word of its acceptance. It was published in the August 1967 issue of Galaxy *and brought me one of the most cherishable reader comments I have ever received: the famed science writer Willy Ley, encountering me at a New York literary party, praised at great length the accuracy and richness of texture of my portrait of life in the early Paleozoic. I am not exactly indifferent to most people's praise of my work, but, although I absorb it with pleasure, I tend to forget it quickly; hearing Willy Ley tell me in rumbling Teutonic tones how well I had brought the era of trilobites to life for him is a memory that still glows brightly for me many decades later. The story also brought me my first Hugo and Nebula nominations, though competition for both awards was stiff that year and I finished as a runner-up. At that point in my career, though, simply getting on the final ballot was exciting.*

Despite Willy Ley's warm praise, there was at least one inaccuracy in the story. It takes place in the late Cambrian period, which according to modern geological theory was about 550 million years ago. Yet in my original proposal for Fred Pohl I placed the scene "approximately two and a half billion years ago," and even in the published story I set the Cambrian two billion years in the past. That was not a case of ignorance, but of a writer's outsmarting himself, for what I was doing was implying a revision, after the development of time travel, of our entire geological time scale. But I found no convenient way of working into the story a statement to the effect that scientists had once believed the Cambrian to have been 550 million years ago but now knew it to be two billion, which in fact is now known not to be true, and in the end I just used the greater time scale without explaining what I was up to. This, of course, brought some critical comments from present-day geologists otherwise pleased with the work. So when the story was reprinted in the first of its many anthology appearances I cut the time span in half, putting the late Cambrian at one *billion years ago—still a revisionist notion, but one less likely to draw attack. And I have kept it that way in all further printings of the story, as well as in the expansion to novel form that I carried out in the spring of 1967, under the same title, for Doubleday.*

1.

Barrett was the uncrowned King of Hawksbill Station. He had been there the longest; he had suffered the most; he had the deepest inner resources of strength. Before his accident, he had been able to whip any man in the place. Now he was a cripple, but he still had that aura of power that gave him command. When there were problems at the Station, they were brought to Barrett. That was axiomatic. He was the king.

He ruled over quite a kingdom, too. In effect it was the whole world, pole to pole, meridian to meridian. For what it was worth. It wasn't worth very much.

Now it was raining again. Barrett shrugged himself to his feet in the quick, easy gesture that cost him an infinite amount of carefully concealed agony, and shuffled to the door of his hut. Rain made him impatient: the pounding of those great greasy drops against the corrugated tin roof was enough even to drive a Jim Barrett loony. He nudged the door open. Standing in the doorway, Barrett looked out over his kingdom.

Barren rock, nearly to the horizon. A shield of raw dolomite going on and on. Raindrops danced and bounced on that continental slab of rock. No trees. No grass. Behind Barrett's hut lay the sea, gray and vast. The sky was gray too, even when it wasn't raining.

He hobbled out into the rain. Manipulating his crutch was getting to be a simple matter for him now. He leaned comfortably, letting his crushed left foot dangle. A rockslide had pinned him last year during a trip to the edge of the Inland Sea. Back home, Barrett would have been fitted with prosthetics and that would have been the end of it: a new ankle, a new instep, refurbished ligaments and tendons. But home was a billion years away, and home there's no returning.

The rain hit him hard. Barrett was a big man, six and a half feet tall, with hooded dark eyes, a jutting nose, a chin that was a monarch among chins. He had weighed two hundred fifty pounds in his prime, in the good old agitating days when he had carried banners and pounded out manifestos. But now he was past sixty and beginning to shrink a little, the skin getting loose around the places where the mighty muscles used to be. It was hard to keep your weight in Hawksbill Station. The food was nutritious, but it lacked intensity. A man got to miss steak. Eating brachiopod stew and trilobite hash wasn't the same thing at all. Barrett was past all bitterness, though. That was another reason why the men regarded him as the leader. He didn't scowl. He didn't rant. He was resigned to his fate, tolerant of eternal exile, and so he could help the others get over that difficult, heart-clawing period of transition.

A figure arrived, jogging through the rain: Norton. The doctrinaire Khrushchevist with the Trotskyite leanings. A small, excitable man who frequently appointed himself messenger whenever there was news at the Station. He sprinted toward Barrett's hut, slipping and sliding over the naked rocks.

Barrett held up a meaty hand. "Whoa, Charley. Take it easy or you'll break your neck!"

Norton halted in front of the hut. The rain had pasted the widely spaced strands of his brown hair to his skull. His eyes had the fixed, glossy look of fanaticism—or perhaps just astigmatism. He gasped for breath and staggered into the hut, shaking himself like a wet puppy. He obviously had run all the way from the main building of the

Station, three hundred yards away—a long dash over rock that slippery.

"Why are you standing around in the rain?" Norton asked.

"To get wet," said Barrett, following him inside. "What's the news?"

"The Hammer's glowing. We're getting company."

"How do you know it's a live shipment?"

"It's been glowing for half an hour. That means they're taking precautions. They're sending a new prisoner. Anyway, no supplies shipment is due."

Barrett nodded. "Okay. I'll come over. If it's a new man, we'll bunk him in with Latimer."

Norton managed a rasping laugh. "Maybe he's a materialist. Latimer will drive him crazy with all that mystic nonsense. We could put him with Altman instead."

"And he'll be raped in half an hour."

"Altman's off that kick now," said Norton. "He's trying to create a real woman, not looking for second-rate substitutes."

"Maybe our new man doesn't have any spare ribs."

"Very funny, Jim." Norton did not look amused. "You know what I want the new man to be? A conservative, that's what. A black-souled reactionary straight out of Adam Smith. God, that's what I want!"

"Wouldn't you be happy with a fellow Bolshevik?"

"This place is full of Bolsheviks," said Norton. "Of all shades from pale pink to flagrant scarlet. Don't you think I'm sick of them? Sitting around fishing for trilobites and discussing the relative merits of Kerensky and Malenkov? I need somebody to *talk* to, Jim. Somebody I can fight with."

"All right," Barrett said, slipping into his rain gear. "I'll see what I can do about hocusing a debating partner out of the Hammer for you. A rip-roaring Objectivist, okay?" He laughed. "You know something, maybe there's been a revolution Up Front since we got our last man? Maybe the left is in and the right is out, and they'll start shipping us nothing but reactionaries. How would you like that? Fifty or a hundred storm troopers, Charley? Plenty of material to debate economics with. And the place will fill up with more and more of them, until we're outnumbered, and then maybe they'll have a *putsch* and get rid of all the stinking leftists sent here by the old regime, and—"

Barrett stopped. Norton was staring at him in amazement, his faded eyes wide, his hand compulsively smoothing his thinning hair to hide his embarrassment. Barrett realized that he had just committed one of the most heinous crimes possible at Hawksbill Station: he had started to run off at the mouth. There hadn't been any call for his little outburst. What made it more troublesome was the fact that *he* was the one who had permitted himself such a luxury. He was supposed to be the strong one of this place, the stabilizer, the man of absolute integrity and principle and sanity on whom the others could lean. And suddenly he had lost control. It was a bad sign. His dead foot was throbbing again; possibly that was the reason.

In a tight voice he said, "Let's go. Maybe the new man is here already."

They stepped outside. The rain was beginning to let up; the storm was moving out to sea. In the east, over what would one day be the Atlantic, the sky was still clotted with gray mist, but to the west a different grayness was emerging, the shade of normal gray that meant dry weather. Before he had come out here, Barrett had expected to find the sky practically black, because there'd be fewer dust particles to bounce the light around and turn things blue. But the sky seemed to be a weary beige. So much for *a priori* theories.

Through the thinning rain they walked toward the main building. Norton accommodated himself to Barrett's limping pace, and Barrett, wielding his crutch furiously, did his damndest not to let his infirmity slow them up. He nearly lost his footing twice, and fought hard not to let Norton see.

Hawksbill Station spread out before them.

It covered about five hundred acres. In the center of everything was the main building, an ample dome that contained most of their equipment and supplies. At widely paced intervals, rising from the rock shield like grotesque giant green mushrooms, were the plastic blisters of the individual dwellings. Some, like Barrett's, were shielded by tin sheeting salvaged from shipments from Up Front. Others stood unprotected, just as they had come from the mouth of the extruder.

The huts numbered about eighty. At that moment, there were 140 inmates in Hawksbill Station, pretty close to the all-time high. Up Front hadn't sent back any hut-building materials for a long time, and so all the newer arrivals had to double up with bunkmates. Barrett and all those whose exile had begun before 2014 had the privilege of private dwellings, if they wanted them. (Some did not wish to live alone; Barrett, to preserve his own authority, felt that he was required to.) As new exiles arrived, they bunked in with those who currently lived alone, in reverse order of seniority. Most of the 2015 exiles had been forced to take roommates now. Another dozen deportees and the 2014 group would be doubling up. Of course, there were deaths all up and down the line, and there were plenty who were eager to have company in their huts.

Barrett felt, though, that a man who has to be sentenced to life imprisonment ought to have the privilege of privacy if he desires it. One of his biggest problems here was keeping people from cracking up because there was too little privacy. Propinquity could be intolerable in a place like this.

Norton pointed toward the big shiny-skinned green dome of the main building. "There's Altman going in now. And Rudiger. And Hutchett. Something's happening!"

Barrett stepped up his pace. Some of the men entering the building saw his bulky figure coming over the rise in the rock, and waved to him. Barrett lifted a massive hand in reply. He felt mounting excitement. It was a big event at the Station whenever a new man arrived. Nobody had come for six months, now. That was the longest gap he could remember. It had started to seem as though no one would ever come again.

That would be a catastrophe. New men were all that stood between the older inmates and insanity. New men brought news from the future, news from the world that was entirely left behind. They contributed new personalities to a group that always was in danger of going stale.

And, Barrett knew, some men—he was not one—lived in the deluded hope that the next arrival might just be a woman.

That was why they flocked to the main building when the Hammer began to glow. Barrett hobbled down the path. The rain died away just as he reached the entrance.

Within, sixty or seventy Station residents crowded the chamber of the Hammer—just about every man in the place who was able in body and mind, and still alert enough to show curiosity about a newcomer. They shouted their greetings to Barrett. He nodded, smiled, deflected their questions with amiable gestures.

"Who's it going to be this time, Jim?"

"Maybe a girl, huh? Around nineteen years old, blonde, built like—"

"I hope he can play stochastic chess, anyway."

"Look at the glow! It's deepening!"

Barrett, like the others, stared at the Hammer. The complex, involuted collection of unfathomable instruments burned a bright cherry-red now, betokening the surge of who knew how many kilowatts being pumped in at the far end of the line. The glow had spread to the Anvil now, that broad aluminum bedplate on which all shipments from the future were dropped. In another moment—

"Condition Crimson!" somebody yelled. "Here he comes!"

2.

A BILLION YEARS UP THE time-line, power was flooding into the real Hammer of which this was only the partial replica. A man—or something else—stood in the center of the real Anvil, waiting for the Hawksbill Field to unfold him and kick him back to the early Paleozoic. The effect of time travel was very much like being hit with a gigantic hammer and driven clear through the walls of the continuum: hence the governing metaphors for the parts of the machine.

Setting up Hawksbill Station had been a long, slow job. The Hammer had knocked a pathway and had sent back the nucleus of the receiving station first. Since there was no receiving station on hand to receive the receiving station, a certain amount of waste had occurred. It wasn't necessary to have a Hammer and Anvil on the receiving end, except as a fine control to prevent temporal spread; without the equipment, the field wandered a little, and it was possible to scatter consecutive shipments over a span of twenty or thirty years. There was plenty of such temporal garbage all around Hawksbill Station: stuff that had been intended for the original installation, but which because of tuning imprecisions in the pre-Hammer days had landed a couple of decades (and a couple of hundred miles) away from the intended site.

Despite such difficulties, they had finally sent through enough components to the master temporal site to allow for the construction of a receiving station. Then the first prisoners had gone through: technicians who knew how to put the Hammer and Anvil together. Of course, it was their privilege to refuse to cooperate. But it was to their own advantage to assemble the receiving station, thus making it possible for them to be sure of getting further supplies from Up Front. They had done the job. After that, outfitting Hawksbill Station had been easy.

Now the Hammer glowed, meaning that they had activated the Hawksbill Field on the sending end, somewhere up around 2028 or 2030 AD. All the sending was done there. All the receiving was done here. It didn't work the other way. Nobody really knew why, although there was a lot of superficially profound talk about the rules of entropy.

There was a whining, hissing sound as the edges of the Hawksbill Field began to ionize the atmosphere in the room. Then came the expected thunderclap of implosion, caused by an imperfect overlapping of the quantity of air that was subtracted from this era and the quantity of air was being thrust into it. And then abruptly, a man dropped out of the Hammer and lay stunned and limp, on the gleaming Anvil.

He looked young, which surprised Barrett considerably. He seemed to be well under thirty. Generally, only middle-aged men were sent to Hawksbill Station. Incorrigibles, who had to be separated from humanity for the general good. The youngest man in the place now had been close to forty when he arrived. The sight of this lean, clean-cut boy drew a hiss of anguish from a couple of the men in the room, and Barrett understood the constellation of emotions that pained them.

The new man sat up. He stirred like a child coming out of a long, deep sleep. He looked around.

His face was very pale. His thin lips seemed bloodless. His blue eyes blinked rapidly. His jaws worked as though he wanted to say something, but could not find the words.

There were no physiological harmful effects to time travel, but it could be a rough jolt to the consciousness. The last moments before the Hammer descended were very much like the final moments beneath the guillotine, since exile to Hawksbill Station was tantamount to a sentence of death. The departing prisoner took his last look at the world of rocket transport and artificial organs, at the world in which he had lived and loved and agitated for a political cause, and then he was rammed into an inconceivably remote past on a one-way journey. It was a gloomy business, and it was not very surprising that the newcomers arrived in a state of emotional shock.

Barrett elbowed his way through the crowd. Automatically the others made way for him. He reached the lip of the Anvil and leaned over it, extending a hand to the new man. His broad smile was met by a look of blank bewilderment.

"I'm Jim Barrett. Welcome to Hawksbill Station. Here—get off that thing before a load of groceries lands on top of you." Wincing a little as he shifted his weight, Barrett pulled the new man down from the Anvil. It was altogether likely for the idiots Up Front to shoot another shipment along a minute after sending a man.

Barrett beckoned to Mel Rudiger, and the plump anarchist handed the new man an alcohol capsule. He took it and pressed it to his arm without a word. Charley Norton offered him a candy bar. The man shook it off. He looked groggy—a real case of temporal shock, Barrett thought, possibly the worst he had ever seen. The newcomer hadn't even spoken yet. Could the effect really be that extreme?

Barrett said, "We'll go to the infirmary and check you out. Then I'll assign you your quarters. There's time for you to find your way around and meet everybody later on. What's your name?"

"Hahn. Lew Hahn."

"I can't hear you."

"Hahn," the man repeated, still only barely audible.

"When are you from, Lew?"

"2029."

"You feel pretty sick?"

"I feel awful. I don't even believe this is happening to me. There's no such place as Hawksbill Station, is there?"

"I'm afraid there is," Barrett said. "At least, for most of us. A few of the boys think it's all an illusion induced by drugs. But I have my doubts of that. If it's an illusion, it's damned good. Look."

He put one arm around Hahn's shoulders and guided him through the press of prisoners, out of the Hammer chamber and toward the nearby infirmary. Although Hahn looked thin, even fragile, Barrett was surprised to feel the rippling muscles in those shoulders. He suspected that this man was a lot less helpless and ineffectual than he seemed to be right now. He *had* to be: he had earned banishment to Hawksbill Station.

They passed the open door of the building. "Look out there," Barrett commanded.

Hahn looked. He passed a hand across his eyes as though to clear away unseen cobwebs, and looked again.

"A Late Cambrian landscape," said Barrett quietly. "This view would be a geologist's dream, except that geologists don't tend to become political prisoners, it seems. Out in front of you is what they call Appalachia. It's a strip of rock a few hundred miles wide and a few thousand miles long, running from the Gulf of Mexico to Newfoundland. To the east we've got the Atlantic Ocean. A little way to the west we've got a thing called the Appalachian Geosyncline, which is a trough five hundred miles wide full of water. Somewhere about two thousand miles to the west there's another trough that they call the Cordilleran Geosyncline. It's full of water too, and at this particular stage of geological history the patch of land between the geosynclines is below sea level, so where Appalachia ends we've got the Inland Sea, currently, running way out to the west. On the far side of the Inland Sea is a narrow north-south land mass called Cascadia that's going to be California and Oregon and Washington someday. Don't hold your breath till it happens. I hope you like seafood, Lew."

Hahn stared, and Barrett, standing beside him at the doorway, stared also. You never got used to the alienness of this place, not even after you had lived here twenty years, as Barrett had. It was Earth, and yet it was not really Earth at all, because it was somber and empty and unreal. The gray oceans swarmed with life, of course. But there was nothing on land except occasional patches of moss in the occasional patches of soil that had formed on the bare rock. Even a few cockroaches would be welcome; but insects, it seemed, were still a couple of geological periods in the future. To land dwellers, this was a dead world, a world unborn.

Shaking his head, Hahn moved away from the door. Barrett led him down the corridor and into the small, brightly lit room that served as the infirmary. Doc Quesada was waiting. Quesada wasn't really a doctor, but he had been a medical technician once, and that was good enough. He was a compact, swarthy man with a look of complete self-assurance. He hadn't lost too many patients, all things considered. Barrett had watched him removing appendixes with total aplomb. In his white smock, Quesada looked sufficiently medical to fit the role.

Barrett said, "Doc, this is Lew Hahn. He's in temporal shock. Fix him up."

Quesada nudged the newcomer onto a webfoam cradle and unzipped his blue jersey. Then he reached for his medical kit. Hawksbill Station was well equipped for most medical emergencies, now. The people Up Front had no wish to be inhumane, and they sent back all sorts of useful things, like anesthetics and surgical clamps and medicines and dermal probes. Barrett could remember a time at the beginning when there had been nothing much here but the empty huts, and a man who hurt himself was in real trouble.

"He's had a drink already," said Barrett.

"I see that," Quesada murmured. He scratched at his short-cropped, bristly mustache. The little diagnostat in the cradle had gone rapidly to work, flashing information about Hahn's blood pressure, potassium count, dilation index, and much else. Quesada seemed to comprehend the barrage of facts. After a moment he said to Hahn, "You aren't really sick, are you? Just shaken up a little. I don't blame you.

Here—I'll give you a quick jolt to calm your nerves, and you'll be all right. As all right as any of us ever are."

He put a tube to Hahn's carotid and thumbed the snout. The subsonic whirred, and a tranquilizing compound slid into the man's bloodstream. Hahn shivered.

Quesada said, "Let him rest for five minutes. Then he'll be over the hump."

They left Hahn in his cradle and went out of the infirmary. In the hall, Barrett looked down at the little medic and said, "What's the report on Valdosto?"

Valdosto had gone into psychotic collapse several weeks before. Quesada was keeping him drugged and trying to bring him slowly back to the reality of Hawksbill Station. Shrugging, he replied, "The status is quo. I let him out from under the dream juice this morning and he was the same as he's been."

"You don't think he'll come out of it?"

"I doubt it. He's cracked for keeps. They could paste him together Up Front, but—"

"Yeah," Barrett said. If he could get Up Front at all, Valdosto wouldn't have cracked. "Keep him happy, then. If he can't be sane, he can at least be comfortable. What about Altman? Still got the shakes?"

"He's building a woman," Quesada said.

"That's what Charley Norton told me. What's he using? A rag, a bone—"

"I gave him some surplus chemicals. Chosen for their color, mainly. He's got some foul green copper compounds and a little bit of ethyl alcohol and six or seven other things, and he collected some soil and threw in a lot of dead shellfish, and he's sculpting it all into what he claims is female shape and waiting for lightning to strike it."

"In other words, he's gone crazy," Barrett said.

"I think that's a safe assumption. But he's not molesting his friends any more, anyway. You didn't think his homosexual phase would last much longer, as I recall."

"No, but I didn't think he'd go off the deep end. If a man needs sex and he can find some consenting playmates here, that's quite all right with me. But when he starts putting a woman together out of some dirt and rotten brachiopod meat it means we've lost him. It's too bad."

Quesada's dark eyes flickered. "We're all going to go that way sooner or later, Jim."

"I haven't. You haven't."

"Give us time. I've only been here eleven years."

"Altman's been here only eight. Valdosto even less."

"Some shells crack faster than others," said Quesada.

"Here's our new friend."

Hahn had come out of the infirmary to join them. He still looked pale, but the fright was gone from his eyes. He was beginning to adjust to the unthinkable. He said, "I couldn't help overhearing your conversation. Is there a lot of mental illness here?"

"Some of the men haven't been able to find anything meaningful to do here," Barrett said. "It eats them away. Quesada here has his medical work. I've got administrative duties. A couple of the fellows are studying the sea life. We've got a newspaper to keep some busy. But there are always those who just let themselves slide into despair, and they crack up. I'd say we have thirty or forty certifiable maniacs here at the moment, out of 140 residents."

"That's not so bad," Hahn said. "Considering the inherent instability of the men who get sent here, and the unusual conditions of life here."

Barrett laughed. "Hey, you're suddenly pretty articulate, aren't you? What was in the stuff Doc Quesada jolted you with?"

"I didn't mean to sound superior," Hahn said quickly. "Maybe that came out a little too smug. I mean—"

"Forget it. What did you do Up Front, anyway?"

"I was an economist."

"Just what we need," said Quesada. "He can help us solve our balance-of-payments problem."

Barrett said, "If you were an economist, you'll have plenty to discuss here. This place is full of economic theorists who'll want to bounce their ideas off you. Some of them are almost sane, too. Come with me and I'll show you where you're going to stay."

3.

THE PATIO FROM THE MAIN building to the hut of Donald Latimer was mainly downhill, for which Barrett was grateful even though he knew that he'd have to negotiate the uphill return in a little while. Latimer's hut was on the eastern side of the Station, looking out over the ocean. They walked slowly toward it. Hahn was solicitous of Barrett's game leg, and Barrett was irritated by the exaggerated care the younger man took to keep pace with him.

He was puzzled by this Hahn. The man was full of seeming contradictions—showing up here with the worst case of arrival shock Barrett had ever seen, then snapping out of it with remarkable quickness; looking frail and shy, but hiding solid muscles inside his jersey; giving an outer appearance of incompetence, but speaking with calm control. Barrett wondered what this young man had done to earn him the trip to Hawksbill Station, but there was time for such inquiries later. All the time in the world.

Hahn said, "Is everything like this? Just rock and ocean?"

"That's all. Land life hasn't evolved yet. Everything's wonderfully simple, isn't it? No clutter. No urban sprawl. There's some moss moving onto land, but not much."

"And in the sea? Swimming dinosaurs?"

Barrett shook his head. "There won't be any vertebrates for millions of years. We don't even have fish yet, let alone reptiles out there. All we can offer is that which creepeth. Some shellfish, some big fellows that look like squids, and trilobites. Seven hundred billion different species of trilobites. We've got a man named Rudiger—he's the one who gave you the drink—who's making a collection of them. He's writing the world's definitive text on trilobites."

"But nobody will ever read it in—in the future."

"Up Front, we say."

"Up Front."

"'That's the pity of it," said Barrett. "We told Rudiger to inscribe his book on imperishable plates of gold and hope that it's found by paleontologists. But he says the odds are against it. A billion years of geology will chew his plates to hell before they can be found."

Hahn sniffed. "Why does the air smell so strange?"

"It's a different mix," Barrett said. "We've analyzed it. More nitrogen, a little less oxygen, hardly any CO_2 at all. But that isn't really why it smells odd to you. The thing is, it's pure air, unpolluted by the exhalations of life. Nobody's been respiring into it but us lads, and there aren't enough of us to matter."

Smiling, Hahn said, "I feel a little cheated that it's so empty. I expected lush jungles of weird plants, and pterodactyls swooping through the air, and maybe a tyrannosaur crashing into a fence around the Station."

"No jungles. No pterodactyls. No tyrannosaurs. No fences. You didn't do your homework."

"Sorry."

"This is the Late Cambrian. Sea life exclusively."

"It was very kind of them to pick such a peaceful era as the dumping ground for political prisoners," Hahn said. "I was afraid it would be all teeth and claws."

"Kind, hell! They were looking for an era where we couldn't do any harm. That meant tossing us back before the evolution of mammals, just in case we'd accidentally get hold of the ancestor of all humanity and snuff him out. And while they were at it, they decided to stash us so far in the past that we'd be beyond all land life, on the theory that maybe even if we slaughtered a baby dinosaur it might affect the entire course of the future."

"They don't mind if we catch a few trilobites?"

"Evidently they think it's safe," Barrett said. "It looks as though they were right. Hawksbill Station has been here for twenty-five years, and it doesn't seem as though we've tampered with future history in any measurable way. Of course, they're careful not to send us any women."

"Why is that?"

"So we don't start reproducing and perpetuating ourselves. Wouldn't that mess up the time-lines? A successful human outpost in One Billion B.C., that's had all that time to evolve and mutate and grow? By the time the twenty-first century came around, our descendants would be in charge and the other kind of human being would probably be in penal servitude, and there'd be more paradoxes created than you could shake a trilobite at. So they don't send the women here. There's a prison camp for women, too, but it's a few hundred million years up the time line in the Late Silurian, and never the twain shall meet. That's why Ned Altman's trying to build a woman out of dust and garbage."

"God made Adam out of less."

"Altman isn't God," Barrett said. "That's the root of his whole problem. Look, here's the hut where you're going to stay. I'm rooming you with Don Latimer. He's a very sensitive, interesting, pleasant person. He used to be a physicist before he got into politics, and he's been here about a dozen years, and I might as well warn you that he's developed a strong and somewhat cockeyed mystic streak lately. The fellow he was rooming with killed himself last year, and since then he's been trying to find some way out of here through extrasensory powers."

"Is he serious?"

"I'm afraid he is. And we try to take him seriously. We all humor each other at Hawksbill Station; it's the only way we avoid a mass psychosis. Latimer will probably try to get you to collaborate with him on his project. If you don't like living with him, I can arrange a transfer for you. But I want to see how he reacts to someone new at the Station. I'd like you to give him a chance."

"Maybe I'll even help him find his psionic gateway."

"If you do, take me along," said Barrett. They both laughed. Then he rapped at Latimer's door. There was no answer, and after a moment Barrett pushed the door open. Hawksbill Station had no locks.

Latimer sat in the middle of the bare rock floor, cross-legged, meditating. He was a slender, gentle-faced man just beginning to look old. Right now he seemed a million miles away, ignoring them completely. Hahn shrugged. Barrett put a finger to his lips. They waited in silence for a few minutes, and then Latimer showed signs of coming up from his trance.

He got to his feet in a single flowing motion, without using his hands. In a low, courteous voice he said to Hahn, "Have you just arrived?"

"Within the last hour. I'm Lew Hahn."

"Donald Latimer. I regret that I have to make your acquaintance in these surroundings. But maybe we won't have to tolerate this illegal imprisonment much longer."

Barrett said, "Don, Lew is going to bunk with you. I think you'll get along well. He was an economist in 2029 until they gave him the Hammer."

"Where did you live?" Latimer asked, animation coming into his eyes.

"San Francisco."

The glow faded. Latimer said, "Were you ever in Toronto? I'm from there. I had a daughter—she'd be twenty-three now, Nella Latimer—I wondered if you knew her."

"No. I'm, sorry."

"It wasn't very likely. But I'd love to know what kind of a woman she became. She was a little girl when I last saw her. Now I guess she's married. Or perhaps they've sent her to the other Station. Nella Latimer—you're sure you didn't know her?"

Barrett left them together. It looked as though they'd get along. He told Latimer to bring Hahn up to the main building at dinner for introductions, and went out. A chilly drizzle had begun again. Barrett made his way slowly, painfully up the hill. It had been sad to see the light flicker from Latimer's eyes when Hahn said he didn't know his daughter. Most of the time, men at Hawksbill Station tried not to speak about their families, preferring to keep those tormenting memories well repressed. But the arrival of newcomers generally stirred old ties. There was never any news of relatives, and no way to obtain any, because it was impossible for the Station to communicate with anyone Up Front. No way to ask for the photo of a loved one, no way to request specific medicines, no way to obtain a certain book or a coveted tape. In a mindless, impersonal way, Up Front sent periodic shipments to the Station of things thought useful—reading matter, medical supplies, technical equipment, food. Occasionally they were startling in their generosity, as when they sent a case of Burgundy, or a box of sensory spools, or a recharger for the power pack. Such gifts usually meant a brief thaw in the world situation, which customarily produced a short-lived desire to be kind to the boys in Hawksbill Station. But they had a policy about sending information about relatives. Or about contemporary newspapers. Fine wine, yes; a tridim of a daughter who would never be seen again, no.

For all Up Front knew, there was no one alive in Hawksbill Station. A plague could have killed every one off ten years ago, but there was no way of telling. That was why the shipments still came back. The government whirred and clicked with predictable continuity. The government, whatever else it might be, was not malicious. There were other kinds of totalitarianism beside bloody repressive tyranny.

Pausing at the top of the hill, Barrett caught his breath. Naturally, the alien air no longer smelled strange to him. He filled his lungs with it. Once again the rain ceased. Through the grayness came the sunshine, making the naked rocks sparkle. Barrett closed his eyes a moment and leaned on his crutch, and saw as though on an inner screen the creatures with many legs climbing up out of the sea, and the mossy carpets spreading, and the flowerless plants uncoiling and spreading their scaly branches, and the dull hides of eerie amphibians glistening on the shores, and the tropic heat of the coal-forming epoch descending like a glove over the world.

All that lay far in the future. Dinosaurs. Little chittering mammals. Pithecanthropus in the forests of Java. Sargon and Hannibal and Attila, and Orville Wright, and Thomas Edison, and Edmond Hawksbill. And finally a benign government that would find the thoughts of some men so intolerable that the only safe place to which they could be banished was a rock at the beginning of time. The government was too civilized to put men to death for subversive activities, and too cowardly to let them remain alive. The compromise was the living death of Hawksbill Station. A billion years of impassable time was suitable insulation even for the most nihilistic idea.

Grimacing, Barrett struggled the rest of the way back toward his hut. He had long since come to accept his exile, but accepting his ruined foot was another matter entirely. The idle wish to find a way to regain the freedom of his own time no longer possessed him; but he wished with all his soul that the blank-faced administrators Up Front would send back a kit that would allow him to rebuild his foot.

He entered his hut and flung his crutch aside, sinking down instantly on his cot. There had been no cots when he had come to Hawksbill Station. He had come here in the fourth year of the Station, when there were only a dozen buildings and little in the way of creature comforts. It had been a miserable place then, but the steady accretion of shipments from Up Front had made it relatively tolerable. Of the fifty or so prisoners who had preceded Barrett to Hawksbill, none remained alive. He had held highest seniority for almost ten years. Time moved here at a one-to-one correlation with time Up Front; the Hammer was locked on this point of time, so that Hahn, arriving here today more than twenty years after Barrett, had departed from a year Up Front more than twenty years after the time of Barrett's expulsion. Barrett had not had the heart to begin pumping Hahn for news of 2029 so soon. He would learn all he needed to know, and small cheer it would be, anyway.

Barrett reached for a book. But the fatigue of hobbling around the Station had taken more out him than he realized. He looked at the page for a moment. Then he put it away, and closed his eyes and dozed.

4.

THAT EVENING, AS EVERY EVENING, the men of Hawksbill Station gathered in the main building for dinner and recreation. It was not mandatory, and some men chose to eat alone. But tonight nearly everyone who was in full possession of his faculties was there, because this was one of the infrequent occasions when a newcomer had arrived to be questioned about the world of men.

Hahn looked uneasy about his sudden notoriety. He seemed to be basically shy, unwilling to accept all the attention now being thrust upon him. There he sat in the middle of the group, while men twenty and thirty years his senior crowded in on him with their questions, and it was obvious that he wasn't enjoying the session.

Sitting to one side, Barrett took little part in the discussion. His curiosity about Up Front's ideological shifts had ebbed a long time ago. It was hard for him to realize that he had once been so passionately concerned about concepts like syndicalism and the dictatorship of the proletariat and the guaranteed annual wage that he had been willing to risk imprisonment over them. His concern for humanity had not waned, merely the degree of his involvement in the twenty-first century's political problems. After twenty years at Hawksbill Station, Up Front had become unreal to Jim Barrett, and his energies centered around the crises and challenges of what he had come to think of as "his own" time—the late Cambrian.

So he listened, but more with an ear for what the talk revealed about Lew Hahn than for what it revealed about current events Up Front. And what it revealed about Lew Hahn was mainly a matter of what was not revealed.

Hahn didn't say much. He seemed to be feinting and evading.

Charley Norton wanted to know, "Is there any sign of a weakening of the phony conservatism yet? I mean, they've been promising the end of big government for thirty years and it gets bigger all the time."

Hahn moved restlessly in his chair. "They still promise. As soon as conditions become stabilized—"

"Which is when?"

"I don't know. I suppose they're just making words."

"What about the Martian Commune?" demanded Sid Hutchett. "Have they been infiltrating agents onto Earth?"

"I couldn't really say."

"How about the Gross Global Product?" Mel Rudiger wanted to know. "What's its curve? Still holding level, or has it started to drop?"

Hahn tugged at his ear. "I think it's slowly edging down."

"Where does the index stand?" Rudiger asked. "The last figures we had, for '25, it was at 909. But in four years—"

"It might be something like 875 now," said Hahn.

It struck Barrett as a little odd that an economist would be so hazy about the basic economic statistic. Of course, he didn't know how long Hahn had been imprisoned before getting the Hammer. Maybe he simply wasn't up on recent figures. Barrett held his peace.

Charley Norton wanted to find out some things about the legal rights of citizens. Hahn couldn't tell him. Rudiger asked about the impact of weather control—whether the supposedly conservative government of liberators was still ramming programmed weather down the mouths of the citizens—and Hahn wasn't sure. Hahn couldn't rightly say much about the functions of the judiciary, whether it had recovered any of the power stripped from it by the Enabling Act of '18. He didn't have any comments to offer on the tricky subject of population control. In fact, his performance was striking for its lack of hard information.

"He isn't saying much at all," Charley Norton grumbled to the silent Barrett. "He's putting up a smokescreen. But either he's not telling what he knows, or he doesn't know."

"Maybe he's not very bright," Barrett suggested.

"What did he do to get here? He must have had some kind of deep commitment. But it doesn't show, Jim! He's an intelligent kid, but he doesn't seem plugged in to anything that ever mattered to any of us."

Doc Quesada offered a thought. "Suppose he isn't political at all. Suppose they're sending a different kind of prisoner back here now. Axe murderers, or something. A quiet kid who very quietly chopped up sixteen people one Sunday morning. Naturally he isn't interested in politics."

Barrett shook his head. "I doubt that. I think he's just clamming up because he's shy or ill at ease. It's his first night here, remember. He's just been kicked out of his own world and there's no going back. He may have left a wife and baby behind, you know. He may simply not give a damn tonight about sitting up there and spouting the latest word on abstract philosophical theory, when all he wants to do is go off and cry his eyes out. I say we ought to leave him alone."

Quesada and Norton looked convinced. They shook their heads in agreement; but Barrett didn't voice his opinion to the room in general. He let the quizzing of Hahn continue until it petered out of its own accord. The men began to drift away. A couple of them went back to convert Hahn's vague generalities into the lead story for the next handwritten edition of the Hawksbill Station *Times*. Rudiger stood on a table and shouted out that he was going night-fishing, and four men asked to join him. Charley Norton sought out his usual debating partner, the nihilist Ken Belardi, and reopened, like a festering wound, their discussion of planning versus chaos, which bored them both to the point of screaming. The nightly games of stochastic chess began. The loners who had made rare visits to the main building simply to see the new man went back to their huts to do whatever it was they did in them alone each night.

Hahn stood apart, fidgeting and uncertain.

Barrett went up to him. "I guess you didn't really want to be quizzed tonight," he said.

"I'm sorry I couldn't have been more informative. I've been out of circulation a while, you see."

"But you were politically active, weren't you?"

"Oh, yes," Hahn said. "Of course." He flicked his tongue over his lips. "What's supposed to happen now?"

"Nothing in particular. We don't have organized activities here. Doc and I are going out on sick call. Care to join us?"

"What does it involve?" asked Hahn.

"Visiting some of the worst cases. It can be grim, but you'll get a panoramic view of Hawksbill Station in a hurry."

"I'd like to go."

Barrett gestured to Quesada and the three of them left the building. This was a nightly ritual for Barrett, difficult as it was since he had hurt his foot. Before turning in, he visited the goofy ones and the psycho ones and the catatonic ones, tucked them in, wish them a good night and a healed mind in the morning. Someone had to show them that he cared. Barrett did.

Outside, Hahn peered up at the moon. It was nearly full tonight, shining like a burnished coin, its face a pale salmon color and hardly pockmarked at all.

"It looks so different here," Hahn said. "The craters—where are the craters?"

"Most of them haven't been formed yet," said Barrett. "A billion years is a long time even for the moon. Most of its upheavals are still ahead. We think it may still have an atmosphere, too. That's why it looks pink to us. Of course, Up Front hasn't bothered to send us much in the way of astronomical equipment. We can only guess."

Hahn started to say something. He cut himself off after one blurted syllable.

Quesada said, "Don't hold it back. What were you about to suggest?"

Hahn laughed in self-mockery. "That you ought to fly up there and take a look. It struck me as odd that you'd spend all these years here theorizing about whether the moon's got an atmosphere, and wouldn't ever once go up to look. But I forgot."

"It would be useful if we got a commute ship from Up Front," Barrett said. "But it hasn't occurred to them. All we can do is look. The moon's a popular place in '29, is it?"

"The biggest resort in the System," said Hahn. "I was there on my honeymoon. Leah and I—"

He stopped again.

Barrett said hurriedly. "This is Bruce Valdosto's hut. He cracked up a few weeks ago. When we go in, stand behind us so he doesn't see you. He might be violent with a stranger. He's unpredictable."

Valdosto was a husky man in his late forties, with swarthy skin, coarse curling black hair, and the broadest shoulders any man had ever had. Sitting down, he looked even burlier than Jim Barrett, which was saying a great deal. But Valdosto had short, stumpy legs, the legs of a man of ordinary stature tacked to the trunk of a giant, which spoiled the effect completely. In his years Up Front he had totally refused any prosthesis. He believed in living with deformities. Right now he was strapped into a webfoam cradle. His domed forehead was flecked with beads of sweat, his eyes were glittering beadily in the darkness. He was a very sick man. Once he had been clear-minded enough to throw a sleet-bomb into a meeting of the Council of Syndics, giving a dozen of them a bad case of gamma poisoning, but now he scarcely knew up from down, right from left.

Barrett leaned over him and said, "How are you, Bruce?"

"Who's that?"

"Jim. It's a beautiful night, Bruce. How'd you like to come outside and get some fresh air? The moon's almost full."

"I've got to rest. The committee meeting tomorrow—"

"It's been postponed."

"But how can it? The Revolution—"

"That's been postponed too. Indefinitely."

"Are they disbanding the cells?" Valdosto asked harshly.

"We don't know yet. We're waiting for orders. Come outside, Bruce. The air will do you good."

Muttering, Valdosto let himself be unlaced. Quesada and Barrett pulled him to his feet and propelled him through the door of the hut. Barrett caught sight of Hahn in the shadows, his face somber with shock.

They stood together outside the hut. Barrett pointed to the moon. "It's got such a lovely color here. Not like the dead thing Up Front. And look, look down there, Bruce. The sea breaking on the rocky shore. Rudiger's out fishing. I can see his boat by moonlight."

"Striped bass," said Valdosto. "Sunnies. Maybe he'll catch some sunnies."

"There aren't any sunnies here. They haven't evolved yet." Barrett fished in his pocket and drew out something ridged and glossy, about two inches long. It was the exoskeleton of a small trilobite. He offered it to Valdosto, who shook his head.

"Don't give me that cockeyed crab."

"It's a trilobite, Bruce. It's extinct, but so are we. We're a billion years in our own past."

"You must be crazy," Valdosto said in a calm, low voice that belied his wild-eyed appearance. He took the trilobite from Barrett and hurled it against the rocks. "Cockeyed crab," he muttered.

Quesada shook his head sadly. He and Barrett led the sick man into the hut again. Valdosto did not protest as the medic gave him the sedative. His weary mind, rebelling entirely against the monstrous concept that he had been exiled to the inconceivably remote past, welcomed sleep.

When they went out Barrett saw Hahn holding the trilobite on his palm and staring at it in wonder. Hahn offered it to him, but Barrett brushed it away.

"Keep it if you like," he said. "There are more where I got that one."

They went on. They found Ned Altman beside his hut, crouching on his knees and patting his hands over the crude, lopsided form of what, from its exaggerated breasts and hips, appeared to be the image of a woman. He stood up when they appeared. Altman was a neat little man with yellow hair and nearly invisible white eyebrows. Unlike anyone else in the Station, he had actually been a government man once, fifteen years ago, before seeing through the myth of syndicalist capitalism and joining one of the underground factions. Eight years at Hawksbill Station had done things to him.

Altman pointed to his golem and said, "I hoped there'd be lightning in the rain today. That'll do it, you know. But there isn't much lightning this time of year. She'll get up alive, and then I'll need you, Doc, to give her shots and trim away some of the tough places."

Quesada forced a smile. "I'll be glad to do it, Ned. But you know the terms."

"Sure. When I'm through with her, you get her. You think I'm a goddamn monopolist? I'll share her. There'll be a waiting list. Just so you don't forget who made her, though. She'll remain mine, whenever I need her." He noticed Hahn. "Who are you?"

"He's new," Barrett said. "Lew Hahn. He came this afternoon."

"Ned Altman," said Altman with a courtly bow. "Formerly in government service. You're pretty young, aren't you? How's your sex orientation? Hetero?"

Hahn winced. "I'm afraid so."

"It's okay. I wouldn't touch you. I've got a project going here. But I just want you to know, I'll put you on my list. You're young and you've probably got stronger needs than some of us. I won't forget about you, even though you're new here."

Quesada coughed. "You ought to get some rest now, Ned. Maybe there'll be lightning tomorrow."

Altman did not resist. The doctor took him inside and put him to bed while Hahn and Barrett surveyed the man's handiwork. Hahn pointed toward the figure's middle.

"He's left out something essential," he said. "If he's planning to make love to this girl after he's finished creating her, he'd better—"

"It was there yesterday," said Barrett. "He must be changing orientation again." Quesada emerged from the hut. They went on, down the rocky path.

Barrett did not make the complete circuit that night. Ordinarily, he would have gone all the way down to Latimer's hut overlooking the sea, for Latimer was on his list of sick ones. But Barrett had visited Latimer once that day, and he didn't think his aching good leg was up to another hike that far. So after he and Quesada and Hahn had been to all of the easily accessible huts, and visited the man who prayed for alien beings to rescue him and the man who was trying to break into a parallel universe where everything was as it ought to be in the world and the man who lay on his cot sobbing for all his wakeful hours, Barrett said good night to his companions and allowed Quesada to escort Hahn back to his hut without him.

After observing Hahn for half a day, Barrett realized he did not know much more about him than when he had first dropped onto the Anvil. That was odd. But maybe Hahn would open up a little more after he'd been here a while. Barrett stared up at the salmon moon, and reached into his pocket to finger the little trilobite before he remembered that he had given it to Hahn. He shuffled into his hut. He wondered how long ago Hahn had taken that lunar honeymoon trip.

5.

RUDIGER'S CATCH WAS SPREAD OUT in front of the main building the next morning when Barrett came up for breakfast. He had had a good night's fishing, obviously. He usually did. Rudiger went out three or four nights a week, in the little dinghy that he had cobbled together a few years ago from salvaged materials, and he took with him a team of friends whom he had trained in the deft use of the trawling nets.

It was an irony that Rudiger, the anarchist, the man who believed in individualism and the abolition of all political institutions, should be so good at leading a team of fishermen. Rudiger didn't care for teamwork in the abstract. But it was hard to manipulate the nets alone, he had discovered. Hawksbill Station had many little ironies of that sort. Political theorists tend to swallow their theories when forced back on pragmatic measures of survival.

The prize of the catch was a cephalopod about a dozen feet long— a rigid conical tube out of which some limp squidlike tentacles dangled. Plenty of meat on that one, Barrett thought. Dozens of trilobites were arrayed around it, ranging in size from the inch-long kind to the three-footers with their baroquely involuted exo-skeletons. Rudiger fished both for food and for science; evidently these trilobites were discards— species that he already had studied, or he wouldn't have left them here to go into the food hoppers. His hut was stacked ceiling-high with trilobites. It kept him sane to collect and analyze them, and no one begrudged him his hobby.

Near the heap of trilobites were some clusters of hinged brachiopods, looking like scallops that had gone awry, and a pile of snails. The warm, shallow waters just off the coastal shelf teemed with life, in striking contrast to the barren land. Rudiger had also brought in a mound of shiny black seaweed. Barrett hoped someone would gather all this stuff up and get it into their heat-sink cooler before it spoiled. The bacteria of decay worked a lot slower here than they did Up Front, but a few hours in the mild air would do Rudiger's haul no good.

Today Barrett planned to recruit some men for the annual Inland Sea expedition. Traditionally, he led that trek himself, but his injury made it impossible for him even to consider going any more. Each year, a dozen or so able-bodied men went out on a wide-ranging reconnaissance that took them in a big circle, looping northwestward until they reached the sea, then coming around to the south and back to the Station. One purpose of the trip was to gather any temporal garbage that might have materialized in the vicinity of the Station during the past year. There was no way of knowing how wide a margin of error had been allowed during the early attempts to set up the Station, and the scattershot technique of hurling material into the past had been pretty unreliable. New stuff was turning up all the time that had been aimed for Minus One Billion, Two Thousand Oh Five AD, but which didn't get there until a few decades later. Hawksbill Station needed all the spare equipment it could get, and Barrett didn't miss a chance to round up any of the debris.

There was another reason for the Inland Sea expeditions, though. They served as a focus for the year, an annual ritual, something to peg a custom to. It was a rite of spring here. The dozen strongest men, going on foot to the distant rock-rimmed shores of the tepid sea that drowned the middle of North America, were performing the closest thing Hawksbill Station had to a religious function, although they did nothing more mystical when they reached the Inland Sea than to net a few trilobites and eat them. The trip meant more to Barrett himself than he had even suspected, also. He realized that now, when he was unable to go. He had led every such expedition for twenty years.

But last year he had gone scrabbling over boulders loosened by the tireless action of the waves, venturing into risky territory for no rational reason that he could name, and his aging muscles had betrayed him. Often at night he woke sweating to escape from the dream in which he relived that ugly moment: slipping and sliding, clawing at the rocks, a mass of stone dislodged from somewhere and crashing down with improbably agonizing impact on his foot, pinning him, crushing him. He could not forget the sound of grinding bones. Nor was he likely to lose the memory of the homeward march, across hundreds of miles of bare rock, his bulky body slung between the bowed forms of his companions. He thought he would lose the foot, but Quesada had spared him from the amputation. He simply could not touch the foot to the ground and put weight on it now, or ever again. It might have been simpler to have the dead appendage sliced off. Quesada vetoed that, though. "Who knows," he had said, "some day they might send us a transplant kit. I can't rebuild a leg that's been amputated." So Barrett had kept his crushed foot. But he had never been quite the same since, and now someone else would have to lead the march.

Who would it be? he asked himself.

Quesada was the likeliest. Next to Barrett, he was the strongest man here, in all the ways that it was important to be strong. But Quesada couldn't be spared at the Station. It might be handy to have a medic along on the trip, but it was vital to have one here. After some reflection Barrett put down Charley Norton as the leader. He added Ken Belardi—someone for Norton to talk to. Rudiger? A tower of strength last year after Barrett had been injured; Barrett didn't particularly want to let Rudiger leave the Station so long; he needed able men for the expedition, true, but he didn't want to strip the home base down to invalids, crackpots, and psychotics. Rudiger stayed. Two of his fellow fishermen went on the list. So did Sid Hutchett and Arny Jean-Claude.

Barrett thought about putting Don Latimer in the group. Latimer was coming to be something of a borderline mental case, but he was rational enough except when he lapsed into his psionic meditations, and he'd pull his own weight on the expedition. On the other hand, Latimer was Lew Hahn's roommate, and Barrett wanted Latimer around to observe Hahn at close range. He toyed with the idea of sending both of them out, but nixed it. Hahn was still an unknown quantity. It was too risky to let him go with the Inland Sea party this year. Probably he'd be in next spring's group, though.

Finally Barrett had his dozen men chosen. He chalked their names on the slate in front of the mess hall, and found Charley Norton at breakfast to tell him he was in charge.

It felt strange to know that he'd have to stay home while the others went. It was an admission that he was beginning to abdicate after running this place so long. A crippled old man was what he was, whether he liked to admit it to himself or not, and that was something he'd have to come to terms with soon.

In the afternoon, the men of the Inland Sea expedition gathered to select their gear and plan their route. Barrett kept away from the meeting. This was Charley Norton's show, now. He'd made eight or ten trips, and he knew what to do. Barrett didn't want to interfere.

But some masochistic compulsion in him drove him to take a trek of his own. If he couldn't see the western waters this year, the least he could do was pay a visit to the Atlantic, in his own back yard. Barrett stopped off in the infirmary and, finding Quesada elsewhere, helped himself to a tube of neural depressant. He scrambled along the eastern trail until he was a few hundred yards from the main building, dropped his trousers, and quickly gave each thigh a jolt of the drug, first the good leg, then the gimpy one. That would numb the muscles just enough so that he'd be able to take an extended hike without feeling the fire of fatigue in his protesting joints. He'd pay for it, he knew, eight hours from now, when the depressant wore off and the full impact of his exertion hit him like a million daggers. But he was willing to accept that price.

The road to the sea was a long, lonely one. Hawksbill Station was perched on the eastern rim of Appalachia, more than eight hundred feet above sea level. During the first half dozen years, the men of the Station had reached the ocean by a suicidal route across sheer rock faces, but Barrett had incited a ten-year project to carve a path. Now wide steps descended to the Atlantic. Chopping them out of the rock had kept a lot of men busy for a long time, too busy to worry or to slip into insanity. Barrett regretted that he couldn't conceive some comparable works project to occupy them nowadays.

The steps formed a succession of shallow platforms that switchbacked to the edge of the water. Even for a healthy man it was a strenuous walk. For Barrett in his present condition it was an ordeal. It took him two hours to descend a distance that normally could be traversed in a quarter of that time. When he reached the bottom, he sank down exhaustedly on a flat rock licked by the waves, and dropped his crutch. The fingers of his left hand were cramped and gnarled from gripping the crutch, and his entire body was bathed in sweat.

The water looked gray and somehow oily. Barrett could not explain the prevailing colorlessness of the Late Cambrian world, with its somber sky and somber land and somber sea, but his heart quietly ached for a glimpse of green vegetation again. He missed chlorophyll. The dark wavelets lapped against his rock, pushing a mass of floating black seaweed back and forth. The sea stretched to infinity. He didn't have the faintest idea how much of Europe, if any, was above water in this epoch. At the best of times most of the planet was submerged; here, only a few hundred million years after the white-hot rocks of the land had pushed into view, it was likely that all that was above water on Earth was a strip of territory here and there. Had the Himalayas been born yet? The Rockies? The Andes? He knew the approximate outlines of Late Cambrian North America, but the rest was a mystery. Blanks in knowledge were not easy to fill when the only link with Up Front was by one-way transport; Hawksbill Station had to rely on the random assortment of reading matter that came back in time, and it was furiously frustrating to lack information that any college geology text could supply.

As he watched, a big trilobite unexpectedly came scuttering up out of the water. It was the spike-tailed kind, about a yard long, with an eggplant-purple shell and a bristling arrangement of slender spines along the margins. There seemed to be a lot of legs underneath. The trilobite crawled up on the shore—no sand, no beach, just a shelf of rock—and advanced until it was eight or ten feet from the waves.

Good for you, Barrett thought. Maybe you're the first one who ever came out on land to see what it was like. The pioneer. The trailblazer.

It occurred to him that this adventurous trilobite might well be the ancestor of all the land-dwelling creatures of the eons to come. It was biological nonsense, but Barrett's weary mind conjured a picture of an evolutionary procession, with fish and amphibians and reptiles and mammals and man all stemming in unbroken sequence from this grotesque armored thing that moved in uncertain circles near his feet.

And if I were to step on you, he thought?

A quick motion—the sound of crunching chitin—the wild scrabbling of a host of little legs—

And the whole chain of life snapped in its first link. Evolution undone. No land creatures ever developed. With the descent of that heavy foot all the future would change and there would never have been any Hawksbill Station, no human race, no James Edward Barrett. In an instant he would have both revenge on those who had condemned him to live out his days in this place, and release from his sentence.

He did nothing. The trilobite completed its slow perambulation of the shoreline rocks and scattered back into the sea unharmed.

The soft voice of Don Latimer said, "I saw you sitting down here, Jim. Do you mind if I join you?"

Barrett swung around, momentarily surprised. Latimer had come down from his hilltop but so quietly that Barrett hadn't heard a thing. He recovered and grinned and beckoned Latimer to an adjoining rock.

"You fishing?" Latimer asked.

"Just sitting. An old man sunning himself."

"You took a hike like that just to sun yourself?" Latimer laughed. "Come off it. You're trying to get away from it all, and you probably wish I hadn't disturbed you."

"That's not so. Stay here. How's your new roommate getting along?"

"It's been strange," said Latimer. "That's one reason I came down here to talk to you." He leaned forward and peered searchingly into Barrett's eyes. "Jim, tell me: do you think I'm a madman?"

"Why should I?"

"The ESP-ing business. My attempt to break through to another realm of consciousness. I know you're tough-minded and skeptical. You probably think it's all a lot of nonsense."

Barrett shrugged and said, "If you want the blunt truth, I do. I don't have the remotest belief that you're going to get us anywhere, Don. I think it's a complete waste of time and energy for you to sit there for hours harnessing your psionic powers, or whatever it is you do. But no, I don't think you're crazy. I think you're entitled to your obsession and that you're going about a basically futile thing in a reasonably level-headed way. Fair enough?"

"More than fair. I don't ask you to put any credence in my research, but I don't want you to think I'm a total lunatic for trying it. It's important that you regard me as sane, or else what I want to tell you about Hahn won't be valid to you."

"I don't see the connection."

"It's this," said Latimer. "On the basis of one evening's acquaintance, I've formed an opinion about Hahn. It's the kind of an opinion that might be formed by a garden-variety paranoid, and if you think I'm nuts you're likely to discount my idea about Hahn."

"I don't think you're nuts. What's your idea?"

"That he's spying on us."

Barrett had to work hard to keep from emitting the guffaw that would shatter Latimer's fragile self-esteem. "Spying?" he said casually. "You can't mean that. How can anyone spy here? I mean, how can he report his findings?"

"I don't know," Latimer said. "But he asked me a million questions last night. About you, about Quesada, about some of the sick men. He wanted to know everything."

"The normal curiosity of a new man."

"Jim, he was taking notes. I saw him after he thought I was asleep. He sat up for two hours writing it all down in a little book."

Barrett frowned. "Maybe he's going to write a novel about us."

"I'm serious," Latimer said. "Questions—notes. And he's shifty. Try to get him to talk about himself!"

"I did. I didn't learn much."

"Do you know why he's been sent here?"

"No."

"Neither do I," said Latimer. "Political crimes, he said, but he was vague as hell. He hardly seemed to know what the present government was up to, let alone what his own opinions were toward it. I don't detect any passionate philosophical convictions in Mr. Hahn. And you know as well as I do that Hawksbill Station is the refuse heap for revolutionaries and agitators and subversives and all sorts of similar trash, but that we've never had any other kind of prisoner here."

"I agree that Hahn's a puzzle. But who could he be spying for? He's got no way to file a report, if he's a government agent. He's stranded here for keeps, same as the rest of us."

"Maybe he was sent to keep an eye on us—to make sure we aren't cooking up some way to escape. Maybe he's a volunteer who willingly gave up his twenty-first-century life so he could come among us and thwart anything we might be hatching. Perhaps they're afraid we've invented forward time travel. Or that we've become a threat to the sequence of the time-lines. Anything. So Hahn comes among us to snoop around and block any dangers before they arrive."

Barrett felt a twinge of alarm. He saw how close to paranoia Latimer was hewing, now: in half a dozen sentences he had journeyed from the rational expression of some justifiable suspicions to the fretful fear that the men from Up Front were going to take steps to choke off the escape route that he was so close to perfecting.

He kept his voice level as he told Latimer, "I don't think you need to worry, Don. Hahn's an odd one, but he's not here to make trouble for us. The fellows Up Front have already made all the trouble they ever will."

"Would you keep an eye on him, anyway?"

"You know I will. And don't hesitate to let me know if Hahn does anything else out of the ordinary. You're in a better spot to notice than anyone else."

"I'll be watching," Latimer said. "We can't tolerate any spies from Up Front among us." He got to his feet and gave Barrett a pleasant smile. "I'll let you get back to your sunning now, Jim."

Latimer went up the path. Barrett eyed him until he was close to the top, only a faint dot against the stony backdrop. After a long while Barrett seized his crutch and levered himself to his feet. He stood staring down at the surf, dipping the tip of his crutch into the water to send a couple of little crawling things scurrying away. At length he turned and began the long, slow climb back to the Station.

6.

A COUPLE OF DAYS PASSED before Barrett had the chance to draw Lew Hahn aside for a spot of political discussion. The Inland Sea party had set out, and in a way that was too bad, for Barrett could have used Charley Norton's services in penetrating Hahn's armor. Norton was the most gifted theorist around, a man who could weave a tissue of dialectic from the least promising material. If anyone could find out the depth of Hahn's Marxist commitment, if any, it was Norton. But Norton was leading the expedition, so Barrett had to do the interrogating himself. His Marxism was a trifle rusty, and he couldn't thread his path through the Leninist, Stalinist, Trotskyite, Khrushchevist, Maoist, Berenkovskyite and Mgumbweist schools with Charley Norton's skills. Yet he knew what questions to ask.

He picked a rainy evening when Hahn seemed to be in a fairly outgoing mood. There had been an hour's entertainment that night, an ingenious computer-composed film that Sid Hutchett had programmed last week. Up Front had been kind enough to ship back a modest computer, and Hutchett had rigged it to do animations by specifying line widths and lengths, shades of gray, and progression of raster units. It was a simple but remarkably clever business, and it brightened a dull night.

Afterward, sensing that Hahn was relaxed enough to lower his guard a bit, Barrett said, "Hutchett's a rare one. Did you meet him before he went on the trip?"

"Tall fellow with a sharp nose and no chin?"

"That's the one. A clever boy. He was the top computer man for the Continental Liberation Front until they caught him in '19. He programmed that fake broadcast in which Chancellor Dantell denounced his own regime. Remember?"

"I'm not sure I do." Hahn frowned. "How long ago was this?"

"The broadcast was in 2018. Would that be before your time? Only eleven years ago—"

"I was nineteen then," said Hahn. "I guess I wasn't very politically sophisticated."

"Too busy studying economics, I guess."

Hahn grinned. "That's right. Deep in the dismal science."

"And you never heard that broadcast? Or even heard *of* it?"

"I must have forgotten."

"The biggest hoax of the century," Barrett said, "and you forgot it. You know the Continental Liberation Front, of course."

"Of course." Hahn looked uneasy.

"Which group did you say you were with?"

"The People's Crusade for Liberty."

"I don't know it. One of the newer groups?"

"Less than five years old. It started in California."

"What's its program?"

"Oh, the usual," Hahn said. "Free elections, representative government, an opening of the security files, restoration of civil liberties."

"And the economic orientation? Pure Marxist or one of the offshoots?"

"Not really any, I guess. We believed in a kind of—well, capitalism with some government restraints."

"A little to the right of state socialism, and a little to the left of laissez faire?" Barrett suggested.

"Something like that."

"But that system was tried and failed, wasn't it? It had its day. It led inevitably to total socialism, which produced the compensating backlash of syndicalist capitalism, and then we got a government that pretended to be libertarian while actually stifling all individual liberties in the name of freedom. So if your group simply wanted to turn the clock back to 1955, say, there couldn't be much to its ideas."

Hahn looked bored. "You've got to understand I wasn't in the top ideological councils."

"Just an economist?"

"That's it. I drew up plans for the conversion to our system."

"Basing your work on the modified liberalism of Ricardo?"

"Well, in a sense."

"And avoiding the tendency to fascism that was found in the thinking of Keynes?"

"You could say so," Hahn said. He stood up, flashing a quick, vague smile. "Look, Jim, I'd love to argue this further with you some other time, but I've really got to go now. Ned Altman talked me into coming around and helping him do a lightning-dance to bring that pile of dirt to life. So if you don't mind—"

Hahn beat a hasty retreat.

Barrett was more perplexed then ever, now. Hahn hadn't been "arguing" anything. He had been carrying on a lame and feeble conversation, letting himself be pushed hither and thither by Barrett's questions. And he had spouted a lot of nonsense. He didn't seem to know Keynes from Ricardo, nor to care about it, which was odd for a self-professed economist. He didn't have a shred of an idea of what his own political party stood for. He had so little revolutionary background that he was unaware even of Hutchett's astonishing hoax of eleven years back.

He seemed phony from top to bottom.

How was it possible that this kid had been deemed worthy of exile to Hawksbill Station, anyhow? Only the top firebrands went there. Sentencing a man to Hawksbill was like sentencing him to death, and it wasn't done lightly. Barrett couldn't imagine why Hahn was here. He seemed genuinely distressed at being exiled, and evidently he had left a beloved young wife behind, but nothing else rang true about the man.

Was he as Latimer suggested—some kind of spy?

Barrett rejected the idea out of hand. He didn't want Latimer's paranoia infecting him. The government wasn't likely to send anyone on a one-way trip to the Late Cambrian just to spy on a bunch of aging revolutionaries who could never make trouble again. But what *was* Hahn doing here, then?

He would bear further watching, Barrett thought.

Barrett took care of some of the watching himself. But he had plenty of assistance. Latimer. Altman. Six or seven others. Latimer had recruited most of the ambulatory psycho cases, the ones who were superficially functional but full of all kinds of fears and credulities.

They were keeping an eye on the new man.

On the fifth day after his arrival, Hahn went out fishing in Rudiger's crew. Barrett stood for a long time on the edge of the world, watching the little boat bobbing in the surging Atlantic. Rudiger never went far from shore—eight hundred, a thousand yards out—but the water was rough even there. The waves came rolling in with X thousand miles of gathered impact behind them. A continental shelf sloped off at a wide angle, so that even at a substantial distance off shore the water wasn't very deep. Rudiger had taken soundings up to a mile out, and had reported depths no greater than 160 feet. Nobody had gone past a mile.

It wasn't that they were afraid of falling off the side of the world if they went too far east. It was simply that a mile was a long distance to row in an open boat, using stubby oars made from old packing cases. Up Front hadn't thought to spare an outboard motor for them.

Looking toward the horizon, Barrett had an odd thought. He had been told that the women's equivalent of Hawksbill Station was safely segregated out of reach, a couple of hundred million years up the time-line. But how did he know that? There could be another Station somewhere else in this very year, and they'd never know about it. A camp of women, say, living on the far side of the ocean, or even across the Inland Sea.

It wasn't very likely, he knew. With the entire past to pick from, the edgy men Up Front wouldn't take any chance that the two groups of exiles might get together and spawn a tribe of little subversives. They'd take every precaution to put an impenetrable barrier of epochs between them. Yet Barrett thought he could make it sound convincing to the other men. With a little effort he could get them to believe in the existence of several simultaneous Hawksbill Stations scattered on this level of time.

Which could be our salvation, he thought.

The instances of degenerative psychosis were beginning to snowball, now. Too many men had been here too long, and one crackup was starting to feed the next, in this blank lifeless world where humans were never meant to live. The men needed projects to keep them going. They were starting to slip off into harebrained projects, like Altman's Frankenstein girlfriend and Latimer's psi pursuit.

Suppose, Barrett thought, I could get them steamed up about reaching the other continents?

A round-the-world expedition. Maybe they could build some kind of big ship. That would keep a lot of men busy for a long time. And they'd need navigational equipment—compasses, sextants, chronometers, whatnot. Somebody would have to design an improvised radio, too. It was the kind of project that might take thirty or forty years. A focus for our energies, Barrett thought. Of course, I won't live to see the ship set sail. But even so, it's a way of staving off collapse. We've built our staircase to the sea. Now we need something bigger to do. Idle hands make for idle minds . . . sick minds . . .

He liked the idea he had hatched. For several weeks, now, Barrett had been worrying about the deteriorating state of affairs in the Station, and looking for some way to cope with it. Now he thought he had his way.

Turning, he saw Latimer and Altman standing behind him.

"How long have you been there?" he asked.

"Two minutes," said Latimer. "We brought you something to look at."

Altman nodded vigorously. "You ought to read it. We brought it for you to read."

"What is it?"

Latimer handed over a folded sheaf of papers. "I found this tucked away in Hahn's bunk after he went out with Rudiger. I know I'm not supposed to be invading his privacy, but I had to have a look at what he's been writing. There it is. He's a spy, all right."

Barrett glanced at the papers in his hand. "I'll read it a little later. What is it about?"

"It's a description of the Station, and a profile of most of the men in it," said Latimer. He smiled frostily. "Hahn's private opinion of me is that I've gone mad. His private opinion of you is a little more flattering, but not much."

Altman said, "He's also been hanging around the Hammer."

"What?"

"I saw him going there late last night. He went into the building. I followed him. He was looking at the Hammer."

"Why didn't you tell me that right away?" Barrett snapped.

"I wasn't sure it was important," Altman said. "I had to talk it over with Don first. And I couldn't do that until Hahn had gone out fishing."

Sweat burst out on Barrett's face. "Listen, Ned, if you ever catch Hahn going near the time travel equipment again, you let me know in a hurry. Without consulting Don or anyone else. Clear?"

"Clear," said Altman. He giggled. "You know what I think? They've decided to exterminate us Up Front. Hahn's been sent here to check us out as a suicide volunteer. Then they're going to send a bomb through the Hammer and blow the Station up. We ought to wreck the Hammer and Anvil before they get a chance."

"But why would they send a suicide volunteer?" Latimer asked. "Unless they've got some way to rescue their spy—"

"In any case we shouldn't take any chance," Altman argued. "Wreck the Hammer. Make it impossible for them to bomb us from Up Front."

"That might be a good idea. But—"

"Shut up, both of you," Barrett growled. "Let me look at these papers."

He walked a few steps away from them and sat down on a shelf of rock. He unfolded the sheaf. He began to read.

7.

HAHN HAD A CRAMPED, CRABBED handwriting that packed a maximum of information into a minimum of space, as though he regarded it as a mortal sin to waste paper. Fair enough; paper was a scarce commodity here, and evidently Hahn had brought these sheets with him from Up Front. His script was clear, though. So were his opinions. Painfully so.

He had written an analysis of conditions at Hawksbill Station, setting forth in about five thousand words everything that Barrett knew was going sour here. He had neatly ticked off the men as aging revolutionaries in whom the old fervor had turned rancid; he listed the ones who were certifiably psycho, and the ones who were on the edge, and the ones who were hanging on, like Quesada and Norton and Rudiger. Barrett was interested to see that Hahn rated even those three as suffering from severe strain and likely to fly apart at any moment. To him, Quesada and Norton and Rudiger seemed just about as stable as when they had first dropped onto the Anvil of Hawksbill Station; but there was possibly the distorting effect of his own blurred perceptions. To an outsider like Hahn, the view was different and perhaps more accurate.

Barrett forced himself not to skip ahead to Hahn's evaluation of him.

He wasn't pleased when he came to it. "Barrett," Hahn had written, "is like a mighty beam that's been gnawed from within by termites. He looks solid, but one good push would break him apart. A recent injury to his foot has evidently had a bad effect on him. The other men say he used to be physically vigorous and derived much of his authority from his size and strength. Now he can hardly walk. But I feel the trouble with Barrett is inherent in the life of Hawksbill Station, and doesn't have much to do with his lameness. He's been cut off from normal human drives for too long. The exercise of power here has provided the illusion of stability for him, but it's power in a vacuum, and things have happened within Barrett of which he's totally unaware. He's in bad need of therapy. He may be beyond help."

Barrett read that several times. *Gnawed from within by termites . . . one good push . . . things have happened within him . . . bad need of therapy . . . beyond help.*

He was less angered than he thought he should have been. Hahn was entitled to his views. Barrett finally stopped rereading his profile and pushed his way to the last page of Hahn's essay. It ended with the words, "Therefore I recommend prompt termination of the Hawksbill Station penal colony, and, where possible, the therapeutic rehabilitation of its inmates."

What the hell was this?

It sounded like the report of a parole commissioner! But there was no parole from Hawksbill Station. That final sentence let all the viability of what had gone before bleed away. Hahn was pretending to be composing a report to the government Up Front, obviously. But a wall a billion years thick made filing of that report impossible. So Hahn was suffering from delusions, just like Altman and Valdosto and the others. In his fevered mind he believed he could send messages Up Front, pompous documents delineating the flaws and foibles of his fellow prisoners.

That raised a chilling prospect. Hahn might be crazy, but he hadn't been in the Station long enough to have gone crazy here. He must have brought his insanity with him.

What if they had stopped using Hawksbill Station as a camp for political prisoners, Barrett asked himself, and were starting to use it as an insane asylum?

A cascade of psychos descending on them. Men who had gone honorably buggy under the stress of confinement would have to make room for ordinary bedlamites. Barrett shivered. He folded up Hahn's papers and handed them to Latimer, who was sitting a few yards away, watching him intently.

"What did you think of that?" Latimer asked.

"I think it's hard to evaluate. But possibly friend Hahn is emotionally disturbed. Put this stuff back exactly where you got it, Don. And don't give Hahn the faintest inkling that you've read or removed it."

"Right."

"And come to me whenever you think there's something I ought to know about him," Barrett said. "He may be a very sick boy. He may need all the help we can give."

THE FISHING EXPEDITION RETURNED IN early afternoon. Barrett saw that the dinghy was overflowing with the haul, and Hahn, coming into the camp with his arms full of gaffed trilobites, looked sunburned and pleased with his outing. Barrett came over to inspect the catch. Rudiger was in an effusive mood, and held up a bright red crustacean that might have been the great-great-grandfather of all boiled lobsters, except that it had no front claws and a wicked-looking triple spike where a tail should have been. It was about two feet long, and ugly.

"A new species!" Rudiger crowed. "There's nothing like this in any museum. I wish I could put it where it would be found. Some mountaintop, maybe."

"If it could be found, it would have been found," Barrett reminded him. "Some paleontologist of the twentieth century would have dug it out. So forget it, Mel."

Hahn said, "I've been wondering about that point. How is it nobody Up Front ever dug up the fossil remains of Hawksbill Station? Aren't they worried that one of the early fossil hunters will find it in the Cambrian strata and raise a fuss?"

Barrett shook his head. "For one thing, no paleontologist from the beginning of the science to the founding of the Station in 2005 ever *did* dig up Hawksbill. That's a matter of record, so there was nothing to worry about. If it came to light after 2005, why, everyone would know what it was. No paradox there."

"Besides," said Rudiger sadly, "in another billion years this whole strip of rock will be on the floor of the Atlantic, with a couple of miles of sediment over it. There's not a chance we'll be found. Or that anyone Up Front will ever see this guy I caught today. Not that I give a damn. I've seen him. I'll dissect him. Their loss."

"But you regret the fact that science will never know of this species," Hahn said.

"Sure I do. But is it my fault? Science does know of this species. Me. I'm science. I'm the leading paleontologist of this epoch. Can I help it if I can't publish my discoveries in the professional journals?" He scowled and walked away, carrying the big red crustacean.

Hahn and Barrett looked at each other. They smiled, in a natural mutual response to Rudiger's grumbled outburst. Then Barrett's smile faded.

. . . termites . . . one good push . . . therapy . . .

"Something wrong?" Hahn asked.

"Why?"

"You looked so bleak, all of a sudden."

"My foot gave me a twinge," Barrett said. "It does that, you know. Here. I'll give you a hand carrying those things. We'll have fresh trilobite cocktail tonight."

8.

A LITTLE BEFORE MIDNIGHT, BARRETT was awakened by footsteps outside his hut. As he sat up, groping for the luminescence switch, Ned Altman came blundering through the door. Barrett blinked at him. "What's the matter?"

"Hahn!" Altman rasped. "He's fooling around with the Hammer again. We just saw him go into the building."

Barrett shed his sleepiness like a seal bursting out of water. Ignoring the insistent throb in his left leg, he pulled himself from his bed and grabbed some clothing. He was more apprehensive than he wanted Altman to see. If Hahn, fooling around with the temporal mechanism, accidentally smashed the Hammer, they might never get replacement equipment from Up Front. Which would mean that all future shipments of supplies—if there were any—would come as random shoots that might land in any old year. What business did Hahn have with the machine, anyway?

Altman said, "Latimer's up there keeping an eye on him. He got suspicious when Hahn didn't come back to the hut, and he got me, and we went looking for him. And there he was, sniffing around the Hammer."

"Doing what?"

"I don't know. As soon as we saw him go in, I came down here to get you. Don's watching."

Barrett stumped his way out of the hut and did his best to run toward the main building. Pain shot like trails of hot acid up the lower half of his body. The crutch dug mercilessly into his left armpit as he leaned all his weight into it. His crippled foot, swinging freely, burned with a cold glow. His right leg, which was carrying most of the burden, creaked and popped. Altman ran breathlessly alongside him. The Station was terribly silent at this hour.

As they passed Quesada's hut, Barrett considered waking the medic and taking him along. He decided against it. Whatever trouble Hahn might be up to, Barrett felt he could handle it himself. There was some strength left in the old gnawed beam, after all.

Latimer stood at the entrance to the main dome. He was right at the edge of panic, or perhaps over the edge. He seemed to be gibbering with fear and shock. Barrett had never seen a man gibber before.

He clamped a big paw on Latimer's thin shoulder and said harshly, "Where is he? Where's Hahn?"

"He—disappeared."

"What do you mean? Where did he go?"

Latimer moaned. His face was fish-belly white. "He got onto the Anvil," Latimer blurted. "The light came on—the glow. And then Hahn disappeared!"

"No," Barrett said. "It isn't possible. You must be mistaken."

"I saw him go!"

"He's hiding somewhere in the building," Barrett insisted. "Close that door! Search for him!"

Altman said, "He probably did disappear, Jim. If Don says he disappeared—"

"He climbed right on the Anvil. Then everything turned red and he was gone."

Barrett clenched his fists. There was a white-hot blaze just behind his forehead that almost made him forget about his foot. He saw his mistake, now. He had depended for his espionage on two men who were patently and unmistakably insane, and that had been itself a not very sane thing to do. A man is known by his choice of lieutenants. Well, he had relied on Altman and Latimer, and now they were giving him the sort of information that such spies could be counted on to supply.

"You're hallucinating," he told Latimer curtly. "Ned, go wake Quesada and get him here right away. You, Don, you stand here by the entrance, and if Hahn shows up I want you to scream at the top of your lungs. I'm going to search the building for him."

"Wait," Latimer said. He seemed to be in control of himself again. "Jim, do you remember when I asked you if you thought I was crazy? You said you didn't. You trusted me. Well, don't stop trusting me now. I tell you I'm not hallucinating. I saw Hahn disappear. I can't explain it, but I'm rational enough to know what I saw."

In a milder tone Barrett said, "All right. Maybe so. Stay by the door, anyway. I'll run a quick check."

He started to make the circuit of the dome, beginning with the room where the Hammer was located. Everything seemed to be in order there. No Hawksbill Field glow was in evidence, and nothing had been disturbed. The room had no closets or cupboards in which Hahn could be hiding. When he had inspected it thoroughly, Barrett moved on, looking into the infirmary, the mess hall, the kitchen, the recreation room. He looked high and low. No Hahn. Of course, there were plenty of places in those rooms where Hahn might have secreted himself, but Barrett doubted that he was there. So it had all been some feverish fantasy of Latimer's, then. He completed the route and found himself back at the main entrance. Latimer still stood guard there. He had been joined by a sleepy Quesada. Altman, pale and shaky-looking, was just outside the door.

"What's happening?" Quesada asked.

"I'm not sure," said Barrett. "Don and Ned had the idea they saw Lew Hahn fooling around with the time equipment. I've checked the building, and he's not here, so maybe they made a little mistake. I suggest you take them both into the infirmary and give them a shot of something to settle their nerves, and we'll all try to get back to sleep."

Latimer said, "I tell you, I saw—"

"Shut up!" Altman broke in. "Listen! What's the noise?"

Barrett listened. The sound was clear and loud: the hissing whine of ionization. It was the sound produced by a functioning Hawksbill Field. Suddenly there were goose-pimples on his flesh. In a low voice he said, "The field's on. We're probably getting some supplies."

"At this hour?" said Latimer.

"We don't know what time it is Up Front. All of you stay here. I'll check the Hammer."

"Perhaps I ought to go with you," Quesada suggested mildly.

"Stay here!" Barrett thundered. He paused, embarrassed at his own explosive show of wrath. "It only takes one of us. I'll be right back."

Without waiting for further dissent, he pivoted and limped down the hall to the Hammer room. He shouldered the door open and looked in. There was no need for him to switch on the light. The red glow of the Hawksbill Field illuminated everything.

Barrett stationed himself just within the door. Hardly daring to breathe, he stared fixedly at the Hammer, watching as the glow deepened through various shades of pink toward crimson, and then spread until it enfolded the waiting Anvil beneath it. An endless moment passed.

Then came the implosive thunderclap, and Lew Hahn dropped out of nowhere and lay for a moment in temporal shock on the broad plate of the Anvil.

9.

IN THE DARKNESS, HAHN DID not notice Barrett at first. He sat up slowly, shaking off the stunning effects of a trip through time. After a few seconds he pushed himself toward the lip of the Anvil and let his legs dangle over it. He swung them to get the circulation going. He took a series of deep breaths. Finally he slipped to the floor. The glow of the field had gone out in the moment of his arrival, and so he moved warily, as though not wanting to bump into anything.

Abruptly Barrett switched on the light and said, "What have you been up to, Hahn?"

The younger man recoiled as though he had been jabbed in the gut. He gasped, hopped backward a few steps, and flung up both hands in a defensive gesture.

"Answer me," Barrett said.

Hahn regained his equilibrium. He shot a quick glance past Barrett's bulky form toward the hallway and said, "Let me go, will you? I can't explain now."

"You'd better explain now."

"It'll be easier for everyone if I don't," said Hahn. "Please. Let me pass."

Barrett continued to block the door. "I want to know where you've been. What have you been doing with the Hammer?"

"Nothing. Just studying it."

"You weren't in this room a minute ago. Then you appeared. Where'd you come from, Hahn?"

"You're mistaken. I was standing right behind the Hammer. I didn't—"

"I saw you drop down on the Anvil. You took a time trip, didn't you?"

"No."

"Don't lie to me! You've got some way of going forward in time, isn't that so? You've been spying on us, and you just went somewhere to file your report—somewhere—and now you're back."

Hahn's forehead was glistening. He said, "I warn you, don't ask too many questions. You'll know everything in due time. This isn't the time. Please, now. Let me pass."

"I want answers first," Barrett said. He realized that he was trembling. He already knew the answers, and they were answers that shook him to the core of his soul. He knew where Hahn had been.

But Hahn had to admit it himself.

Hahn said nothing. He took a couple of hesitant steps toward Barrett, who did not move. He seemed to be gathering momentum for a rush at the doorway.

Barrett said, "You aren't getting out of here until you tell me what I want to know."

Hahn charged.

Barrett planted himself squarely, crutch braced against the doorframe, his good foot flat on the floor, and waited for the younger man to reach him. He figured he outweighed Hahn by eighty pounds. That might be enough to balance the fact that he was spotting Hahn thirty years and one leg. They came together, and Barrett drove his hands down onto Hahn's shoulders, trying to hold him, to force him back into the room.

Hahn gave an inch or two. He looked up at Barrett without speaking and pushed forward again.

"Don't—don't—" Barrett grunted. "I won't let you—"

"I don't want to do this," Hahn said.

He pushed again. Barrett felt himself buckling under the impact. He dug his hands as hard as he could into Hahn's shoulders, and tried to shove the other man backward into the room, but Hahn held firm and all of Barrett's energy was converted into a backward thrust rebounding on himself. He lost control of his crutch, and it slithered out from under his arm. For one agonizing moment Barrett's full weight rested on the crushed uselessness of his left foot, and then, as though his limbs were melting away beneath him, he began to sink toward the floor. He landed with a reverberating crash.

Quesada, Altman, and Latimer came rushing in. Barrett writhed in pain on the floor. Hahn stood over him, looking unhappy, his hands locked together.

"I'm sorry," he said. "You shouldn't have tried to muscle me like that."

Barrett glowered at him. "You were traveling in time, weren't you? You can answer me now!"

"Yes," Hahn said at last. "I went Up Front."

An hour later, after Quesada had pumped him with enough neural depressants to keep him from jumping out of his skin, Barrett got the full story. Hahn hadn't wanted to reveal it so soon, but he had changed his mind after his little scuffle.

It was all very simple. Time travel now worked in both directions. The glib, impressive noises about the flow of entropy had turned out to be just noises.

"How long has this been known?" Barrett asked.

"At least five years. We aren't sure yet exactly when the breakthrough came. After we're finished going through all the suppressed records of the former government—"

"The former government?"

Hahn nodded. "The revolution came in January. Not really a violent one, either. The syndicalists just mildewed from within, and when they got the first push they fell over."

"Was it mildew?" Barrett asked, coloring. "Or termites? Keep your metaphors straight."

Hahn glanced away. "Anyway, the government fell. We've got a provisional liberal regime in office now. Don't ask me much about it. I'm not a political theorist. I'm not even an economist. You guessed as much."

"What are you; then?"

"A policeman," Hahn said. "Part of the commission that's investigating the prison system of the former government. Including this prison."

Barrett looked at Quesada, then at Hahn. Thoughts were streaming turbulently through him, and he could not remember when he had last been so overwhelmed by events. He had to work hard to keep from breaking into the shakes again. His voice quavered a little as he said, "You came back to observe Hawksbill Station, right? And you went Up Front tonight to tell them what you saw here. You think we're a pretty sad bunch, eh?"

"You've all been under heavy stress here," Hahn said. "Considering the circumstances of your imprisonment—"

Quesada broke in. "If there's a liberal government in power, now, and it's possible to travel both ways in time, then am I right in assuming that the Hawksbill prisoners are going to be sent Up Front?"

"Of course," said Hahn. "It'll be done as soon as possible. That's been the whole purpose of my reconnaissance mission. To find out if you people were still alive, first, and then to see what shape you're in, how badly in need of treatment you are. You'll be given every available benefit of modern therapy, naturally. No expense spared to—"

Barrett scarcely paid attention to Hahn's words. He had been fearing something like this all night, ever since Altman had told him

Hahn was monkeying with the Hammer, but he had never fully allowed himself to believe that it could really be possible.

He saw his kingdom crumbling, now.

He saw himself returned to a world he could not begin to comprehend—a lame Rip van Winkle, coming back after twenty years.

He saw himself leaving a place that had become his home.

Barrett said tiredly, "You know, some of the men aren't going to be able to adapt to the shock of freedom. It might just kill them to be dumped into the real world again. I mean advanced psychos—Valdosto, and such."

"Yes," Hahn said. "I've mentioned them in my report."

"It'll be necessary to get them ready for a return in gradual stages. It might take several years to condition them to the idea. It might even take longer than that."

"I'm no therapist," said Hahn. "Whatever the doctors think is right for them is what'll be done. Maybe it will be necessary to keep them here. I can see where it would be pretty potent to send them back, after they've spent all these years believing there's no return."

"More than that," said Barrett. "There's a lot of work that can be done here. Scientific works. Exploration. I don't think Hawksbill Station ought to be closed down."

"No one said it would be. We have every intention of keeping it going. But not as a prison. The prison concept is out."

"Good," Barrett said. He fumbled for his crutch, found it, and got heavily to his feet. Quesada moved toward him as though to steady him, but Barrett shook him off. "Let's go outside," he said.

They left the building. A gray mist had come in over the Station, and a fine drizzle had begun to fall. Barrett looked around at the scattering of huts. At the ocean, dimly visible to the east in the faint moonlight. He thought of Charley Norton and the party that had gone on the annual expedition to the Inland Sea. That bunch was going to be in for a real surprise, when they got back here in a few weeks and discovered that everybody was free to go home.

Very strangely, Barrett felt a sudden pressure forming around his eyelids, as of tears trying to force their way out into the open.

Then he turned to Hahn and Quesada. In a low voice he said, "Have you followed what I've been trying to tell you? Someone's got to stay here and ease the transition for the sick men who won't be able to stand the shock of return. Someone's got to keep the base running. Someone's got to explain things to the new men who'll be coming back here, the scientists."

"Naturally," Hahn said.

"The one who does that—the one who stays behind—I think it ought to be someone who knows the Station well, someone who's fit to return Up Front, but who's willing to make the sacrifice and stay. Do you follow me? A volunteer." They were smiling at him now. Barrett wondered if there might not be something patronizing about those smiles. He wondered if he might not be a little too transparent. To hell with both of them, he thought. He sucked the Cambrian air into his lungs until his chest swelled grandly.

"I'm offering to stay," Barrett said in a loud tone. He glared at them to keep them from objecting. But they wouldn't dare object, he knew. In Hawksbill Station, he was the king. And he meant to keep it that way. "I'll be the volunteer," he said. "I'll be the one who stays."

He looked out over his kingdom from the top of the hill.

AGAINST THE CURRENT

Because I started so young—I was in my late teens when I began getting stories professionally published—my career as a science fiction writer has been one of the longest on record, if you leave aside such probably unmatchable ones as those of Jack Williamson (who began writing in 1928 and went right on for 75 years plus, until his death a few years ago at the age of 98) and Frederik Pohl (whose earliest published story dates from 1939 and who was still at it to the end of his days, 74 years later.) Ray Bradbury, whose career got under way in 1941, is another whose career span exceeds mine by quite some distance. But it is now some 65 years since editors began saying yes to my SF stories, and through a lucky combination of longevity and precocity I have been able to exceed in the duration of my writing career those of such major figures of the field as Isaac Asimov, Robert A. Heinlein, Theodore Sturgeon, and Poul Anderson, though I have no intention of trying to break the flabbergasting Williamson record.

There were some changes along the route of my six-decade career. Not only had there been some growth in literary ability, I hope, but there had been a steady slowdown in productivity from what was, at the beginning, a virtually inhuman pace. As I said in the introduction of an earlier collection of mine, "Despite the rigors of college work, I wrote short stories steadily throughout 1954—one in April, two in May, three in June, two in October after the summer break . . . and by June of 1955 I was writing a story a week." A pace of a story a week would add up to fifty or so stories a year. But then we find, "I wrote 'Alaree' in March of 1956—one of eight stories that

I managed to produce that month, while still carrying a full class load in college." And then the topper: "June of 1956: the new college graduate, in his first official month as a full-time professional writer, turns out no less than eighteen stories plus two small nonfiction pieces—an average of just about one a day, considering that I always took Saturdays and Sundays off—and sells them all."

Well, that had to stop. Not only were there not enough science fiction magazines in existence to absorb eighteen stories a month by one writer, but I wasn't going to be 21 forever, either, and no writer even of first-magnitude prolificity has ever been able to manage to keep up an eighteen-story-a-month pace for very long. My output of short stories gradually dropped to a more normal sort, partly because I had begun writing novels as well, partly because many of the old-line magazines that had encouraged my voluminous production had gone out of business, and partly because I just couldn't keep hammering away at that frantic rate indefinitely. Writers, like everybody else, want to take things a little easier as the years mount up. Shakespeare and Hemingway didn't write anything in their sixties. (They were dead by then.) Asimov, Heinlein, Pohl, and Bradbury all slowed down some as time went along. So did I.

Gradually, over the years, I came to write less and less, though I've continued to write steadily, by and large, except for the sabbatical years from 1974 to 1978. The pace slowed so much that bibliographers will find just a dozen stories emerging from me in the entire decade beginning in 1995, and nearly all of those were the result of some direct request from an editor rather than my own burning desire to add one more short story to my long list. Indeed, I wrote no short stories at all between the summer of 1996 and "Millennium" in December 1998, except for a couple related to my Majipoor *and* Roma Eterna *story sequences that had to be written to complete those books and others of their kind. And the four stories that I wrote over the next few years were instigated by editorial request rather than by some inner hunger to write.*

But even an aging writer who feels that he has said just about all he wants to say in the way of science fiction over the many decades of his career still does occasionally feel the irresistible pull of a story that demands to be written. At least, that was my experience one sunny day in the fall of 2006 when, while reading a fifty-year-old anthology of fantasy stories that Ray

Bradbury had edited, the idea of writing a story about a man who gets into his car and drives off into the past popped into my mind.

I wasn't looking for story ideas. I had not let myself get drawn into any new writing obligations since finishing a longish story early in 2005, and the rest of that year and most of 2006 had glided by without any new Silverberg fiction entering the world. But suddenly the story that I would call "Against the Current" was taking shape willy-nilly in my mind, and the only response that seemed appropriate was, "Why not write it?" So I did. Over the next week or so it came forth virtually of its own accord, an experience that has been, I have to confess, exceedingly rare for me in modern times. I didn't stop to ask myself how it might be possible to get into one's car and drive into one's past. That would have spoiled the fun. All I wanted to do was tell the story as it told itself to me, and whether the story was science fiction (i.e. the car has been rigged to act as a sort of time machine) or fantasy (i.e. the car simply does what it does, no explanations offered) was irrelevant to me. I figured this story was a gift from the gods, and I wasn't minded to look a gift story in the mouth.

The magazine most receptive to out-of-genre stories like this, over the years, has been Fantasy and Science Fiction. *I had been an infrequent but regular contributor to* F&SF *since 1957, when the brilliant Anthony Boucher was its editor. It had published such stories of mine as "Sundance" and "Born with the Dead," and it had serialized my novels* The Stochastic Man *and* Lord Valentine's Castle. *Its editor and publisher now was Gordon van Gelder, with whom I had come to strike up a pleasant and curious friendship. (We are both involuntary early risers, and we have breakfast together at the World Science Fiction Convention each year in the dawn hours, while the rest of the convention-goers are still fast asleep.) I sent it to Gordon and he published it in his October–November 2007 issue.*

ABOUT HALF PAST FOUR IN the afternoon Rackman felt a sudden red blaze of pain in both his temples at once, the sort of stabbing jab that you would expect to feel if a narrow metal spike had been driven through your head. It was gone as quickly as it had come, but it left him feeling queasy and puzzled and a little frightened, and, since things were slow at the dealership just then anyway, he decided it might be best to call it a day and head for home.

He stepped out into perfect summer weather, a sunny, cloudless day, and headed across the lot to look for Gene, his manager, who had been over by the SUVs making a tally of the leftovers. But Gene was nowhere in sight. The only person Rackman saw out there was a pudgy salesman named Freitas, who so far as he recalled had given notice a couple of weeks ago. Evidently he wasn't gone yet, though.

"I'm not feeling so good and I'm going home early," Rackman announced. "If Gene's around here somewhere, will you tell him that?"

"Sure thing, Mr. Rackman."

Rackman circled around the edge of the lot toward the staff parking area. He still felt queasy, and somewhat muddled too, with a slight headache lingering after that sudden weird stab of pain. Everything seemed just a bit askew. The SUVs, for instance—there were more of the things than there should be, considering that he had just run a big clearance on them. They were lined up like a whopping great phalanx of tanks. How come so many? He filed away a mental note to ask Gene about that tomorrow.

He put his card in the ignition slot and the sleek silver Prius glided smoothly, silently, out of the lot, off to the nearby freeway entrance. By the time he reached the Caldecott Tunnel twenty minutes later the last traces of the pain in his temple were gone, and he moved on easily through Oakland toward the bridge and San Francisco across the bay.

At the Bay Bridge toll plaza they had taken down all the overhead signs that denoted the FasTrak lanes. That was odd, he thought. Probably one of their mysterious maintenance routines. Rackman headed into his usual lane anyway, but there was a tolltaker in the booth—why?—and as he started to roll past the man toward the FasTrak scanner just beyond he got such an incandescent glare from him that he braked to a halt.

The FasTrak toll scanner wasn't where it should be, right back of the tollbooth on the left. It wasn't there at all.

Feeling a little bewildered now, Rackman pulled a five-dollar bill from his wallet, handed it to the man, got what seemed to be too many singles in change, and drove out onto the bridge. There was very little traffic. As he approached the Treasure Island tunnel, though, it struck him that he couldn't remember having seen any of the towering construction cranes that ran alongside the torso of the not-quite-finished new bridge just north of the old one. Nor was there any sign of them—or any trace of the new bridge itself, for that matter, when he glanced into his rear-view mirror.

This is peculiar, Rackman thought. Really, really peculiar.

On the far side of the tunnel the sky was darker, as though dusk were already descending—at 5:10 on a summer day?—and by the time he was approaching the San Francisco end of the bridge the light was all but gone. Even stranger, a little rain was starting to come down. Rain falls in the Bay Area in August about once every twenty years. The morning forecast hadn't said anything about rain. Rackman's hand trembled a little as he turned his wipers on. I am having what could be called a waking dream, Rackman thought, some very vivid hallucination, and when I'm off the bridge I better pull over and take a few deep breaths.

The skyline of the city just ahead of him looked somehow diminished, as though a number of the bigger buildings were missing. And the exit ramps presented more puzzles. A lot of stuff that had been torn down for the retro-fitting of the old bridge seemed to have been put back in place. He couldn't find his Folsom Street off-ramp, but the long-gone Main Street one, which they had closed after the 1989 earthquake, lay right in front of him. He took it and pulled the Prius to curbside as soon as he was down at street level. The rain had stopped—the streets were dry, as if the rain had never been—but the air seemed clinging and clammy, not like dry summer air at all. It enfolded him, contained him in a strange tight grip. His cheeks were flushed and he was perspiring heavily.

Deep breaths, yes. Calm. Calm. You're only five blocks from your condo.

Only he wasn't. Most of the high-rise office buildings were missing, all right, and none of the residential towers south of the off-ramp complex were there, just block after block of parking lots and some ramshackle warehouses. It was night now, and the empty neighborhood was almost completely dark. Everything was the way it had looked around here fifteen, twenty years before. His bewilderment was beginning to turn into terror. The street signs said that he was at his own corner. So where was the thirty-story building where he lived?

Better call Jenny, he thought.

He would tell her—delicately—that he was going through something very baffling, a feeling of, well, disorientation, that in fact he was pretty seriously mixed up, that she had better come get him and take him home.

But his cell phone didn't seem to be working. All he got was a dull buzzing sound. He looked at it, stunned. He felt as though some part of him had been amputated.

Rackman was angry now as well as frightened. Things like this weren't supposed to happen to him. He was 57 years old, healthy, solvent, a solid citizen, owner of a thriving Toyota dealership across the bay, married to a lovely and loving woman. Everyone said he looked ten years younger than he really was. He worked out three times a week and ran in the Bay-to-Breakers Race every year and once in a while he even did a marathon. But the drive across the bridge had been all wrong and he didn't know where his condo building had gone and his cell phone was on the fritz, and here he was lost in this dark forlorn neighborhood of empty lots and abandoned warehouses with a wintry wind blowing—hey, hadn't it been sticky and humid a few minute ago?—on what had started out as a summer day. And he had the feeling that things were going to get worse before they got better. If indeed they got better at all.

He swung around and drove toward Union Square. Traffic was surprisingly light for downtown San Francisco. He spotted a phone booth, parked nearby, fumbled a coin into the slot, and dialed his number. The phone made ugly noises and a robot voice told him that the number he had dialed was not a working number. Cursing, Rackman tried again, tapping the numbers in with utmost care.

"We're sorry," the voice said again, "the number you have reached is not—"

A telephone book dangled before him. He riffled through it—Jenny had her own listing, under Burke—but though half a dozen J Burkes were in the book, five of them lived in the wrong part of town, and when he dialed the sixth number, which had no address listed, an answering machine responded in a birdlike chirping voice that certainly wasn't Jenny's. Something led him then to look for his own listing. No, that wasn't there either. A curious calmness came over him at that discovery. There were no FasTrak lanes at the toll plaza, and the dismantled freeway ramps were still here, and the neighborhood where he lived hadn't been developed yet, and neither he nor Jenny was listed in the San Francisco phone book, and therefore either he had gone seriously crazy or else somehow this had to be fifteen or even twenty years ago, which was pretty much just another way of saying the same thing. If this really is fifteen or twenty years ago, Rackman thought, then Jenny would be living in Sacramento and I'd be across the bay in El Cerrito and still married to Helene. But what the hell kind of thing was that to be thinking, *If this really is fifteen or twenty years ago*?

He considered taking himself to the nearest emergency room and telling them he was having a breakdown, but he knew that once he put himself in the hands of the medics, there'd be no extricating himself: they'd subject him to a million tests, reports would be filed with this agency and that, his driver's license might be yanked, bad things would happen to his credit rating. It would be much smarter, he thought, to check himself into a hotel room, take a shower, rest, try to figure all this out, wait for things to get back to normal.

Rackman headed for the Hilton, a couple of blocks away. Though night had fallen just a little while ago, the sun was high overhead now, and the weather had changed again, too: it was sharp and cool, autumn just shading into winter. He was getting a different season and a different time of day every fifteen minutes or so, it seemed. The Hilton desk clerk, tall and balding and starchy-looking, had such a self-important manner that as Rackman requested a room he felt a little abashed at not having any luggage with him, but the clerk didn't appear to give a damn about that, simply handed him the registration form and asked him for his credit card. Rackman put his Visa down on the counter and began to fill out the form.

"Sir?" the desk clerk said, after a moment.

Rackman looked up. The clerk was staring at his credit card. It was the translucent kind, and he tipped it this way and that, puzzledly holding it against the light. "Problem?" Rackman asked, and the clerk muttered something about how unusual the card looked.

Then his expression darkened. "Wait just a second," he said, very coldly now, and tapped the imprinted expiration date on the card. "What is *this* supposed to be? Expires July, 2010? *2010,* sir? *2010?* Are we having a little joke, sir?" He flipped the card across the counter at Rackman the way he might have done if it had been covered with some noxious substance.

Another surge of terror hit him. He backed away, moving quickly through the lobby and into the street. Of course he might have tried to pay cash, he supposed, but the room would surely be something like $225 a night, and he had only about $350 on him. If his credit card was useless, he'd need to hang on to his cash at least until he understood what was happening to him. Instead of the Hilton, he would go to some cheaper place, perhaps one of the motels up on Lombard Street.

On his way back to his car Rackman glanced at a newspaper in a sidewalk rack. President Reagan was on the front page, under a headline about the invasion of Grenada. The date on the paper was Wednesday, October 26, 1983. Sure, he thought. 1983. This hallucination isn't missing a trick. I am in 1983 and Reagan is President again, with 1979 just up the road, 1965, 1957, 1950—

In 1950 Rackman hadn't even been born yet. He wondered what was going to happen to him when he got back to a time earlier than his own birth.

He stopped at the first motel on Lombard that had a VACANCY sign and registered for a room. The price was only $75, but when he put two fifties down on the counter, the clerk, a pleasant, smiling

Latino woman, gave him a pleasant smile and tapped her finger against the swirls of pink coloration next to President Grant's portrait. "Somebody has stuck you with some very funny bills, sir. But you know that I can't take them. If you can pay by credit card, though, Visa, American Express—"

Of course she couldn't take them. Rackman remembered, now, that all the paper money had changed five or ten years back, new designs, bigger portraits, distinctive patches of pink or blue ink on their front sides that had once been boringly monochromatic. And these bills of his had the tiny date "2004" in the corner.

So far as the world of 1983 was concerned, the money he was carrying was nothing but play money.

1983.

Jenny, who is up in Sacramento in 1983 and has no idea yet that he even exists, had been 25 that year. Already he was more than twice her age. And she would get younger and younger as he went ever onward, if that was what was going to continue to happen.

Maybe it wouldn't. Soon, perhaps, the pendulum would begin to swing the other way, carrying him back to his own time, to his own life. What if it didn't, though? What if it just kept on going?

In that case, Rackman thought, Jenny was lost to him, with everything that had bound them together now unhappened. Rackman reached out suddenly, grasping the air as though reaching for Jenny, but all he grasped was air. There was no Jenny for him any longer. He had lost her, yes. And he would lose everything else of what he had thought of as his life as well, his whole past peeling away strip by strip. He had no reason to think that the pendulum *would* swing back. Already the exact details of Jenny's features were blurring in his mind. He struggled to recall them: the quizzical blue eyes, the slender nose, the wide, generous mouth, the slim, supple body. She seemed to be drifting past him in the fog, caught in an inexorable current carrying her ever farther away.

HE SLEPT IN HIS CAR that night, up by the Marina, where he hoped no one would bother him. No one did. Morning light awakened him after a few hours—his wristwatch said it was 9:45 P.M. on the same

August day when all this had started, but he knew better now than to regard what his watch told him as having any meaning—and when he stepped outside the day was dry and clear, with a blue summer sky overhead and the sort of harsh wind blowing that only San Francisco can manage on a summer day. He was getting used to the ever-changing weather by now, though, the swift parade of seasons tumbling upon him one after another. Each new one would hold him for a little while in that odd *enclosed* way, but then it would release its grasp and nudge him onward into the next one.

He checked the newspaper box on the corner. *San Francisco Chronicle,* Tuesday, May 1, 1973. Big front-page story: Nixon dismisses White House counsel John Dean and accepts the resignations of aides John Ehrlichman and H. R. Haldeman. Right, he thought. Dean, Ehrlichman, Haldeman: Watergate. So a whole decade had vanished while he slept. He had slipped all the way back to 1973. He wasn't even surprised. He had entered some realm beyond all possibility of surprise.

Taking out his wallet, Rackman checked his driver's license. Still the same, expires 03-11-11, photo of his familiar 50-something face. His car was still a silver 2009 Prius. Certain things hadn't changed. But the Prius stood out like a shriek among the other parked cars, every last one of them some clunky-looking old model of the kind that he dimly remembered from his youth. What we have here is 1973, he thought. Probably not for long, though.

He hadn't had anything to eat since lunchtime, ten hours and thirty-five years ago. He drove over to Chestnut Street, marveling at the quiet old-fashioned look of all the shopfronts, and parked right outside Joe's, which he knew had been out of business since maybe the Clinton years. There were no parking meters on the street. Rackman ordered a salad, a Joe's Special, and a glass of red wine, and paid for it with a ten-dollar bill of the old black-and-white kind that he happened to have. Meal plus wine, $8.50, he thought. That sounded about right for this long ago. It was a very consistent kind of hallucination. He left a dollar tip.

Rackman remembered pretty well what he had been doing in the spring of 1973. He was 22 that year, out of college almost a year, working in Cody's Books on Telegraph Avenue in Berkeley while waiting to get into law school, for which he had been turned down the first time around but which he had high hopes of entering that autumn. He and Al Mortenson, another young Cody's clerk—nice steady guy, easy to get along with—were rooming together in a little upstairs apartment on Dana, two or three blocks from the bookshop.

What ever had happened to old Al? Rackman had lost touch with him many years back. A powerful urge seized him now to drive across to Berkeley and look for him. He hadn't spoken with anyone except those two hotel clerks since he had left the car lot, what felt like a million years ago, and a terrible icy loneliness was beginning to settle over him as he went spinning onward through his constantly unraveling world. He needed to reach out to someone, anyone, for whatever help he could find. Al might be a good man to consult. Al was levelheaded; Al was unflusterable; Al was *steady*. What about driving over to Berkeley now and looking for Al at the Dana Street place?—"I know you don't recognize me, Al, but I'm actually Phil Rackman, only I'm from 2008, and I'm having some sort of bad trip and I need to sit down in a quiet place with a good friend like you and figure out what's going on." Rackman wondered what that would accomplish. Probably nothing, but at least it might provide him with half an hour of companionship, sympathy, even understanding. At worst Al would think he was a lunatic and he would wind up under sedation at Alta Bates Hospital while they tried to find his next of kin. If he really was sliding constantly backward in time he would slip away from Alta Bates too, Rackman thought, and if not, if he was simply unhinged, maybe a hospital was where he belonged.

He went to Berkeley. The season drifted back from spring to late winter while he was crossing the bridge: in Berkeley the acacias were in bloom, great clusters of golden yellow flowers, and that was a January thing. The sight of Berkeley in early 1973, a year that had in fact been the last gasp of the Sixties, gave him a shiver: the Day-Glo rock-concert posters on all the walls, the flower-child costumes, the huge, bizarre helmets of shaggy hair that everyone was wearing. The streets were strangely clean, hardly any litter, no graffiti. It all was like a movie set, a careful, loving reconstruction of the era. He had no business being here. He was entirely out of place. And yet he had lived here once. This street belonged to his own past. He had lost Jenny, he had lost his nice condominium, he had lost his car dealership, but other things that he had thought were lost, like this Day-Glo tie-dyed world of his youth, were coming back to him. Only they weren't coming back for long, he knew. One by one they would present themselves, tantalizing flashes of a returning past, and then they'd go streaming onward, lost to him like everything else, lost for a second and terribly final time.

He guessed from the position of the pale winter sun, just coming up over the hills to the east, that the time was eight or nine in the morning. If so, Al would probably still be at home. The Dana Street place looked just as Rackman remembered it, a tidy little frame building, the landlady's tiny but immaculate garden of pretty succulents out front, the redwood deck, the staircase on the side that led to the upstairs apartment. As he started upward an unsettling burst of panic swept through him at the possibility that he might be going to come face to face with his own younger self. But in a moment his trepidation passed. It wouldn't happen, he told himself. It was just *too* impossible. There had to be a limit to this thing somewhere.

A kid answered his knock, sleepy-looking and impossibly young, a tall lanky guy in jeans and a t-shirt, with a long oval face almost completely engulfed in an immense spherical mass of jet-black hair that covered his forehead and his cheeks and his chin, a wild woolly tangle that left only eyes and nose and lips visible. A golden peace-symbol amulet dangled on a silver chain around his neck. My God, Rackman thought, this really is the Al I knew in 1973. Like a ghost out of time. But *I* am the ghost. *I* am the ghost.

"Yes?" the kid at the door said vaguely.

"Al Mortenson, right?"

"Yes." He said it in an uneasy way, chilly, distant, grudging.

What the hell, some unknown elderly guy at the door, an utter stranger wanting God only knew what, eight or nine in the morning:

even the unflappable Al might be a little suspicious. Rackman saw no option but to launch straight into his story. "I realize this is going to sound very strange to you. But I ask you to bear with me. Do I look in any way familiar to you, Al?"

He wouldn't, naturally. He was much stockier than the Phil Rackman of 1973, his full-face beard was ancient history and his once-luxurious russet hair was close-cropped and gray, and he was wearing a checked suit of the kind that nobody, not even a middle-aged man, would have worn in 1973. But he began to speak, quietly, earnestly, intensely, persuasively, his best one-foot-in-the-door salesman approach, the approach he might have used if he had been trying to sell his biggest model SUV to a frail old lady from the Rossmoor retirement home. Starting off by casually mentioning Al's roommate Phil Rackman—"he isn't here, by any chance, is he?"—no, he wasn't, thank God—and then asking Al once again to prepare himself for a very peculiar tale indeed, giving him no chance to reply, and swiftly and smoothly working around to the notion that he himself was Phil Rackman, not Phil's father but the actual Phil Rackman who had been his roommate back in 1973, only in fact he was the Phil Rackman of the year 2008 who had without warning become caught up in what could only be described as an inexplicable toboggan-slide backward across time.

Even through that forest of facial hair Al's reactions were readily discernible: puzzlement at first, then annoyance verging on anger, then a show of curiosity, a flicker of interest at the possibility of such a wild thing—hey, man, far out! Cool!—and then, gradually, gradually, gradually bringing himself to the tipping point, completing the transition from skepticism verging on hostility to mild curiosity to fascination to stunned acceptance, as Rackman began to conjure up remembered episodes of their shared life that only he could have known. That time in the summer of '72 when he and Al and their current girlfriends had gone camping in the Sierra and had been happily screwing away on a flat smooth granite outcropping next to a mountain stream in what they thought was total seclusion, 8000 feet above sea level, when a wide-eyed party of Boy Scouts came marching past them down the trail; and that long-legged girl from Oregon Rackman had picked up one weekend who turned out to be double-jointed, or whatever, and showed them both the most amazing sexual tricks; and the great moment when they and some friends had scored half a pound of hash and gave a party that lasted three days running without time out for sleep; and the time when he and Al had hitchhiked down to Big Sur, he with big, cuddly Ginny Beardsley and Al with hot little Nikki Rosenzweig, during Easter break, and the four of them had dropped a little acid and gone absolutely gonzo berserk together in a secluded redwood grove—

"No," Al said. "That hasn't happened yet. Easter is still three months away. And I don't know any Nikki Rosenzweig."

Rackman rolled his eyes lasciviously. "You will, kiddo. Believe me, you will! Ginny will introduce you, and—and—"

"So you even know my own future."

"For me it isn't the future," Rackman said. "It's the long-ago past. When you and I were rooming together right here on Dana Street and having the time of our lives."

"But how is this possible?"

"You think I know, old pal? All I know is that it's happening. I'm me, really me, sliding backward in time. It's the truth. Look at my face, Al. Run a computer simulation in your mind, if you can—hell, people don't have their own computers yet, do they?—well, just try to age me up, in your imagination, gray hair, more weight, but the same nose, Al, the same mouth—" He shook his head. "Wait a second. Look at this." He drew out his driver's license and thrust it at the other man. "You see the name? The photo? You see the birthdate? *You see the expiration date?* March 2011? Here, look at these fifty-dollar bills! The dates on them. This credit card, this Visa. Do you even know what a Visa is? Did we have them back in 1973?"

"Christ," Al said, in a husky, barely audible whisper. "Jesus Christ, Phil.—It's okay if I call you Phil, right?"

"Phil, yes."

"Look, Phil—" That same thin ghostly whisper, the voice of a man in shock. Rackman had never, in the old days, seen Al this badly shaken up. "The bookstore's about to open. I've got to get to work.

You come in, wait here, make yourself at home." Then a little manic laugh: "You *are* at home, aren't you? In a manner of speaking. So wait here. Rest. Relax. Smoke some of my dope, if you want. You probably know where I keep it. Meet me at Cody's at one, and we can go out to lunch and talk about all this, okay? I want to know all about it. What year did you say you came from? 2011?"

"2008."

"2008. Christ, this is so wild!—You'll stay here, then?"

"And if my younger self walks in on me?"

"Don't worry. You're safe. He's in Los Angeles this week."

"Groovy," Rackman said, wondering if anyone still said things like that. "Go on, then. Go to work. I'll see you later."

THE TWO ROOMS, AL'S AND his own just across the hall, were like museum exhibits: the posters for Fillmore West concerts, the antique stereo set and the stack of LP records, the tie-dyed shirts and bell-bottom pants scattered in the corner, the bong on the dresser, the macrame wall-hangings, the musty aroma of last night's incense. Rackman poked around, lost in dreamy nostalgia and at times close to tears as he looked at this artifact of that ancient era and that one, *The Teachings of Don Juan, The White Album, The Whole Earth Catalog.* His own copies. He still had the Castaneda book somewhere; he remembered the beer stain on the cover. He peered into the dresser drawer where Al kept his stash, scooped up a pinch of it in his fingers and sniffed it, smiled, put it back. It was years since he had smoked. Decadcs.

He ran his hand over his cheek. His stubble was starting to bother him. He hadn't shaved since yesterday morning on Rackman body time. He knew there'd be a shaver in the bathroom, though—he was pretty sure he had left it there even after he began growing his Seventies beard—and, yes, there was his old Norelco three-headed job. He felt better with clean cheeks. Rackman stuffed the shaver into his inside jacket pocket, knowing he'd want it in the days ahead.

Then he found himself wondering whether he had parked in a tow-away zone. They had always been very tough about illegally parked cars in Berkeley. You could try to assassinate the president and get off with a six-month sentence, but God help you if you parked in a tow-away zone. And if they took his car away, he'd be in an even worse pickle than he already was. The car was his one link to the world he had left behind, his time capsule, his home, now, actually.

The car was still where he had left it. But he was afraid to leave it for long. It might slip away from him in the next time-shift. He got in, thinking to wait in it until it was time to meet Al for lunch. But although it was still just mid-morning he felt drowsiness overcoming him, and almost instantly he dozed off. When he awakened he saw that it was dark outside. He must have slept the day away. The dashboard clock told him it was 1:15 P.M., but that was useless, meaningless. Probably it was early evening, too late for lunch with Al. Maybe they could have dinner instead.

On the way over to the bookstore, marveling every step of the way at the utter weirdness of everybody he passed in the streets, the strange beards, the flamboyant globes of hair, the gaudy clothing, Rackman began to see that it would be very embarrassing to tell Al that he had grown up to own a suburban automobile dealership. He had planned to become a legal advocate for important social causes, or perhaps a public defender, or an investigator of corporate malfeasance. Everybody had noble plans like that, back then. Going into the car business hadn't been on anyone's screen.

Then he saw that he didn't have to tell Al anything about what he had come to do for a living. It was a long story and not one that Al was likely to find interesting. Al wouldn't care that he had become a car dealer. Al was sufficiently blown away by the mere fact that his former roommate Phil Rackman had dropped in on him out of the future that morning.

He entered the bookstore and spotted Al over near the cash register. But when he waved he got only a blank stare in return.

"I'm sorry I missed our lunch date, Al. I guess I just nodded off. It's been a pretty tiring day for me, you know."

There was no trace of recognition on Al's face.

"Sir? There must be some mistake."

"Al Mortenson? Who lives on Dana Street?"

"I'm Al Mortenson, yes. I live in Bowles Hall, though."

Bowles Hall was a campus dormitory. Undergraduates lived there. This Al hadn't graduated yet.

This Al's hair was different too, Rackman saw now. A tighter cut, more disciplined, more forehead showing. And his beard was much longer, cascading down over his chest, hiding the peace symbol. He might have had a haircut during the day but he couldn't have grown four inches more of beard.

There was a stack of newspapers on the counter next to the register, the *New York Times.* Rackman flicked a glance at the top one. *November 10, 1971.*

I haven't just slept away the afternoon, Rackman thought. I've slept away all of 1972. He and Al hadn't rented the Dana Street place until after graduation, in June of '72.

Fumbling, trying to recover, always the nice helpful guy, Al said, "You aren't Mr. Chesley, are you? Bud Chesley's father?"

Bud Chesley had been a classmate of theirs, a jock, big, broad-shouldered. The main thing that Rackman remembered about him was that he had been one of about six men on campus who were in favor of the war in Vietnam. Rackman seemed to recall that in his senior year Al had roomed with Chesley in Bowles, before he and Al had known each other.

"No," Rackman said leadenly. "I'm not Mr. Chesley. I'm really sorry to have bothered you."

So it was hopeless, then. He had suspected it all along, but now, feeling the past tugging at him as he hurried back to his car, it was certain. The slippage made any sort of human interaction lasting more than half an hour or so impossible to sustain. He struggled with it, trying to tug back, to hold fast against the sliding, hoping that perhaps he could root himself somehow in the present and then begin the climb forward again until he reached the place where he belonged. But he could feel the slippage continuing, not at any consistent rate but in sudden unpredictable bursts, and there was nothing he could do about it. There were times when he was completely unaware of it until it had happened and other times when he could see the seasons rocketing right by in front of his eyes.

Without any particular destination in mind Rackman returned to his car, wandered around Berkeley until he found himself heading down Ashby Avenue to the freeway, and drove back into San Francisco. The toll was only a quarter. Astonishing. The cars around him on the bridge all seemed like collector's items, with yellow-and-black license plates, three digits, three letters. He wondered what a highway patrolman would say about his own plates, if he recognized them as California plates at all.

Halfway across the bridge Rackman turned the radio on, hoping the car might be able to pick up a news broadcast out of 2008, but no, no, when he got KCBS he heard the announcer talking about President Johnson, Secretary of State Rusk, Vietnam, Israel refusing to give back Jerusalem after the recent war with the Arab countries, Dr. Martin Luther King calling for calm following a night of racial strife in Hartford, Connecticut. It was hard to remember some of the history exactly, but Rackman knew that Dr. King had been assassinated in 1968, so he figured that just in the course of crossing the bridge he probably had slid back into 1967 or even 1966. He had been in high school then. All the sweaty anguish of that whole lunatic era came swimming back into his mind, the Robert Kennedy assassination too, the body counts on the nightly news, Malcolm X, peace marches, the strident 1968 political convention in Chicago, the race riots, Nixon, Hubert Humphrey, Mao Tse-tung, spacemen in orbit around the moon, Lady Bird Johnson, Cassius Clay. *Hey hey hey, LBJ, how many kids did you kill today?* The noise, the hard-edged excitement, the daily anxiety. It felt like the Pleistocene to him now. But he had driven right into the thick of it.

The slippage continued. The long hair went away, the granny glasses, the Day-Glo posters, the tie-dyed clothes. John F. Kennedy came and went in reverse. Night and day seemed to follow one another in random sequence. Rackman ate his meals randomly too, no idea whether it was breakfast or lunch or dinner that he needed. He had lost all track of personal time. He caught naps in his car, kept a low profile, said very little to anyone. A careless restaurant cashier took one of his gussied-up fifties without demur and gave him a stack of spendable bills in change. He doled those bills out parsimoniously, watching what he spent even though meals, like the bridge toll, like the cost of a newspaper, like everything else back here, were astoundingly cheap, a nickel or a dime for this, fifty cents for that.

San Francisco was smaller, dingier, a little old 1950s-style town, no trace of the high-rise buildings now. Everything was muted, old-fashioned, the simpler, more innocent textures of his childhood. He half expected it all to be in black and white, as an old newsreel would be, and perhaps to flicker a little. But he took in smells, breezes, sounds, that no newsreel could have captured. This wasn't any newsreel and it wasn't any hallucination, either. This was the world itself, dense, deep, real. All too real, unthinkably real. And there was no place for him in it.

Men wore hats, women's coats had padded shoulders. Shop windows sparkled. There was a Christmas bustle in the streets. A little while later, though, the sky brightened and the dry, cold winds of San Francisco summer came whistling eastward at him again out of the Pacific, and then, presto jingo, the previous winter's rainy season was upon him. He wondered which year's winter it was.

It was 1953, the newspaper told him. The corner newspaper rack was his only friend. It provided him with guidance, information about his present position in time. That was Eisenhower on the front page. The Korean war was still going on, here in 1953. And Stalin: Stalin had just died. Rackman remembered Eisenhower, the president of his childhood, kindly old Ike. Truman's bespectacled face would be next. Rackman had been born during Truman's second term. He had no recollection of the Truman presidency but he could recall the salty old Harry of later years, who went walking every day, gabbing with reporters about anything that came into his head.

What is going to happen to me, Rackman wondered, when I get back past my own birthdate?

Maybe he would come to some glittering gateway, a giant sizzling special effect throwing off fireworks across the whole horizon, with a blue-white sheen of nothingness stretching into infinity beyond it.

And when he passed through it he would disappear into oblivion and that would be that. He'd find out soon enough. He couldn't be much more than a year or two away from the day of his birth.

Without knowing or caring where he was going Rackman began to drive south out of San Francisco, the poky little San Francisco of this far-off day, heading out of town on what once had been Highway 101, the freeway that led to the airport and San Jose and, eventually, Los Angeles. It wasn't a freeway now, just an oddly charming little four-lane road. The billboards that lined it on both sides looked like ads from old *National Geographics*. The curving rows of small ticky-tacky houses on the hillsides hadn't been built yet. There was almost nothing except open fields everywhere, down here south of the city. The ballpark wasn't there—the Giants still played in New York in this era, he recalled—and when he went past the airport, he almost failed to notice it, it was such a piffling little small-town place. Only when a DC-3 passed overhead like a huge droning mosquito did he realize that that collection of tin sheds over to the left was what would one day be SFO.

Rackman knew that he was still slipping and slipping as he went, that the pace of slippage seemed to be picking up, that if that glittering gateway existed he had already gone beyond it. He was somewhere near 1945 now or maybe even earlier—they were honking at his car on the road in amazement, as though it was a spaceship that had dropped down from Mars—and now a clear, cold understanding of what was in store for him was growing in his mind.

He wouldn't disappear through any gateway. It didn't matter that he hadn't been born yet in the year he was currently traveling through, because he wasn't growing any younger as he drifted backward. And the deep past waited for him. He saw that he would just go endlessly onward, cut loose from the restraints that time imposed, drifting on and on back into antiquity. While he was driving southward, heading for San Jose or Los Angeles or wherever it was that he might be going next, the years would roll along backward, the twentieth century would be gobbled up in the nineteenth, California's great cities would melt away—he had already seen that happening in San

Francisco—and the whole state would revert to the days of Mexican rule, a bunch of little villages clustered around the Catholic missions, and then the villages and the missions would disappear too. A day or two later for him, California would be an emptiness, nobody here but simple Indian tribes. Farther to the east, in the center of the continent, great herds of bison would roam. Still farther east would be the territory of the Thirteen Colonies, gradually shriveling back into tiny pioneering settlements and then vanishing also.

Well, he thought, if he could get himself across the country quickly enough, he might be able to reach New York City—Nieuw Amsterdam, it would probably be by then—while it still existed. There he might be able to arrange a voyage across to Europe before the continent reverted entirely to its pre-Columbian status. But what then? All that he could envisage was a perpetual journey backward, backward, ever backward: the Renaissance, the Dark Ages, Rome, Greece, Babylon, Egypt, the Ice Age. A couple of summers ago he and Jenny had taken a holiday in France, down in the Dordogne, where they had looked at the painted caves of the Cro-Magnon men, the colorful images of bulls and bison and spotted horses and mammoths. No one knew what those pictures meant, why they had been painted. Now he would go back and find out at first hand the answer to the enigmas of the prehistoric caves. How very cool that sounded, how interesting, a nice fantasy, except that if you gave it half a second's thought it was appalling. To whom would he impart that knowledge? What good would it do him, or anyone?

The deep past was waiting for him, yes. But would he get there? Even a Prius wasn't going to make it all the way across North America on a single tank of gas, and soon there weren't going to be any gas stations, and even if there were he would have no valid money to pay for gas, or food, or anything else. Pretty soon there would be no roads, either. He couldn't *walk* to New York. In that wilderness he wouldn't last three days.

He had kept himself in motion up until this moment, staying just ahead of the vast gray grimness that was threatening to invade his soul, but it was catching up with him now. Rackman went through ten or fifteen minutes that might have been the darkest, bleakest moments of his life. Then—was it something about the sweet simplicity of this little road, no longer the roaring Highway 101 but now just a dusty, narrow two-laner with hardly any traffic?—there came an unexpected change in his mood. He grew indifferent to his fate. In an odd way he found himself actually welcoming whatever might come. The prospect before him looked pretty terrifying, yes. But it might just be exciting, too. He had liked his life, he had liked it very much, but it had been torn away from him, he knew not how or why. This was his life now. He had no choice about that. The best thing to do, Rackman thought, was to take it one century at a time and try to enjoy the ride.

What he needed right now was a little breather: come to a halt if only for a short while, pause and regroup. Stop and pass the time, so to speak, as he got himself ready for the next phase of his new existence. He pulled over by the side of the road and turned off the ignition and sat there quietly, thinking about nothing at all.

After a while a youngish man on a motorcycle pulled up alongside him. The motorcycle was hardly more than a souped-up bike. The man was wearing a khaki blouse and khaki trousers, all pleats and flounces, a very old-fashioned outfit, something like a scoutmaster's uniform. He himself had an old-fashioned look, too, dark hair parted in the middle like an actor in a silent movie.

Then Rackman noticed the California Highway Patrol badge on the man's shoulder. He opened the car window. The patrolman leaned toward him and gave him an earnest smile, a Boy Scout smile. Even the smile was old-fashioned. You couldn't help believing the sincerity of it. "Is there any difficulty, sir? May I be of any assistance?"

So polite, so formal. *Sir.* Everyone had been calling him *sir* since this trip had started, the desk clerks, the people in restaurants, Al Mortenson, and now this CHP man. So respectful, everybody was, back here in prehistory.

"No," Rackman said. "No problem. Everything's fine."

The patrolman didn't seem to hear him. He had turned his complete attention to Rackman's car itself, the glossy silver Prius, the car out of the future. The look of it was apparently sinking in for the first time. He was staring at the car in disbelief, in befuddlement, in unconcealed jaw-sagging awe, gawking at its fluid streamlined shape, at its gleaming futuristic dashboard. Then he turned back to Rackman himself, taking in the look of his clothing, his haircut, his checked jacket, his patterned shirt. The man's eyes seemed to glaze. Rackman knew that there had to be something about his whole appearance that seemed as wrong to the patrolman as the patrolman's did to him. He could see the man working to get himself under control. The car must have him completely flummoxed, Rackman thought. The patrolman began to say something but it was a moment before he could put his voice in gear. Then he said, hoarsely, like a rusty automaton determined to go through its routine no matter what, "I want you to know, sir, that if you are having any problem with your—ah—your car, we are here to assist you in whatever way we can."

To assist you. That was a good one.

Rackman managed a faint smile. "Thanks, but the car's okay," he said. "And I'm okay too. I just stopped off here to rest a bit, that's all. I've got a long trip ahead of me." He started the car. Silently, smoothly, the Prius floated forward into the morning light and the night that would quickly follow it and into the random succession of days and nights and springs and winters and autumns and summers beyond, forward into the mysteries, dark and dreadful and splendid, that lay before him.

ABOUT THE AUTHOR

ROBERT SILVERBERG IS ONE OF science fiction's most beloved writers, and the author of such contemporary classics as *Dying Inside, Downward to the Earth, Lord Valentine's Castle,* and *At Winter's End.* He is a former president of the Science Fiction and Fantasy Writers of America and the winner of five Nebula Awards and five Hugo Awards. In 2005, the Science Fiction and Fantasy Writers of America presented him with the Grand Master Award.